SPARK

S.L. SCOTT

- It only takes a spark to start a fire. -

Design: RBA Designs

Photographer: Art-of-Photo

Editing:

Jenny Sims, Editing4Indies

Marion Archer, Making Manuscripts

Marla Esposito, Proofing Style

Kristen Johnson, Proofreader

ALSO BY S.L. SCOTT

To keep up to date with her writing and more, her website is
www.slscottauthor.com

To receive the Scott Scoop about all of her publishing adventures,
free books, giveaways, steals and more, sign up here:
http://bit.ly/2TheScoop

Join S.L.'s Facebook group here: S.L. Scott Books

The Crow Brothers

Spark

Tulsa

Rivers

Hard to Resist Series

The Resistance

The Reckoning

The Redemption

The Revolution

The Rebellion

The Kingwood Duet

SAVAGE

SAVIOR

SACRED

SOLACE

Sleeping with Mr. Sexy

Morning Glory

PROLOGUE

Jet Crow

Subtle scents of cinnamon mix with the taste of whiskey on her skin. I lick her from collarbone to the back of her ear, her moans enticing me to take more than a gentle share of what I want.

I'm well past hooking up with groupies, but something drew me to the beautiful brunette. Under the bright spotlight of that stage, my eyes found hers as I sang about finding the missing piece of me. Maybe it was the way she pretended not to care—catching my eyes and then turning away as if she was too shy to come speak to me, but too good to be bothered. It didn't matter. I was already caught up in her as much as she was caught up in me.

The set ended, and I made my way over to the mystery woman, the one who hid in the dark of the bar just as two shots were served. I took the shot of Fireball and then took her home shortly after.

Fuck. She feels good.

Hard little body, but soft in all the right places. Tits that fill my large hands and legs that spread enough for me to squeeze between her thighs. I bet she wouldn't reach my shoulders in heels. Speaking of, "Keep them on."

I like the feel of the leather against my lower back, the hard heel scraping across my skin when she tries to power play me by tightening around my waist and pulling me closer. I didn't ask her to my bedroom. I didn't have a chance. What started out as laughing while we shared a two a.m. snack of Cheetos, hummus, and whiskey turned into me eating her as a snack on top of my kitchen counter. I don't ever do that with a one-nighter, but damn if she didn't make me want to break more rules with her.

She kisses me like a woman in need of water, taking as much as she wants while pressing her heels into my ass. The heat between us emanates until I'm dragging my shirt off to try to cool down.

I knew she was different the moment she opened her mouth back at the bar. "You sing rock with so much soul. Who hurt you?"

"No one gets close enough to do me any harm."

"That's a pity."

"It's a pity I've never been hurt?"

"No, it's a pity you've never loved anyone enough to get hurt."

My heart started beating for what felt like the first time as I looked into her sultry eyes. I could blame the booze, but I can't lie to myself. She had me thinking twice about things I never considered once before.

Who was this woman?

Even with our stomachs full, we weren't satisfied. She dragged me by the belt down the hall to my bedroom. Her clothes were off and mine quickly followed before we tumbled into bed.

Fast. I want to fuck her fast and hard, but every time our eyes connect, there's such sadness found in her grays that I slow down. Wanting her to hold the contact, I cup her cheek. "Hannah?"

Her eyes slowly open, the long lashes framing the lust I find between them. "What?" she asks between heavy breaths.

"Are you okay?"

"I'm good."

"Just making sure."

She runs her hands up my neck and into the hair on the back of my head. "I'm sure." Pulling me down to her, our mouths are just a few inches apart when she whispers, "I want you. I want to do this."

Shy isn't something I'd call her, considering we were in my bed two hours after meeting. I like a woman who knows what she wants, and Hannah knows. And fuck if it isn't a turn-on that she wants me.

I nod before kissing her, getting lost in the soft caresses of her tongue mingling with mine and the feel of her nails lightly scraping my scalp as she holds me close.

We don't know each other, but I already know when I slip my fingers under the lace and into her wetness, she purrs for me. When I kiss behind her left ear, her back arches. When I press my erection against her to seek relief, her kisses become more frenzied.

When I slide my bare chest down hers, leaving a wet trail of kisses and taking the lace that divides us down as I go lower, her breath audibly catches. My body reacts—hardening for her, craving her.

Reaching over, she takes the glass of whiskey on the nightstand and sips, her eyes staying on mine as I slip the thong from her ankles and spread her legs wider. And somehow, desire replaces her sadness. In the dim light, her gray eyes appear bluer. I close my eyes and breathe her in —cinnamon.

She hands me the glass, and I take it. Finishing the amber liquid, I let it coat my mouth and burn on the way down. The ice clatters in the glass, so I fish it out and let it roll around my tongue while she watches. Placing it between my lips, I run it between hers. Her fingers tighten in my hair, tugging, urging me for more. "You like that, baby?"

"So much."

I crush the ice and swallow, ready to swallow her instead. I take her sweet pussy with my mouth, kissing and sucking until she's squirming under me. I flick my gaze up and visually trace her breasts and then go higher to see the underside of her jaw as she presses her head into the pillow beneath her.

Playing her body with my tongue like my fingers play my guitar, I set her on fire, feeling the burn deep inside. "I want to be buried inside you."

"I want that, Jet. I want you," she says, her body sinking into the mattress as she comes back to me from the high.

I grab a condom from where I tossed a few on the night-stand when we came crashing in here on a high of alcohol to continue what was started in the kitchen. Sticking the packet between my teeth, I rip it open and sit up.

Hannah lifts on her elbows, eyeing my body unashamedly. "Three crows," she says, eyeing my tattoos. "For three brothers."

"We all have them."

"They're sexy on your bicep." A wry grin appears. "How are you so fit if you drink every night?"

Chuckling, I continue to cover my cock and reply, "I do a lot of damn sit-ups."

"Every last damn one you do is worth it."

"What's your trick for staying in shape?" I ask, bending over and biting her hip just enough to tease her into thinking I'll break the skin. I won't, but I like the indentation from my teeth on her body.

"I like to fuck."

Shit. "You've got a dirty mouth."

"Maybe Jet Crow's just the one to help me clean it up."

Positioning myself above her, I angle my hips until I'm pressing against her entrance. "I have no intention of keeping this clean when it's so much more fun to play dirty."

Lying back, her chest rises and falls heavy with each breath. Her words starting to stick to her throat when she speaks. "With that handsome face, I have no doubt you use your looks to get what you want."

"I know how to use more than my looks," I start, pushing in just enough to feel her heat wash through me, "to get what I want." I push the rest of the way when her thighs butterfly for me. Seated deep inside her body, I close my eyes, the warm sensations taking over. On instinct, I move, and she moans.

I pick up my pace, but when I rise up on my elbows, I pause. *Fuck.* I shake my head.

"What is it, Jet? What's wrong?"

"Nothing," I'm quick to reply, hoping she doesn't see how much she's affecting me. What the fuck? I just met her, but when I close my eyes, it's not just the high of good sex taking over my mind. Normally, I don't pay a lot of attention to the body beneath me. Why should I? They only want me for one thing. But with Hannah? The girl with the haunted eyes? I want to erase the sadness. I want to replace her melancholy with other emotions.

What. The. Fuck?

Just fucking move.

We have chemistry, but I want more than just a physical connection with this woman. I want to know why she was alone tonight. Why she was drinking shots at the bar? Why she ordered me one before she knew me? I just want to know her.

Fucking move, Crow.

I do. Finally. But it's tainted with thoughts of tomorrow and hoping she stays tonight. Fuck.

This is just sex. Sex. Just a good time. *Focus.*

God, she feels amazing. *Too good.* "So good."

A warm hand caresses my cheek, and I open my eyes to find hers on me already. She smiles. "So good." Lifting up, she kisses me, dragging me out of my head and into her world. Her mystery is an aphrodisiac, and I want to learn all her secrets. Will she let me into her mind? It's a place I could lose myself forever in if I'm not careful.

Hannah isn't just another pretty face. She won me over the first time I saw her with that come-hither stare and devilish tilt of her lips.

We exhaust ourselves, pouring my soul into hers while hers fills me. As I hold her in the aftermath of ecstasy, I whisper into her hair, "Stay."

Turning her head, there's just enough light to see a flicker of happiness flaming in her eyes. "Ask me tomorrow," she replies with a small teasing smile as she closes her eyes and snuggles her back to my chest.

"I will."

I did. When her eyes open the next morning, I toss my cigarette out the window, lean forward, and ask her to stay.

While she gets dressed, I tell her I want to know her mind as well as I know her body. I confess too much too soon, more than I have to anyone in years.

She listened with a sly smile peeking through, her eyes brighter in the daylight, her worries seem to have lifted. When she kneels before me, she says, "You were the best time I ever had."

I'm tempted to tell her she's my worst. I hate feeling this way—reliant. Somehow, I've kept my emotions in check, a lock without a key for years.

Then she shows up with the right bow and shoulder, her cuts and tip fitting inside, the anatomy of a key made to unlock the deepest parts of me.

My chance starts slipping away as she does. I offer her coffee, to make her breakfast, and then I offer her a ride back to her car downtown where she parked behind the small bar where we met. I offer her anything to keep her from leaving. I don't offer my heart and I don't beg, but I offer her what I can.

The blue electric car surprises me. I mistakenly took her for a sports car or something less reliable and more rebellious. Her sexually carefree demeanor juxtaposed against her mysterious side fascinates me. Hearing the alarm click off and watching her open the car door, I know she's different. I felt it last night; not just in the way we connected, but in the way she makes me feel. "Maybe I'll see you around?"

"Maybe. I just moved here."

"I can show you around."

"I don't have a lot of free time right now, so I don't get out much."

Her jeans hug the curves of her hips, and I like the way she'd knotted my band's shirt, causing it to hug her upper body and exposing the skin of her stomach. Those boots that rubbed against my ass last night look just as sexy on her today. "Well, if you do, maybe you can come see the band play again."

Just before she slides into the driver's seat, she stops and looks back at me. Resting my elbow out the open window, I watch the sway of her hips as she comes back to me. *Come back to me.*

She lifts up on her toes and kisses me, our tongues meeting slick against each other's. Leaning back, she says, "I had a good time with you, Jet." Lowering back on her heels, she looks disappointed, that sadness making her eyes gray again. I miss the fire of the blue.

"I had a good time, too."

"My life is complicated. It's really not even my own these days."

I'm pathetic for saying anything to get more time with her, but it's worth a shot to explore our connection from last night. "Maybe I can help uncomplicate things."

"I wish you could. My cousin is sick, and I'm here to help her out. She needs me, but she also has a young son. His mom's illness has taken a toll. I need to be there for him."

"Sorry to hear that."

When she touches me, I savor the feel of her nails trailing through my hair. For a foolish split second, I think she's changed her mind, my chest feeling fuller as hope expands. Then the bubble bursts as she says, "If I get some free time, you'll be the first person I look up."

"We could make it easy and exchange numbers."

"That comes with expectations, and I don't want to hurt or disappoint you. If last night is all we get, it was pretty damn good."

"Yeah," I reply, already disappointed I won't know how to contact her. I sit back, take her hand, and bring it to my lips. I kiss it once and then again, pressing the tip of my tongue to her skin. "Take care of yourself."

Maybe I don't hide my feelings as well as I thought. Lifting up once more, she kisses my temple, then whispers, "The weather is too nice for such a sorrowful goodbye."

"Then let's not say it at all."

Nodding, she pushes away gently and returns to her car, opens the door, and slips in. With one foot still firmly on the ground, she looks back. "Take care of yourself, Jet."

1

Jet Crow

Six Months Later . . .

SOME SHOWS ARE BETTER than others. It's a little-known fact that we keep under wraps. No one needs to know when we screw up or miss a beat. Years ago, when the youngest Crow brother, Tulsa, played La Zona Rosa drunk, Rivers and myself covered. By adding more electric and heavy bass, we eventually drowned out any wrong chords.

When Rivers broke a string just before debuting a new song where he played the solo, I traded guitars with him and played a four-string bass like it was made that way.

I've had my fair share of fuckups, but sometimes, life throws you a bone, and it all seems to come together like the music was made to sound that way. My life has worked this way as well. *So far.*

At twenty-six, I've not had to show up for a nine-to-five ever. Nope, this band thing has worked out pretty well, keeping all three of us out of trouble, for the most part—we don't discuss the minor arrests among us, at least not much outside of teasing each other—and paying our rent since we started The Crow Brothers band seven years back. Tulsa was barely a junior in high school, but he had college chicks lined up like groupies every night of the week. I made him promise to go straight home from the gig. That's what my mom would have wanted. Tulsa is hardheaded, though. Mom always said he was a lot like my dad.

And he's a lucky bastard to have such cool big brothers.

Tonight, as I look around the packed bar and listen as the chords come together, making my melody come to life, I know I'm the lucky one.

We've been through hell and back together, but here we are, building something out of nothing from pure determination, and I'll toss in some talent for good measure.

We're booked almost every night of the week. We choose where and when we play, setting our own schedule. Rivers is just as good about managing us as he is playing guitar.

The only issue we have is keeping a drummer. With egos as big as ours, it's easy to get lost in the noise. Also, the pay is decent but not great. We can pay our rent, and that's about it. We play for the love of it, but it's time to get the payoff.

Leaning in the shadows on the back right side and across from the bar, Johnny Outlaw, front man of the legendary band, The Resistance, and rock god, drinks a beer while catching our show. I didn't see him come in and have no idea if he caught the opener, but he's been here for four songs since.

I heard he started Outlaw Records and is scouting bands to add to his new label. Scouting. *Scouting us?* Our song ends, and I turn around while tightening a string. "Johnny Outlaw is in the audience. Don't screw up." The pressure to impress him looms heavy. He could give us the break we need to not have to play downtown Austin every night. He could be our ticket to a full-length album and tour. He could be the ticket we need to hit the big time. Fuck, don't screw this up. I tap my pedal and lean up to the microphone.

It all comes together like it should—my tone, the melody, the rhythm, and the beat. I close my eyes and get lost in the music that bleeds from me. When I finish the song and look his way, Johnny's gone.

Fuck.

I try to save my soured mood and finish the show, but fuck if I'm not bummed. It was right—the sound, the song, and the crowd. I don't tell my brothers. I let them play their hearts out, hoping it makes up for the loss of mine at the moment.

All is not lost when I lean in to sing and a pretty woman at the bar catches my eye. I know that sweet face. It's one I never thought I'd see again.

Hannah.

I only ever got the one name out of her, but it's hung on at the outskirts of my thoughts, hoping to get more than one night.

Six months of silence has given me the distance to let her go while still having her cross my mind too often for my liking. Seeing the brunette beauty again has tempered my disappointment of Johnny Outlaw leaving in the middle of our gig.

She's not drinking, and there's no smile while her eyes stay on mine, never deviating far from me.

The last chord is strummed, and I thank the crowd as I set my guitar on the stand.

Rivers says, "Outlaw left."

"I know. Give me a few minutes. I'll be right back."

Tulsa says, "Grab me a shot while you're at it."

I flip him off and hop off the stage. Hannah's eyes are set on me like mine are set on her. As I work my way around a few tables and through the crowd to see her, I'm grabbed, claws poking the underside of my bicep. Marcy, a bad habit of mine, is whispering in my ear. "You look so good tonight, Jet. When you sing, I get so we—"

Extricating myself from her hold, I go easy. "Sorry. I can't tonight."

When I turn, I'm face to face with the woman I want to see. "Hey."

"Hi," she replies as her gaze lifts over my shoulder.

Marcy comes around, standing next to us, and looks Hannah over. "Maybe later, Jet?"

"Can't. Sorry, Marcy."

"Too bad." Her full lips press against my cheek, and her hand squeezes my ass before she saunters off, showing off what the good Lord gave her.

Hannah watches the exchange but doesn't say anything. When Marcy is gone, I ask, "Can I buy you a drink?"

"No. Thank you." I find her discomfort makes me uneasy. I shove my hands in my pockets and say, "I'm glad to see you. I didn't think I would."

"Yeah, about that. I'm sorry."

"Me too. I had a good time."

Whatever mission she was on, her body softens, giving me a little peek into that woman who I once shared whiskey and an unforgettable night with. "I did too, Jet. Look," she says and then pauses. "I wish this was a social call—"

Reaching out, I touch her wrist. "You're here on business?"

"I couldn't find a phone number." Glancing at our

connection, she doesn't seem to want to pull away, but then she does anyway. "In my research."

"Research?" When I tilt my head, thinking I must have heard her wrong, her expression becomes as serious as her tone. "What's this about?"

"Your son."

"I don't have a son." Wait . . . my mind fumbles through the one night I had with Hannah and back again. Running a hand through my hair, I ask, "Are you pregnant?"

"No. We used protection." The relief I find is short-lived when she adds, "You have a son."

This time, I laugh, but I'm really not finding this conversation very funny. "What are you doing, Hannah? You show up here after six months dropping bombs like they're raindrops. I don't have a son, so I don't know what kind of joke this is, but it's not funny."

I turn to leave, but stop when she says, "You have a six-year-old son named Alfie." Her words become white noise in the crowded bar.

"Dark hair like yours . . .

Green eyes . . .

Cute . . .

Wants to meet you . . . Jet?"

Slowly, I turn while trying to recall seven years back when I struggle to remember a week ago. One thing I'm sure of is that I don't have a kid. "You're going to need to fill in some blanks for me. Why are you here telling me about some kid that I supposedly have with another woman some seven years back?"

"I understand this is news to you, but you are a dad. Don't worry, though. I'm here to help."

"I don't need help other than you telling me what the fuck is going on."

"It's late, so if you have a few minutes, I can explain while you sign some paperwork."

My annoyance is hitting a high. First, we lose Johnny Outlaw's interest, and now, this girl I thought was a pretty cool chick is here making up some crazy bullshit story. "Paperwork? For what?"

"For custody. Clearly, this is unexpected. I'm sorry to barge back into your life like this, but time is of the essence. I just have the paperwork in the car—"

"Slow down. Come with me." I go back to the stage and hop up. Looking back, I tell her, "Meet me out back in ten. I need to load up our equipment."

She nods, and I see her making her way behind Rivers. As I wrap my cord in a circle, my mind reels over the thought of having a son. I can't. I would know. Six fucking years is a long time to raise a kid and not tell the father. *And how the hell would Hannah know? Who is she?*

Tulsa grabs the last amp and asks, "What was that about? It didn't look good."

"I don't know. I'm going to need a few minutes when we're done in here."

"Don't take long. I have a girl waiting for me."

"Use a condom."

He stops in his tracks. "Um, don't you think I'm a little old for sex advice?"

"No," I state firmly. "Use a fucking condom every fucking time."

As I walk to the side of the stage to leave, he follows close behind. "What the fuck are you talking about? What's going on?"

"I don't know, but I'm about to find out."

When I go outside, Hannah is standing off to the side of Tulsa's old '81 Ford Bronco. I help secure the equipment and slam the tailgate shut. Rivers leans against the side. "I'll help him unload into the garage. My 4Runner should be out of the shop this week. This loading and unloading the same night is bullshit." He glances at Hannah. "What's going on? Taking her home?"

"No. Hey, don't say anything to Tuls, but . . ." I nod behind me at Hannah. "She says I have a kid."

"What?" he spouts too loud for my liking.

"Keep it down."

"Sorry, but fuck, Jet. You knocked her up?"

"No. It's not hers. Look, I don't know the full story. I need to talk to her and get it."

"Yeah. Guess so. I'll help Tulsa unload. Fill me in later."

"Maybe tomorrow. It's almost one. I don't know how long this will take."

We shake hands, a handshake that comes with two slow slides, three fist bumps, and a quick chest hit as we bring it in. "Talk tomorrow, bro."

I walk around to the driver's side where Tulsa sits. "I'm going to grab a coffee. I'll see you tomorrow."

"She's hot. Looks familiar. Have I hooked up with her?"

"No, fucker. I have," I reply, walking away as he starts the engine.

My brothers take off, leaving Hannah and me standing in the alley alone. A good fifteen feet is between us, but neither of us makes a move to close the distance. Looking at her now, I'm reminded of how beautiful she was that day as we said goodbye. The wind blows, and she shivers. I say, "There's a coffee shop on the next block. We can talk there."

She comes toward me, and we start walking when she catches up. "What's your last name?" I ask, tracking the cracks in the cement.

"Nichols," she whispers loud enough for me to hear.

I glance over at her. She's just as pretty as my memories held, that haunted sorrow still residing in her eyes. She was more confident that night and a free spirit the next day. Now, she's the bearer of news that could be good or bad. I'm unsure what to think, so I just say what's on my mind. "I have a son?"

A flicker of a smile crosses her lips but leaves even quicker. Reaching over, she touches my arm, and we both stop. "I didn't know who you were when we slept together."

"And you know now? You know me, Hannah Nichols?"

"The world has a screwed-up way of working sometimes. I was never told your name—"

"What were you told and by whom?"

"I was told you walked away."

Anger rises inside me, my chest heating. I start walking, hoping I can cool off enough on the way so I don't take it out on her, though she seems to be the most likely recipient since she's bringing these lies to me. "I wouldn't fucking leave, so whoever your source is lied to you."

"I'm not here to argue."

"Why are you here, and who's the mother?"

"I'm here because of Cassie Barnett."

Hearing Cassie's name after all these years is sobering. I know the name well. I knew the woman better. It was a short-lived love affair. I broke her heart before she had a chance to break mine, apparently. I was twenty and didn't know a good thing when I had it. "Cassie Barnett." I say her name just to taste the sound of it again. But nothing makes sense. "How do you know her?"

"She's my . . ." She sucks in a jagged breath and looks away while tilting her head back. If I'm not mistaken, her eyes are suddenly glassy with tears. "She's my cousin."

Whoa. This world just got a little too small for my liking. "You're cousins?"

"Yes. We were."

"Were? I'm confused. Just spell it out for me."

"I have temporary custody of Cassie's son, Alfie," she says, stopping again. When I turn back to her, she adds, "Your son."

"No, I don't think so," I reply, scoffing at the thought. "Cassie and I broke up a long time ago. If we had a kid, she would've told me, so I think you have the wrong guy."

She seems hesitant and looks down. Tucking some hair behind her ear, she lowers her voice. "I need you to sign paperwork formalizing custody. This shouldn't be an issue since you're claiming he's not yours anyway."

Something is off, not sitting right in my gut. A lump forms in my throat, my thoughts jumping to conclusions I'm not ready to face. "Where's Cassie? Why do you have custody of her kid?"

She looks away, her hair falling to the side and hiding her face from view. "She passed away a few weeks ago."

After that punch to the heart, I'm left speechless and staring at the woman in front of me. "Cassie . . . She's gone?" The deafening cheers from the bar still ring in my ears as her words rumble around my head. "How?"

"Mr. Crow, it's late."

Mr. Crow? "One in the morning, but here we are, *Ms.* Nichols."

"I was given . . . we—"

"We?"

"My aunt and I."

"Cassie's mom?"

"Yes."

Rubbing the bridge of my nose, I remember Cassie's mother well. "She never liked me."

"I've heard." It's not a hateful response, but factual. I hurt Cassie, so I'm not surprised that she and her mother didn't have nice things to say about me.

"We only have seven days left to locate Alfie's next of kin and get the paperwork signed."

"Or what happens?"

"He'll be removed by Child Protective Services. We'll have to start legal proceedings to get him back."

Her pain is evident. Sighing, I feel bad that I can't help her. "I'm sorry. I can only imagine how horrible this is for you, but I can't sign custody *over* when I'm not his dad. Cassie would have told me if we had a kid." *I think. Surely, she would have . . .*

Hannah's smile is as tight as her grip on her handbag. "Time is running out. All you have to do is sign the papers for us to get custody. You'll never have to hear from us again."

Before tonight, I would have loved to hear from Hannah again. But this? *A son? Why didn't she tell me?*

"Hannah, if the kid is mine, I'll take him. If I'd known I'd had a kid, I would have been a part of his life. Cassie would know that, too. But I haven't heard from her in years. That's why I'm finding it hard to believe he's actually mine."

She shifts, glancing at the back door of the bar and then to the opening at the end of the alley. I might be as uncomfortable as she looks, which makes me think we're not going to make it to get coffee. When she turns back, she says, "I'm not here to ruin your life. I'm here so Alfie's life isn't ruined. Will you sign the paperwork?"

"Cassie and I broke up well over six years ago, so I can't . . ." Doing the math, I remember she said the kid is six. "We weren't together long, but would she really withhold something so important?"

Determination crosses her expression, and her chin lifts. Stubborn little thing. "I don't know what to believe, but I'm caught between what I've been told and . . ."

"And?"

"And the man I once spent the night with."

"I'm still that man, Hannah."

"We shouldn't speak as if we actually know each other. We don't. That night was—"

"Amazing. I won't let you call it anything less than what it was."

Her demeanor relaxes before me. "I won't because it was amazing. But that doesn't change what we need to discuss. Alfie's your son, but he doesn't know you, and you don't know him. Will you please just sign the paperwork, Jet?"

"I can't sign paperwork that could be false. If he is some other man's child, I will be committing a crime by denying a different man access to his son. If he is, in fact, my son . . . *If he's mine* . . . I was never told about him. I wouldn't walk away, not like that."

"We don't want to disrupt his life more than it already has been. I'm asking you to sign custody of him over to me. That was Cassie's wish in her will. And he's all my aunt has left. I'm her niece, not her daughter or her grandson."

Shifting so she's out of my shadow, I'd forgotten how small she was until it felt like I was towering over her. "I'm sorry to hear about Cassie, but if he's my son, I won't just sign my responsibility over in a stack of legal paperwork."

Her eyes reflect not just her sadness, but also the desperation to get this deal done. The only problem is, this isn't a deal to close, but a life to discuss.

2

Hannah Nichols

Jet Crow is too handsome for his own good. His good looks have become a distraction to my purpose.

The last time we were together, I got so close to falling for his lines and good time that I cut the ties starting to bind us together before it was too late. I've made the mistake of falling for a musician before, so I refuse to date or trust another musical Romeo. They're all the same. Players who don't understand the definition of commitment, much less live by it. Even when they say they love you, don't believe it. I was a fool before. Not anymore.

Regardless of how amazing our one-night stand was.

But here's Jet Crow with that dark hair and soul-soothing eyes staring into mine. Lips that once kissed me everywhere are licked just before he realizes we are now on opposing sides. With large hands, hands I remember holding me together after falling apart from ecstasy, hanging at his sides, I can tell he's in shock, trying to process how his world just got flipped upside down.

I thought this would be easy. Jet walked away years ago. He wouldn't want to take on a kid now. He'd sign Alfie over. End of story. *But no. Just my luck. He wants to pretend to take the moral high ground.*

Something in his eyes makes me want to believe that maybe he didn't know. That makes no sense, though. My aunt wouldn't lie to me while her daughter was on her deathbed, would she? Would Cassie just go along with some story where he's painted as the villain? Or is he the bad guy?

Jet Crow would. Just like he did to Cassie years ago. He's like every other guy I've dated. He uses his looks and charms to get what he wants and then betrays women. Eileen said he's a cheater and a liar. I have to forget the time we spent together because it doesn't matter now. I may have fallen into his bed, but I won't fall for his act as Cassie once did.

Despite the memories of that magical night we spent in his bed, discovering everything that makes him lose the control he's holding so tightly to now, I stiffen my resolve. My aunt and I haven't always gotten along . . . not in a few years, but this could heal us, so I can't let Aunt Eileen down. She made me promise to help hold onto the last part of her daughter that exists in this world. "I can see it's a lot to take in, that you're struggling to wrap your head around a responsibility that you never wanted or asked for." Breathing out, I drop my guard, trying to ignore the pain I see filter in his eyes and appeal to his more reasonable side. "His grandmother and I are here for him, ready to take on parenting and give him the solid foundation he needs."

"You say that as if I can't."

No, Jet. I'm saying this because I doubt you would. "Can you?" Stepping closer, I plead with my eyes while trying to show him the light. "You play shows how many nights a week, Jet? Can you really fit a child into your lifestyle? You were born to play music. You're truly mesmerizing on that stage. Are you ready to set your dreams aside for the next ten or fifteen years?"

"Why is it one or the other?"

"Because I've been there for the past seven months and lived it. I had to quit my job in Dallas to move down to take care of Alfie because his mother couldn't."

"So how will you take care of him financially? How is your situation better than mine? Where will he be when you find another job and who will take care of him?"

Resting my hand gently on his chest, I reply, "His grandmother. Eileen took early retirement to take care of Cassie. She just got a part-time job. She doesn't make a ton of money, but he'll be cared for and fed, have a good home, and he lives in a great school district. What district do you live in?"

I hate that he shifts away from me, but he does, his frustration seen in the tensing of his jaw. His eyes find mine before he turns back around. When he does, he says, "Maybe we're getting ahead of ourselves." He crosses his arms over his chest and narrows his eyes. "You say you have seven days to secure custody. I suggest we get a paternity test done tomorrow."

"It's not necessary. He's your son."

"You're that confident? How do you know?"

"Because I've seen him."

"Then maybe I deserve to see my own flesh and blood as well."

"Okay," I whisper. He's right. He does. Whether he chose to walk out seven years ago or he was pushed out, he deserves to see the son who cannot be mistaken for anyone else's but his. I pull up my photo app, but his hand covers mine.

"In person."

"Fine." I hold my phone out. "Add your number and I'll text you a location and time tomorrow."

"Sure." While he's adding his number, I take the time to look at him. His shoulders are broad, his hair not shaggy but not too short. The light shining overhead from the bar's backdoor highlights the shadow of his jaw. His lashes dark like his hair.

He's tall.

Six foot three to my five foot three.

I'm tempted to stand against him to verify, but I don't. My gaze slips lower. I have clear memories of that six-pack stomach. By how fitted his shirt is, I'm thinking it's still there if not even better. It's cooler at this hour of the night, but the sleeves of his shirt expose his cut biceps.

When he hands my phone back, he says, "I'll wait for your text."

I nod and look down. He's been nicer than I expected. A motorcycle farther down the alley roars to life, and I look up. "I should go."

"I'll walk you. Where are you parked?"

"I'll be fine."

"I know you will be, but humor me, Hannah."

I exhale, the pressure of this dreaded conversation feeling more like it's over as we stroll toward the street ahead. I shouldn't like how much I like seeing him again, but I've thought of him so much, so many times over the past six months. The way he playfully bit the tips of my fingers when I fed him Cheetos and then licked the orange dust from them. His kisses on the back of my neck seared my skin that night, and now each place his lips touched still warms under the memories. The image I'll never forget is when I sat in my car and looked back. He shared his soul in that exchange, wide open to be accepted or rejected. It pained me to leave, but I was in no condition to stay.

In the dimly lit bar and dark of his bedroom is one thing. Seeing the real me, the damaged parts, in the light of day is another.

I'll take this walk with him. It's more for me, so I slow my pace wanting to savor every second of something I now know can never be. "I'm parked around the corner."

We don't talk, the weight of reality escorting us along the way. When we reach my car, I step off the sidewalk but stop before opening the door. "I'll see you tomorrow, Jet."

He's a musical god I once prayed to by tasting his skin as he came on mine.

Tonight though, standing before me is not the man I saw on stage six months ago or an hour earlier. He's not that guy who got drunk on whiskey and wine just to have what I was having and then charmed me right into his bed.

In the wee hours of a Thursday in Austin, a man with flaws and feelings restrained in the hard muscles of his build has been given a choice to make, one that will change his life and mine forever. I worry what he'll decide, and what I could lose, but I say what I feel because his kindness deserves a return, "Thank you for walking with me."

"No problem."

"I'll see you tomorrow, Jet."

"Tomorrow . . ." He sounds as if he wants to say more but doesn't, so I get in my car and start the engine.

I hate being the bad guy. I hate that Cassie died. I hate that Alfie is in the middle of this mess. A timer was always ticking when it came to Jet and me. A clock was counting down that night, not only stealing my days away, but also my happiness. A few stolen hours with him gave me hope only to find out he's the one who caused my family so much pain.

The reality is hard to come to terms with, especially when I remember him so differently. I didn't know him then, but I thought I got a glimpse of who he was.

So now when I watch him walk away after exchanging numbers, my resolve lessens, wishing our lives hadn't turned out this way.

———

CAN I have my coffee first?

I feel bad that she wants answers and was up worrying, but Aunt Eileen needs to give me a moment. With my forehead in my palm, I slump over the table. "I slept terribly, and I have a headache." Though it's not my head that's hurting, but a dull ache in my chest.

She sits across the table from me and covers my hand. "Please tell me he's not fighting us on this. He walked out once, and I have no intention of letting him back into our lives."

"It will be resolved today."

Her hands slam down on the wood tabletop. "He abandoned his child and my daughter."

Standing, I go to the cupboard and grab the ibuprofen. "You've told me, Aunt Eileen." I hate when she gets like this. There's no reasoning with her or calming her down once she's riled up. I take a coffee mug and fill it with tap water.

When I turn around, she's glaring at me. I grip the side of the sink. She says, "He broke Cassie's poor heart, probably caused her to get cancer. Don't go soft, Hannah. Alfie needs us. He needs people who love him and care about him. People who care about his mother, not disrespect her or her memory." She huffs and turns to leave the kitchen. "Can you imagine the garbage he would feed our sweet Alfie about Cassie?" She looks back once. "We're his only saving grace, Hannah. Don't let me down."

She should have let me get a cup of coffee so my patience wouldn't be worn so thin. I'm in no mood for a fight, but if she's starting one, I'll finish it. "Don't speak to me that way. I was here when you needed me."

"When *Cassie* needed you."

"You needed me. Alfie needed someone to take care of him, to feed him, to spend time with him and play."

"Are you saying I didn't give him enough attention? I refuse to spoil the child."

"Giving him some of your time isn't spoiling him. It's called caring."

"How dare you, Hannah Lynn Nichols. You have no idea what I've given up because of caring for others. So don't come here lecturing me—"

"I'm sorry."

The scowl digs deeper into the lines of her face. Cassie's illness aged my aunt well beyond her years. I understand the worry and concern, the sadness, and the love for a child after spending so much time with Alfie. I've got to cool down and remember she's lost her daughter and now fears losing her grandson.

I repeat myself as tears fall from the corners of her eyes. "I'm sorry, Aunt Eileen. I know you care. I'm just tired and stressed. I loved Cassie, and I miss her. I look at Alfie, and I'm worried I'll lose him as well."

"We won't," she corrects. "We'll fight him if he fights us. Promise me you'll help me save Alfred from that loser of a man."

"I promise. I'll do whatever I can to make sure we keep custody."

She tugs at the hem of her blouse and straightens the

front of her pants before her expression matches the formality of her outfit. Coming over to me, she evens out the collar of my T-shirt and then touches my face. "Thank you, Hannah dear. It's good to see the Nichols fighting spirit in you for once. Family always comes first. Remember that."

Family . . . my father has only seen me once since I've been back and that was because it was Christmas. He didn't bother to stay long. He had work to do and was gone as soon as dinner finished.

I don't think I'll ever understand him. How can his business and money mean more to him than his own daughter?

As she leaves the kitchen, she adds, "You should really change into a dress instead of hiding under sloppiness. You're such a pretty girl. You should show the world."

I've learned to let her little digs—comments that are insults wrapped up as advice—go to save my sanity growing up. I understand why my mother left my father. It's the same reason I left the first chance I got. My mom had better luck, and I wish I could have gone with her. She begged me to. My father stopped her, stopped me at the door holding my favorite Barbie in one hand and my gymnastics tote bag stuffed with my favorite leotard and tights in the other.

She had no money to fight my father for custody. His insurance company was booming, and she walked away with twenty dollars. I still consider her the lucky one because she got out. She remarried and had another kid when I was ten.

But summers? They were ours. Summers with her were my favorite time of year. I realized I didn't need to accept every negative word said to me. Some people, like my dad's sister, Eileen, were just cruel and cold. Saying goodbye to my mother and little brother was the worst.

And now? I'm stuck in the middle of a different custody

battle, trying to save Alfie from drowning in the negativity. I want to show him the ocean, let him run free in the sunshine. I want him to feel like I felt in the summertime. *Loved. Cherished. Affirmed.*

That's the life I want to give him, the one he deserves. Cassie asked *me* to raise him in her absence, so I can't expend energy where it won't do me any good. I'll need it for the battle ahead.

Thinking of the energy I need, I finally pour my first cup of coffee and down one more while getting ready for the day.

After texting Jet the time and place, I've gone through at least four outfits and none feel right. I take my aunt's suggestion and pull a sky blue dress from the hanger, put it on, wrap my waist with a thin leather silver belt, and slip on a green sweater to end this battle. I slide on a pair of wedges because height means power, and if shoes give me any kind of advantage against Jet Crow, then I'll take it.

3

Jet

I could have asked one or both of my brothers to come with me, but I didn't. This just feels like something I should do on my own.

You don't find out every day you have a kid. Feels right to find out first before he's subjected to the crazy that are my brothers. If this kid is mine, I don't want him overwhelmed. He might need time to adjust to me much less the Crow clan.

Sitting in my truck, I stare at the building in front of me —DNA Testing Lab. Hannah said I'll be able to tell he's mine just by looking at him. If that's true, then why did she ask me to meet her here?

I guess it's good to be sure.

A familiar blue car pulls in a few spaces down from mine. I'm tempted to lean over and get a better look inside, but I don't. I try to play it cool, but my heart's thudding against my chest. I'm twenty-six years old, and the idea of being a dad is way out of my comfort zone. *But if I am?*

Shit.

Why am I so nervous?

Hannah's right. My whole life is about to change, but I think I'm okay with it.

I pop the lock and get out. After closing the door, I run my hands down the front of my thighs. I'm nervous. I'm fucking nervous. I'm never nervous. I play in front of hundreds of people every night. I've played in front of thousands before and didn't miss a beat.

This is different. Today, I *might* be about to hop right on this parenting train and hope I don't fuck this whole thing up. He lost his mother. For him, I'll need to be both. I'll need to be everything he needs and hope it's enough.

Not sure what to do, I put my hands in my pockets and wait in front of my car. Hannah gets out, and she steals my breath away. She's springtime come to life in a pretty blue dress and green sweater. Her long brown hair is worn in a ponytail high on her head, and her lips are sweet pink.

"Hi," I dare to say, not sure how to react and trying not to sound like an idiot.

"Hey. How are you?" she asks, walking to the back door and opening it.

"Nervous."

She laughs. "Me too." Turning her attention to the back seat, she says, "Come on, Alfie. It's okay."

A little hand reaches up, and she holds it as he jumps out.

This is it.

I might have a son. I never thought this would be the way I'd meet my child.

Did Cassie know she was pregnant the last time I saw her? Is that why she was so angry with me? Why she came at me after we had already broken up?

Had she intended to tell me the last time I spoke to her, but instead, got mad and walked away? Was it anger that blinded her to what she knew she should do—tell me that she was pregnant with my child?

Knowing I'll never get answers is what drives me mad. I barely slept last night because the more I thought about this kid and how he needed his dad, the more I realized that maybe I needed him too. Maybe he was my redemption for all the trouble I've been in. Maybe he's a gift from the heavens, my mom watching over my brothers and me and giving us something good again. Something we wouldn't want to screw up. Something for me to make the changes we probably need to make with my life.

Do I want to live my life content, or do I want to make it amazing?

This doesn't just affect my life, though. My brothers and the band will forever change—whether good or bad remains to be seen.

I became the man of Mom's house when she needed backup with my brothers. I became more after she died.

I've *played* that role before, but *this* could be real. This could be my role for life. That's a lot to take on when just last night I was fucking around on stage barely getting by paying my bills but loving every second of playing those songs in front of a crowd.

I'm satisfied right now. Sure, I want more—a deal and some security—but this has been a good life. I can live off what I'm paid to pursue my passion.

I can't if I'm supporting two. Kids have needs, expenses, and need more than love to give them the life they deserve.

Am I equipped to do that? Am I ready to do it?

I quit college after two years so Rivers and Tulsa could

go—tough decisions a twenty-one-year-old had to make for the future of his family.

I understand sacrifice. When needed, I've always found a way.

Will that be enough?

I've missed so much that I'm unsure if he'll even accept me into his life at this point.

Lying in bed last night, I couldn't turn my brain off. I imagined every possible scenario when meeting Alfie.

Will I be enough?

What if he hates me?

What if he's a terror?

What if . . .

If he's a Crow, that's enough for me. There's no way to predict how much things will change, but I'll do my damned best for him, to do right by this kid.

Standing here, my hands are sweating. Nothing prepared me for this.

My nerves, my fears settle when I see his little face.

It's not bewilderment on his face, though. It's recognition and a smile. While I stare at this kid like I'm seeing myself at that same age, he says, "I know you."

"You do?" I reply, my nerves put to rest.

"Where's your ka-tar?"

Chuckling, I ask, "My guitar? It's at home." I kneel, though there's still some distance between us. "Do you like the guitar, Alfie?"

"I like music. Will you play for me?"

"Sure. Anytime, buddy." My gaze slides to Hannah. Standing back up, I ask, "Are you wanting proof?"

Moving Alfie in front of her, she holds him as if she's trying to keep him with her forever. "Are you?"

I could go in and take a paternity test, but I don't have to.

Not only is Alfie a little version of me with his dark hair and the matching and frustrating cowlick at the crown of his head, but everything from his eye shape to dimples are versions of mine too. He may have the color of his mother's eyes, but the rest is all me. "I don't need it."

She signals to the car. "I brought the paperwork for you to sign." I don't have to say anything for her to know how I'm feeling. Her arms tighten around him, and her words are quick. "It's just two lines to sign, and then we can let you get back to your life."

"You were right last night."

"About?" she asks, a faint tremble weakening her strong façade.

"My life will never be the same." With my eyes on my son, my heart expands, and I add, "It will be better. I'm willing to do what I need when it comes to raising Alfie."

He flies from her arms and runs into mine with a hard thump against my chest. For a kid who's never met his father, this was not what I expected.

I stand with my son in my arms—taking in his small build, and kid smell, and arms that squeeze me as hard as I'm embracing him—and know this is right.

I catch a glimpse of Hannah with tears in her eyes, matching the ones in mine, just before I close my eyes and tuck my head against his shoulder.

I've not been around many kids since I was one and don't have many friends with them, so I didn't know I'd feel this way. How is it that a heart that feels so normal one minute can be so open and welcoming in such an unexpected way the next?

"You're squeezing too hard," Alfie says, causing me to laugh.

"Sorry, little dude." Keeping him eye level, I continue

holding him in my arms to look at him up close. I see a little of Rivers's chin, too much of Tulsa's mischief in his smile, and Cassie's eyes. "The Crow genes are strong." I glance at Hannah, who shifts, appearing not to know what to do with herself.

She exhales a deep breath and wipes the corner of her eye with the back of her hand. "Yeah." Her reply is so quiet that I barely hear her.

Setting Alfie down, I whisper, "I need to talk to Hannah in private, okay?"

He nods and sits down on the curb. It's only about seven or eight feet away, but an overwhelming need to protect him comes over me. Much like she felt when she was holding him. I fight it because I need to talk to her where he can't hear. I lean against her car. When she turns toward me, I keep my voice low. "I won't give him away."

"I had a feeling," she replies, glancing back at Alfie. When her eyes return to mine, she sighs. "He's like my own child. I love him, Jet."

A foreign stab deep inside makes me rub my hand over my chest. "I meant what I said yesterday. I won't keep him from you. You're all he knows. You and Cassie's mom. He needs you. You're his family."

When a tear starts to slip down her cheek, I reach out reflexively to stop it from falling. "Don't cry, Hannah. We have to be strong for Alfie. We have to work together to make his transition easier."

"Transition?" Her shoulders fly back, and her eyes go wide. "He's not ready for that. You can't just have him. That . . . that . . . that won't work. No." She rushes to Alfie and pulls him up by the hand. "You're not taking him right now if that's what you think."

Alfie's eyes are darting back and forth between us,

unrest settling in his eyes. I don't want to hurt him. Fuck, I don't want to hurt her either, but now that I have my son, I want to be there for him.

She leans down and whispers in his ear. He nods while staring at me. The secrets between them make me uncomfortable, so I step up. "What do I need to do to bring him home with me?"

Hannah says, "He doesn't have his stuff or his clothes. He just came from school."

"He's in school so soon after his moth—"

"He likes school. We thought it best if he was up for it, then he should go to play, to learn, and to be with his friends."

I'm at a loss. This kid, *my* kid has lost his mother and found me all in the span of two weeks. *Am I doing the right thing?* Maybe he does need Hannah and his grandmother right now. Maybe it's too soon for me to change his life after his world has already been altered forever.

Shit. What do I do?

She opens the back door and directs him inside. Seeing his car seat causes me to pause. There are so many things I don't know. Am I ready to be a dad? Am I ready to be a father to a six-year-old?

The door is about to close, but I halt it and lean in. He reaches out and rests his hand on my shoulder. "It's okay to be just okay, Jet."

The light he shines inside the darker recesses of my heart is too bright and reflects in my smile. "There's a lot of stuff Hannah and I will be working through to make this transition as smooth and easy as possible for you. I know I speak for both of us when I say that you and your happiness are most important."

"So will I stay with Grandma and Hannah, or am I coming home with you?"

He's smart. So much smarter than I thought kids his age would be. He's had to be, considering what he's survived. I rub the back of his head, leaning my forehead to his. "I want you to live with me. I want to see you every day." As much as it pains me, I put my fate in his hands. "I want to see you every day, Alfie. But for now"—and it pains me to say it —"you might have to stay with your cousin and grand-mother. Is that okay?"

He tilts his head, *just the way I do,* and says, "Mommy would read me books, lots of books, and sometimes, she would whisper secrets in my ear. Do you want to hear one of our secrets?"

"Can you tell me, or is that breaking some secret code?"

He giggles. "She told me I could tell you this secret."

"What is it?"

"She told me I was lucky to have you. Are you lucky to have me?"

Hearing that Cassie said that makes me think she didn't think of me as the monster I've been led to believe, and relief courses through me. Hannah and I will need to talk more about this, but right now, I have the cutest kid wanting to hear he's loved and wanted. It's easy to answer him. "The luckiest, buddy. We all are, and I can't wait to get to know everything about you."

"Will you show me how to play a ka-tar?"

My smile returns. "I'd like that."

He looks past me at Hannah, guilt changing his features. His fingers twist in his lap, and he whispers, "I love Hannah."

From over my shoulder, she sniffles. "I'll always love you,

Alfie. No matter what happens or where you live, I'm not going anywhere. I'll always be here for you."

I may be breaking her heart, but her kindness still shows. I'm thinking she's rubbed off on Alfie, and for that, I can only be grateful. I lean in and kiss the top of his head. "Thanks for going easy on me, kid."

He giggles. "When will I see you again?"

"Very soon. Hannah and I still have to work it out but soon. You take care of her and your grandma, okay?"

He grabs a juice box and takes a noisy sip, then says, "I will. I'm the man of the house. My mommy told me so."

Every time he mentions Cassie, I can't help but feel devastated inside—for his loss, everyone else's, and mine. I'm struggling to be kind when I know damn well that if she hadn't passed away, I might never have known I have a son. Hearing she said one kind thing about me to him doesn't soothe the anger I feel inside, but for him, I'm going to have to remember the good times we had together. "Bye, Alfie."

"Bye."

I shut the door and close my eyes, needing a second to gather my thoughts and push down the sadness I feel from having to say that farewell. I keep my tone down just in case he can hear through the closed window. "He's an amazing kid. I appreciate everything you, Cassie, and your aunt have done for him, but I'm ready to step in and be a parent to him."

"You say that with such conviction now, but nothing in your life is child-ready, much less your schedule. What are you going to do if you have a show?"

"What every other single parent who works does. I'll find help."

"So just like that. You have all the answers, and there's no changing your mind even in the best interest of Alfie?"

"There's no changing my mind. I'm sorry. I know you thought you'd get a different answer, but I'm not letting someone else raise my son just because it might be difficult for me."

"You don't have a bed for him or know his routine," she starts before the tears fall. "What happens when he misses his mom? You don't even have photos of her."

"I don't have a lot of things, but I have him, and we'll get through it together. Beds, photos, everything he needs, I'll get him. I'd like your help, but if you think it's too much—"

"Jet?" Her shoulders shake with a gentle sob.

She's beautiful dressed in tears, but never seeing her sadness again has become my mission. I wish I could make her happy, but it seems I only know how to ruin her life. "Yeah?"

Turning her back to the car, she comes around and uses my body as a shield. I assume so Alfie can't see or hear. "I can see how much you care for him. I can also see how happy he is to finally meet you, but I must warn you, we're still going to fight for him."

"I have no doubt. I don't know what rights I have other than biology, but I hope you understand why I want to be there for him."

"I don't fully, not yet, but as his father, you have that right."

"So you think I'm the bad guy?"

"I have a weakness for bad boys, or I wouldn't have slept with you. As for the bad *guy*, I guess we'll see."

"I don't remember much sleeping."

She laughs. "There was very little." The laughter fades with her smile. "I hope you know that this may be a battle, but it's not a war. At the end of the day, we'll be there for him however we can be. I just hope it's each night. I can't imagine going to bed without seeing his sweet face and kissing his cheek."

"I want to be responsible for my son. There will be changes, but hopefully, they will be what's best for Alfie."

"I hope so too." She reaches out as if she's about to touch me, but her arm goes back to her side. "I need to go, but I'll text you the information regarding the process to claim custody."

Stepping back, I take the top of the door and open it wide for her. "Thanks." I wave once more. "See you, Alfie."

He waves, and the door shuts.

My gaze and Hannah's connect once more before she starts the car and backs up. I watch as they drive away, wondering if I should have insisted he stay?

I did that once with her, and it didn't work. I have a feeling it wouldn't have worked with her regarding him today. Either way, I can't help but feel my whole world just drove away.

4

Jet

Hannah and I exchange texts twice in the next forty-eight hours. Both times regarding Alfie with her insisting he stay where he is until the family court judge hears our case next Wednesday.

Five days.

I think about arguing, but I'd do the same if our roles were reversed. Despite our personal feelings on the matter, she's let him call me four times each day, including some video chat where I give him a quick tour of my small home on one, played a song for him so he can see the "ka-tar" he's so fascinated by on another, and then introduced him to his uncles yesterday. It's not how any of us ever envisioned meeting family, but this is where we are, and I wanted him to meet Rivers and Tulsa so he knew he had more than just me. He has a family who welcomes him with open arms and open hearts.

I'm already learning so much about him in these calls

that I get even more excited to bring him home. Speaking of home. "Star Wars or plain sheets?"

With a huge stuffed animal in the shape of a shark in his hands, Tulsa replies, "Are there Metallica sheets?"

"He's six."

Tulsa tosses the sheets into a pile of pillows. "And your point is?"

Rivers knocks into me when he comes from behind, grabs the discarded sheets, and puts them back on the shelf. "We were listening to Metallica at six."

"Not when Mom was around." I laugh from the memory of my mom yelling at us to turn down what she called racket. Being the oldest, I have the most memories of her out of the three of us. Rivers once claimed it wasn't fair. But neither was her death when I was only nineteen.

While the guys goof around in the aisle of Target, I stand with pillows in one hand, gray flannel sheets in the other, and a gamut of emotions twisting in my head.

My mom should be here. She'd know what to buy for Alfie's room. She'd know what he needed and what was junk. She'd be able to help me. I try to brush it off because it doesn't matter what I wish. Nothing will bring her back.

A drunk driver made sure of that the night of Rivers's seventeenth birthday. I find him down the aisle grabbing a mattress pad for the twin bed in my spare room, Alfie's soon-to-be room. He carries a lot of guilt with him, guilt that's caused more than his fair share of pain. He was a kid . . . I can't dwell on this.

I'm going to make sure that Alfie has a good life. I tried my best with my brothers. They're happy and the best friends and brothers a guy could ask for, even if disorderly and sometimes embarrassing. Tulsa lands a pillow to the back of Rivers's head just as I say, "You guys are going to get us kicked out."

When Rivers turns, Tulsa takes off. Rivers laughs. "He's such a pussy."

"C'mon, I need help here."

After I throw the pile of bedding in the cart, I grab some essentials, like the seat I saw Hannah had. Of course, this came with Tulsa flirting with the girl who works in the department. He walked away with not only her number, but also a coupon for twenty percent off. It's going to be needed. I'm wondering how we can add a gig to our already full schedule for the added expenses of raising a child.

The trip to the store took longer than planned, and now we're rushing to get ready for tonight. After tossing all the bags in the spare room, I jump in the shower.

Hannah crosses my mind when I close my eyes. I lose track of time, my body hardening and demanding release when I remember how she felt pressed to the wall as the water rained down over us—the feel of her tits as I squeezed them, when I pinched the nipples, the sound of her moan echoing off the cold tile. I remember so much about her because she's too hard to forget.

Smart. Her beauty caught my eye. The ability she seemed to possess of seeing the real me in the lyrics that night, the person I tried to hide from others is what kept me there.

Gorgeous inside and out. Her whole body shook, whiskey tipping over the edge of the glass when she laughed at my bad jokes. She kissed me, pulling me to her smiling lips, her happiness spilling over. Her eyes were bright, and she was playful as we ate junk food and got drunker.

She'd been so goddamn gorgeous in that blue dress and even more stunning wrapped in my sheets with a glistening sheen of sweat from sex, kisses, and a hot summer night too long ago.

The window was cracked open, humidity filling the room. We were drunk on each other, careless with our hearts and bodies. The way the tips of her fingers ran over my unshaven face as if it was slick as ice. She didn't complain about the stubble or when I got up to smoke. I sat in a chair by the window, holding my cigarette through the opening, and watched her.

My pace picks up, getting closer to coming like every other time I let Hannah devour my thoughts the way I devoured her that night.

She's not like the other women who've entangled me. Her grays held a longing for something unforeseeable by a mere bystander to her beauty like me.

When I sobered, I started laying the foundation. With each minute that ticked by, I added a brick, building a wall to protect myself from the only person who seemed to be able to navigate my carefully constructed foundation. She perplexed me, making me want to know how she spent her time when she wasn't caring for her family. Does she go out often? Hook up with others? Was she seeing other people? I felt like a spider caught in her web. That's when I knew she would be the one to damage me. Would I let her?

Yes.

As she sobered, her touches became rough, her patience more hurried as dawn consumed the moonlight. When I took her from behind, her pussy tightened around me. Her moans for more became louder. My name was a curse, a blessing, a sin, a saint. I became all those as she became one thing to me—my salvation.

Could she save me? Would she be the one who could change me? Make me believe in something more than the life I was living. Would she be the one who would hurt me just to teach me the pain of having loved someone so hard that her absence could collapse me?

One night is all we'll ever have. She'll torture me mentally for eternity because I'm taking what she loves most away from her. Before this situation with Alfie, she intrigued me, making me think I wanted more with her. Often. I had believed it impossible six months ago, perceiving in her eyes that she didn't want more than one night.

I'd be lying if I said I hadn't thought about her since then, even when fucking another woman.

Our fate has now been sealed. It must be this way.

If I could, I'd work out a way to make this better between us now. There is no way I'll keep Alfie from his cousin and grandmother. Of all people, I know how important a mother is to a boy. *What about when Hannah starts her own family?*

Fuck.

No. Don't think about that. Don't think about Hannah that way at all.

This is not about us.

This is only about Alfie.

TULSA GRABS a beer from the mini-fridge backstage and twists the top off. After a long pull, he says, "I think he sucks, but he's all we've got."

"How do we live in the Live Music Capital of the World, but we can't find a drummer who can hit basic beats?"

He shrugs. "I can fill in again."

Tulsa is our backup. He learned drums before guitar, but his lazy ass hates carrying the drum kit around. He also claims chicks love when you pull out a guitar and sing to them.

He's right. It's worked for me many times.

I try not to harass him too much about playing the drums, but we're getting desperate.

Right when he gets comfortable on a ripped vinyl recliner, the bar manager comes in. "C'mon. We need to wrap it up. We're behind tonight."

Tulsa's shoes hit the ground. Rivers pops a mint and follows him out. The bar is elongated, and there's a good crowd considering it's a Tuesday off 3rd Street. I grab my guitar and sling it over my shoulder. Tulsa takes his spot, back left. Rivers to my right, the guitar strap settling on his shoulders. I nod to the drummer, a fill-in we hired, and count. "Four. Three. Two. One."

We're supposed to hit the first note together, hence the countdown, but the drummer misses it for the second night in a row. Fuck it. I was pissed last night, but tonight, I'm over it. We need to find a steady drummer. In the meantime, the show must go on.

This bar is small, but I like it. Ten tables deep. Five wide at the most. One spotlight hits just to the left of me. I could shift, but I don't mind sharing with my brothers. I can see better when it's not directly in my eyes anyway.

I turn around and start singing into the microphone. Never let the audience in on the screw-up. We recover, but the feedback from the speakers is throwing my rhythm. One shitty mess up after another. We keep playing, praying it comes together.

Our sound guy graduated from college with honors in computer science a few weeks back. He got offered a job out in San Jose he couldn't refuse, leaving us high and dry ever since. I'm about to hop the stage to get rid of the reverb when some guy gets up from a table and steps behind the board. I'm about to warn him not to fucking touch it, but then I see who it is.

Johnny Outlaw.

He's back.

Fuck, yes!

I'd fist pump, but I'm not screwing up this second chance.

He puts his hand up and mouths, "I've got this." Two turns of some dials and the quality of our indie rock sound returns. When I see him nodding to the beat of the song like he's enjoying it, I ease back into the rhythm and do what I do best—play guitar and sing.

Our last song wraps, and if I didn't have to clear the stage, I'd hop down and talk to him. I should play it cool anyway. If Johnny wants to talk to us, he will.

And he does.

When I come back in from loading the Bronco, he's winding a cord like he's a roadie. "Need some help?" he asks.

"Always. Free help is hard to come by."

Laughing, he says, "I bet."

I try to keep it casual, though I'm kind of freaking out inside. He's a master guitarist, lyricist, and all-around musical heavyweight in the industry. Cool is my MO, though. I pick up my guitar and glance over. "You know your way around the board."

"I've had a little practice."

His friend, who is sitting on the edge of the stage, laughs. I set my guitar down and make the introduction. "I'm Jet Crow."

"Jack Dalton, but you can call me Johnny."

"So you're looking for a job, Johnny?" I tease.

"No. I'm pretty set right now." He's a big guy, not a typical build for . . . well, for anyone. Looks like he would take most guys in a fight. Lean and tall, but not scrawny. Works out. I stand to my full height and hit his. He says, "We heard if we were to see one band while we're in Austin, it was The Crow Brothers."

"Our reputation precedes us. In a good way, for once," I reply.

This time he laughs, and I start to relax. He asks, "Are you really brothers or is that just a name?"

"Some days, I'd like to disown them, but they're all mine."

"It's cool that you formed a band with your brothers."

"As hard of a time as I give them, I wouldn't want to play with anyone else. Unless you're hiring?" I start laughing.

He gets my humor and volleys back, "We're set for now. How long have you guys been performing?"

"We've been hitting it steady for seven years now."

He nods, analyzing me and then turning his attention to the guys packing up on stage. "Why don't you have a crew?"

"We're saving money."

"For studio fees?"

"Something like that."

Signaling back to his table, he says, "Once you're done, we'd love to buy you guys a round of drinks and discuss your music."

"Our music?"

"Business. Maybe recording music on my dime."

"Okay," I reply. "We'll hit up your table when we're done."

He asks, "What do you drink?"

"Whatever's on draft." I take another amp and start for the back. Tulsa is coming inside from the back door when I stop him. "Don't leave. Outlaw's here again and wants to buy us a beer."

"Johnny Outlaw?" he asks, trying to look over my shoulder to the crowd in the bar. "Fucking right, he's back. I'll go park and meet you guys."

When the pedals and last bits of our gig are in his truck, Rivers and I head inside.

Some asshole is homing in on our opportunity. Ripped jeans, baggy shirt stretched out at the collar, and leaning over the table Johnny's sitting at as if he had a personal invite. The guys don't seem interested in whatever this punk is peddling. Johnny says, "Good to meet you, Hunter. We'll keep your band in mind."

"Cool. Cool. Yeah. Come see us play," he says again.

From their body language, they're done with the intruder. Rivers and I take the available seats at their table and pull a spare from another for Tulsa when he gets here. Rivers rests his arm on the back of a chair and asks, "Who are you guys?"

This Hunter guy starts to laugh like he's a part of the conversation. The other guy stands, becoming a barricade between Johnny and Hunter. "We got the information. Now if you don't mind, this is a private conversation."

"Yeah. Cool. Cool. Come see us play before you leave town," he repeats.

When he's gone, Johnny looks around, side to side and over his shoulder before the other guy—lighter hair, familiar to me from photos only—asks Rivers, "Have you heard of the band The Resistance?"

Rivers laughs. "Who hasn't?"

Johnny says, "We haven't met." Sticking his hand out, he says, "I'm Johnny."

As if you can see the pieces fall together all at once in Rivers's eyes, his mouth falls open.

Johnny.

The Resistance.

I nod, already mocking him for not figuring it out sooner.

"Oh, fuck," Rivers exclaims. "You're Johnny Outlaw."

Johnny's nodding in response but lowers his head again and tugs on the bill of his hat. "Yes, if you could keep it down, that would really help us out."

The other guy sits forward. "We don't have security detail tonight. We're just out scouting covertly. We'd like to keep it that way if possible. I'm Tommy—"

"The band's manager," Rivers says. "You're a legend."

"Hear that, Outlaw? I'm a legend." Turning back to Rivers, he asks, "I like you. What's your name?"

"Rivers Crow."

"Rivers is a unique name. So is Jet. What's your brother's name?"

Rivers responds, "Tulsa. Cheesy as it sounds, we were named after the places we were conceived. I was made in Twin Rivers, California. My parents took a road trip that summer. Nine months later, they got a surprise."

By the grins on their faces, they're entertained. The manager asks, "So your parents joined the mile-high club on a jet?"

"Yeaaaaah, let's not talk about that."

Johnny says, "We don't have much time. We've heard you play twice now. You're good. Really good."

"Thank you, sir," Tulsa replies, spinning the chair around and sitting.

The guys laugh, and Johnny says, "You don't have to call me sir. I'm a guitarist like you."

"No, you're Johnny fucking Outlaw is who you are."

Our laughter doesn't compete with the murmuring in the bar. Looking around, I'm still trying to reason through how in the world I'm sitting across from the legendary Johnny Outlaw, when he asks, "What do you think about continuing this conversation somewhere more private?"

Maybe Tulsa's in as much shock as I am because we just stare at him. The other guy asks, "Would you be interested in meeting tomorrow? Maybe we can have a meal."

"Yeah, sure. We can do that." Then to Johnny, I say, "I taught myself how to play guitar listening to The Resistance's debut album. Man, that album was fucking brilliant. So strong. Heavy notes and the lyrics—poetry."

Johnny chuckles, looking down as if the compliment actually means something to him. "I like you, Jet." He stands and hits the back of his hand against his friend's chest. "This is Tommy, by the way. He's our manager." Tommy drops a card on the table, and then Johnny continues. "We've drawn more attention than I prefer in my off hours. I'm launching a label and I like your sound. We leave town tomorrow afternoon. I'd really like to talk to you about a potential collaboration. Give Tommy a call and let's meet up before we fly out."

I stand and shake his hand. "We will."

"Cool."

Turning to Tommy, I shake his hand. "Thanks. Nice meeting you."

Tommy shakes our hands. "Great set tonight."

"Thanks," Rivers replies.

Johnny says, "Good meeting you guys. Really great sound."

"You too, man," Tulsa says, "Wow. You really want to talk to us."

Johnny laughs again. "I dig your music. Great set."

We stand there with our mouths hanging open, trying to process how we were actually sitting at a table with them in a run-down bar in downtown Austin on a random Tuesday night. They want us to call them, and even better, potentially collaborate. Flashes go off around us as they work their way out in a hurry.

Tulsa and I face each other. He pushes me in that way he always does when he's in shock. "What the fuck just happened?"

"I think Johnny Outlaw just said he wants to work with us."

"Holy fuck. No fucking way." He jumps, his arm in the air. "Yes, fucking way!"

The crowd around us cheers, and he slams one of the shots the waitress sets in front of us. With a wink, the waitress asks, "Give Johnny my number, will ya?"

Tulsa makes his move. "First, I'm gonna need it, honey."

Her hand presses to his chest with her tray tucked under her arm. "I gave it to you two years ago, Tulsa Crow, and you never called me. Even after the fun night we had."

"How about a redo?"

Annnnd it's working, like it always does for him. Rivers and I roll our eyes and watch him work his magic.

First, her stance loosens, and then she smiles and begins to flirt right back. "If you can figure out my name, I'm sure my number is still in your phone."

I'm laughing too hard to help my brother out. I know for a fact he doesn't know her name. "She's got you there, bro."

Swinging his arm around her waist, he pulls her close. "I'm gonna call you tomorrow, Jen. Save a day this coming week and I'll take you dancing on my night off."

Her smile is bright and wide, her eyes . . . I've seen that

look before. She's in love, or at least temporary lust. The Crow Bros have that effect on women. She leans in mighty close and says, "You got it, Tulsa." She kisses him on the cheek and saunters off happy as a clam to snag a rare second date with the youngest Crow.

"I don't know how you do it, T, but you are the luckiest damn bastard I ever did know." Rivers asks, "How'd you remember her name?"

"I didn't. Lucky guess." He wipes his brow. "That was the easy part. It's figuring out which Jen when I have about a hundred in my contacts."

I push the shot to Tulsa. "You need this more."

He takes another. "Dude, Johnny fucking Outlaw. Whoa. Tonight is everything."

He's right. We've known for a while that our sound is good and we've paid our dues. We book consistent gigs, are known around town, and had a fairly successful EP release.

We play cohesively and can write songs without too much angst most of the time. If we could find a drummer to fill our band, I've always thought we could go somewhere. And I want that for my brothers. I want it for myself. But the responsibility I've always felt toward making that happen only increased when Mom died. She'd be so proud of this opportunity. As am I. We've done the hard yards for a few years now, and I think we're ready to be found. Ready to move forward.

Wrapping my arms around their shoulders, I correct him. "Nah, it's just the beginning."

"Damn right."

5

Jet

As much as I wanted to celebrate with Tulsa and Rivers, I have my judge-appointed meeting tomorrow to determine custody. I'm the only one required to be there, but they said they'd come for support. My brothers better not be late or hungover.

Lying in bed, I look over at the time: 3:12 a.m.

My body is exhausted, but my mind is too troubled to rest. I could lose Alfie and have him taken away before I even have a chance to be his dad.

I deserve the opportunity . . . no, not opportunity. Right. I have the right to be in his life more than some distant relative he gets to occasionally visit.

I'm his dad.

Nothing decided later today will change that. It will only change where he lives. That's all.

Scrubbing my hands over my face, I roll to the side, sit up, and sigh. There's so much on my mind, but Alfie's at the forefront with Hannah right behind.

Grabbing my cigarettes and lighter from the nightstand, I park myself next to the window and crack it open. Our winter's been mild, but tonight feels colder than usual.

My worries come in degrees matching the weather. The meeting tomorrow feels a lot like the fate of our band is also going to be decided.

One deal.

That's all it will take for us to finally get ahead. Maybe even enough to set aside for the upcoming expenses. I have some money saved, but is there a minimum required for me to win custody? Alfie's had a hard time with losing his mother. I don't want him to be miserable living with me because I can't afford to buy him something he wants.

I'm not sure how I'll be as a parent. Being raised by a single mom meant my brothers and I weren't spoiled, but I have six years to make up for.

Time together is more important. A roof. Food on the table. Love. That's what my mom always told us and showed us. Family. That's most important.

I stab the cigarette into the ashtray until the fire burns out, and then I wave away the smoky air so it slips through the open window. I'm tempted to leave it open. It's only me to concern myself with these days because I've not had anyone in my bed since Hannah left. I couldn't taint what we had by bringing someone home with me. It felt like a betrayal to what we shared. It was more than sex to me . . . My hang-up on this girl is getting really fucking old. I need to get over it, to get over her because she's not coming back.

Closing the window, I flip the lock and climb under the covers, forcing my mind to give in to the dark and try for sleep.

I'm not sure what time I finally do, but I wake up just after nine, which is about three hours earlier than usual.

This is good because when I check my messages, we have a breakfast meeting. This means I'll still have time to put Alfie's room together and get dressed for the custody hearing.

New sheets and a blanket are in the washing machine, and I'm getting ready when I get a text from Hannah. Sometimes when I see her name pop up, my heart stops because I think the worst. I'm denied before getting my day in court, she's found his real father, or she regrets ever meeting me. Relief washes over me when I read her message: *No matter what happens today, I want you to know that I think you're a good person for stepping up as you have.*

I don't need praise for being a decent human, a parent, a father, but I appreciate the sentiment. I reply: *This has been hard on all of us. You've done a lot for us this week when I know it was hard on you. Thank you.*

She doesn't send another, and I find myself feeling disappointed. I think we're supposed to be enemies, considering we're on opposing sides of this legal matter, but it's hard to hate her when just the sight of her brings back all the feelings I was beginning to form months ago.

Is that what that is? Feelings. *Feelings for her?*

We lost a shot at something more six months ago. Now life is too messy for us to get involved. *Fuck. Shake this off.* It was only one night. I grab my shoes and shake my head. I managed to get this far in life without the ridiculous notion of love coming along, though Rivers might argue. He was always the hopeless sap out of the three of us. I've watched him go in and out of a relationship with the same woman for years. Since he's single now, guess it's not a good time for anyone, especially not the woman fighting me for custody of my kid.

Nope. Hannah Nichols is a definite no-go.

As a musician, I'm well aware that timing is everything or the whole rhythm is off. Doesn't matter what happened between us before. All that matters is that we're a song gone wrong.

It's best if I focus on Alfie and my career. Love can go bother someone else who has time for it.

———

SINCE WE GET to the restaurant midmorning, it's not busy. Sitting in the back dining room of Matt's El Rancho, the waiter sets five glasses of water, salsa, and chips on the table. "Gracias."

Tulsa's knee is bouncing, his tapping foot hitting an unbalanced leg of the table, causing it to wobble.

"Dude," Rivers says, glaring at him. "Stop it. You're making me nervous."

"I can't help it."

"Help it anyway," I add, on edge as well. "It's just a meeting. We're not auditioning for them. They heard us play. They liked the music. This is all preliminary stuff. We're not signing any contracts, so fucking chill."

"Okay. Okay." He sits up when he sees the guys walk in. "Shit. I feel like our entire future hinges on this meeting, and we don't even know if they want us."

"It's just a meeting," I repeat, trying to kid myself. "That's all."

Johnny and Tommy walk in, but Tommy stops and turns back, that guy who was pestering them last night at the bar trailing them. Tommy directs him out the door while Johnny looks at ease as he works his way over. *A meeting.* That's all, I remind myself once more before standing up. After we all greet each other, we sit back down.

Johnny says, "Thanks for meeting us."

It's not like you get asked to meet with rock legends every day, but I play it off and shrug. "Yeah, of course."

"Tommy's coming. We were followed from the hotel."

"I saw. Everything all right?"

"Tommy will handle it." He lowers his voice. "Anyway, as I said last night, Tommy and I really like your sound. We've started a label—Outlaw Records—and we want to sign a few bands that fit what we're looking for."

"And you think we might be a good fit?" I drag the palms of my hands down my jeans, anxious to hear the answer.

"No," he replies. "We don't *think*. We know."

Tulsa is the ideal poker opponent because he can't contain his reactions. "No way! Really?"

I kick his shoe, but Rivers and I are laughing. I like to visit cloud nine like Tulsa has always had the freedom to do. As the oldest, I had to be responsible. I went through bouts of the opposite, but for the most part, I stepped up when our father stepped out.

Tommy joins us, leaning forward, and asks, "You put out an EP, but have you gone through the process for a full album before?"

The waiter takes our order before I can answer. When we're alone again, I reply, "We've started several times. We could have done one for ego and gotten a few local shops to carry it and uploaded it online, but we wanted to do an album when it was right and had some coverage. That's not happened for us yet, and it's too expensive to do on our own right now."

Tulsa adds, "We almost signed with a label once after playing South by Southwest, but the contract sucked, so we didn't."

"Smart. Don't sell your soul to sell a song." Johnny picks

up the water in front of him and takes a long pull before saying, "I think that's what makes us unique. We've been there. We started from nothing, literally playing keggers and dive bars. My band played anywhere that paid or gave us exposure. We're not looking to fuck over the artist."

Rivers says, "To be blunt, though, what's in it for you?"

Johnny replies, "We'll help protect your interests and long-term royalties, but this is a business. If we're sharing our connections, from producers to marketing, and fronting the costs, we need to make money on the back end. It's all in the contract, and we can have it sent over."

I say, "Send it over. We'd like to see it."

Tommy says, "No problem. We'll get one out to you tomorrow."

Johnny leans in. "I'd like to produce the album myself. I'll be there in the studio with you developing and growing the sound."

I glance at Tulsa who is staring wide-eyed and shocked. I lean forward and lower my voice. "Why do you want to work with us? And what is the offer that you're setting down on the table?"

Tommy clears his throat, and then replies, "Five-year contract, two albums, possibly three based on sales of the first two. We work like the publishing world works. You'll get an advance and a negotiated percentage of royalties after we recoup our investment."

Johnny adds, "We want to be a label that works with the artist, not against them. We need you making music and doing interviews. Basically, showing up every day ready to play, learn, and create. We're not talking part-time work here. A lot goes into making a successful album, and we'd rather have you focused on that than figuring out how you're going to pay your bills."

Rivers says, "Sounds amazing, but wanting our undivided attention needs to pay the bills."

The side of Johnny's mouth slides up. Tommy outright laughs, hitting Johnny on the back. "I like these guys. They remind me of you, Dex, and Cory." Then he turns back to us. "It's all negotiable. Doesn't mean we'll accept the counteroffer, but it will cover your normal living expenses."

Tulsa asks, "What's the downside?"

Johnny sits back and replies, "We record in LA, and you'll be in the studio daily until the album's cut."

"I have a son," I say. I don't even know where that comes from. The case with Alfie is fragile at best with no determined outcome, but the words don't feel entirely foreign like they used to.

"I have a son named James," he adds.

"Mine is Alfred. We call him Alfie."

"That's an old-fashioned name. After a relative?"

Pausing, I answer as honestly as I can without revealing too much, "Mother's choice."

"Cool. So what are your thoughts on working out a deal?"

Tulsa nudges me, but when I look at Rivers, some of the excitement has worn off. He understands the situation with me is complicated, but he also knows that Alfie isn't just a factor; he's the only thing that matters. Until I have answers, I can't make a decision.

"I'm not sure what to say. I mean, I appreciate the offer, but I'm not sure how to swing living bi-coastal. My son will be living with me full time. There's just a lot to work out." I pause, but then add, "His mother recently passed away."

Johnny's the first to speak. "I'm sorry to hear that."

Nodding, I crack my knuckles under the table. "So am I. The rest is . . . complicated."

There's a pause in the conversation until Tommy says, "All great songs come from somewhere deep. I'm sure there's a song in there somewhere."

Johnny says, "We won't say no based on not having the answers right now. The last thing we want is to cause a problem for you."

Tommy sits back, his body sinking against the chair. "I'm sure we can find some options to handle the transition and get you some help. If you're seriously considering the offer, then let us get back to LA and talk to our business manager." He glances at Johnny. "Rochelle might have some ideas."

Johnny seems to be mulling over the suggestion. "She'll get you what you need, but I'd like to know what your initial thoughts are after hearing the loose details."

Rivers speaks up first, "I can't lie. Making music where I don't have to worry about my bills sounds damn good."

Tulsa adds, "We're getting the shot we've always wanted from musicians we've respected most of our lives."

Shaking his head, Johnny laughs. "We're not that old."

He has a great sense of humor. "There's no doubt we want to work with you guys." Rivers's shoe hits the toe of mine, nudging me on. "My kid is a priority. I have to do what's best for him, so send us your offer and we'll consider our options."

The food is delivered, and Johnny says, "I miss Tex-Mex food so fucking much. With business out of the way, let's eat."

Conversation over the meal is full of laughs and music talk. I like Johnny and Tommy. As famous as Johnny Outlaw is, fame hasn't gone to his head. His drive is obvious, and his passion is seen and heard when he talks about music as an art, something internal that possesses a part of one's soul.

I know what he means. It didn't matter that I quit college

as long as I had music. I didn't need to be rich because I was living a good life.

After stuffing ourselves, they head for the airport, and we head home. On the drive, Tulsa says, "It's everything we've been working for, Jet."

I hear the concern in his voice, the future pending based on mine. I hate that I'm the reason for his worry. "The advance might cover rent and hiring someone to help me with Alfie when we play gigs, or when we're in the studio."

From the back seat, Rivers asks, "When we need to be in LA, he can come with us?"

I'm already tearing him away from the home he knows. Can I take him to LA for three weeks as well? "I'm already stressed about the hearing. Let's wait to hear about custody before planning. We'll know before we receive the contracts."

"What about the offer?" Tulsa asks, but I already see that shit-eating grin on his face. He knows what I'm going to say before I even say it.

I glance at Rivers, and my grin can't be hidden. "If it's decent money, and they seemed like they wouldn't screw us over, then we just scored ourselves a deal."

Reaching out the window, he bangs his hand on the side of the truck and hollers. "Look at us now."

Rivers adds, "The Crow Brothers are heading for the big time. LA or bust, baby."

6

Jet

Staring down into the wide green eyes of my son, tears threaten mine while my hand tightens around his. He asks, "Does that make me a Crow?"

I tap his nose. "You've always been a Crow, but you're lucky to have such a cool last name like Barnett." Kneeling, I add, "Looks like you're coming home with me, little man."

He smiles, reassuring me, reminding me of his mother. Cassie and I were casual, or so I thought. I guess she was a little more serious than I was even though I've never had a bad thought about her. She told me I broke her heart, so when she kicked me to the curb, I was left dumbfounded. I thought I must have deserved it, that I wasn't good enough for her. Back then, I was all ego and attitude on the surface, but on the inside, I was struggling to deal with my mother's death. I'm not sure I'm any better now, but let's hope so since I was just given a chance to earn full custody of this little human.

I've thought a lot about the time I spent with Cassie,

thinking of this child and wishing I'd known she was pregnant before we went our separate ways.

Alfred Jet Barnett.

My son was born eight months after the fight that ended us for good.

Almost seven years later, he gives my hand a little squeeze and says, "It'll be okay. I'll make ramen noodles."

"You know how to make ramen?"

"Yes. Hannah says it's good, and they make us feel less sad on bad days."

"Are you having a bad day?"

"I was happy, but then I saw Grandma and Hannah. They're sad. That makes me sad."

"They want what's best for you. We all decided that for the time being that all of us getting time with you will be best." Glancing across the aisle of the courtroom, the woman whose happiness was traded for mine stands staring down at her hands. I miss those hands, the softness of her hands against the roughness of mine.

Fuck. It's not just her hands I miss.

I miss her.

She pulls a tissue from her pocket and wipes her eyes, making me feel bad for how things turned out, my heart hurting for hers. It makes me wonder how she would feel about me if she had won.

We didn't know how entangled our lives were when we first met. They've become more twisted since. When our eyes meet now, I understand the sadness I saw in them then, but I've layered more troubles to make them grayer.

Alfie is my son, though. I get that Hannah Nichols is protective of him. She was there when I wasn't, but it wasn't by my choice but his mother's. I'm here now, and it wouldn't be right to let someone else raise him when I created him. He's not just a responsibility. He's a part of me.

Hannah may be sad to lose him full time, but we're both stuck in this odd temporary arrangement of shared custody for the next two months. I'm determined to make her see that I can be what he needs long after this deal expires.

When I stand, she leaves her aunt's side, comes over, and bends in front of Alfie. Taking his free hand, she says, "My number is in your bag. Call me anytime you want—day or night. If you need anything—"

I say, "I'll make sure he gets whatever he needs."

Standing up, she tightens her mouth into a straight line, her eyes blazing with the things she wants to say. Her tongue is still slick, willing to burn me with an insult. "You're new to parenting."

"I'll learn."

"What happens when he gets a fever?"

"I'll call his doctor."

"What about if he falls off his bike?"

Crossing my arms over my chest in annoyance, I reply, "I'll make sure he's wearing a helmet before getting on."

"And if he scrapes his knee?"

"Then he scrapes his knee and we'll bandage it."

"What about—"

"Is this a pop quiz?"

Her shoulders fall, and she looks down. "I'm sorry. I just—"

That's when I see her, the real her, the girl I once knew for a night when the world wasn't trying to ruin everything good we had. Reaching out, I touch her wrist, tempted to encircle it with my hand. It's small enough, at least in comparison. It's probably just a memory making me want things I can't have. I shove down my personal wants because they don't matter anymore. When she looks up, I say, "I understand. I won't let anything happen to him."

Her aunt snaps, "Hannah."

"I'll be right there," she replies, looking back. Eileen Barnett has not said two words to me since she walked in. She barely acknowledges my existence, but she had plenty of nasty things to tell the judge while I sat there and bit my tongue.

All of it bullshit she's made up in her head.

I defended myself as if I was charged with the crime of taking her daughter out on a few dates. I was nineteen when I met Cassie. I wasn't in love, but I liked her a lot. Her mother never approved of me, and even then, my gut told me she was behind the change in Cassie's feelings for me too.

Hannah dips down again to hug Alfie, so tight as if she'll never see him again. Desperation coats her voice and mingles with the tears she's stifling. "I'll see you in a few days, okay?"

"Okay," he replies with his arms around her neck. He kisses her on the head and smiles. "I'm going to make ramen noodles for Jet. Just like I make for you."

"Your specialty." Her smile is wide, but I can see it's put on for him. When she stands again, she says to me, "Two days. Please have him ready at noon."

"We're not enemies, Hannah."

Her hands fly to cover Alfie's ears, and she grits her teeth. "Don't talk about us in front of him. There is not an 'us' except when it comes to him. For him, we have to stand as a united front, not talk of being enemies."

Her anger is palpable, but I have a feeling it's more than anger she's feeling. The pain is heard in her voice. I want to make her feel better, to ease the heartbreak that rivals her joy, but I also have a right to spend time with my son and a chance to get to know him without an audience judging everything I do. Time with him was stolen from me prior to now, and I intend to make up for it. "We should get going."

Stepping back, she gives us space. "You have my number if you have any questions, Mr. Crow." *We're back to Mr. Crow again?*

"You don't have to be formal with me. Jet will do."

"I'm not sure—"

She was damn sure of my name when she called it out three times. "It seems our past is clearly another time and place, far from this reality."

Reaching to cover Alfie's ears again, she snaps, "I made a mistake."

Her claws come out when she feels threatened. Good to know. "We weren't a mistake. You may have walked away that day, but I could see it meant more than you were letting on. You were just too caught up in your head to recognize what we were."

"Caught up in my head? My cousin was fighting for her life. I've not had the luxury of being caught up in my own head in longer than I can remember. So don't come at me like we were more than . . ." She stops talking and looks around. Her aunt is impatiently waiting at the doors to leave. Her hands tighten over Alfie's ears, who's looking a little annoyed, and she whispers, "For Alfie's sake and mine, let's forget anything ever happened between us."

Impossible, sweet Hannah. She really has no clue . . . Leaning in, I whisper in her ear, "It will be hard to forget one of the best nights of my life, but I guess I'll try."

My confession seems to catch her off guard. Her lips part as I pull back, and she stares into my eyes. Just when I think she's about to say something, she takes a deep breath

80

S.L. SCOTT

instead and drops her hands to her sides. "He should be in bed by seven, and his favorite nightlight is in the bag. Make sure he brushes his teeth both morning and ni—"

"Got it. See you Friday."

Alfie smiles. "Bye, Hannah."

"Love you," she says, causing me to look back. Her eyes dart from Alfie's to mine.

"Love you, too," he replies as we walk out of the courtroom and into the lobby where my brothers have been waiting. He's looking around, over his shoulder, and back down the open lobby. I know he's looking for his grandma. "Where's Grandma?"

Though I wish she didn't, she can hate me all she wants, but Alfie, he doesn't deserve anything less than love and support. "I don't know, buddy. Maybe she's outside. Let's go look."

Rivers says, "Go get the truck, Tulsa."

Tulsa doesn't question the order. He feels the tension. We all do.

When we exit, she's still nowhere to be found. I really hope she doesn't make this situation worse by her actions, judging by her words inside.

My brother's Bronco is parked at the curb, so we follow Rivers down the steps. I stop Alfie just out of hearing distance from everybody else and squat so I'm at eye level. "My home is your home. Are you ready to go see it?"

Out of the corners of my eyes, I see her walking to her car in the distance. Her aunt is waving her hands, furious if I'm reading her body language correctly. "Hey, there's your grandma."

"Grandma," he shouts, dashing toward her.

Standing there, I watch carefully. I won't let her hurt him. He won't be a casualty in her war. I'm relieved when she hugs him. He jumps up into Hannah's arms, and she squeezes him tight, just as tight as he hugs her.

She dabs her eyes with tissues and then to him, she nods my way. When he comes running back, I feel her eyes on me and look up. Giving her a little wave, I open the door for him. "Climb in."

He asks, "How about ice cream?"

I laugh. "Nice try, kid. Dinner first. Ice cream after."

"Oh, man," he says, sounding disappointed as we start walking again. "I thought this would be fun."

"Fun and spoiled are two different things."

"That's what Hannah always says."

"Hannah's pretty wise."

"She's pretty, too," he says, surprising me.

Chuckling, I nudge his shoe with mine. "You're too young to be into girls."

Tulsa adds, "Anyway, she's your cousin, Alfie. That means off-limits."

Alfie's quick to reply, "For me, but for Jet she's on-limits."

After the shock wears off that he actually just said that, I ruffle his hair. "Hey," I start, "what do you know about on-limits?"

"I'm six, not dumb. I know all about the birds and the bees. Grandma has HBO."

Good grief, this kid. He's going to keep me on my toes. Goodbye single days. Hello parenting. "Remind me to cancel Cinemax, Rivers."

Rivers laughs as I slide into the back after Alfie, as he takes the passenger seat. My legs are cramped back here, and I'm tempted to kick my little brother out of the prime real estate up front, but this transition time with Alfie is important. So I stay after I give a hard shove with my knee into the back of the seat. "A little legroom would be nice."

"Welcome to my world, bro."

This is like living in an alternate universe. I'm usually the one in charge, but things have changed dramatically over the last week. I'll be in charge, but it's not just my brothers and me anymore. Life won't be all fun and games, playing music late into the night, or going home with a chick after a gig when the right opportunities come around.

Surprisingly, I'm not bothered by the change. Alfie comes first.

7

Jet

I'm a sucker for those big eyes and little dimples when he smiles. Alfie got his wish. After we finish two scoops of ice cream with whipped cream and chocolate sauce, I sit back and rub my stomach. "Not sure I'm going to have room for dinner now."

Alfie mimics me, even groaning a little like I did. "Yeah, I might just hit the hay."

I laugh. He's got a good sense of humor. "It's been a big day. You okay?"

"I guess. I—" He looks around the living room.

I don't live in a particularly nice house, but it's been home for a few years. Affordable. Decent neighborhood. Low bills that allow me to live alone instead of with my brothers, who share a place a few miles away. I never needed much but looking at him makes me want to give him more. "You what, buddy?"

His shoulders sag, and he looks down at his lap, his fingers twisting the hem of his shirt. "Hannah said I should be grateful to have so many people who love me. I got uncles too, but . . ."

"But?"

"I miss my mom."

"I'm sure you do. I lost my mom too. I know it hurts a lot." I pull him close just as he begins to sniffle. His head is tucked against my side, and I add, "We don't know each other well, but I'm here for you, Alfie. I'm not just your dad, but also a friend. You can talk to me about anything, including your mom and your feelings."

He looks up, tears welling over his bottom lids and falling down his cheeks. "My mommy said if I didn't have her, I'd have you; that you and Hannah would take care of me."

Comments like this and the "lucky to have you" one from the other day surprise me, considering all the bad things Hannah's been told about me. Cassie apparently hated me, but she didn't turn our kid against me. I guess I should be thankful for small favors.

I still wish I could have been there for him, for her even, all along. Been there when she got sick. Met Hannah the way we should have. Maybe then things wouldn't be like they are now. "I will. We're in this together." I hope Hannah and I can work together.

He asks, "What's *this*?"

"Life."

"We're in life together?"

"Yes. Our blood bonds us. The blood that runs through me runs through you. That makes us family. And family always sticks together."

For a little kid, he seems to have a deep understanding beyond his years. He nods, a shared knowing look between us.

The stress from today must just be too much because the sugar rush never comes. When he yawns, I check the time. Just after eight. Hannah would flip if she knew he was up this late. "C'mon, I think that ice cream can tide you over until tomorrow. It's late, and it's been a long day. Time for bed."

We make our way to his room. As he stands in the center, I open his bag and dig out his toothbrush and paste. "Bathroom's across the hall. Are you potty trained?"

"I'm not a baby," he replies defensively.

Throwing my hands up in surrender, I try to restrain my smile. "Okay. Okay. I didn't know."

While he brushes his teeth, I pull his nightlight out and plug it in. His stuffed Snoopy is tossed on the bed, and pajamas are set out. We muddle through the routine without issue, and when he climbs into bed, I kneel next to him. "Hey Alfie?"

"Yeah?"

"I'm new to all this dad stuff. Maybe you can help me out and show me the ropes to parenting a big boy."

"Didn't your dad show you?"

"Long story for another day."

His hand touches my nose and then his own. "Will my nose be big like yours?"

Reactively grabbing my nose, I ask, "Is it that big?"

He giggles his answer. "Bigger than mine."

I tap his nose. "That is a fact. As for size, I think yours will grow to be the size you're meant to have."

"You're tall. Uncle Tulsa and Uncle Rivers are tall. Mom was small like Hannah. Will I be big or small?"

"Only time will tell. The one thing I do know is that we won't find out tonight. We can measure you tomorrow and start keeping track, but you need to get some sleep tonight."

"I didn't make ramen noodles. Since we're in life together, I can make them tomorrow."

Chuckling, I pull the covers higher to his chin. "Yes, we're in life together." I kiss the top of his head and kneel back. It reminds me of how my mom used to kiss my head at bedtime, and how much I missed that once I was *too old* for her to do it. How much I missed when she told me she loved me. Alfie will never receive that kiss from his mom again or hear her tell him she loves him, and it breaks my heart. Technically, I've only known him minutes, but already, he's in my heart. "Is it too soon to tell you I love you?"

"Mommy told me that you should always tell people you love them if you feel it. I wish I could tell her."

"Don't worry, buddy. She knows." Kissing his head, I say, "I love you."

"I like you, Jet."

I smile. We'll get there in time. "Good night."

"Night."

After shutting the door, I walk back into the living room and stand there, not sure what I'm supposed to do. Is this what it's like to be a parent? Never knowing what to do next and winging it day by day?

I look back toward the bedroom where Alfie is sleeping. A week ago, I thought we'd lost the biggest opportunity of our lives. Johnny Outlaw was there and then gone the next song.

When Hannah walked in, the words she said would change my life forever—you have a son—and I realized right then the opportunity I had been given.

Just a week after meeting him, I'm now worrying daily about the son I want to get to know and how I'm going to provide for him. I can't scrape by anymore. It's not just about me. If the advance from Outlaw Records isn't enough, do I give up my dreams to give my kid what he needs?

Yes is the only answer.

I'll do whatever I need to do. I'll do everything my father never did.

My phone buzzes with a text. When I look down, I see Hannah's name. Seeing it flash on my screen reminds me of the sadness I'm used to seeing in her eyes. I feel it inside me. Despite the good of discovering that this little person exists in my world, something missing still remains.

The text buzzes again. *How's Alfie settling in?*

She's tenacious. It's only been three hours since she saw him, so I can already tell this woman is going to drive me mad. I may be new at this parenting thing, but damn, give me a chance to screw up before you harass me.

Before I have time to respond, a shadow crosses my front window. Tossing my phone on the couch, I open the door, and find the woman taking up too many of my thoughts pacing my porch. "Can't resist me?" I wing it with a bad line.

"You wish," Hannah snaps, stopping and crossing her arms over her chest.

Leaning against the doorframe, I mimic her arm position, and smirk. "Then to what do I owe the displeasure?"

"I was worried about Alfie. You didn't text me."

My brow shoots to the sky. "I didn't know I was supposed to. Anyway, you didn't give me much of a chance." My annoyance comes out with a sigh. "For the record, he's fine." Refusing to give her ammo against me on night one, I give her all she needs, "We had dinner, and he went to bed."

Her body loses the fight, and she appears to relax for the first time since the night we first met. She's been so uptight this last week, understandably so, but I still don't think it's warranted. I'm tempted to offer her a beer and some company, but I'm not sure that's a good idea, though. "I should go back inside. It's getting late."

"You don't normally play until after ten. Eight thirty must be early for you."

The little hint of sarcasm in her tone betrays the curiosity in her eyes. Sliding my hands into my pockets, I drop my defenses. "I don't want to argue with you, Hannah."

"I shouldn't have come here. I just . . . I was thinking about Cassie."

"I've been thinking about her a lot as well."

Her eyes close and reopen with what looks like tears filling them. "She was an amazing mother. She would push herself harder than she should have in the end just to be there for him as much as she could."

I'm starting to see the crack in her armor. "I'm sorry for your loss."

"I thought I would feel better if I was close to him because I miss him already."

"This is new territory for both of us. We have to work together for the next sixty days, but I need you to let me get to know Alfie. I had the first six years taken from me, so I want this time with him to matter. I need it to build our relationship."

"You're right. You deserve that. I'm sorry."

"It's all right that you're here. He was good tonight and settled in easily. It could have been the opposite, and it might be tomorrow, but we're all taking it day by day." Looking at her car in my driveway, I realize she remembered the way. "It's good to see you again."

The nicety seems to give her pause, but as if the weight of the world returns, she squares her body to me. "I shouldn't have come. I don't know what I was thinking." She rushes for the steps.

"Hey, Hannah?"

Keeping her back to me, she looks over her shoulder.

"I won't keep him from you."

Her gaze moves ahead of her when she turns away. "Thanks," she whispers. I'm tempted to say more just to see her eyes again, but then she leaves.

At one time, I had the nerve to ask her to stay. She didn't. This time, I don't ask, and I don't watch her leave. I move inside, lock the door behind me, and then decide to make the most of a rare night at home. I go to bed because I have a feeling I'm going to be up early.

8

Jet

"Jet . . . Jet . . . Jeeet?"

Daylight infiltrates my darker dreams, and my eyes slowly open to find two little green peepers so close that I startle. "Fuck."

"You swear."

"Shit. Sorry." Fuck. I can't swear in front of Alfie. "What are you doing in here?"

"Daylight's burnin'. That's what Grandma says."

"What time is it?" I try to look around him to the nightstand, but his hair is pretty crazy, exactly like mine in the morning. "Do you shower in the morning?"

"I take a bath at night when Hannah makes me. Are you going to make me?"

Chuckling, I ruffle his hair up even more. "Yep."

"Dang."

Climbing onto the bed, he says, "I thought it would be more fun being here," and sits next to me.

I adjust my pillows and lean against the wall. "Hopefully,

it will be fun, but I also have to make sure you're clean, healthy, and a good human."

"What's a good human?"

"A good human is a person who is nice and treats others well."

He reaches over and ruffles my hair, making me laugh. "Are you a good or bad human, Jet?"

I pause. I'm good inside. I live a life I'm not ashamed of, but I have regrets. Looking at him, I wonder if maybe I am bad, at least for him, like his grandma and Hannah think. "I do my best to treat others the way I like to be treated."

"What does that mean?"

"You ask a lot of questions. I think I need coffee before we keep going."

Perking up, he says, "There's coffee in the kitchen."

My eyes go wide. "You made coffee?"

"You have a big bed."

"I'm a big guy, but let's get back to the coffee."

"Hannah needs coffee in the morning before she does anything. She says grown-ups need it to function."

"She's right." Reaching over, I pull him close and give him a little noogie on the head. "You're a handful." He's giggling while I flip the covers off and grab Alfie, holding him over my shoulder. "C'mon you. Coffee for me. Milk for you."

Wiggling and full of more giggles, he squeals. When I set him down on top of the bar, I ask, "Hungry?"

"I ate cereal."

"You know how to make cereal?"

"I'm six, not a—"

"Not a baby. Gotcha." I pull eggs and milk out of the fridge to scramble, and a mixing bowl and fork. Alfie's eyes stay on me. I can't tell if it's because I'm new to him or if he's just not used to having a man around. "You'll be honest with me, right, Alfie?"

"Yes. Lying is bad."

"Yes, lying is bad. I'm going to ask you a lot of questions like you ask me. I want you to know you can always be honest. You won't get in trouble for telling the truth." I look up after I pour the eggs in a pan on top of the hot stove. "You can ask me anything you want to know as well. This is new for both of us. What do you say we work as a team?"

He hops off the counter. "I've never been on a team before."

"No sports?"

"No. It was too much money and too much time away from my mom when she was sick. That's what Grandma would say."

"What about Hannah?"

"Hannah wasn't there yet. When Mom got really sick, Grandma had Hannah come live with us."

"When was that? Do you remember?"

"My birthday. She took me to the zoo."

"August fifth." I mentally tally how many months back from this month, March, that is. Seven. We hooked up Labor Day weekend. What made her go out that night?

Hannah was struggling, wanting to forget what was happening for one night. If only I'd known then, maybe I could have helped. Maybe our conversation would have led me to her cousin and Alfie.

Regrets. If I could have a redo . . . Looking at this brave kid, I ask, "Do you have photos of your mom?"

Dashing off before I barely finish, I worry I've upset him. I click off the burner and start for the hall when he comes running out of his room and right back to the kitchen. Holding up photos, he says, "I have these."

"Come show me." I sit on the couch, and he sits next to me, not even denting the cushion he's so little. Makes me wonder if he's the size of most six-year-olds or if he's on the smaller side. My mom told me I was a big baby but a small child. High school was good to me. College even better.

Crows are built big.

Mentally, I add his health and medical history to my checklist of things to do and research. "What do you have there? Photos?"

"This one was when my mom had me. That's me. The baby in her arms. She was happy that day. See her smile?"

I haven't seen Cassie since the day we ended our relationship. Seeing her again reminds me of how beautiful she was—dark blond hair and those green eyes she shares with Alfie. Taking the photo in hand, I say, "I bet you were the happiest day of her life."

"What about you?"

"What about me?"

"Was I the happiest day of your life?"

Seeing the anticipation in his expression, the hope in his eyes, and those dimples, I nod. "Meeting you was the best day of my life, Alfie." It's not a realization. It's a feeling deep inside. An emptiness I didn't know I had is suddenly full and overflowing for this kid. How is it so instantaneous? I don't even know him, but it's as if my heart has all along. I wrap my arm around him and pull him to my side. "Today's even better."

He doesn't reply, but he doesn't need to. Sometimes, a quiet moment is all that's needed. I hand his photo back to him, and he shows me the other photos, five in total. I ask, "I was thinking we could get a frame for one of these. What do you think?"

"This one."

He holds up the most recent picture taken, one of him lying next to her in bed. I'm thinking it was not too long ago by her appearance—the tan she once had long gone, frailer than anyone ever should be, and her hair thinned. "You sure?"

"She's pretty like a princess."

Staring at the photo, I realize he doesn't see her as sick; he sees her as his mom. She's still smiling because he's there, and he sees that love shining through. Taking the photo, I say, "She's very pretty just like a princess." I stand and put the photo on the shelf, propping it up against some of my albums so we can see it. "How's this spot?"

He smiles and gives me two thumbs-up.

I walk back into the kitchen and start the flame on the burner to finish cooking my eggs. "Hey, Alfie?"

"Yeah?" Leaning back on the couch, he puts his hands behind his head and kicks his feet up on the coffee table, reminding me a lot of Tulsa.

"I'll let you take today off since we're in that transition phase Hannah mentioned, but tomorrow, I think you should go back to school."

"I'll let you take me to the zoo."

"You'll let me?" I laugh. This kid. If I didn't know better, he could be Tulsa's kid through and through. "If I take you to the zoo today, you're going back to school tomorrow."

"Oh, man. Bummer."

"School is Monday through Friday, buddy. I think it's good if we get back on schedule."

He sighs exasperatedly. "Okay."

"But today, we get to have fun. Tell me about this zoo."

Bolting upright, he animatedly tells me about the jaguars and hundred-year-old tortoises. How the Austin Zoo is a rehab sanctuary. An hour later, we're there, and he's showing me around as he knows the layout by heart. On the train a few hours later, I get a text. Hannah: *How's your first day on the job?*

It's interesting, or maybe I'm just reading more into it, but she actually seems friendly. Alfie's lucky to have her in his corner. I reply: *The hours are tough, but it's been a good day.*

And it has. I've smiled and laughed more than I have in a long time even though I've always thought of myself as a happy guy. With Alfie around, it's a different kind of happy—his innocence is refreshing. It's incredible to see the world through his untainted eyes.

I think this parenting gig is going to work out A-OK. She replies: *Good to hear. I noticed you have a show tonight. What are you going to do with Alfie?*

Shit. With all the crazy of the past few days, I had forgotten about tonight. As we roll back into the train terminal, my phone rings. I help Alfie off and answer as I walk through the gate, "You have got to be one of the most impatient women I've ever known, and I've known a few."

"I just bet you have. Anyway, I'd be happy to come hang out with him, stay while you're gone. I mean, I'm not trying to intrude. It's not my day with him or anything."

"It's okay. I appreciate the offer." Checking the time, it's just past two. "We're at the zoo right now, but I do need to make arrangements."

"You took him to the zoo?"

I cringe, wondering if I just screwed up by telling her the truth. "I know he's supposed to be in school and stuff, but—"

"It's really thoughtful of you to do that."

"He's been thrown into the care of a stranger."

"I spent a lot of time trying to prepare him for it. We talked about you. A lot."

"Thank you. He's been really good. I brought him to the zoo because I thought it would be a good way for us to get to know each other better."

"How's that going?"

"Like we've known each other his whole life."

I can only see her in my mind, but the mouth that drew me to her is smiling. "Then it was worth skipping school. Anyway, it's only one time, but he'll remember you taking him long after today."

"Hope so."

"As I was saying, I don't want to intrude on your day, but if you want, I can make him dinner."

"I promised to let him make ramen noodles." Given I'll be performing later, I'll have to eat more before I go on set. Ramen noodles will definitely not be enough by any stretch of the imagination. "You can come over a little early and eat with us. I'd appreciate the help after and I can pay you."

The silence stretches between us, and then she says, "You don't have to pay me to spend time with Alfie. I miss him. Last night and today have been too quiet."

Helping me seems to be helping her. Watching him run ahead, I realize wherever he ends up, he'll be surrounded by love. "He's lucky to have you. I have to head out by nine, so what time do you want to come over?"

"He gets hungry early. If you wait too long, he'll fill up on snacks."

"How about six?"

"I'll be there. Can I bring anything?"

I kind of love how at ease she is, as if we might be friends right now. "I don't have anything to drink but beer, but you're welcome to it if you want."

I'm rewarded with a chuckle. "Thanks. See you later."

"See you later."

Alfie tugs on my shirt. "Why are you smiling? Is it the birds? They don't have crows here, but they have peacocks by the snack bar."

I don't even know what this kid is talking about, but he makes me laugh. "C'mon. We need to go to the store before heading home."

"Ahhh."

"What's ahhh?"

"I don't want to leave."

"Hannah's coming over for dinner."

Well, that turned his frown upside down. Cocking an eyebrow, I nudge him as we walk toward the exit. "What's with that grin on your face?"

"Hannah's coming over. Figured that's why you were smiling too."

With a peacock in sight, he runs ahead to get a closer look. "Look, Jet!"

"Awesome, little dude." My smile remains long after he's left my side. If I'm being honest, he's right. I am smiling because Hannah's coming over. But looking at this kid with skinny knee-knockers, a head full of wild hair, and better insight than most adults I know, it stays.

9

Hannah

Jet Crow ... Good lord, that man.

I've lost so much time in memories of him. It's hard to stand my ground when all I want to do is lie down with him ... on top of me. Again.

I can't even listen to his music anymore. My body starts aching in ways I can't satisfy when I hear his deep voice singing.

His lips.

His mouth.

His tongue.

God. My body warms, remembering when he whispered in my ear, "It will be hard to forget the best night of my life."

Taking a slow inhale, I close my eyes, wanting to touch him again as he touches me. Strong hands with rough, callused fingers drag over my soft skin, tiny triggers fueling my desires. Feverish.

My breathing picks up.

My body is his and not my own.

My thoughts buried back in his bed. There's no escaping the hunger I have for Jet.

I crave him.

I ache for him.

I'll burn for him just to taste the fire, shaming myself for giving in once again.

"*Ah.*" I try to catch my harsh breath and slow my racing heart. I exhale a deep breath, releasing the remaining pent-up energy.

Straightening the lace that hugs my hips, I rest my arms on the bed beside me as I come down from the high of a release. I stare at the ceiling fan, my body exhausted, but alive and still tingling between my legs. A pulse still beats to the rhythm we once created together, my body remembering every tender and beautiful moment we once shared.

I've got to learn to embrace hate a little better, or I'm never going to be able to keep my real feelings hidden from the world, from Eileen, and from Jet.

The sound of cabinets slamming is heard. It was the washing machine lid being dropped earlier. The front door before that.

I've been hiding in my room all day. I shouldn't. I know I shouldn't. I understand Aunt Eileen is upset, but I'm upset too. First, we lost Cassie. Now, we lost custody of Alfie.

I need to mourn in my own way without having to discuss or defend Jet Crow. If I go out there, that's what will end up happening, and I'm just not ready. I wouldn't know what to say anyway.

I'm conflicted.

He has a right to raise his son. From all that I've seen and discovered on my own, Jet's a good guy who wants to do right by his son. Who am I to discount that desire? But damn it, I miss Alfie and worry about him constantly.

All the things I've heard about the man over the past seven years, when pieced together, don't make up the man I met, the man I've come to think about too much.

Sitting up, I decide it's time to deal with the inevitable. I start to freshen up before heading into the firing line, also known as the kitchen, but then my phone rings. It's been a few months since I've seen that name and heard my friend's voice, so I answer quickly, "Hi there, stranger."

Dave Carson, friend and one time savior. "Hey there. It's been a while. Wanted to check in."

"Too long. Things are . . . what they are." He'll want to know, so I just tell him without waiting to be asked. "Cassie passed away."

"Oh, wow. I'm sorry, Hannah. I should have called sooner."

"No. We knew it was just a matter of time. She was so young, and it's a terrible way to die, but in a way, we got to prepare Alfie." I was "prepared," but it hasn't made it any less painful.

"I'm sorry. I really am."

"Thank you." I'm so happy to hear from him. "How are you?"

"Good. Working a lot."

"Oh yeah, where?"

"A recording studio over on Oltorf. I have the night shift. Musicians are a funny bunch. It's the busiest and shittiest shift, but I get to record for free when it's not in use."

"That's cool. Are you recording an album?"

"I'm working on an EP, but I won't be able to do anything with it for at least another year. I need money for that."

I smile, but I feel the tightness. I take the blame for him not being with the band he started. My ex did damage to me and managed to fuck his best friend over in the process. "I'm sorry."

"Don't do that, Hannah. You don't owe anyone an apology. I left because of an asshole I thought was a friend. How can I play my music with someone I don't trust? I can't. Anyway, at least I get to create music I like now. That band had changed too much for me to be proud of anymore. Good for them for working like they do. Fuck him though for trading us in for a shot at fame."

"Yeah. Screw him." The words aren't as harsh, but the feeling behind it is the same.

"Hey, so let's hang out sometime and catch up."

"Yeah, I'd like that. I'll text you soon."

"Cool." He pauses, then says, "I'm sorry about Cassie."

"I appreciate it. Take care, Dave."

"See ya around, Han."

When I hang up, I think about how far Dave and I have come, not just in our friendship, but what we went through together. I'll always be grateful to him for his kindness when I had no one else.

Smiling, I now feel truly ready to face the day. I walk into the kitchen and greet my aunt with the smile that's still on my face. "Good afternoon."

"You burned the day away."

"Guess I did." It's easier to stand my ground with my aunt than it ever has been with Jet. It's an interesting detail I'll explore about the time I'm trying to fall asleep, but my mind won't rest. Basically like every night lately.

She asks, "Have you seen Cassie's journal?"

"No." The question surprises me. We're not allowed to go into Cassie's room, and Eileen would freak out if we touched anything. "I can help find it if you'd like."

"No. No. No. I'll find it."

"Do you want to read it?"

She stops and shoots me a look. As if her mission has changed, she faces me and narrows her eyes. "How do you think Alfie is faring with him?"

Him . . . Jet. "I think Alfie is fine with his father."

"Are you taking his side again?"

Filling a glass with water, I attempt to calm the fire in her eyes. "I'm not taking anyone's side but Alfie's. Jet took him to the zoo today. You know how much he loves it there."

"He's just trying to buy his affection."

I sigh. "I don't want to fight over this. He lost six years with him—"

"Because he chose to leave my pregnant daughter."

"Are you sure?"

Offense crinkles the skin on her face. "How dare you say she would lie!"

"I didn't say Cassie would lie. I'm just starting to think there are two sides to this story."

"Not when it comes to this. That man is a lowlife lothario, and he'll turn Alfie into one if we don't intervene. If you're truly on Alfie's side, you'll protect him from his sperm donor."

"Ew." I could argue, but there's no point. She's made up her mind, and there's no changing it. "I'm going to have dinner with them and watch Alfie while Jet plays a show tonight."

"See? Not even twenty-four hours and he's shuffling his kid off like he doesn't matter."

"He has to pay rent—"

"You seemed to have lost all reasoning, Hannah. This is exactly how he tempted my daughter into his sins. I'll be speaking with the lawyer today to figure out our next step."

"This is it. We've been given more than I thought we'd

get. We have shared custody for the next sixty days. We need to make this transition as easy as possible on Alfie."

She gasps, her hand covering her mouth. "Transition? There is no transitioning. I'm fighting. If you don't intend to fight with me, you should probably consider returning to Dallas." On that final not so veiled threat, she turns and goes to her room. The door is not handled gently when it closes behind her.

I want to do some door slamming of my own, but I need to shower and get ready to go to Jet's house.

Wrapped in a towel and freshly showered, I open my laptop to do what was inevitable—find a job. As soon as I sit down, my phone rings. It takes me a second to shake the shock. "Hi . . . Dad."

"Eileen just called me hysterical. What have you done, Hannah?"

Seeing him at Christmas was one thing, but this is the first call I've had from him in years, and it's to gripe at me for how I'm apparently treating *his* sister. The pain runs deep. I didn't even get a hi, hello, or how are you? "I told her the truth. We have time and half custody. I have no control over that."

"I know the outcome, but you need to make sure you win full custody until we get that matter of the will out of the way."

"You mean Cassie's wishes," I say, snarky.

"Eileen said you were going soft on that loser. Keep your eyes on the prize."

"Alfie's not a prize. He's a kid. His mother's wishes should matter."

"So you want to raise him as your own? You can't support yourself."

I swear they're the same person. "I want what's best for him. That's all."

"Stay focused. I'm busy. I can't field calls from hysterical women because my own daughter has forgotten what responsibility means."

"I'm done here."

"Good. So am I."

The line goes dead, just like our relationship. Why does he hate me so much? Did he hate my mother so much that he'd crush me just to get revenge?

I shut my computer, disheartened by everything. Finishing my last two years of college will have to wait another year. I'm almost out of money, and despite what my aunt thinks, I plan to be in Alfie's life however I can. If that means coming back home for good, then I guess I'm staying in Austin longer than I planned. I need to start thinking long term and moving out once I have a job.

"Donuts?"

I walk in, right past Jet and his ridiculously handsome, make no effort just woke up looking this incredible sexy self. Gracious, I'm horny. I really need to get control of these rampant and sexually charged thoughts. If I'm not careful, he'll be naked in my mind in no time, or better yet, in his bed with me climbing—I shake my head. "Dessert. They're Alfie's favorite."

"Round Rock Donuts. Man, I haven't had those in years. So good." As soon as I set the box down, he lifts the lid and starts to reach for one.

I slap his hand. "Not until after dinner, mister."

He looks over his shoulder. Seemingly satisfied that

we're alone, he whispers, "Do you know how hot it is when you call me mister?"

My belly and lower clenches as his words act as an aphrodisiac and the dull pulse becomes a throb between my legs. His breath is heavy against the bare skin of my shoulder. I clear my throat and try to hide the fact that my nipples are hard buttons pressed against my bra when all I want is Jet pressing them.

Shoot. Solo time is not getting the job done.

He's supposed to be the enemy.

I can't forget that, but he makes it hard to focus. "You shouldn't say such things. You need to forget our past."

"You keep saying that as if it will make your wish come true. It won't. I can't forget, Hannah."

"You have a million girls who would rather have your smooth lines laid upon them."

Opening the fridge, he sets two bottles of Dos Equis on the counter in front of me. "See, that's where you are absolutely right. Girls." With a bottle opener in hand, he pops one cap and then the other off. "I want a woman. *Again.*" Pressing the green glass to his lips, he tilts the bottle back.

Watching the golden lager slide from the neck of the bottle into his mouth is mesmerizing. But seeing his Adam's apple dip deep along his throat and then up again as he swallows is a vision I'd pay money for . . . and one I'll store for later.

I push away from the counter and quickstep around him. "Alfie?"

When Alfie comes running out of his room, he runs to me. "Hannah."

I envelop him in my arms. It's only been twenty-four hours, but it feels good to hug him. "Hey, buddy. How are you?"

"Jet got me a table. I can do drawings on it, and I don't have to clean up my mess on it."

Glancing up at Jet, I catch his eyes already on me. I turn my attention back to Alfie. "That's great, but you know how fast a mess can get out of hand if you let it."

"Yeah, I already cleaned my room, except the table." Jumping up, he asks, "Will you cook ramen with me?"

"Absolutely. That's why I'm here, chef."

Although I know Jet's brothers don't live here, I almost expected them to be here all the time, hanging out, drinking and eating together. I like that it's just the three of us. While Jet's grating ginger and the carrot, I'm put in charge of boiling two eggs and mincing garlic. Alfie is opening the yakisoba noodles.

Jet's cutting board is almost bumped up to mine while we work side by side like a team. *What would it be like to cook like this every night? Just the three of us? A team.* I glance up at him quickly but am caught. One you're-so-busted eyebrow is raised at me, and I look away with a smile on my face.

Not two seconds later, his shoe is against the side of mine, and I'm not in a hurry to move.

Dinner is delicious, but I wonder if a noodle soup can tide Jet over through a gig, though. "Are you still hungry?"

"No, I'm good for now," he says, looking content.

I stand. "Very well. I can clean the dishes. Why don't you two dig into the donuts?"

"Yay!" Alfie hops off the barstool and grabs the box from the kitchen counter and runs into the living room. "Jet said there's a game on. Can we eat in front of the TV?"

He never cared about sports before, but living in the lion's den will rub off in many ways. Alfie's waiting for me to answer, but it's not right if I do. I look at Jet and then turn back. "Your house. Your rules."

"Go on, little man," he says. "I'll be right there."

The TV turns on, and Jet comes to stand next to me at the sink. "It must be hard to hand off a role you've had for so long. I'm sorry you've been put in the middle."

Focusing on the plate in my hand, I run the soapy sponge over it and scrub. "You don't have to apologize to me. You didn't create this situation. Anyway, I'm exactly where I want to be, so you don't need to worry about me."

He's close. So close I can feel his presence overshadowing me from behind. I don't look back, and I don't continue the conversation. Not more than ten or so seconds tick by before I can breathe again.

I look up and watch him sit next to Alfie on the couch. While taking a bite of donut, Jet looks up. We exchange a little smile when our eyes meet in a silent but peaceful surrender. I smile before finishing the dishes and letting a son and his dad share donuts for dessert. Seven rolls around too soon.

Wired on sugar, Alfie's running laps around the backyard while we look on and laugh. Jet says, "I'm thinking about getting him a trampoline. Mom used to send us outside to jump on ours even if it was raining. She'd call us wild and tell us to release some energy. It used to work for us. Any thoughts?"

"That makes sense. What about waiting for a week, though? He's only been with you one day, and it probably feels like he's on vacation or having a sleepover. I can't deny he's taken to you quickly, but he's used to a certain routine. I worry how he'll adapt after a normal day when you're there and not me. If there's one thing Cassie showed me in how she parented Alfie, it was not to indulge unnecessarily. If you think a trampoline will make this transition easier, then get one. He's happy in the present, but I want to make sure he's happy in the long run."

"He's never looked at me like I'm a stranger." He pulls a cigarette and lighter from his shirt pocket and lights up. There's no breeze tonight, and the smoke fills the air around us.

Just as I close my eyes to inhale him into my lungs, he waves it off. "Sorry about that. I need to quit." Signaling toward Alfie, he looks regretful. "He's already told me he wants me to. I might give it a try."

"He's having a good influence on you." I grin and tap his side with my elbow. "About time someone did."

I like the smile I receive in return, the tension missing from his jaw. "We had a good day." He drops the barely smoked cigarette to the cement patio and snubs it out with his shoe. Picking it up, he tosses the remains in a bucket full of sand and butts. "*I* had a good day because of him."

"He has that effect." I'm tempted to tell him that's how he makes me feel but don't. He's making it awfully hard to keep my guard up since I realized he's not my enemy. With each passing hour we spend together, I'm starting to believe that he just might be my ally.

10

Hannah

Cassie was an amazing mom.

She read to him every night until her last day. She loved spending any time she could with him. I relate. I love him like he's my own.

After reading two books to Alfie and having him read the third, he fell asleep in the middle. Kneeling on the floor, I rest my head on the bed while he sleeps. The room is quiet, and my body relaxes. It would be easy to let my worries fade away and fall asleep in the peace of the room.

Maybe I'll just rest my eyes for a minute. I'm about to close them when I hear a light strum from the living room. I'm not home, I remind myself. I can't get too comfortable although it would be so easy to do so. Pushing myself up, I lean down and kiss Alfie's head. "I love you," I whisper, and then sneak out of the room, closing the door quietly behind me.

Standing in the hall, I'm not sure if I should make a show of my presence or walk out unannounced. I look a little farther down the hall and see his bedroom light on. Taking a few steps, I peek in. I feel almost guilty spying like this when he's not back here, but I just want to see the scene of the crime from that night.

I can't even kid myself when it comes to being with him too many months ago. It was the best sex I'd ever had. The bed is messy, the sheet tangled, but it looks the same—some clothes on the floor, miscellaneous items from money to cologne on the dresser, and the blinds cracked open even though it's dark outside.

"Whatcha doin'?"

"Ack!" My hands fly to my chest. "Oh, my God." I squeal too loud and then try to rein in my thundering heart, hoping I didn't wake Alfie. Whacking Jet on the arm, I say, "You scared the hell out of me, Jet."

"Sorry about that." He chuckles but ends up with that same smirk on his face as the night I fell for his lines and right into his bed. "But really, what are you doing in my bedroom? Reminiscing?"

I ignore the way he's raised one of his eyebrows like he just busted me doing something that might be a compliment to him. I refuse to give his ego a boost. "I thought I heard a noise. I guess it was just you playing guitar." He doesn't need to know that he's right. Ugh. I can already imagine that smile curling up at the sides. Nope. I will not give him the satisfaction.

"Noise?" Jerking back, he replaces his look of offense with narrowed eyes and a look of determination on his face. "I don't think so, sweetheart. I think you were spying on me to gather information to use against me."

Remembering how close we are to Alfie's bedroom door, I grab Jet by the upper arm and pull him toward the living room. As soon as we round the corner, I reply, "I didn't come over here to spy on you. I was invited. And don't call me sweetheart."

"From what I remember—"

"I don't care what you remember. This relationship is strictly platonic."

His gaze slides down to my hand, which I still have firmly wrapped around his incredibly sexy and strong bicep. I drop my hand to my side quickly and send a quick prayer to the heavens that my cheeks aren't as red hot as they feel. "Starting now."

"Have it your way, sweet—Hannah." He walks to the front door and opens it. Standing just outside on the porch, he says, "Maybe we should hang out here so we don't wake Alfie. I have some time to kill, and I need to tune my guitar."

I go out but leave the door cracked. "The swing looks inviting. Do you mind?"

"Make yourself at home."

Sitting on the rustic swing, I don't worry about it breaking. The paint may be peeling, but I can tell by the bolts and structure it's built to last. Pushing off, I watch as he sits on the edge of a lawn chair and messes with a guitar string. He glances up, catching me watching him, and asks, "You heard of the band, The Resistance?"

"Of course."

Something changes in his eyes, an excitement seen as well as heard in his voice. "They want to sign us to a recording deal."

I drag my feet, bringing the swing to a halt. "What? No way!"

"We were sent the contracts today."

"That's amazing. Congratulations."

"Thanks." He strums mindlessly, but it's music to my

ears. Talent comes naturally to him. "I haven't looked over it since I was out most of the day."

"You think you'll sign?"

"I want to, but there are other things to consider."

Kicking off with my feet, I say, "Alfie."

Turning his attention back to the guitar, he nods. "I think like most guys, I've had thoughts about how I would feel if a girl told me she was pregnant and how I would react." Another strum, then his palm goes flat, cutting off the sound.

I've had the same thoughts if I got pregnant and how I would handle it. "How would you react?"

I like the way he looks into my eyes when he talks to me. I've seen him do it to others. For as much as I want to consider him a rebel musician who can be easily judged as irresponsible, Jet's not like that. He's respectful, and I've never heard him say a mean word. Granted, I'm not around him all the time, but as an observer, he's different from my ex by a million miles and a few years of maturity.

He replies, "I would've been there however the mom needed or wanted. I'd support her the best I could. I would never walk away from my kid, though. You were told otherwise. I just don't know why."

Neither do I. What would she gain by lying about something so important? Cassie struggled financially. I think Jet would have helped if he had known. This is such a mess. I wish I knew what to believe.

I may never know the truth. The sincerity in his eyes makes me want to believe him, but if I do, am I betraying Cassie and Aunt Eileen?

My rambling thoughts are cut off when he says, "I understand you're caught in the middle and stuck with me when it comes to Alfie. You don't have to believe me, but I hope you give me a chance to show you who I am and not just believe what you're told."

"What are the chances out of all the people in Austin, we hooked up only to find ourselves pitted against each other six months later?"

We'll never truly get answers to how the world works, but I wish I could get a little insight into why I was put in the middle of this complicated mess.

Jet sets his guitar down and joins me on the swing. We swing back and forth a few times before he says, "I'm not going to talk about the sex that night because you get all flustered—"

"I do not."

"You do. Like now. Your cheeks turn red, and you look at me with little lusty memories filling your head."

So what if he's right. I'll never cop to it. Bumping against him, I take my annoyance out on him. Is it sad that I'm not really annoyed and acting like a fifth grader hitting the guy I like?

Like?

I can't like Jet Crow.

Nothing good will come of it.

There's no denying good has already come from it. No confession will change the circumstances, though. I'm not supposed to like him or maybe I'm not allowed to like him without feeling like I'm a traitor to my family.

He's laughing lightly. When it subsides, he adds, "I was going to say that besides the sex you can't stop thinking about, we had more than just a physical connection."

"Jet," I caution before we end up in a downward spiral of emotions we won't know how to escape. "We shouldn't talk about things we can't change."

"Why can't we change things?"

"Alfie needs us. He's so at ease with you already, but I have to focus on his well-being and what's best for him."

"Fine. We'll talk about Alfie." His tone flips to match his expression—hard lines across his brow and tight jaw as he gazes into the distance.

I want his eyes back on me. I want to ease those lines, smoothing them with care, like I'd want to do with our relationship. I'm close to going inside, worried it doesn't matter what I say or do. We're always going to be stuck in this purgatory. It's best just to face it and accept that this is it between us. "He's a great kid."

"The best." His shoulders appear to bear the same burdens, but like me, he fights his way back to what this is—reality. A small smile finally shines through the darkness. "It was fascinating to watch him today. His mind zooms from one thing to the next. He's all over the place and smart."

"So smart. Before I came to stay with them, he was already so self-sufficient. Cassie had been sick for a few years, and in the time before she got too weak, she taught him to take care of himself."

"He made his cereal before I woke up."

"If you're not careful, he'll have you convinced he can do anything and that he's a regular adult."

Understanding crosses his expression. "I can see that. I'll make sure to keep him six as long as I can."

Playing along, I say, "I promise to do the same."

"You've done a lot for him, Hannah. Thank you."

"You don't have to thank me. I love him."

"I know you do. He loves you, too. He talks about you all the time. I definitely have a lot to live up to."

"That's where you're wrong. He's happy to have a dad in his life. You're new."

"And shiny?"

I agree. "It's hard to compete with shiny."

"There's no one to compete with." He nudges me. "You're his Hannah. When I become the bad guy and he gets in trouble, you can swoop in and be the fun one."

"He has Tulsa for that."

"True." I start laughing with her. It feels good to laugh this hard.

"The truth is, I'm not sure where I fit in anymore."

He touches my hand. "Right here, Hannah."

The sincerity of his words is sharp like arrows to my heart, reawakening every part of me to what's right in front of me. "With you?"

"For Alfie," he says quieter, all signs of the laughter I love to hear gone.

"Of course. Yeah." I stand from the swing, my foolish heart about to beat out of my chest. "That's what I meant." I lie, trying to cover for my wrong assumption. I let hope tempt me down a path I knew better to travel. "You should probably get going."

The squeak of the swing gets my attention. When I look back, he's still sitting there, patting the spot I vacated seconds before. "I have a little time. Swing with me, Hannah."

He's enticing, but I think I should resist the offer after embarrassing myself not even a minute earlier. "I have some research I need to get back to."

Pressing the heels of his shoes against the cement, the swing comes to a full stop. "What kind of research?"

"Nosy much?" I quirk an eyebrow and crack a smile.

"Yes. I'm very nosy when it comes to you."

His words are harmless, nothing more than a flirtation, but he's not laughing like I am. We're not in the same place we once were, so I can't fall under his spell . . . not again. I'll keep my heart in check and my tone all business. "I didn't expect to move here permanently when I came to Austin to help with Alfie. I've been here seven months and burned through my savings."

"You need a job?"

"Yes." Shifting, I lean against the doorframe. "With this new arrangement in place . . ." My heart clenches and my eyes burn with tears I haven't had time to cry. "And Cassie passing, I need to figure out my next step."

Leaning forward and resting his forearms on his legs, he clasps his hands together and looks up. "Can I ask you something, Hannah?"

"Yes."

"Why are you the one fighting for Alfie and not Eileen?"

Cassie's wish versus my aunt's demands. Just thinking about my and Eileen's fights has my hands sweating from anxiety. "It's complicated."

He looks down and nods. "Okay." Pushing up off the swing, he says, "I need to get ready to leave soon."

When he's only a few inches away, his heat emanates as it blankets me in the subtle scent of his cologne, his breath has a faint smell of Marlboro cigarettes and spearmint gum.

My body freezes, my heart stopping, my breath catching under the intense soul-shattering gaze as he drinks me in and then shifts to the side. "Do you mind?" he asks with a sly smile.

I can't look away, caught up in him. "Huh?"

"The door. Can I open the door?"

"Yeah, sure," I reply not understanding.

When he laughs, he says, "Hannah, you're blocking the door."

Blocking the door . . . Oh! "Ohhh, sorry." I move out of

the way and let him by. Inwardly, I roll my eyes at myself. Ugh. So embarrassing.

Just inside the house, he stops and looks back. "Sometimes I see that same woman I met all those months ago. Your eyes are just as sad, but every so often, I see the blue shine through. It's a good look for you."

And without much effort on his part, my heart leaps through that doorway and becomes putty right in his hands again.

He's right, though. I am sad. I'm sad that I met him when I did, when there was no chance of it becoming more. I'm sad because I lost my cousin to a cruel, painful disease. *I'm sad because her little boy won't have her in his life forever.* But Alfie has Jet, and for that? I'm not sad at all. Alfie has a good man who will love him selflessly, and I can't feel anything but thankful for that.

But my heart?

One moment, I'm holding my own against the intimidating Jet Crow. The next, my whole *hate-the-man* stance flies out the window.

Damn him.

11

Jet

Leaning against the tailgate of my truck, I toss the half-smoked cigarette and grind out the flame. A flame burned out too soon reminds me of the woman inside my house.

I grab my guitar case from the back and shake my head. It's fucking ridiculous that one woman can consume my thoughts as she has.

Hannah Nichols is a chick, just like any other. One night is generally a good policy to live by when it comes to letting women into my life. More than once becomes an obligation I have no current intentions of having right now. Add a major life change into the mix, and two nights is out of the fucking question.

I made that mistake with Marcy. Even tonight, she came catcalling, drunk with that look in her eyes. I could have fucked her in the parking lot. She offered. Or taken her in a bathroom stall with other people next door. Another offer that didn't appeal to me.

That's not who I am. A woman worth sticking my dick in

is worth an actual date, but that's not what Marcy wants. She wanted to fuck tonight when she came up after the show trying to pull my shirt up and my jeans down. Her sharp nails scratched my side when I removed her hands.

When I told her to find some other guy, a slap followed but was caught before impact. That was when the fun we'd had in the past was just that—over and done and in the past.

She doesn't want me. Not really. She wants anyone who she can show off. She wants to cling to my minor fame around town. But ultimately, she wants something she knows she'll never have again—me.

She's a bad habit that never should have been and will never be again.

Marcy is nothing like Hannah.

That's a big fucking problem for me since Hannah is the one who doesn't see us as ever being more than opposing teams.

It would be wise for me not to think of her, but when I saw her standing outside my bedroom, my thoughts ran wild, sticking to me like glue all night. She was buried in every riff of my guitar, the notes that made the melody, the cheering of the crowd. She was at the forefront of my mind as if my muse had tracked me down just to haunt me even more.

What would have happened if I'd invited her all the way in? What would she have done if I had kissed her in the hallway? What harm would be done if we'd snuck in an encore? No one would know but the two of us.

The two of us . . . Hannah is the kind of trouble I don't need right now. Being conflicted keeps her tied up in her head. Eileen is whispering shit in her ear that's just not true. I can argue all day long, but Hannah is torn between us.

Why would I torture myself by pursuing a woman who can't see my truth?

Just because she's sexy as fuck doesn't mean she's worth the time trying to convince her I'm worth the effort. The only problem is I don't believe that shit myself.

Smart. Gorgeous. Strong. Independent. Feisty. She's worth the trouble.

She's the sort of woman I want in my life. And if I'm honest, I can see how good it would be to have a partner to come home to. For me and for Alfie. *She's worth every effort, but she doesn't want me.*

Maybe in time she'll see in me what I see in her—worth the effort.

Until then, two's a good number—Alfie and me.

I open the front door, expecting to get an irritated glare or a snarky remark. It would almost be warranted, considering it's almost two in the morning.

But that's not what I get.

Instead, I'm greeted with the stunning sight of a sleeping siren. Closing the door behind me, I'm as quiet as can be as I lock up. I set my guitar down and sit in a chair. What do I do? Wake her? Let her sleep? Move her to my bed? Send her home?

Sending her home is the last thing I want. I wonder how pissed off she'll be if I don't wake her. Leaning back, I like seeing her face free from worries and her body relaxed. I don't want her to be uncomfortable, but she might kick my ass if I wake her.

I decide to leave her be for now. I brush my teeth and strip down to my boxers, kicking my clothes to the corner of the bathroom. I grab a pillow from my bed and go back into the living room to set it down.

She's still asleep when I return. I watch her a minute

before I get up and stand over her. Reaching down, I lift her into my arms. Light as a feather. I need to feed this woman more ramen and put some weight on her.

Just as I start to walk down the hall, her eyes open and her arms go around my neck. "What are you doing?"

"Taking you to bed."

So what if I phrase it a specific way . . . I chuckle without shaking her.

"Okay," she says, her eyes dipping closed.

Okay?

Don't think my whole body doesn't react to that response. I set her on the bed and pull the sheet and blanket over her as she snuggles in. I'm surprised she's "okay" with this. When her breathing deepens I move to leave, but she reaches up and captures my hand. "Stay."

Stay.

One word.

One request.

It would be so easy to slide in behind her and hold her until morning. I would sleep better than I have since she left the last time. The offer is tempting, just like she is.

But I'm thinking she's not fully awake. If she was, she wouldn't be asleep in my bed like everything's A-OK. Her hand soon falls away, and she's asleep before I have a chance to talk myself into climbing in this bed with her.

I close the door when I leave and peek in on Alfie. The nightlight allows me to see his sleeping form. Pulling the covers over an exposed foot, I also kiss his head before sneaking back out.

After grabbing a blanket from the closet, I settle on the couch with my pillow and cover up the best I can. My legs are too damn long, but sleeping out here is the right thing to do. Hannah would be furious if she found me sleeping next to her in the morning.

"Sleep on the couch," I repeat, really for myself. I'll stay here, even if the couch is lumpy and my feet hang off the side. I left a little piece of my heart in that back bedroom, but it doesn't make sense why I'd even think that. Hannah and I are a lost cause that's not going to be found between the sheets despite how good we are when we're together.

I have to learn to stay away just like she wants.

MY EYES BURN.

My body tenses.

My mind is filled with too much groggy fog to reason through. *What the fuck hour is it?* Squinting an eye open, I'm greeted with an angel in a Crow Bros tee, flowing chestnut hair cascades over the side of her sweet face. I close my eye to see if she remains and if I can get lost in the dirty dreams I'm about to have. When she disappears behind my lids, I reopen my eyes to discover a dream come true. "Hannah."

"How do you like your eggs?" Soft pink lips. Clear blue eyes. Her voice is only a whisper of the sweet sound of her melodic tone.

Reaching forward, I'm still precariously balanced between sleep and reality. Just to test if I'm awake, I touch her leg and my hand is promptly smacked. She stands and walks away. "He'll take scrambled, Alfie."

I lift on my elbow and see Alfie standing next to her at the stove, their backs to me. I forgot I was on the couch. No wonder my back hurts. "Good morning to you, too."

"Morning, Jet. Hannah stayed. It was like a sleepover, but she slept in your room and not mine."

Hannah smiles. "Next time, buddy."

Alfie runs over and sits on the coffee table where Hannah was. "I have school today. Hannah's going to take me. Will you pick me up?"

Ruffling his hair, I smile. "Course, bud. What time?"

He looks at Hannah, and my eyes follow. Hannah twirls a spatula like a pro. God, that woman's sexy. "We could use a drummer," I say. "Got any rhythm?" I know she does in the bedroom, but with the kid around, I keep it to myself.

With a wiggle of her hips, she smiles, and it's so damn enticing. "I've got a few moves. But I don't know anything about drumming." Signaling toward Alfie, she adds, "School ends at two forty-five. You should get there around two thirty to find parking. You'll have to wait for his class to come out, and when the teacher sees you, she'll release Alfie into your care."

"Sounds complicated."

"It's not." She laughs. "Safety precautions. I'll add you to the approved pick-up list."

I sit all the way up and run my hands through my hair. I'm sure I look awesome at six thirty in the morning. Not really. "Approved pick-up list?"

"You have to be on the list to pick up Alfie."

"Right. Safety precautions." Maybe it's because I'm running on four hours sleep, but I'm not feeling cut out for this job right now. Looking back at Hannah and Alfie, she's moving through this routine like it's second nature with a smile on her face.

Catching me watching them, she sets a plate down on the bar and tells him to eat. There's something in her eyes I'm not able to read from here, so silently I ask, "What?"

After taking a seat next to me, she leans in and quietly says, "You can do this, Jet."

She sees through me, right into my mind, touching on my insecurities. "Do what?"

Nodding toward Alfie, she gives me a reassuring smile. "It's easier than it sounds. Showing up is what matters most."

I have a feeling it's not just school she's talking about. Her wisdom extends beyond the words. Moving the tips of my fingers under the tips of hers resting on her thigh, I tap. "Message received."

Not sure what happens, but her smile fades and her lips part as she stares at our hands. When I see how she stiffens, I pull back. "I'm sorry."

"No, it's okay." Licking her lips, she tugs one side of the bottom one under her teeth. She's standing too soon for my liking.

Alfie drops his dishes in the sink with a clatter and says, "All done. Come eat your eggs, Jet."

"I'll eat, but you need to brush your teeth."

When he rushes down the hall, I get up and find a plate waiting for me with a mug of coffee next to it. "You cook, you make coffee, and you're great with kids."

"Don't say it, Crow. I have dreams of my own to pursue."

Guess they don't include me . . . we'll see about that. I take a sip. Perfect brew. "What are your dreams?"

She pauses, studying me. "My dreams?"

"Yeah. Your dreams."

"Sorry," she says, looking down, the shirt she snagged from me suddenly the most fascinating thing ever. Seeming to realize she's paused too long, she adds, "It's been a while since anyone asked about me."

"Why is that?"

"Because if it wasn't about Cassie or something she needs, I was told what I needed to do for Alfie."

"He's six. He doesn't need much but love, I reckon."

Agreeing, she stands, shoving her hands in her back pockets. "He's changed me for the better. I've screwed up my life, but he loves me like I haven't."

"How old are you, Hannah?"

Feigning offense, she places her hand on her chest and her lips go wide into the prettiest smile. The shirt engulfs her small frame, the collar hanging wide and exposing some of her shoulder. I'll never ask for it back. It looks a lot better on her than on me. "I do declare, Mr. Crow, that a lady never gives up her secrets."

I'm just about to tell her I can guess, but Alfie walks back in and says, "Hannah's twenty-four."

Pretending to be a monster, she goes after him with wiggly fingers. "You weren't supposed to tell him." When she catches him, he's giggling uncontrollably while trying to form words to make her stop. Setting him free, she asks, "Can you give me and Jet another minute to chat? Maybe draw a giggle monster to show me?"

Nodding with excitement, he runs back to his room. She turns back to me. "There. Now you know."

"I still don't know about your dreams."

"It's too early to get into all that, don't you think?"

"Too early to start living your dream? I don't think so."

"Let me ask you something. Did you always know you wanted to play music, to be in a band, to perform for live audiences?"

Leaning against the counter, I reply, "Yes. That's why when money was tight I quit college. I couldn't see how sitting in an auditorium learning about gravitational dynamics would help me land a recording deal. Playing music every night whether to a coffeehouse or at the Austin Music Awards would. Every time I got on stage, I got more comfortable, I honed my skills, my talent, and I figured out our sound."

She sits back down and looks my way. "What about Alfie? I want him to go to college."

"He will go to college. Just like Rivers and Tulsa."

"They have degrees?"

"Rivers does. Tulsa graduates next December. He can't go full time with our gigs, so it's taken a little longer. I haven't gone back, but I think you understand the sacrifices you're willing to make to take care of others."

It's the minutest of nods, but I see it as her gaze falls to the floor.

We're in uncomfortable territory for her, and as much as I'd love to delve deeper, I won't risk her shutting down just when we're getting somewhere. "It's not just the coffee that makes you a catch, you know?"

She hates attention and starts dusting imaginary lint from her jeans. "What else makes me a catch, Jet?"

I return to the couch, setting my mug on the table in front of me. "Everything."

"Everything?" She snorts, and I think I fall a little more for her.

"You're not what you think, Hannah."

"What do I think?"

"You think you're hardened and in control all the time. That everything rolls off your back, no problem. Your feelings play like a movie in your eyes—sadness, conflict, happiness, and anger, sometimes directed at me. You give them life, beautiful complicated emotions."

She stands, scoffing as if I couldn't possibly be referring to her. "You don't know what you're saying."

I take the dare and touch her leg, my hand spanning the inside of her right calf to stop her from leaving. She rests her hand on my shoulder and whispers, "You don't know me."

When she walks away, I ask, "What if I want to?"

Her modus operandi is back in play, and she ignores the comment and continues like she didn't hear me. "I made up the bed. You should get some sleep. I'll text you the details to pick up Alfie later."

"So that's it?"

I watch her hesitate and then nod. "That's all it can be." The sound of her talking to Alfie carries. "Are you ready?"

"Yes," he replies.

When he returns to the living room, I catch him and whisk him into my arms. He's happy. This kid is so damn happy, even at an ungodly hour. Carrying him upside down, I ask, "Have you seen Alfie, Hannah?"

Coming back with his jacket and backpack, she takes his lunch from the counter and pretends to look around. "Nope, haven't seen him."

"Now where could he be?"

He's a giggly monster. "I'm here. I'm here."

"I think I hear something."

"Where?" Hannah plays along.

Alfie flails his arms while laughing even more. "Here. Here. Here."

Spinning him right side up, I come face to face with him. "Ohhhh here you are."

He rubs his hand up the side of my cheek. "Ouch," he teases.

Taking his hand, I kiss his palm. "Better?"

"I get to come here after school, right?"

"You do. I'll pick you up from school."

Hannah walks by and tugs his shirt. "C'mon, kiddo. We have to get going or we'll be late."

I hug him to me. It's purely selfish. "You have a good day and work hard. Okay?"

When I set him down, he runs to the front door and takes her hand. Eyeing her, I ask, "You stealing that shirt?"

"I am." Walking out the door, I see the smile she tries to hide. *That smile. The ghost of a smile. That was for me.* God, she's gorgeous.

"See you later, gators."

"Bye," Alfie calls back and closes the door.

Taking the mug with me into the kitchen, I devour the eggs they made for me and then head to bed. I need sleep. With a full belly and running on only a few hours sleep, I make my way to my bedroom.

The bed is made, but I mess it up when I climb in. Lying here in the darkish room, I focus my senses. The scent is faint, but I can smell her on my pillow.

I could lie here all day breathing in her perfume as if she's still here, and it would never come close to having the real thing. I close my eyes, and her words come back to me. *"Showing up is what matters most."*

Show up.

Not just for Alfie, but her.

Show up.

12

Jet

On Tuesday, I'm standing in front of the school at two forty-five, as directed.

I picked up Alfie on Friday. Hannah came over after he fell asleep to watch him while I played my gig. He never knew I was gone, and she dashed out the door as soon as I walked in.

Other than that, I haven't seen him since Saturday morning when I dropped him off at Hannah and Eileen's for their scheduled days. The band's busiest nights are the weekend, so Hannah offered to take him those days to help us out. This week, I'll only have him until Thursday.

The band flies to LA on Friday morning to meet with Johnny and the rest of the band to get a plan in place. We received the contract, but I haven't had time to go over it fully. After a brief review, I'm still stuck on how I'm going to care for Alfie if I'm stuck in a studio or on tour. My brothers and I toured for years, but we were only responsible for us. There were no strings or attachments holding us back or tying us down, except for Rivers. On our last tour, his girl was still in school, so it was me and my brothers with our ex-drummer. We were four guys with few cares riding high on our popularity while doing something we love.

The next time will be different. There's talk of touring with the The Resistance and opening for them. That means stadiums and arenas, which is a whole other ballgame.

I may have stars in my eyes this time around, but I'm not going in blind. Touring is taxing on the body and mind, but it kills relationships, as Rivers can attest to. Only the strongest bonds will survive. Alfie has to remain a priority, and I have no problem doing that. I think deep down, Hannah knows that, but at some point, when I know where we're heading career wise, I'll have to sit down and work this out *with* her. She needs to be a part of the decision too.

A few walls have come tumbling down over the past week. I think she wants to hate me more than she does. At least that's what I'm counting on.

The doors open, and the classes file out one by one. Alfie's is third, and he's already jumping up and down, excited to see me. I may not be jumping, but I'm just as excited, something I could've never imagined before meeting him.

His teacher waves to me, and I see two other teachers next to her waving. I look behind me, but no one is standing there. I'm used to attention when I'm at a show, but the school setting perplexes me. Alfie is tapped on the shoulder, the signal he's free to go. He runs around a baby stroller and two moms and straight into my arms. "I did a pitcher for you, Jet."

"A picture, buddy."

"I made one for the fridge. Look." He holds up green

construction paper, and I turn my head all the way to the right.

"Heeey, that's pretty good. It's a guitar."

"It's your ka-tar. We were told to draw something that makes us happy."

Hugging him, I reply, "My guitar makes you happy?"

"When you play, it makes you happy, and that makes me happy."

"You've got a big heart, Alfie." When I set him down, I hold the artwork in one hand and his hand in the other. "Who are the people drawn in the corner?"

"Our family."

"Are those your uncles?"

We cross the street to where I've parked the truck. "No, silly, that's me and you and Hannah."

I almost stumble over my own feet. The drawn people are all holding hands, with him holding Hannah's and me holding her other one. *If only life was that simple.*

I navigate to a different topic, one I'm more comfortable talking about. "I like that you drew a star and a sun."

"The star is Mommy. She's in heaven."

Stopping in front of my truck, I feel my chest squeeze. I'm always at a loss for what to say about Cassie. I don't want him not to talk about her, but I also don't want to say the wrong thing or screw up.

When I open the door for him to climb in, I wait for him to settle and then buckle him up. "You know, Alfie, we haven't talked much about my mom, but she's in heaven too."

"Is she my grandma?"

"Yes. Louisa. That was her name."

"Do you have pitchers?"

"Pictures." Chuckling, I rest my weight on the truck door. "I do. I can show you when we get home."

"Grandma Eileen once said I was born with only one, but I knew she was wrong because my teachers told me everyone has two. Brandon Lowery has three because his grandpa married a nurse."

What the fuck? I don't even know what to say to that. I just rub my temple instead and let him keep talking. He says, "I don't argue with Grandma, or I get sent to my room."

"Look, little man, I know it's tough to have all these changes at this moment, but your mommy meant a lot to Eileen. She loved your mommy very much."

"Did you?"

"Sonic or Wendy's for dinner? I'm thinking Sonic, but I'm open if you have a preference."

"Happy meal?"

"You got it." *Shit.* This kid catches me off guard, but I can't let him see me sweat. I also can't make him think his questions aren't valid. *Fuck.* I sound like a psychologist. I shut the door and walk around the back of the truck. Stopping at the tailgate, I pretend to secure it because I need a damn second to figure out what to say if he bombs me like that again.

I slide into the driver's seat and start the engine. With my arm on the back of my seat, I turn around, and look at him in his booster chair in the back. His eyes reveal his curiosity, and I owe him an actual answer. "I loved your mom, Alfie." I just say it.

He did nothing to deserve anything less than to hear good things about his mother, but would she really tell him bad things about me? In my gut, I feel she wouldn't. He also doesn't act like I'm a monster. The kid accepted me the second he saw me, so that's what I'll hold onto. That's what I'll believe in—him.

Turning back to pull out of the parking spot, I freeze when he says, "She said she loved you."

First, my eyes find his in the rearview mirror, and then I turn around again. "She did?"

"She said I would like you. I do, Jet. I like you."

"When did she say that?"

"I would sneak into her bed at night. I was careful not to wake Hannah."

"Where was Hannah?"

"In our room."

"You shared with her?"

He nods. "I have a room, but I liked Mommy's room, but sometimes her machines kept me awake. Hannah would let me sleep in her bed when I was scared or couldn't sleep."

"How often were you scared?"

"Most nights I have bad dreams."

He hasn't here, not at my house. I check on him all the time. "Do you still have bad dreams?"

Shrugging, he replies, "Not really."

I find some relief in his answer. I'm not a psychologist, but he seems to be internalizing his emotions. He's dealt with more than any kid should have to yet remains positive on the outside. Is it an act he puts on, or is he starting to heal in some ways? And I'm still curious what Cassie had to say about me. "Tell me about when you would sneak with your mommy."

He says, "We would read together, and she would teach me all the things she wanted me to know before she goes."

"She taught you about me?"

Another nod. When he starts losing interest in the

conversation, I start driving. "What did she say about me?" I glance at him in the mirror.

He smiles. "She said she loved you, and you loved her, and that love made me." I'm about to say something, but he adds, "If Hannah loves you and you love Hannah, will I get a baby brother?"

My foot almost slams on the brake, bringing us to a skidding stop, but I keep driving, flustered by how I should reply. I swear he can hear my thoughts scrambling around my head over the rumbling of this truck. "Umm, do you want one?"

"You got two. All I want is one."

I'm four years older than Tulsa and two years older than Rivers. I had two baby brothers by the time I was Alfie's age. This is brand new for both of us and too soon to think about what might happen, much less adding another kid into the mix, another kid with Hannah apparently. "Hannah and I are friends, Alfie. Like you have friends at school."

"Oh," he says, sighing and looking out the window.

We pull into the parking lot of the fast food joint, and I look back again. "Hey, this is good—you and me. As for more kids, I'm not sure what will happen, but I'm happy to have you."

"I'm happy to have you, Jet."

Squeezing his hand, I say, "I want you to know that I like you too, Alfie." I want to push him for more information about what Cassie told him, but by the way he's looking out the window, he's ready to eat. So am I. "Nuggets or burger?"

"Nuggets."

STUBBING the cigarette into the bucket of sand, I say, "I'll fly back every few days if I have to."

Rivers shakes his head. "You can't be gone when we're trying to record. The whole project will be put on hold every three days."

"I don't know how to manage this. I was fucking around with music, having a good time without any real responsibilities. Without any heads-up or warning, I became a father less than two weeks ago."

We continue to talk while watching Tulsa teach Alfie how to throw a baseball. Rivers pats my back. "Normally, I'd give you a hard time about what's happened, but you're doing the right thing, Jet."

"He's a great kid, and I had nothing to do with it."

"Sure, you did. It's your genes mixed up in that kid."

"Let's hope he gets his mother's sensibilities. If he's anything like me when he becomes a teen, I'm fucked."

Laughing, he says, "Karma's a bitch."

"Karma sure is." We sit a minute, more on my mind than I know what to address. I go with the heavy stuff that's been weighing down my heart. "It's bullshit that she was taken from him." I look over at him. "I can't believe she's gone."

"I've been trying to think back to the time you were dating. She wasn't around long."

"No. Even though we were dating, we didn't see each other that many times. We were gone for part of the tour that month."

"Man, this whole thing is heavy. How are you holding up?"

"I'm doing fine, but Alfie deserves a mother."

"You know we're here whenever you or Alfie needs us. As for the contract, if it doesn't work out, it's not meant for us anyway."

Rivers has always been more reasonable than Tulsa or me. I think my mom's accident made him grow up faster than he should have. We all reacted differently or acted out differently, I should say. He looked inward for answers, and I did everything I could to bury myself in whiskey and women, lost my soul to music, and gave in to the demons of my parents' death.

I hit my low on the road while sitting in a drunk tank in Nacogdoches. Rivers was only seventeen and busy fighting with his girlfriend on the phone. Tulsa wasn't old enough to bail me out, so he had to convince the bar manager to bail me out after paying him our earnings.

Rivers needed a big brother he could count on, and Tulsa needed a father figure. I became both that day. My role in Alfie's life comes more naturally this time around. "I won't hold you guys back. If you have to sign without me, I'll still do what I can, whatever you need me to do. I just can't take the risk of hurting Alfie. He's already lost one parent . . ."

"We're not just a band, Jet. We're brothers. All for one and one for all." We stand, our bodies mimicking each other's—hands in pockets, nearly the same height. Nudging me with his elbow, he adds, "Enough of this sappy shit. Let's eat and go over the contract."

Saved from getting any deeper by the doorbell, I announce dinner. "Pizzas are here."

With full bellies, we start reading through the contract. Alfie is playing a video game while sitting next to me.

Rivers says, "We can make this work, but you'll need help. It's good money, so Tulsa and I talked already, and we'll give up a portion of our share to hire someone."

Alfie asks, "Hire someone for what?" Raising his hand, he sits up eagerly. "I'll help."

"You've been a big help around here already, Alfie, but we're talking about help with you. Your schedule. Your school. If I sign this contract, I won't always be able to pick you up from school or read you books at night."

The controller is set aside, and he clings to my arm, leaning his head against me. "I just got you. Don't leave me."

To say he's adapted well is an understatement. I wrap my arm around him and kiss the top of his head. "I play music for my job, and sometimes that requires travel. That means I won't be here, in my house, with you. But it's only for a little bit of the time. You can't travel all over when you're in school and who will watch you at night when I'm on stage?"

"Me. I'm a big boy," he says, pouting. "You told me so."

"You are, buddy," I reply, catching Rivers's troubled gaze. He and Tulsa know me better than anyone. They know what I'm thinking. Music is in my soul, but this kid is my flesh and blood. After all those years stolen from us, if I leave now, that may damage us even more.

Alfie asks, "Why can't I go with you?"

"We play in a lot of places that kids can't hang out in, and to make an album, we will have to fly to LA for a month or so."

"What's LA?"

"Los Angeles. It's a city in California, which is a long way from Texas." I can't do it. I can't leave him, especially not when I'm trying to win custody of him.

His tiny shoulders slump even more. "Everybody leaves me." The words punch a hole right through my heart, and then he follows with another. "Is it because I said I like you?"

Pulling him onto my lap, I try my best to reassure him. "No, that's not it at all." I don't know how to sugarcoat, and I think he's had enough of that in the past. "I love you, Alfie. I want what's best for you because you are the most important thing in my life. If it's not good for you, it's not good for me. We're a team, buddy. Your last name may be Barnett, but you're still a Crow."

Green eyes peer up at me. "What is famous?"

"Where did you hear famous?"

"Uncle Tulsa."

I scowl at Tulsa. A kid doesn't need to worry about that shit. Fame is hollow. Music has depth. I don't need fame to find success. If I can make a living, I'm good. "It's when everyone knows who you are. I don't need fame." I shoot Tulsa a glare and then turn back to Alfie. "I need to be able to give you what you need."

"I don't need anything. Promise."

"You know we leave this week, but you won't even notice I'm gone because you'll be with Hannah and Grandma. Then I'll be back just in time to pick you up." It's really more for me that I hug him, but if he feels an ounce of how much I care about him, I'm winning.

Tulsa stands, an idea firmly planted in his mischievous eyes. "Rivers is right. Together we have enough in this offer to keep us going for the next year. Even if we take say twenty-five percent to hire someone we trust, someone to help out, we're still banking."

Alfie bolts upright with a matching look in his eyes. He's going to be so much trouble if he turns out anything like Tulsa. I can't help but laugh, though. And then he says, "Hannah."

My laughter is gone, not liking her name being dragged in out of nowhere. "What about Hannah?"

Whipping around to look back at me, he tilts his head and scrunches his face, and then it dawns on me too. "Hannah."

My eyes dart to Rivers, who nods, and then to Tulsa, who has a shit-eating grin on his face. "The kid's on to something," he says. Walking around the coffee table, Tulsa takes Alfie and swings him onto his back. "Come on, little monkey. Let's give your dad and uncle time to talk. Anyway, I want to show you how to style your hair so all the girls will go nuts for you."

"I don't want girls to go nuts, Uncle Tulsa."

"I second that," I say, sitting up. "He's got some time before we need to worry about that."

Tulsa laughs. "Fine. I'll race you out back."

Alfie replies, "I'm going to win again."

"We'll see about that."

Who's the kid here? Fuck, I'm lucky for my brothers, and Alfie's lucky to have them as uncles.

The screen door slams closed behind them, and Rivers says, "Hannah's a good idea."

She always was.

"He loves her. We can trust her to take care of him. I don't get the impression she's working right now." He asks, "Do you think she'd consider the job?"

"She's been looking for a job. I need help. This could be either a brilliant idea or a disastrous mistake."

"Sounds like a match made in . . ." He doesn't finish that sentence. He's starting to pick up on my feelings for her, feelings I can't afford to risk expressing out loud.

She's not a cruel person, but she and her aunt still want to win custody. "I'm not sure if it's wise to involve her. It could be used against me in the custody case."

"Parents work, Jet. They can't fault you for needing help. Your hours are different from the usual parent, but you're there when they aren't."

"It's an interesting idea. Maybe this is my shot at proving

I can be all he needs while keeping her involved in his life. Eileen Barnett wants me gone, but the more family the better when it comes to surrounding him with love."

"I know dick about kids, but he seems so . . . happy. Yeah, he misses his mom, but is it normal for him to have just coped so well with coming here? He's a good kid."

"He is. Doing this could screw up everything."

"Signing this deal could make all the years of hard work pay off. It wouldn't be a matter of paying the light bill or getting the truck fixed. It would be a matter of do I buy the house with the view or the one with the swimming pool. This could change everything in a better way for you and Alfie."

"He trusts and loves her. She loves him. This would show the judge that I'm willing to put his interests ahead of my own by putting our differences aside and working together." I stand and lean to the side to catch sight of Alfie and Tulsa in the backyard playing. "If Hannah would be willing to work with me to take care of Alfie, we could record the album and release it on Outlaw Records nationally. This could be the best thing that ever happened for us."

"Exactly."

I'm not naïve. I know the risk I'm taking. "Man, the possibility of our dreams coming true hinges on one thing . . . or should I say person—Hannah."

13

Jet

Our knees bump together under the table, but she's always the first to move away. I persist, liking this game of cat and mouse we're playing. I finish my last bite of bacon and notice her plate is still more than half full.

By looking at Hannah's plate, I start to wonder if she has a small appetite or just doesn't like to eat in front of me. I don't know why chicks feel they aren't allowed to eat. I've never once heard a guy bragging about banging a bag of bones. "Are you going to eat that?" I ask, pushing away my empty plate.

"Probably not." Her voice is quiet this morning, and I don't think she's looked me in the eyes once since she arrived.

"What's going on?"

"Nothing." Her voice pitches defensively.

"Maybe you're hungry."

"I'm perfectly fine."

Apparently . . . "Are you uncomfortable?"

"No," she scoffs, waving her hand as if I'm ridiculous for even suspecting such a thing.

"I'm not hungry, and I'm not uncomfortable, Jet." Her eyes still haven't met mine. "I'm wondering why I'm here." Bam! I'm leveled to a complete halt when she finally looks my way. "Breakfast on exchange day isn't part of the deal if that's what you're wanting."

"What's wrong?"

"Why am I here?"

"I wanted to talk to you about Alfie."

"That could have been done over the phone or through text."

Her defenses are sky high, making me doubt my decision to ask her to work with me, much less to breakfast this morning. "I thought it would be easier to talk face to face."

"What do you want to talk about?" she snaps.

"Maybe we should talk when you're in a better mood."

"Don't you get it? I'm not going to be in a better mood. I never planned for any of this."

Rolling my eyes, I sigh. "Tell me about it."

My comment strikes her, not like the quip I intended it to be but as a missile that hits its target. She leans forward and that ire in her eyes softens into something kinder. "I'm sorry. That was insensitive of me. I realize you've been dealing with more of a shock and adjustment than I have." Her gaze disappears into the distance, and she exhales, releasing the tension that was keeping her shoulders firmly squared since she sat down. "I'm just dealing with a lot, and I'm tired."

"You can talk to me, Hannah. You think you can't, keeping up pretenses like we're on opposing sides, but we're not. We both want what's best for that little boy. That's being on the same side. As for how that's done, we'll figure it out. In the meantime, the woman before me is not the woman I've been getting to know. Your sadness has changed."

"To what?"

She looks at me as if I can solve her problems with a simple answer. I can't, but I can do my best. "Distraught. You've been itching to leave since you got here, but I don't think I'm causing the pain you're dealing with." I dare to slide my hand across the table until the tips of my fingers are touching the tips of hers.

Her eyes watch and then stare as we sit in silence. When those beautiful eyes finally meet mine again, the fire is gone, but the smoke remains. "My aunt and I have been fighting all week. Before she was testing my allegiance, telling me I might need to go back to Dallas, but this morning she told me I should."

"What? No."

"What do you mean no?"

Shit. "Alfie needs you . . ." I don't want her to go. She's the only thing that's keeping this situation sane. I'm a fool for even considering what I'm about to do, much less doing it. Have I let my feelings get so caught up in her that I'll risk exposing them to take her side? *Yes.* "So do I."

"So do you, what?" Surprise followed by amusement fills her questioning eyes, reversing her bad mood. "You need me?"

"Yes. That's why I asked you here."

"Oh. Ummm . . . I'm not sure we should talk about this. I told you before that we can't be together. I mean, just because, you know, we like it doesn't mean we should." Her fried eggs suddenly become her whole world; her attention dedicated to the cold food as she rambles. "It would be complicated." As she moves her eggs around with her fork, I spy blue eyes under long lashes taking me in. "And I'm not sure how to—"

I put her out of her misery. Signaling between us, I say, "I didn't mean to talk about us. *Us*."

"Not us?"

"No."

Her hand is pulled back, and her head drops down in humiliation. "God, I'm such a fool."

"No, you aren't. I'm sorry if I made you feel—"

Snapping upright, she's quick with the reply, "No, you didn't make me feel anything."

"*Okay . . .*" This girl's got a chip on her shoulder like none other I've ever seen. It protects her from the bad, but I'm starting to wonder if it keeps out the good as well. "As you know, we fly to LA today, but before I go, I wanted to talk to you about Alfie. We signed the contract." If I'm not mistaken, despite all the combative snips that have come my way, I see joy in her expression. It must be exhausting to be here some days. Holding onto anger seems to be her specialty, but she can't hold onto it around me for long. The cracks in her armor are growing, which benefits me. I prefer her smile more than her scowl any damn day.

That little piece of joy I found a moment earlier disappears. "You're leaving Alfie? You can't come into his life and then vanish like he doesn't matter."

"I wouldn't. Thanks for the thinking the best of me, though," I say, letting my words drip with sarcasm.

"What do you plan to do then?"

"I've been thinking about it. Also because Alfie will say something if I don't."

"Just tell me, Jet."

"He lost his mother. I don't want him to feel like he's losing me as well. I also don't want him to lose you. To add to the complication, I don't want him flying back and forth all the time."

"Neither do I."

Here goes everything . . . "This trip is only a few days, but when it's time, I've been told we'll be out for three weeks to a month to record. We'll play them the songs we currently have, and if they approve of those for the release, the recording sessions will be during the sixty day period to add the last four to six."

"You just said you weren't going to abandon him."

"I'm not. We've come up with an idea. What if you were to take care of him full time?"

"What?" Her head shakes as if the idea is incomprehensible, then she asks, "How does that fix the problem of you leaving? That's exactly what you'll be doing to him —leaving him."

I'm smart enough not to tell a woman to calm down when she's fired up. I slip on my kid gloves and proceed with caution. "You and Alfie would come to LA." Mouth open.

Eyes wider than the plate in front of her.

Cogs turning so fast that I expect to see smoke come out of her ears.

Still so damn beautiful. I'm almost tempted to kiss that stunned look right off her face, but I like my dick the way it is—not kicked in—so I stay on track as much as I can. "There's only two months of school left. I looked into a homeschool program for this year that will keep him on track to start back in the fall." I can't take all the credit for that one. Rivers mentioned homeschooling, but I did the research.

A furrow anchors her brow, and I can't read her. "I don't even know what to say. I can't afford to take off to LA to follow your dreams."

"You would be there to take care of Alfie."

"I have no money, Jet."

I hate using information against her, but in this case, I take the chance it will allow her to see the opportunity instead of the negativity. "You said your aunt told you to go back to Dallas. I assume you don't have a job anymore, maybe not even a place to live. I'm offering you a job, Hannah. I'll pay you a salary and your expenses. You'll have your own room and time off. When I'm not recording or doing business, I'll be with Alfie."

Hands are waving. It's always quite the sight when she gets flustered, and I've thrown a real curveball at her this time. "Wait. Wait. Wait. You want to pay me to watch Alfie?"

"Yes." As the idea settles between us, I wait anxiously to hear what she says next.

"You know I would take care of him for free."

"I do."

"But I need a job, and if I get one somewhere else, that means I can't watch him whenever I want, only on my time off."

"That's not good."

"No, it's not. How much are you offering to pay?"

"I was thinking we could figure it out together."

"The minimum is three weeks? The maximum is one month?"

"I can't guarantee the timeline until I learn more from this trip."

Staring toward the front door of the diner, her thoughts aren't anywhere near here. That she's still here, though, is a good thing, and that she's considering the idea even better. "Apparently, I owe my aunt a thousand dollars for my share of the bills and rent the past couple of months. The free ride was only temporary. This would allow me to pay her back. Will the pay cover what I owe and next months' bills?"

"Wait, back up. Why do you owe your aunt money?"

"For my share of living expenses."

"But you came here to help Cassie and Eileen with Alfie."

Exasperation comes in the form of a sigh. "I know. Look, Jet, I know you think she's horrible, but Cassie was her life. Alfie is a tie to that life. She loves him and is scared he'll be taken from her forever—"

"By his father, someone else who loves him."

"I get it. I do. I promise you I do. It's been part of the problem. If I defend you at all, she thinks I'm on your side."

Sides? There are those fucking sides again. "We're all on Alfie's side. We all want what's best for him."

"I know, and I agree with you. Eileen, on the other hand . . . forget it. As for this job, if I could afford to, I'd do it for free."

"You do a lot for Alfie, and he notices. He's actually the one who suggested I ask you."

Waves of brown hair fall to the side with her head resting in her hand. "I'm not sure what to say, Jet."

"Say yes." Yes. *Yes to the job.* Yes. *Yes to me.*

"Why do you want me? I understand how it benefits Alfie—having both of us beats a stranger. But you'll be stuck with me—in the mornings, cramping your nights, bugging you on your days off. You'll be stuck with me all the time if I'm living with you." As if it just sinks in, she says, "Oh my God. You said I'd have a room. We'll be living together?"

Well, she doesn't look disgusted, so I'll take the compliment. "I'm getting an advance, but not enough to rent two places."

"What happens when you bring someone home?"

"Someone?" My eyebrows shoot straight up. "A girl?"

For someone who thinks so poorly of me, she sure does look hurt by the thought of me with another woman. "You think I fuck anyone who offers?" I'm not hurt by her assumption, but it does disappoint me. "Don't worry about it, honey. I can keep my dick to myself when I'm caring for my kid."

"I didn't mean to suggest—"

"You know exactly what you meant, and so do I."

"Let me ask you, Hannah, have you fucked anyone since we fucked?"

"Is that what we did?"

"I didn't think so until now." I catch the waitress's eyes. *That's all I was to her. A quick fuck. Okay. Lesson learned.* "Check please."

"Jet, I'm sorry. I didn't mean to insinuate—"

"What did you mean then?"

Following a long exhale, she leans forward resting her arms on the table, and whispers, "You can. You can do whatever you want. You don't owe me anything. I was just saying if you want to have company, I'm not sure where we'll go."

"I won't have company, so there's nothing to worry about."

Regrets color her cheeks as if embarrassment has taken over. What does she have to be embarrassed about or regret? *Maybe us?* Probably.

"I have no right to ask anything of you. I know I've been hot and cold with you, but it's not for the reasons you think. I told you I don't want to talk about our time together—"

"When we fucked?" I'm surprised she doesn't get whiplash from making sure no one else in the place is listening. Fuck it. I have nothing to lose. To deepen that blush that's crawling up her chest and neck and heading north to her cheeks, I say, "I don't remember you being so shy when you were naked in my bed."

"When you say things like that . . ." She sighs, but I see how her chest rises and falls deeper than before. "Jet, we can't do this—you and I—we're not in a place where we can ever happen." *Get it together, Crow.* She doesn't want to be in this situation if the sad expression in her eyes is to be believed. *God, this woman.* Why does she affect me so much?

Reaching across the vinyl tabletop, I take her hand in mine, and she doesn't pull away. In fact, she stays and her fingers curl around mine. "We're only rivals because of some fucked-up situation we've found ourselves in. We spent time together in the most intimate way two people can, and you walked away. Now I know why."

"I don't even know why."

"You had so much on your plate already with the pressure of holding a family together that was falling apart. I get it."

"I know it won't make a difference now, but I wanted to be carefree that night. I wanted to forget that Cassie was dying before my eyes and that my aunt was drinking herself into oblivion. I didn't want to see the sadness in Alfie's eyes anymore. I wanted to feel free from everything that night, and you did that for me." Her hand tightens briefly around mine. "That night has meant more to me than you know. I got to be me again, even if it was just for one night."

"I wish I would have known."

"I wish I would have known who you were back then."

"I'm glad you didn't, or we wouldn't have had that night."

A genuine smile appears, not one filled with the pressures of a custody battle or a threat of having to move. Her smile is one that finds comfort in the company she keeps.

Unfortunately, her hand slides back to her side of the

table, and we're back to being on opposite sides again. "*If I come with you and Alfie, it can only be for him, and to help you out. That's it.*"

"That's reasonable. A little disappointing," I say, giving her a wink, "but reasonable."

Scooping a forkful of food, she takes a big bite, mulling the idea while she eats. I'm not sure if I should push my luck by talking or just wait her out. Silence is king, so I wait her out.

Half a glass of orange juice and a full piece of bacon later, she sets her fork down and rests her arms on the table. "I'll do it."

"You'll do it?"

"Yep."

"We didn't even discuss salary."

"Jet," she starts, leaning closer. "You've caught me at a great time. I don't have many options, and you're offering me a job to do something I love, spending time with Alfie. Bonus, I'll have my expenses covered. It may only be for a month, but it's a month I get to spend with him. How can I say no?"

Even though I knew I was helping her out when I decided to suggest this job, selfishly, I also knew I'd get more time with her too. See how selfless she is—she could probably get a job paying more than I do, but here she is sacrificing herself for her little cousin. I kind of feel like an asshole now. Right then, I realize I have to give her the respect she deserves for giving up so much for him, and now for me. "Thank you. I appreciate it more than you know, but Alfie will be over the moon."

The waitress approaches to refill our coffee cups. Hannah adds cream and sugar and stirs casually, her demeanor so different from earlier. "Since Cassie has passed, I need to be there for Alfie. If that means putting my life on hold to help hold his together, so be it."

"Cassie would want you to have a life, Hannah."

The waitress drops off the ticket and takes my card.

"I don't matter . . . he does. He has a chance."

"A chance at what?"

Her tone hardens like her gaze. "Nothing. Let's just focus on the job."

She's done. It's clear there's no use trying to open something up that she's already put the lid on. I drink my coffee, hoping to clear the lump in my throat that formed when she became upset.

I'm shadowed when the waitress returns with my card. I sign the receipt and look up and straight into the cloudy eyes of Hannah.

With her chin tilted high and the chip on her shoulder back in place, she says, "If you have a chance, let me know when you land in LA."

I've been known to have a cocky side, and Hannah Nichols brings it out in me. "Why is that?"

She rolls her eyes. "Why do you make this so hard?"

"Speaking of making things hard—"

"God, you're incorrigible, Jet Crow."

"Jet will do."

Another eye roll, a little more epic, is her first response as she stands up. The second is her saying, "I worry. That's all. There. Are you satisfied?"

The way her waist dips in and her hips curve out, she affects me in ways that I'm apparently supposed to suppress. This is going to be a struggle. "Satisfied isn't quite the word I'd choose."

This time I see a little of the woman I met that night at the bar—the one who escaped her life and entered mine.

The one I've left a door open and maybe my heart for as well. But I don't want to get ahead of myself or scare her off.

Any needs I have come secondary. If she's offering to help us, even if for a short time, I'll back off like she wants and take what I can get.

With her hands on the table, she leans down and whispers, "So this deal means we're in bed together once again. Speaking purely business wise."

The waitress walks by with a pot of coffee in hand but stops to hip bump Hannah. "Stake that claim, girlfriend."

I chuckle. Hannah doesn't. And then she does, not able to hide her embarrassment. "She thinks we're sleeping together."

Popping my imaginary collar, I smirk—good and smug—just how she likes. "Nothing wrong with that."

"You're ridiculous," she says, giggling. "I'm going now." She turns to go but doesn't leave. Turning back, she rubs my shoulder. "Safe travels."

"Thanks. I'll call you when I land."

This time, she does leave. The walk is slow, but I enjoy every step she takes. "A text will do, Jet."

"Fine. Text you later."

She waves over her shoulder, the bell above the door chiming when it's opened. I'm about to get up, but the waitress stops back by and asks, "Are you going to let her get away?"

"Not a chance."

14

Jet

My guitar goes everywhere I go. Even so, for some reason, I didn't expect to play this weekend in California. I thought I'd be stuck in business meetings, working out a schedule, and finalizing our negotiations.

We did most of that, but a few too many beers, a full moon, and a chance to jam with legends led to me with a cigarette hanging out the side of my mouth while rocking acoustically around a fire pit in Ojai.

The Crow Brothers will never forget this night. Never in a million years did I think I'd be getting drunk with the members of The Resistance much less playing music with them.

Saturday night in the wee hours of the morning, my brothers, Johnny, Kaz, a guitarist, Dex, a drummer, and I are still up. Derrick, the fourth member and guitarist, went to bed with his woman a few hours ago, and Tommy's crashed on the couch inside.

Johnny stands with his guitar slung over his shoulder

and a shot of whiskey in hand. "It's been fun, but I want to put a baby in my wife."

Among the laughter, Dex says, "You try to put a baby in Holli while you're drunk, and your ass is grass and sleeping under the stars."

"She can't resist me, except if I stay out here until the sun comes up." He stands and points. "It comes up over that clearing if you hang out a few more hours." He shakes our hands before adding wood to the pit. "Kaz, take care of the fire."

"On it."

He downs the shot and tosses the red cup in the trash. "See you tomorrow, gentlemen."

Dex stands next. "I'm out. See you in the morning."

When it's Kaz, Tulsa, and Rivers left around the pit with me, Kaz says, "We stay out here sometimes when we're writing songs or recording." Kicking his feet up on the low rustic rock wall, he looks up at the stars. "Johnny's studio is outfitted with the best production equipment in LA. Plus, it's quiet out here, away from the paparazzi and fans. The privacy gives us a bit of peace." Turning to me, he says, "You'll like it out here. Anyway, it's easier than making the drive back to LA, especially if we've been drinking."

Tulsa asks, "What about women?"

Twisting a bottle cap between his fingers, Kaz flicks it into the fire. "No single women around here."

I ask, "What's your story?"

"Happy. Lara's career has taken off, so she's busy. My schedule isn't too bad when I'm home. If we're recording or on tour, it's tougher, but she flies out or I'll fly home if we have a day or two off. Any of you hooked up already?"

Laughing, Tulsa replies, "I've got a phone full of special someones." Squeezing Rivers's shoulder, he knocks him a bit. "What about you, Riv? Where you been sneaking off to so much lately?"

"I haven't been sneaking anywhere." He looks down, messing with a blade of grass. Rivers is the quietest Crow Bro. He opens up slower, not like Tulsa who is wide open for the world to know all his business.

Rivers is honest and can't seem to lie to save his life or protect his privacy, so I ask him directly, "Are you seeing anyone on the regular?"

"There might be someone."

That sends the guys to howl over the juicy information. "I knew it, fucker," Tulsa says and then downs his beer.

Rivers says, "I'm not telling you assholes anything more, so you might as well move the conversation along to Jet and Hannah."

My body stills when I hear her name, my heart beating a little harder.

Kaz shows interest and sits up. "What's the story with Hannah?"

"Fucker," I mumble under my breath to Rivers while shaking my head. Hannah is always in the corner of my mind, hiding in the recesses and coming into the light when I'm alone with too much time to think.

She keeps me in the loop with anything to do with Alfie and makes sure he's available to talk at eleven each day and again at six forty-five for me to say good night. He loves his time with her, but he's vocal about missing me. I miss him too. But if I'm not with him, having them together gives me a weird sense of peace and comfort.

"She helps me with my son, watching him while I'm gone."

Kaz doesn't know the history, though it's a short one, involving Alfie and Hannah. I'm not sure it's wise to get into it either since I've been drinking. Liquor lowers my walls, and it becomes hard to keep my inner thoughts out of the story. It's like a bad editorial that will make me sound like an idiot.

Tulsa laughs. "He likes her."

"I don't *like* her. Just because she's good with my kid, thoughtful, and gorgeous . . ." The flames of the fire flicker, fueling my feelings. "Has the clearest blue eyes or the cloudiest grays, lips that I turned from pink to red and swollen." I close my eyes as a million little stolen moments with her feel real once again. She has this tattoo on her right side, near the top of her ribs. It's not visible to anyone unless she's naked and twisted around your body, but damn, it felt like I had conquered new land when I discovered that tiny lotus flower. She made me feel new too. "The way she looks at me like I can do no wrong when all I do is fuck up—"

Opening my eyes I find three pairs staring back at me. No one is laughing. There are no side conversations. Shit. "What?"

Kaz is on his feet and shoveling dirt on the fire. "Nothing, man," he replies, chuckling a bit. "I'm going to bed." He moves around the pit and tosses his can in the trash bin nearby. Before he leaves, he says, "I'm no expert on women, but deep down, I knew when it was right even before I admitted it to myself. Sounds like Hannah might be as good for you as she is for your son. Just my two cents. Night."

Rivers is the first to stand. "C'mon, brothers. Let's get some sleep. I have a feeling tomorrow's going to be busier than they've let on. We dealt with the business side of things this morning. Tonight was about getting to know us. Tomorrow, we show them who we are as a band."

Just past the pool, the guesthouse on the property is about three times larger than my house. Made of stone and custom woodwork that Johnny helped not only design but also build in his free time. He told me earlier in the day to find a hobby that takes my mind off the job.

My hobby has always been music.

"Music is a passion that business will destroy if you let it. Protect it," he said. "Find some other way to release the aggression, so when you're playing your guitar or writing a new song, your head is clear of the shit storm."

I'll hold onto any advice from him. With the hell he's been through and the price he's paid to find his place not just in music but in his own life, he knows what he's talking about.

Tulsa talks Rivers into a game of pool in the living room. My head is swimming after all the drinking, so I make my way upstairs to the bedroom where I dropped my bag earlier. After setting my guitar back in its case, I pull my phone from my pocket, letting liquid courage control my fingers instead of my mind, and text Hannah: *I know you're not awake, but I was thinking about you.*

A text buzzes back, bringing a smug ass smile to my face. It reads: *Was?*

I'm quick to reply: *Am.*

She replies: *Why are you thinking about me?*

Me: *How are you?*

Hannah: *Alfie's fine, if that's what you're asking.*

Me: *I'm not. I know he's in good hands when he's with you. I was asking about you.*

I don't like the long pause. She was fast in replying and now nothing. I crossed a line. *Fuck whiskey.* It really makes me do stupid shi—my phone lights up with a response: *I'm fine. You?*

Me: *Drunk.*

Hannah: *You should probably go to bed before you say some-thing you'll regret.*

Me: *I'll just add it to the tally.*

Hannah: *I have a few of my own to reckon with.*

Me: *Tell me one of yours, and I'll tell you one of mine.*

Hannah: *Maybe one day I'll show you.*

Me: *I like the sound of that.*

Hannah: *I have to get up soon. You should go to bed.*

Me: *I should, but I don't want to. Let's talk until the sun comes up. I heard it would be soon.*

Hannah. *LOL. You are drunk. I'm going back to bed.*

Me: *Wish I was there.*

Hannah: *That's what I was talking about. Go to bed.*

I meant my bed and being with Alfie and hanging out with Hannah, but I don't correct her. She's right as well, so I type: *Good night, Hannah.*

Hannah: *Good night, Jet.*

I drop the phone next to me on the mattress and close my eyes; memories of her bare before me come easy when I let my mind drift. More than her skin was exposed that night. Her mind and heart were wide open for me.

The needle of the record player had been skipping at the end of the album long enough for the sound to create a calming lullaby. I thought she was asleep when I got out of bed to smoke, but she rolled over to face me, that sadness in her eyes from earlier back and permeating the room.

"Why are you so sad?" I asked, truly wanting to know her deepest thoughts, thoughts I had no right to hear.

She smiled. God, how I loved seeing that smile. "You can't fix it, so it doesn't matter."

Since we left the bar, my heart had been beating in ways I tried to hide, ways that were loud in my ears and heavy in my chest. I haven't known her long enough to share feelings attaching too fast. "It matters to me."

"If I told you, Jet, you'd be sad too. I like how you are."

"How am I?"

She climbed out of bed, and her hair was messy. The black that rimmed her eyes had spread beneath her lower lids and her body naked. Fucking breathtaking.

She came to me while I was smoking by the window and held out two fingers, a silent request for the cigarette. "The overcast I need, and the storm I crave."

"Is it that bad?"

"Worse," she replied, her gaze turning down.

I took hold of her hand, denying her what she originally wanted and giving her what she needed.

I tilted my head and took a long drag, holding the cig between my thumb and index finger. Running my other hand over her smooth ass, I pulled her forward, encouraging her to sit on my lap. I expected her to turn around and rest on me, but she didn't.

Sexy fucking nymph.

Hannah straddled me and clasped my face between her hands. Kissing me, she urged my lips to part, and the smoke flowed between us.

Her tongue controlling mine, her body started rocking on top of me. She was damp, so wet for me, making me feel possessive, yearning to take her in ways I probably shouldn't since we'd just met. But damn, when she started grinding harder, my whole body craved her. It would have been so easy to slip inside that slick little pussy, so easy to let her fuck me, her tits bouncing in my face until I pinched those taut pink nipples, causing her to cry out for more.

Fuuuck.

"Get a condom, baby."

She got up and sauntered across the room, not shy about her

body. She had nothing to be shy about. The woman was dangerous curves and tits that begged to be held, squeezed, and fucked.

The needle was moved, and the music began to play again, blending in with the winds that snuck their way in through the crack between the window and the sill.

The moonlight that shone inside highlighted the golden strands of her hair hidden by night. Clustered tips grazed over the pink buds of her breasts as she walked.

When she returned to me, she knelt, her tongue running over her bottom lip. Her grip was tight around my hard cock. Lifting up, she licked the tip but held out her hand again. "Share," she requested, wanting my smoke.

"No. You're too beautiful to taint yourself."

I hated when she fucking looked away, the confident woman disappearing under a cloud of self-doubt. "It's an illusion, Jet. Makeup, clothes, and alcohol."

"I was talking about the beauty inside."

She sat back, seeming to ponder my words as she watched me. I didn't mind silence except when I was with her. Could she hear the thundering of my heart or see my thoughts? Would she forgive me for trespassing against the façade she had in place? Every touch of her body made me crave another until I was buried deep inside again.

Slender fingers with bad intentions crawled over my thighs and she lifted up. Her mouth covered me again, taking my erection deep inside her.

Setting the remainder of the burning cigarette in the ashtray, I slid my hands into her hair, wanting to get lost in her for hours. It would only be minutes. A mere mortal had no defenses in the presence of a goddess like her.

As good as her lips felt wrapped around me, her tongue teasing, I wanted to kiss her while I made love and watch her pretty face while I fucked her until she released that sadness holding her captive.

Watching her take me deep and slide back up, I wasn't going to last. She felt too good, too hot, too wet, making me think about how damp she was between her legs.

She'd steal peeks every time she came up and close her eyes on the way down. I remember thinking that heaven can't feel better.

I was too close, but I managed to stop her, making her wait impatiently until I was sheathed. Then I lifted her by the shoulders until she was seated on my lap, her body embracing the hardest part of me. "Fuck," I muttered with my head falling back as one hand wove into her hair. Bringing her lips to mine, I didn't kiss her. I seduced her mouth with mine, my tongue finding a new home in the welcoming warmth twisted with hers.

I came.

I came.

I came when she came, her body choking everything from me —hidden emotions, an orgasm, and a confession that shouldn't have been voiced. "Stay," I whispered. "Stay with me."

... Just like that night, my body betrays me too quickly. I don't find peace in this California bedroom because Hannah may be fifteen hundred miles away, but our unsettled business remains.

I release my cock, my orgasm hitting hard and covering my stomach while I was lost in a past that will only ever be a memory. My breathing evens and my lids are heavy.

Meandering my way into the bathroom, I clean up, and then fall back into bed. Picking up my phone, I text her: *I once met a woman who for one night turned my world inside out.*

Hannah: *You were lucky it was only for one night. I'm still recovering.*

A grin slides into place. I thought she'd be asleep, but I'm glad she's not. I reply: *Maybe one day we'll find a cure.*

I'm tempted to add together but don't.

I wait but no reply comes, so I close my eyes. I'm about to drift off to sleep, but then my phone buzzes in my hand. Holding the phone above my head, her text reads: *Maybe.*

Maybe is not a no. I'll take it from the girl with sad eyes. I'll take that maybe and turn it into a yes one day.

15

Hannah

I have to stop thinking about him.

My body is sticky. My mind still in a haze as my body recovers.

Maybe—That was not a good text to send. It could give hope or imply that there could be more between us. Maybe he'll take it how it was meant—that one day, I'll find the man made for me, and my history with my ex and with Jet will be replaced with new memories.

Eileen should know my plans. I've not been brave enough to tell her that I've decided to work for him. It's in the name of Alfie, but still, I dread her reaction. No matter how I spin it, she'll shoot bullets right through it.

My family would tell me it's wrong to remember that night like it was yesterday, like we don't have problems and debts to pay.

Jet's right.

He sees right through me. The conflict I try hard to hide that comes in bouts of anger or softens in the light of his kind eyes. I struggle to see him as bad when I only remember the good.

An ultimatum was thrown down during an alcohol-fueled rage, my aunt and dad worse when they're together. My father never takes my side, which is one of the reasons I left the first time.

They're not good solo but get them together, and they're vicious. Two bitter and angry individuals . . . I'm terrible. I'm a terrible niece and a worse daughter. I have to remember that Eileen is grieving. She just makes it so hard sometimes.

I just can't play along anymore. This turmoil is destroying me, stealing my sanity. I hate the hate I'm expected to feel toward him, but they're determined to make Jet Crow enemy number one of the Barnett and Nichols families. I'm told I have to save Alfie from the big bad wolf.

I've realized there are days when I'm not exactly certain who that is. But I'm torn.

I'm so torn between the two sides, the divide too great to bridge.

Would he really abandon Cassie when she was pregnant?

Would he walk away without a second thought of his child? He said he didn't know about him.

Not the man I see, the one I'm getting to know. Jet would have been there for her, like he is for Alfie now. How can I doubt him, though? From the moment he believed Alfie was his, he has *fought* for him. Fought to *keep* him. To raise him. To love him. *He's a good man.*

But can I really be considered a good judge of character? Especially when sexy musicians make me lose my better judgment. For the family, it's probably best if I keep things strictly professional.

Is that even possible? I've seen him carrying the burdens of the custody case. And I've witnessed happiness etched on his face so deep that I smiled just because he was while teaching Alfie to play guitar, and eyes with fire inside burning with desire for me. I've seen so many sides to this complicated man that sexy musician seems shallow compared to who he really is.

Two minutes in his presence has me surrendering my heart. If I had to choose, I'd choose him, and that's not what's expected of me. I have to keep my secrets safe inside. I have to hide my true feelings for him from him and them.

Alfie wasn't given a choice when he lost Cassie. I want his future to be full of hope and full of choices.

Swinging my robe around my shoulders, I sneak out of my room at the early hour and go to the bathroom to shower. I need to wash away the memories of that one night we had together, a night where two people were free to be whoever they wanted, sharing their bodies and forgetting their worries.

For one perfect moment in time, Jet Crow was a great distraction from my problems . . . Now he seems to be at the root of them.

As I glide the bar of soap across my skin, parts of me still tingle with need for the real thing. The relief from loneliness I find by reliving that night, touching myself as he once did until the clenching loosens and my body relaxes, is temporary.

Is he?

Doting father, respectful to women, dedicated to his work and his family—is this just an act he's putting on for us? Surely not. A girl he picked up at a bar is one thing. The woman a judge is forcing him to get along with is another. Either way he sees me, I'm one thing.

Alfie is another altogether. Only the cruelest of monsters

could look in the wide expectant eyes of a six-year-old and break his heart.

Not even six in the morning and my mind is buzzing with theories and questions. I'll be facing my aunt soon, and no other argument than "he seems like a good guy" has been handy. I don't want to be made a fool by defending someone who eventually reveals his true colors as any other than what I've seen.

I wrap a towel around me and go back into my bedroom. It's cold in here. I guess I didn't notice earlier since I was heated under my sheet with naughty images of Jet on my mind.

I'm shameful.

Thank God, Eileen and my dad don't know about my past with Jet. Yep, secrets and lies are all that will keep me safe and in Alfie's life.

Hurrying to dress, I toss my towel on the bed. It falls and takes my phone with it. The phone is lit when I reach down to pick it up, the text messages we sent an hour or two ago still on the screen, my "maybe" still glaring back at me. "Let it go," I tell myself. I set the phone down and finish getting ready.

It calls to me, my attention divided between my last reply and what shirt to wear. I grab The Crow Brothers tee and pull it over my head. As if I'll be busted any moment, I pull on a sweatshirt that reads "But first, coffee" over it. No one has to know I'm wearing it underneath.

Taking my phone in hand, I'm about to shove it in my back pocket but don't. I stop to read the exchange again. Before I can talk myself out of it, I confess my fear and type: *I don't think there's a cure for my broken parts, but I could use a little glue.*

Am I insane? What the hell am I doing?

I try to reason myself out of the reprimand. Logically, I know he's asleep. Maybe that's why it was easier to type this time. It's six here so four a.m. there.

Even though I shouldn't have sent another message, I still can't help but feel a little disappointment when I don't get a response.

"Shake it off." I put the phone in my pocket like I should have done in the first place and regret sending that last text. He's going to wake up and read that . . . God, what have I done? I've opened it up for a conversation like he's going to be able to do anything other than realize I'm not worth the trouble of even working with now. Have I jeopardized the job?

I've got to stop running everything around in my head over and over again. Alfie. I need to focus on him instead. Today is Sunday.

"What do you want to do today?" I ask him an hour later when he comes out of his room and parks himself on the sofa with *Teen Titans Go!* on TV.

"The zoo?"

"You just went to the zoo with Jet."

"Hannah!" I'm cautioned the moment my aunt appears from the hallway. "Do not say *his* name in *my* house."

Fury takes hold of my body as my mind races with all the things I shouldn't say, especially not in front of Alfie. This is life here now, now that Cassie is gone—arguing and anger.

But I refuse to let her demean his father in front of him. I stand to talk to her privately in the kitchen, but Alfie asks, "Why can't Hannah say Jet's name in your house, Grandma?"

From the mouths of babes . . .

I cross my arms over my chest and raise an eyebrow,

letting her take the heat for her rudeness. Her voice goes up a few octaves higher, and she feigns innocence. "Oh, sweet boy, the man who calls himself your father was not nice to your moth—"

"Eileen!" I shout, hoping she doesn't finish that sentence. "Alfie, go get dressed. We're going to have a busy day. Wear something warm."

His gaze flicks back and forth between us twice before he scoots off the couch and goes down the hall. "Close your door, Alfie," I add when he disappears into his bedroom.

When I hear it close, I walk into the kitchen, trying to contain my rage, but everything about her pisses me off right now. Dropping my head down, I close my eyes and rub the bridge of my nose. Raising back up, I take a deep breath and narrow my eyes. "Do not ever speak of his father that way again, or I'll make sure you lose him."

The slap comes fast, the sting across my face registering before the realization that I was hit. A look of horror crosses her face, one that surely matches mine. My gasp is all wrong, not vocal enough with my words caught in my throat.

Grabbing my hands that hold my cheeks in shock, she pleads, "I'm sorry, Hannah. I don't know what came over me. I'm sorry. I just—"

I back away out of her reach. "Get away from me."

"I said I'm sorry."

Tears form from anger, and I state, "You hit me."

"I didn't mean to, but—"

"There are no buts." I move back even more, but she keeps closing the gap.

"Please. You can't defend him. My daughter died—"

"Not because of him."

I turn to go, but she grabs my arm to spin me around.

"You are turning your back on your family, a family that has given you everything."

Shrugging out of her hold, I ask, "Where were you two years ago when I needed someone to help me?"

"You made your bed . . . with that loser," she snaps. "You had to lie in it to learn a lesson."

"I was broken and you shut the door in my face. You didn't care about me until you needed me."

"Cassie needed you. Alfie needed you. He still does. Hannah, you're upset. You need to calm down."

"It's so clear now." I scoff, staring into her eyes. "I laid in that bed you said I needed and suffered. I paid the price for making a bad choice back then." I add, "It must be nice to be so perfect that you can stand in judgment of my personal sins, mistakes that affected no one but me in the end, or to be so stuck in your grief, or whatever this is, that you willingly hate a man who has only shown love to his son."

"I'm protecting Alfred from what I know is coming. That man will walk away from him and never look back just like he did to my daughter."

"The only problem is that you're pushing us away as well." I walk to the hall but stop, still giving her the courtesy she has never shown me. "I'm taking Alfie to the zoo because it makes him happy, and his happiness is mine."

Other than a flicker of regret after she hit me, I see worry creasing her face. "What time will you be back?"

"You had me take responsibility for his well-being. The judge gave me shared custody. With that in mind, I will keep him safe, healthy, and happy. Nothing else is your business."

She knows she's holding the losing hand, so she backs up and pretends none of this has happened. "I'll have dinner ready by five thirty."

Walking to Alfie's room, I say, "We're eating out. Don't wait on us."

She's wise not to say any more. My mind is made up by the time I reach his door. When I open it, I say, "Grab your backpack."

"Am I going to school? I don't wanna."

"No. I'm taking you to the zoo, but we're going to be out late, so I want to be prepared for the morning."

He nods, but then pauses to look at me. Reaching up, his small hand touches my cheek. "I'm sorry."

"Why are you sorry?"

His gaze lowers with his hand and guilt is written across his face. "You fight because of me." Looking back up at me, he says, "Does your cheek hurt?"

My heart hurts. "No. I'm fine." I lie because he should never have to bear the burdens of adults who can't get along. "Go ahead and get ready. We're leaving in a few minutes."

I move to my bedroom. Grabbing a large tote bag, I stuff an outfit and some personal items inside and move into the bathroom to pack my toothbrush and other toiletries.

Just outside his door, I hold my hand out. Alfie, with his backpack on, takes my hand, and we walk back through the living room to the front door.

Eileen says, "I'm sorry, Hannah."

Leading Alfie outside before me, I look back at her. Coffee in hand and toast with jelly in front her as if we didn't have a fight at all. Like life hasn't changed in the least bit, she stands there with a tapping, impatient foot and faux smile on her face.

I reply, "So am I," and close the door behind me. But I'm not sorry for the same shallow reason she is because I've seen her true colors.

I'm sorry I didn't see her more clearly prior to now. I'm

sorry for some of the things I said to Jet, but I'm not sorry for fighting for Alfie. I'm not sorry I left the sad life I was leading in Dallas. I'm not sorry I met Jet before I heard the stories. I'm not sorry I slept with him or spent the time to get to know him. No, I'm not sorry for anything she would shame me for, the same things I was shaming myself for not even an hour ago.

I'm only sorry I didn't do this sooner.

16

Hannah

Sitting on a picnic bench, I watch Alfie run wild. The kid already has so much energy, but the popsicle sends him over the edge. I just need to outlast the sugar rush.

My phone buzzes, and I look down. Jet.

I don't think there's a cure for my broken parts, but I could use a little glue. I had happily blocked out that I sent that text until this reminder. My gaze slides south, my heart beating harder in my chest, anticipating his reply: *I'll be home in time to pick Alfie up from school tomorrow.*

I read it several times before I rest my jaw in my hand, struggling not to recoil in humiliation. I was awake this morning when he first started texting, not able to sleep with all the worries crowding my brain. I've had many emotions since coming to Austin, but they were never conflicted until I met him.

Trying so hard to hold my family together under their judgment of me has been like living inside a pressure cooker. I've been on edge for months, ready to burst well before the judge made my life even more complicated.

I've taken so much of my uncertainty on what to do out on Jet and then dumped that text on him like he's a priest taking confessions.

I obviously crossed a line by sending it. Jet's giving me an out by not acknowledging my mistake, something my aunt would point out in a heartbeat. I'll just pretend I never sent it. Replying, I text: *I'll let him know*.

Jet: *Thanks. You doing okay?*

Me: *All good.*

I used to hate lying. Liars are the worst, and now I've become one. I would never want him to worry, and he will if I open up too much. Remembering my thoughts earlier, I take a risk and call him. He answers after the first ring, "Hey, everything okay?"

"Yeah," I reply, keeping my voice down so Alfie can't hear if he runs by. "I'm fine, but I was wondering, and you can totally say no, if . . ." Am I doing the right thing, or am I dragging him into my mess?

"If what, Hannah?"

I can't afford a hotel, and if we're at Jet's, at least Alfie will have his stuff and room. "Since you won't be home until tomorrow, would it be okay if Alfie and I stay at your house tonight?"

"Why do you want to stay there? Are you sure everything's all right?"

"Yes. Fine. I just want some peace and one-on-one time with Alfie."

"You're welcome there anytime, Hannah, but I hope you're being honest with me."

Honest? I'm a horrible person. Run as far away as you can, Jet. Hesitantly, I ask, "Why would I lie?"

"The other day, you mentioned that your aunt told you to go back to Dallas. Are you still fighting?"

Feeling cornered between a lie I don't want to tell and the truth, I struggle with what to do. If I don't lie, it's like handing him ammo to use against us. Would he do that? I'm at a loss on reading people these days. My instincts tell me to trust him . . . and I do. But everyone else tells me not to. "No, we're fine. Hey, listen, we don't have to stay there. Don't even worry. Never mind—"

"The place is yours whenever you need. The key is under the right black shutter of my window on the side of the house."

"Your bedroom window?"

"Yes," he says, and I can almost see the smile I hear in his tone.

He's being so kind. I need to learn to accept a gift with grace. "Thank you, Jet."

"Anytime. There are pizzas in the freezer, but not much else. I didn't shop since I was leaving town."

"It's okay. I can stop by the store on the way home." Alfie comes barreling back and plops down across from me. "I should go. Thanks again."

"Hey, Hannah?"

"Yeah?"

"You take care of everyone else, but don't forget to take care of yourself."

"I'll try."

"See you tomorrow."

"I'll be gone, but Alfie will be excited to see you."

"Right." He sounds disappointed.

"You know," I start, but I'm not sure what to say. I just don't want to hear him sad. "You'll be traveling and need to eat. Alfie will need to eat. What if we make you dinner? You can come home and relax instead of jumping right back into the chaos."

I've stunned the poor man. Muffled voices are heard on his end, but Jet's still silent. "Jet?"

"I'm here. Sorry. We were taking a break from the studio. I have to get back inside, but dinner sounds good. Really good."

"I'll see you tomorrow then."

"I'll call Alfie later, but yeah, it's a date."

It's a date . . . It's just an expression, a common phrase, and neither of us corrects him, letting it go. "Bye," I say and hang up. Setting my phone down in front of me like it's a hot potato, I ask myself, "What am I doing?"

I'm answered unexpectedly. "Falling for my dad."

I look up and right into his innocent eyes, my mouth falling open. "What do you know about falling?"

Alfie smiles. "Uncle Tulsa talks about the ladies falling for him. Why do grown-ups fall when they like each other? Do you get scraped knees? I got one last week. Jet told me to be more careful so I don't fall again."

"He's a wise man."

I'm still in shock he told me I'm falling for his dad. *No way.*

Getting up, he comes around and rubs my shoulder. "Be more careful, Hannah, so you don't fall again."

"That's the best advice I've received in a long time, buddy." I stand, and we start for the exit. "I appreciate you looking out for my well-being."

"Daddy said since I'm the man of the house at Grandma's, I need to take care of you."

"Me and your grandma?"

"Yes."

That man is something else. After how Eileen's treated

him, how I've treated him, he still says such kind things in front of Alfie.

He adds, "He talks about you and how nice you are."

"He does?"

Shrugging, he says, "Sure," like it's perfectly normal for Jet to discuss me with Alfie. We share custody, but I'm curious if that's all he says. I'm about to dig a little deeper, but he points and says, "The prairie dogs," and runs to the see them.

WITH A HUNDRED DOLLARS left in my account, I spend twenty-five on gas and another twenty-five purchasing stuff for dinner and essentials for Jet's fridge. He and Alfie will need them anyway.

Alfie helps me cook the chicken. He loved teasing me with the bits from the inside. *Boys.*

Fortunately, I bought a tin pan, considering how bare these cabinets are. While it roasts, he watches TV, and I watch him.

Fifty dollars isn't going to get me far. I need to find work until the job with Jet begins. Fingers crossed it begins at all. I'll find out more when he comes home.

Home.

Do I have a home anymore? If I walk away from Eileen, where will we go? I'm not leaving without Alfie, but fifty dollars is not enough to fight for custody. I'll do anything for him.

Watching him giggle from something the rabbit did on TV makes me smile. His innocence needs to be protected. His right to like his dad needs to be defended.

Looking around Jet's home, the level of comfort I feel here isn't lost on me.

There are touches that are all man and so him—grays and black and rich brown woods mixed in. It's eclectic with simple pieces that work together as if planned. I don't really see him designing the space, but it's not a mishmash of college crash pad either.

I wonder if I should sleep on the couch or if I dare get sucked into that little piece of heaven in the back room. Guess I'll decide later.

Our evening comes and goes. Once Alfie's sound asleep, I take a shower. The warm water rinses away some of the dirt of the day, but my soul still feels scathed. I scrub a little harder.

Giving in, I climb under his sheets. I don't know when he washed them last, but I can smell his scent as it lingers on the cotton. *I love it.* I revel in it. Here in the peace of his little home, I don't feel the guilt when I indulge in my memories of him. I get to enjoy them instead.

I'm not one to sleep without pajamas, but I opt for just a pair of panties because I love the way the soft sheets and warm blanket feels against my bare skin.

It's not even ten p.m., but I'm so tired from the lack of sleep at Eileen's lately that I find my eyes are heavy as soon as I lay my head down. Sleep comes even faster as my thoughts and worries fade away.

A chill covers me, and I tug at the blanket that's fallen to my feet. When I can't get warm, I open my eyes, my gaze landing first on the clock—3:30 a.m.—and then to the burning spec of orange by the window, and finally to the figure that's so familiar I recognize him in the dark. "I didn't mean to wake you," he says after blowing smoke through a crack in the window.

Everything about him takes me back to our night without strings attached, problems to solve, or duties to fulfill. It was just us and the moonlight back then. Sleep starts to evade as my mind clears. "I thought you wouldn't be home until later."

"A story for the morning."

My voice is low, fitting for the dark of night. "What are you doing?"

"Watching you." His tone matches mine.

"What do you think about when you watch me?"

"Do you ever think about that night?"

"All the time." I lift on my elbow and rest my head on my hand.

"Me too."

"I like to watch you smoke, though I want you to quit."

"What do you like about it?"

"The way you hold the cigarette pinched between your fingers, and the way you look when you inhale."

He rests forward on his knees and looks at me. With his dark hair and matching eyes, he's a nocturnal animal who sees me so clearly in the dark. "I almost climbed into that bed with you." He stands, stubbing the butt into the ashtray. Moving with so much ease in who he is, he walks to the door. "I'll take the couch."

"You don't have to." I almost take it back as soon as I offer, but when his eyes land back on mine, his brow forming questions he doesn't ask, I leave it out there for him to decide.

"Do you think that's wise, Hannah?"

"No, but the offer still stands."

"What are the conditions?"

"I'll move to the couch before Alfie wakes up. That's the only condition."

And then he does that magical thing that men do—he grabs the shirt at the nape of his neck and pulls it off over his head.

The door is locked, and he's standing at the end of the bed. "Are you sure?"

"Yes."

"I mean are you sure you can handle being in the same bed with me?" he asks, chuckling as he heads for the bathroom.

"Pfft. Don't be ridiculous."

"From the way you're looking at me, I thought I should ask."

"Oh, my God." I roll my eyes and turn to my side. Busted. *So busted.* Don't let him see the truth.

"Don't worry, baby. I'm so tired that I'll fall asleep as soon as I climb in. You'll just have to find something else to ogle."

"Don't even go there with me. I was not ogling."

"Sure, you weren't." He closes the bathroom door, and the faucet is turned on.

While he brushes his teeth, I sit and fume in my irritation. I'm just not sure if I should be irritated with him for catching me or myself for staring in the first place.

Grabbing my pillow, I nestle my head under it. Maybe he won't notice the mortification heating my cheeks.

The bed dips beside me, the weight of his muscular body causing me to roll toward him and crash into him. I remain steady in my hiding, pillow secured over me.

Lifting the pillow up, he bends his neck to catch my wide eyes. "It's okay. I don't mind you checking me out. I like you looking at me."

I squeeze my eyes closed, hoping to wash away some of

my embarrassment. It doesn't work. "I was not checking you out. God, you're so conceited, Jet. Just go to sleep."

As soon as I open my eyes, his are wide this time. "You're naked. In my bed."

Gasping, my hands fly to cover my chest. "Shit." I forgot. Is he mad? Did he see me? All of me? Sinking into the mattress, I try to slide farther down under the covers.

"Just in case you've forgotten, I've seen your body before and tasted all of you."

My head whips to the side so my eyes can find his. "You can't say things like that, Jet."

"I just did and look, nothing bad happened." Sometimes, I think he says stuff like that just to get a rise out of me. And it works every time. I'm about to give him an earful, but he presses a finger to my mouth. "Do you know how fucking sexy it is that you're sleeping naked in my bed?"

A girl can only do so much fantasizing before she needs the real thing. Call me weak because damn I am when it comes to him. I know I shouldn't, but I do it anyway. I don't shrivel like a wallflower under his admiring gaze. I embrace who I am when I'm with him, the woman he reminds me I used to be, and come back up in full view of him.

I'm not drunk, but I feel tipsy around him. I'm tired of the outside world beating me down. I deserve to feel good. I deserve to forget my troubles for a little while.

I deserve to feel good.

I deserve this.

I deserve him.

"Kiss me, Jet."

17

Hannah

Without concerns for repercussions, I invite him into my world once more. I'm tired of the lonely nights when my thirst isn't quite quenched. My hand has never felt as good as his does, and a vibrator has never made my body wet with anticipation or heat with desire.

Jet has.

Jet does.

With the lightest of touches on my arm, he fixes his eyes on mine. I want him, want him until my insides uncoil in sheer bliss, the tightening relenting from his touch. I want him to make me feel everything again.

Lost minutes to tongues dancing in the dark and bodies maneuvering, the holes left behind from the pain of the past start to feel whole again. He pulls back with his head over mine. He doesn't speak at first, choosing to stare into my eyes a good long while and caress my cheek. Kissing the corner of my mouth feels intimate when I thought we'd keep it casual.

Dropping my eyes closed, I try to feel instead of think. His breath rushes across my cheek, the words tickling in their wake. "Stay with me."

The sentiment echoed from the first time we were together. I open my eyes and my worries ease as I look into the sincerity of his. Reaching up, I take his face in my hands, the stubble spikes my skin, the sharpness giving me clarity. "Just tonight."

A smile from him is followed by his lips at my ear, whispering, "I'll take tonight."

I release a breath as if I'd been holding it this whole time, my hips angling toward his. Large hands cover me—one in my hair and one on my hip—as we kiss. Pulling me over him, I find myself positioned on top, our underwear the only thing between us. I sit up, dragging my nails lightly through the hair on his chest as I find where he feels best between my legs.

Magic.

I start to move my hips, slow, *oh so slow*; the pressure of his hardness rubbing exactly where I want him feels so good. I didn't even realize my eyes had closed or my head had fallen back until I feel his hands on my breasts, squeezing and bringing me back to him. He sits up and kisses my nipples—unhurried and appreciative—one and then the other. The sight of him is erotic, arousing me even more.

Looking up at me, he says, "You're the most beautiful woman I've ever seen."

I stop moving, my hold on his shoulders tightening. A lump forms in my throat, and my chest tightens. He sure knows how to make a girl feel good about herself. I just wish I was the person he sees in me.

When I look down, he rests his head against my temple

and adds, "I don't need you to say anything. I know you want to snap with some comeback, but I want the truth to sink in first. I hope you hear my words because I mean them."

Looking into his eyes, I whisper, "I know. That's what scares me."

"Don't be scared. This is right." His expression softens, and he cups my face, his thumbs gently running across my cheeks. "I didn't mean to make you cry."

"You didn't." I laugh. It's light, but there. "Well, you did, but these aren't sad tears, Jet." I slide my arms around a little more so he's wrapped in them. I like him close. I like him . . .

He kisses my collarbone and then the curve of my neck and a little higher. Just below my ear, he whispers, "Do you want this, Hannah? Do you want me?"

"I do, so much."

His tongue flattens, and he covers my skin with coolness from his breath, igniting goose bumps in its trail. Pushing forward, I rest in his capable hands, bending to his will. "I want you, too, so much," he says and then flips me onto my back.

The kindness from his eyes is gone, the low light of the room highlighting his hunger for me. Sitting back, he takes hold of the lace on each side of my hips and starts pulling down. My breath catches when he stops and his eyes lower like my undies. Taking me in from the apex of my thighs, he flashes his gaze up to mine. "I want to eat you. I want to devour you. I want to get drunk on you, baby. Tell me I can take what I want."

"You can have me however you want." Running my fingers through his thick, dark hair, I reply, "But kiss me first." I think he's going to move up and let me get caught up in careless kisses, but he lowers his mouth, his fingers parting me, and starts kissing me where he knows I'll beg for more and more and . . . "Oh God."

Minutes feel like seconds as he holds my hips down and his tongue coaxes my body into submission, eliciting his name just for him by making me come. His hand covers my mouth. Rising above me, he moves it and kisses my lips. "Shh, baby."

I'd forgotten we were stealing time together, forgetting a world existed outside this bedroom. My breath comes out harsh, but I swallow, trying to even my racing heart. "I want to feel you inside me, Jet."

"Do you know what it does to me every time I hear you say my name?"

I don't have to lift much to kiss his neck. Wrapping my leg around his, we slowly roll over until I'm on top of him. "What does it do to you when I say your name, *Jet*?" I want him to ache for me the way he makes me ache for him.

He reaches for his cigarettes and lighter on the night-stand, setting them on the bed. "Grab a condom, baby."

If he only knew all the bad things I'm willing to do just to hear him call me baby more often. When we're tangled up in each other, the good far outweighs any bad the world wants to rain down on the happiness we find in times like tonight.

As I stretch over him, he holds me by the waist so I don't fall over. I get a condom from the drawer and get comfortable on top of him again. "Underwear."

He lifts his middle with me on top. I take them down, and he kicks them to the floor. "Good Lord, you're built like a Greek god." Too tempting, I have to run my hands over every dip and rise of his abdominal muscles.

My ass is squeezed with gusto. "You have the sexiest body and the best fucking ass I've ever seen."

"And since you've seen a lot, I'll take the compliment."

Laughing, he doesn't bother with apologies. He has nothing to be sorry for anyway. He moves me down and rips the wrapper open. The condom covers him, and he moves me back with a little lift so I can slide down.

I hold my breath as he stakes claims deep inside me. God, it feels so good. Having him inside me . . . The feel of his skin below me, the coarse hair of his legs . . . his hard stomach . . . I want this. I want him. *I just hope he leaves my battered heart alone; it's too weak to fight a battle.*

Putting his hands behind his head, he keeps eye contact but then starts claiming me in a new way—through a fixed gaze. "I want to watch you get off on me."

He's never made me feel less than confident in doing whatever I want to do in bed with him, but I hesitate. "Watch?"

"Start slow and then fuck me the way it feels best for you."

I pluck my bottom lip a few times in contemplation, but he feels too good not to want more—faster and deeper.

Finding a rhythm that feels amazing, I use his stomach as leverage to keep it. I watch as he takes a Marlboro from the box and lights it. His eyes never leave mine while taking a deep inhale, slowly exhaling, and savoring every second.

Smoke fills the air above us. He never smokes anywhere but next to the open window or outside, but damn if he's not absolutely the sexiest man I've ever seen doing it in bed.

I burn for him. The yearning builds as I get closer to the finish line. My lids close, but he says, "Open your eyes, baby."

Moving without regret or apologies of my own, I take everything he's willing to give—his body, his lustful eyes, his soul . . . I rock. I ride. I take. I don't give a damn thing until I give him my fall, my orgasm, a little piece of my heart, more of my soul, and his name. "Jet," comes out with a whimper as I grind against him until my need is satisfied.

He answers my earlier question. "When you say my name—in swear or prayer—I see your wounds and want to heal every one of them. I want more than one night every six months. I want you to stay when morning comes."

With his hand out, the lit cigarette held away from me, he sits up, holding me by the back of the neck with my cheek against his. "Fuck me, Hannah. Fuck sense right back into me so when you leave this room I can pretend this was nothing more than fun."

His forehead falls to my shoulder, his body slightly curled toward me, bending to me, bowing to me. With my arms around him, I kiss the top of his head. I want to tell him it's okay, that I feel the same, but I can't. I can't. I can't pretend that this is just fun. It isn't nothing. *It's him. It's us.*

We didn't expect things to get out of hand so quickly. But here we are—our hearts open and our bodies bared.

What he doesn't realize is that my body is open and my heart bared. It would be too much too soon to tell him.

So I fuck him to spite my growing emotions. I fuck him to take away his pain. I fuck and fuck and fuck until we're both coming together, and the lies bind us—the lie that this is only fun.

As soon as we're done, he's gone. The ash leaves a trail on the wood floors as he rushes from the bed to tap out the burning butt into the ashtray on the sill. The cold I'm left with doesn't comfort but leaves enough room for doubt to creep in.

Before I have time to regret what we've done, the warmth of his body cradles mine from behind, and he whispers, "You're amazing."

His soothing words melt the forming chill, and I cover his hands with mine.

My hair is swept to the side, and kisses are placed the length of my neck. I start to shy away, but he holds me tighter. "Stay," dusts across my skin, making me consider it for the first time.

The beat of my heart pounds in my chest, reflecting my nerves. Nothing I'm about to do is right in the light of day, but right here in the dark of his bedroom it feels right. Shifting around so I can see him, I take a breath while admiring those eyes that give so much insight to the man. "Jet?"

"Yes?"

"We've got to keep us a secret."

"Tonight?"

"I'll stay," I reply with a smile sneaking out. "But we have to keep this a secret."

He doesn't even try to hide his relief. "Promise me more than tonight, Hannah."

Running the tips of my fingers over the stubble on his chin, I smile, the thought of waking up next to him too tempting to pass up. I kiss him, loving the feel of his lips pressed against mine and the way his hands span my back, holding me close. "I can't promise you much, but I'll give you tomorrow. I want to give you more, but I've been hurt before."

He tilts his head, his gaze traveling from my mouth to my eyes. "I'll take whatever days you can give and show you how good we can be together."

"You're so optimistic."

"When I look into your clear blue eyes, hope is found in your endless oceans. Give me a chance, Hannah. Give me a chance to be the glue that can hold your broken parts together when you're not strong enough. Let me be the one who gets to put you back together. Just one chance is all I'm asking for."

My heart softens. He did read my confession, my text that I regretted sending. I don't have any regrets now as I look into the warmth of his eyes. He wins me over with his gentleness while wooing me with his words. "What will you do with only one chance?"

"I'll make sure that sadness never touches your heart again."

Leaning my head on his shoulder, I want to shout yes to this amazing man with every part of my being. I place one kiss on his lips, and reply, "How are you so sure?"

"Gut instinct. Following my heart. Throwing caution to the wind. Chemistry. Attraction. Everything up here," he says, tapping his temple, "tells me to proceed with caution because of the situation we're in and because I can see you're worried." Taking my hand, he holds it against his chest. His heartbeat is strong, just like him. "If I can't bring down your walls, I'll climb them to prove you're worth the effort. To me, you are worth everything."

Whispering, I ask, "Why?"

"I know your heart. I see how you put everyone else before yourself. We may not have had an ideal start or taken a traditional path to get here, but we're here, and I'm not asking for your heart. I'm asking for a chance to see what this is, to find out what could be. Will you give it to me?"

After I left him so many months ago, Cassie consumed my mind. I spent days looking after her and Alfie's needs, trying to fill the blanks that her illness had created in their lives. But even then, my nights belonged to Jet. Thoughts of him. Thoughts of the way he touched me, kissed me, owned me.

Then all that fell apart when Cassie told me who Alfie's dad was. The knife further tore my heart open as Eileen used scathing and spiteful words to further dehumanize him.

My heart has felt empty. Now, lying so close to him, feeling his heart beat and hearing his words that he wants to be the one who puts me back together, how can I say no? I've never felt more vulnerable, more exposed to be hurt. We have so much more to learn and to talk about, but he makes me want to stay. He makes me want to take another risk. "How could I ever say no to you?"

"All I need is a yes."

"Yes."

18

Jet

How'd I go from trying to keep my distance to being in a relationship?

She called my house "home" on the phone. I know it was a slip on her part, but damn if it didn't make me wish that it was more for her.

Thinking back to our talk before she fell asleep, I pray that yes she gave me wasn't a dream. I may not have planned for this, but I don't regret telling her how I feel. I never saw Hannah Nichols coming, but now that she's here, I'm not ready to let her go.

I'm curious how she'll feel when the sun rises. With her sleeping soundly next to me, I'm not anxious for the day to invade.

Alfie needs to be up soon, so I decide to let her sleep in. I'm going off two hours of sleep from the plane ride home, but I want to see him. I carefully get out of bed so I don't wake her and get dressed by plucking clothes off the floor and sneaking out the door, closing it behind me.

First priority—coffee. I start the pot and pull on a shirt and jeans before going into Alfie's room. Kneeling, I rub his arm to wake him. "Hey buddy, it's time to get up."

He yawns and then opens his eyes. The smile is instant, and he throws his arms around my neck. "You're home."

"I'm home. Missed you."

"Missed you."

"You hungry?"

He nods, and we make our way to the kitchen. "Hannah's sleeping, so it's just you and me this morning. Eggs?"

"Waffles. Hannah let me choose any flavor I wanted." I check the freezer and see a box of frozen waffles.

"Chocolate chip. Good choice." I pop two in the toaster. "Go get dressed and they'll be ready when you are."

He runs off, and I pour a cup of coffee just as I hear Hannah speaking to him in the hall. "Whoa! Slow down, Alfie."

I pull another mug from the cabinet and fill it, though I leave enough room for the creamer she likes to add. When she comes around the corner, a smile I've only seen in private is on full display. "Good morning," I say, pulling her close by a belt loop.

Glancing over her shoulder and then back at me, she whispers, "Good morning." I go in for a kiss, but she stops me. "We can't. We'll talk after Alfie is at school."

"What are you going to talk about when I'm in school?" Alfie asks, coming in just as the waffles pop up.

"Nothing," she replies quickly, stepping out of his way when he rushes back in for breakfast.

She shakes her head at me, but she's not mad. That little smile she's trying so hard to hide behind the mug comes with music to my ears in the form of a giggle. Alfie is eyeing her while he eats his waffle, but then sets it down. "What's going on?"

"Nothing."

When we reply in unison and a little too guiltily by how quick we both answer, he squints his eyes and looks at us. "Did you get a sunburn, Hannah? Remember when I got a sunburn at the park?"

She starts fanning herself after setting the mug down. "We should go so we're not late. Grab your backpack, Alfie."

"Can I eat in the car?"

"Yes." He takes his waffle and gets his bag by the front door. When he's out of earshot, she turns back to me and whispers, "I was thinking I could come back—"

"I want you to come back," I reply, feeling good about how things are between us.

She nods and starts for the door. I catch Alfie in a hug. "It's good to see you this morning, buddy."

"Will I see you today?"

"I'll pick you up from school." His arms tighten around me, and he squeezes hard for a six-year-old. That's my kid. "I like you, Jet."

"I love you, Alfie."

As I'm setting him down, I hear Hannah exhale a breath and look up. Her hand is covering her heart and tears are in her eyes. Moving closer, I take her hand and hold it. "Are you okay?"

"More than okay." She clears her throat, and our little bubble is popped. "I'll be back soon."

"No hug?" I love pushing her buttons.

"No hug in front of him."

I slap her ass as she walks out the door. "I'll collect later."

Alfie has run ahead on the sidewalk, but Hannah's still

on the porch. She shakes her ass for me. "Good luck with that, Crow."

"I don't need luck, baby." I drag my hand over my stomach, pulling my shirt up along with it. "I got all I need right here."

Her mouth drops open. "Do you really think I'm that weak that I'd fall for a few good abs?"

"A few?" I ask, lifting an eyebrow at her. The gauntlet has been thrown down.

Turning around on the path, she rests her hand on her hip. "Is that how we're going to play this, Jet?" The alarm beeps, and Alfie starts climbing into her car.

"This is exactly how we're going to play this, Ms. Nichols."

With an exaggerated eye roll, she turns around, but then calls over her shoulder, "Game on, Crow. Game. On."

I lean against the doorframe with a smile on my face and cross my arms, watching her walk down that path. This time, she'll be coming back. Yeah, I win. "Bye, guys."

After they drive away, I go back inside. I'm a stinky fuckin' bastard, and since I'm hoping for more action with Hannah when she returns, I jump in the shower.

I'm in, out, and scrub my hair with the towel. I spend some time looking through my closet, but my best shirts went with me to LA and are now dirty. I stop acting like a chick and pull a tee from the shelf.

I keep checking the time, wondering when she'll be back. It shouldn't have taken this long, so I text her: *Got an ETA?*

Hannah: *Do you miss me already?*

Me: *Yep.*

Hannah: *Charmer.*

Me: *Come back so I can show you how charming I can be.*

Hannah: *I think you showed me several times last night.*

Me: *And your point is?*

Hannah: *You're right. I'll be back in a few.*

She isn't, though. I sit on the front porch for the next hour wondering where she is and checking my phone regularly. I finally break down and call her, but she doesn't answer.

Worrying, I pace. I'm about to go inside and busy myself with some housework that needs to be done, but the sound of tires turning into the driveway pulls my attention back. I walk down the steps and greet her by opening the door. "Hey, I was starting to worry."

She unbuckles her seat belt and smiles, but something is off. "We've already jumped to worrying about each other?"

"Guess so."

Standing with the door between us, she hides her eyes behind large sunglasses. When she shifts and lowers her head, I know something's off. Something's wrong. She's quick to duck out from between the car and me. "You don't need to worry about me, Jet. I can take care of myself."

I shut the door, and she clicks the alarm, locking the doors when she walks away. I follow her up the sidewalk but step around her and block the door. "What's wrong?"

"Nothing is wrong."

"Then take your sunglasses off, look me in the eyes, and tell me nothing's wrong. If you do, I'll back off."

She crosses her arms over her chest, her stance firming. "Don't tell me what to do."

"I'm not telling you. I'm asking you what's wrong. Clearly, something is." Taking her wrists, I try to unfold her arms and make her feel more comfortable. "Hey." I tilt my head to the side. "It's me. The guy you said you can't say no to last night. C'mon, Hannah. Talk to me."

Her arms fall to her side, and her head falls forward to rest against my chest. I bring her in and hold her. Kissing the top of her head, I whisper, "You can talk to me about anything. I'm kind of impatient in life and a little bossy, but I'm a good listener."

"A little?" She laughs against my chest, making me laugh.

"Fine. A lot bossy." I open the door and step aside to let her by. "Now tell me what's on your mind."

Once we're inside, she pulls the sunglasses off and drops them in her purse that's dumped on the coffee table. She sits down and finally looks up at me. Her eyes are red and a little puffy from crying. "My cousin died, and I haven't had the time to even mourn."

Kneeling before her, I rest my hands on her knees. "Is that what you've been doing?"

"She was cremated."

I wasn't expecting to hear about Cassie, but looking at the pain on Hannah's face, the gray in her eyes, I realize I should have asked. I'm still not sure what I can and can't ask, but I should have taken the risk. I still don't know if I have the right to ask about her at all. "I don't need you to fix anything, Jet. I just needed to cry."

Getting up, I sit on the couch next to her. "And you did?"

"I did. It makes no sense, but I was driving by the park we used to take Alfie to. I drive by that park every time I go to his school, which is almost every day, sometimes twice, but today . . ." She rubs her eyes and huffs, annoyed with her tears.

"But today what? What happened?"

"I've not been happy in a long time." I pull her onto my lap and keep my arms wrapped around her when she's settled. "How can I be happy when she's no longer alive?

How cruel am I?" She drops her head into her hands as her body gently shakes with little sobs.

"You're not to blame for her death, and you're allowed to be happy. That's what living is about—finding what makes you happy."

Leaning her head on my shoulder, she says, "She's not been gone that long."

"Everyone mourns in their own time and in their own way."

"Alfie won't talk about it."

"He will when he's ready."

Looking back at me, she asks, "Do you ever think about her?"

"All the time, but being honest with you, I'm not sure what to think. She obviously didn't think very highly of me, and I've spent years thinking the best of her."

"Why did you break up?"

I knew this would come up, but I had foolishly convinced myself we'd have more time together before dredging up the past. I can't control what happened, but I can control the outcome. "Hannah, are you sure you want to discuss this?"

"I think I need to."

Seeing her reaction and the questions in her eyes, I need to give her anything that will give her peace. "I have a million excuses, but the bottom line is, I screwed up. I thought we were casual. She thought we were more serious."

"You cheated on her?"

I knew she'd jump to conclusions. The muscles in her back stiffen, causing me to hold her a little tighter. "I wasn't fucking anyone else."

She tries to get up. "What were you doing then?"

"I'm not letting you walk across this room in anger over something you're imagining in your head."

"How do you know what I'm imagining?"

"Because of the bullshit you were fed about me."

"Are you sure it's bullshit?"

"Yes, it's all bullshit. You can ask me anything, and I'll tell you the truth. Not me pleading my side, but the truth."

The tension in her body eases, and she looks me in the eyes again. "Then tell me the truth, and I'll listen."

I love the way her hands lock together behind my neck, and when I lean in to kiss her, she lets me, and she kisses me back. I just got her. I'm not ready to lose her. "She broke up with me, accusing me of a bunch shit I didn't do. Came at me saying she didn't want to waste her time with someone she didn't trust, someone she didn't love. It was heavy, considering how new we were as a couple."

"How long were you together?"

"A month, a month and a half at best. I liked her. We had fun. She was wild, which worked for me at that time in my life."

I see the question on her face, the worry to give it a voice, to release it between us. Once she asks me about love, I'll have to answer. I cared a lot about Cassie, but I'm not so sure, thinking back, that it was love. How will Hannah react to that? I hope I can keep that locked away just a little bit longer for both of our sakes.

She kisses my forehead and cradles my head to her before slipping off my lap. "You don't owe me the details. I just wanted to understand the relationship a little more." She walks to the kitchen and stands on the other side of the bar. "Thank you."

"For what?"

"Letting me talk about whatever I need."

I walk to the opposite side of the bar, resting my hands on it. I can see the fog of burden lifting in her eyes, and a smile appears. "I'm sorry about your cousin. I'm sorry about Cassie passing for Alfie. I'm sorry I hurt her. I never intended to."

"I don't want to keep talking about you and Cassie. When I'm with you, I'm betraying her. I'm betraying my aunt and my family. I just needed a few minutes to mourn her passing." She sniffles, tears beginning to well in her eyes. "But I'm here. I'm here because I've come to know a different man than how you were described. You've been nothing but good to me, Jet. That's why I struggle. That's why I'm conflicted inside."

"I—"

"You don't have to defend yourself to me. I see who you are. I see who you are with Alfie when you think no one is watching. I know you're a good man. Just some days are going to be tougher, days I'm fighting with my aunt over . . . everything. So it's nothing you can fix. I may have been mourning Cassie's death, but I'm also mourning the loss of trust from my family while trying to figure out what is the right thing to do for Alfie. Now I've gone and gotten myself involved with you and . . ." She smiles and comes around. With her hands on my middle, she lifts on her toes and kisses me. "If you didn't realize already, I have feelings for you."

"So no regrets about last night?"

"Regrets?" She laughs. "God, no. I can't wait to do it again."

Bending over, I scoop her into my arms and head for the bedroom. "We have a few hours to kill. Want to burn some daylight?"

"I was thinking some moonlight too."

"Have I told you how amazing I think you are?"

"No, tell me."

Tossing her on the bed, I pull my shirt off and drop my jeans, kicking them off. When I climb on the bed and hover over her, her legs open for me without even asking. Fucking hell, she's a sex goddess. "Exquisite."

Hannah

Thirty minutes.

I have thirty minutes to recover from the best sex of my life.

There is no recovery. I will never feel as whole as I do when we're bonded physically and emotionally during sex. Jet Crow is gifted in all ways, but damn, he sure knows how to please a woman.

Unfortunately, I can't lie here all day or I would. I get moving and take a shower. I'm dressed and fixing Alfie's snack just as he comes barreling in. "Hannah. Hannah. I got to lead the line today. All the way from the classroom to the cafeteria."

"Fantastic. You've wanted to do that all year. What changed today?"

He drops his backpack in the middle of the living room and runs to me. Taking a cracker with cheddar on top in hand, he replies, "Lucy Minken was sick today, so I got to do her job and mine." He shoves the cracker into his mouth while I get him an apple juice box to help wash it down.

I look up when Jet walks in, my breath catching just enough for him to notice and for Alfie not to. My cheeks heat, and I want to burst like a bottle of champagne full of happy bubbles.

His gaze dips to Alfie, and he asks, "What's your job?"

"I get to sweep under the table at lunch," he replies excitedly.

Jet's expression sours. "What the fu—"

"Isn't it great that schools give kids responsibilities?" I say, laughing on the inside from his reaction. "And teaches them to clean up their messes?"

"Yeah, sure. Responsibility," he mumbles. He's smart enough to let it go. Rubbing his eyes, he looks so tired. He detours toward the hall. "Except for two hours on the plane, I haven't slept in almost thirty-six. Mind if I lie down for a bit?"

"No, of course not. Me and the kid have some homework to do anyway."

Alfie asks, "You have homework too?"

"Research, buddy. We'll work while your dad rests."

"What kind of research?"

"Nothing big. Go to sleep. You'll need the energy later." This time, I give him a wink.

Jet moves to come back to me—maybe to kiss me or hug me, touch me in a way he can't around Alfie—but stops and nods down the hall. "If you need anything—"

"We'll be fine. Go rest."

"Thanks."

And there is one of the sweetest smiles that I love. How could anyone question his devotion to Alfie? Many parents would have opted out of the duty of collecting their child when so tired. But he went. *That's love.*

I carry the plate for Alfie and situate his stuff on the coffee table, then pull my laptop from my bag and set up on the couch. Alfie gets busy on his workbook, and I log in to my account to finish my college application.

It's that annoying hour when it's too soon for dinner and too late to snack, too soon to go to bed and too late to nap. It's been two hours since Jet went to sleep, and I'm tempted to take Alfie to the park or somewhere to let him run around when someone knocks on the door.

I'm quick to my feet to answer. I open the door to one of Jet's brothers. I remember seeing him when they played live.

"Uhh," he starts, clearly confused by why I'm here. His lighter eyes and hair contrast the dark of Jet's, but his skin has that same golden brown even in winter. He might be shorter than his older brother, but if he is, it's not by much, and his muscle mass makes up for it. "Is Jet here?"

"Yes."

His hands go to his head and then blow out. "Whoa, I was not expecting you." Offering his hand, he says, "We haven't met, but I'm Jet's brother, Tulsa. You're Hannah, right?"

"Yes," I reply, starting to feel a little ridiculous mimicking myself. I shake his hand and then open the door a little wider. "He's sleeping, and I was watching Alfie—"

"Alfie's here?" he asks, leaning to the side to peek around me. A huge smile, his emotions written all over him, another contrast to his brother, shines when he spies Alfie. "Alfred, my man."

"Uncle Tulsa!"

Alfie runs to him. "Guess you two have become friends."

"Fast friends," Tulsa replies, swinging Alfie onto his back.

"Tulsa's my uncle," Alfie adds, reaching to touch the roof of the front porch.

"He is," I say, smiling. I'm impressed by how close they've become in such a short time. My father was never there for Alfie, and he doesn't have any other male relatives nearby. He deserves this family, this love and acceptance. "You can come in if you'd like."

He turns and sticks two fingers in his mouth, an earsplitting whistle following. "My brother," he says, shrugging.

The third Crow brother catches my eyes when he gets out of the SUV and strides up the sidewalk with the phone to his ear. By the time he reaches the porch, he looks back and forth between the two of us, trying to figure out the situation, and then smiles at Alfie. "My man. I didn't know we'd get the pleasure. How are you, buddy?"

"I got to be line leader today, Uncle Rivers."

"No way," he replies acting shocked and feeding the story. I'm kind of falling for all three of these guys because of their sweetness for Alfie.

Alfie laughs, delighted in the attention. "Way. And if Lucy is sick tomorrow, I get to do it again."

"Whoa! Fingers crossed that Lucy is si—" His eyes dart to mine, but when he sees my displeasure, he adds, "Makes a speedy recovery."

I cross my arms over my chest. "Nice save."

"Rivers Crow and you're Hannah. I've heard a lot about you."

"Oh?" Wonder if Jet has talked to them about me.

"We haven't met, but I'm sorry for your loss."

I'm kind of taken aback by how thoughtful he is. "Thank you. Jet is sleeping, but you're welcome to wait inside if you'd like."

Tulsa tells Alfie to duck, and they move inside. I follow

with Rivers behind me who shuts the door. Alfie is set on his feet, and Tulsa walks with purpose down the hall. Yikes.

Rivers starts laughing when Tulsa barges into the back bedroom and shouts, "Get up, fucker."

"Fuck, Tulsa," Jet yells. "Get the fuck out."

I'm not quick enough to cover Alfie's ears. His eyes go wide, and he looks at me. I say, "Do not repeat those bad words ever. Got it, kid?" He nods his head, making me smile. "Good boy."

Rivers has helped himself to a juice box. When I eye him, he says, "Alfie's a great kid. It's been fun getting to know him."

"His mom did a great job with him."

"And you. Jet's talked about how much you've done for him."

Pulling Alfie close, I wrap my arms around him as he leans his back on me. "He has?"

"All the time. We've heard a lot about you."

"I'm curious what you've—"

Tulsa runs through the living room and out the back door, calling behind him, "C'mon, Alfie. Your dad is a bear today."

Just as Alfie runs out the door, chasing Tulsa, Jet comes from the dark of the hallway. Good grief, he does things to me, things that I hope I can hide from his brothers—things like my throat going suddenly dry and causing me to shift as my body becomes a traitor to me and an ally to him.

And then he winks, and my hands go to cover my heating cheeks. I want to run to him, to cling to his bare chest and chiseled abs, to run my fingers through his sex god hair, and to kiss him until we're falling into bed again. The best part is he's looking at me the same way.

Head tilted down, he's rubbing the back of his neck,

hiding that smirk, but eyes directed at me, he's taking me in head to toe. I just wish I was wearing something cuter than a pair of old ripped jeans and a baggy T-shirt.

I almost forgot Rivers was here until he clears his throat and says, "Yeah, um, so I'll go check . . . I'll just go out back."

As soon as the door closes, I run to Jet and mount him. With my legs wrapped around his middle and his hands squeezing my ass, we kiss. We kiss until our eyes close and time disappears. We kiss until our tongues mingle and our hearts beat faster. My back hits the wall, and he readjusts me, but just the feel of being pressed against his hard muscled body makes me want so much more. Through panting breaths and hands running through his thick hair, I whisper, "You turn me on so much."

His unshaven cheek scrapes my cheek as he runs his nose along the underside of my ear. "You smell so fucking delicious. You think they'll miss us if we disappear for a while?"

My legs tighten around him, and I wiggle, wanting the friction but needing the payoff. "Yes."

The back door squeals in protest when it opens. "Is it clear in here?"

Tulsa.

Jet and I exchange the same sexually frustrated look. I drop my legs, and he tugs the hem of my shirt back into place. After stealing a kiss, he smiles before calling out, "All clear."

He starts to walk away, but at least I get a good view of his ass in those jeans. I slap it, and when he turns back in surprise, I shrug.

"Paybacks are hell, Hannah."

"I'll take my chances."

The guys and Alfie file back inside, and Rivers says, "The

band's coming over."

Jet starts the coffee pot. "What are you talking about? You guys are already here and need to leave. I'm just kicking it with Alfie and Hannah tonight."

I see the way they're looking at him and then at me, trying to figure out what's going on. Considering I'm not even sure what's happening between us, I wish them luck. If they find out, maybe they'll let me know.

In the meantime, I like whatever this is that's happening. Our relationship is growing, evolving into something new, something without anger or emotional bullets waiting to be fired.

When I look at Jet now, I see that guy I met so long ago, the guy I would have fallen for if I had stayed. At the time, that's why I had to go.

Last night, I'm glad I stayed.

Rivers says, "You really need to get some food in this place."

Tulsa is popping grapes, my grapes, he took from the colander near the sink. "The Resistance. They wanted a place to jam, so they're coming over later."

I'm stuck on the fact that I don't have much money left, and he's eating all my grapes when my mind rewinds, and I understand what he actually said. Wait, what? I do a double take. "The who?"

"Not The Who," he says, laughing. "The Resistance."

"The band? They're coming here?"

Jet says the last part in unison with me, but I have a feeling it's for different reasons.

Alfie jumps up and tries to catch a grape with his hand. "Who's resistance?

Tulsa replies, "It's a famous band."

"Like you guys?" Alfie follows up.

Rivers rubs Alfie's head as he walks by. "Band. Yes." He bends down. "Are you gonna play guitar with us?"

"I've been thinking about it," he says, rubbing his chin, which is stinkin' adorable. "I like drums."

Tulsa's arm flies up. "Yes, I win."

Rivers rolls his eyes and adds, "The only time you play drums is by default, Tulsa. Hey Alfie, you hang with me, and I'll show you how your dad taught me to play."

Alfie turns to Jet, who's nearby. "You teached Rivers?"

"Taught," Jet corrects with a smile. "I taught both my little brothers how to play."

When it comes to Jet, he hung the stars, according to Alfie. At first, I thought it was just because he was happy to have another male around since he'd always been around women. But it's not that. I see the love he has for him already. The way he looks up to him, not just because he's taller, but because he truly admires him.

Tulsa and Rivers have the same admiration in their expression when they look at their big brother. *But Jet makes it really easy to admire him. He's kind, generous, and attentive. And if his brothers are anything to go by, Alfie is going to be a fine man, too.*

Alfie's happiness is contagious. He lights up a room without any effort. He's just him, and we all love him for it. But it's not just him who's lucky. It's me. I'm not treated like an outsider or the enemy. I'm treated like a part of the family.

This could have so easily been Cassie. They would have loved her and accepted her into their clan as they've accepted me. It makes me sad to think about me reaping the rewards because of the struggles she went through.

20

Jet

"I'm getting drunk." Tilting my head back, I look for the stars between the clouds. Hannah, who's sitting on a lawn chair next to me, laughs loud enough to get everyone's attention, causing me to laugh. Rolling my head to the side, I say, "You're getting drunk, too."

"I already am." Her eyes are glazing over. Her hands are not covert like she insisted we be this morning. Instead, she's been rubbing the top of my leg, her fingers occasionally dipping between my thighs, getting precariously close to touching a part of me that I won't be able to disguise much longer behind this guitar.

The conversation picks back up around the fire we built to keep us warm this chilly March night. It's nothing compared to the fire pit in Ojai, but it's served us well many times before.

Alfie went to bed hours ago, and we have each checked on him several times since.

Hannah invited her friend, Dave, over. I've heard a little

about him, and he seems nice enough. Plays guitar, which is cool. Friendly and fits in with the group without hand-holding from Hannah.

She chatted with him for a bit early on, but when we pulled out our guitars, he showed his talent. He definitely knows his way around the strings. "Dave, why aren't you in a band?" I ask.

"Bad past and haven't found the right band. You guys needing a new guy?"

Tulsa laughs. "We have more guitarists than we know what to do with."

"I've seen you guys play a few times. You're good."

Johnny says, "They're great. It's time the rest of the world hears The Crow Brothers' music."

They start playing a Stevie Ray Vaughn song, and I glance at Hannah. She was starstruck when she first met the guys, but fuck, so was I. A few hours later, her eyes have been stuck on me as if the other guys don't even exist. I fucking love it. It turns me on to see how much she wants me; her lustful thoughts are felt through the way she touches me with intention and how deep blue her eyes can be.

Johnny transitions from Vaughn to Van Halen, attempting Eddie's infamous "Eruption" solo. When he starts laughing, he stops playing and pretends to toss his guitar into the fire. "Fuck. I'm too drunk for this."

I say, "I think we've all tried it. Eddie's a genius. I don't feel worthy to carry his equipment, much less attempt that solo."

Tulsa stands and gives it a shot.

Laughing, Tommy says, "That hurts my Van Halen loving heart, man. Stop torturing that song."

With Dave here tonight, five guitarists are jamming. It's

fucking awesome to shoot the shit and make music with these guys. But this guy earns full respect when he starts the solo and almost makes it to the end before he looks up and realizes we were gawking at him. He shifts in his chair and says, "I've practiced a few times."

I reach my hand forward. We shake, and I say, "That was awesome."

"Thanks."

Hannah playfully jabs him. "You should be in a band again. You're too good not to play."

"I play. I just don't get paid."

Johnny says, "You should get paid. You're really good. If you're open to gigs or studio opportunities, I'll let you know if I hear of anything."

"Really?"

"Yeah, I heard all I need. I'm happy to recommend you."

"Thanks, man. I think you just made my life."

"I haven't done anything yet, but if I can I will."

Rivers gives it a go before I mutilate it. We're all blaming the beer, having too good of a time to care if we nail it or not.

When everyone's distracted by another song, I lean over to whisper in Hannah's ear. "What you failed to see is that I crave your sharp edges and chipped corners. I'll be the glue for you, but I like you how you are."

A warm caressing hand soothes my cold cheek. "Broken?"

"You've never been broken to me."

"Jet?" It's not sweet Hannah's voice, but another person saying my name.

Shit. I know before I even turn back to find out. Looking over Hannah's head, Marcy is just a few feet away—hands twisting together nervously. Seeing her is sobering. I stand. "What are you doing here?"

The silence of the group is palpable. I want to look at Hannah, to check on her, knowing this has ruined a good night. I don't, though. I go to Marcy to lead her back out the way she came in through the side gate. But I stop when a guy comes around the corner. What the fuck?

He's all smarmy smile and too skinny to hold the joint I can smell he's been smoking. "Fuck, man. You're hard to track down. Jet Crow. Fuck, you're a badass."

I may have had some drinks, but every red flag is flying high over this guy. "Who are you?"

"Oh, damn. Let me introduce myself. Hunter Hix." He drags his hand down the front of dirty pants before holding it out to me.

There's no way in fuck I'm touching him unless it's to throw him out. I look at Marcy. "Did you bring him here?"

"I'm sorry, he—"

"This is my home."

Rivers comes up behind me. "Why don't I walk you out? We'll go back this way."

Hunter shrugs away from my brother. "I'm not doing any harm. Just talking to another musician, an artiste, like myself." Looking past me, he acts like he didn't know Johnny Outlaw would be here. He acts like Marcy didn't sell my information to him to put on this act like he's our best friend and not here to see their band.

But when I see him staring, I follow his gaze. It's not on Johnny like I suspected. It's on Hannah, who's frozen in horror with her hand over her mouth and her eyes as wide as the night sky. I've seen Hannah wary, I've seen her sad, but this? This is pure terror. *Who the fuck is he, and what did he do to her?*

She begins to shake, so I look at my brother. "Tulsa." I don't need to say anything else to him. He heard the command, could see her distress. He grabs her hand and rushes her toward the back door. I push Hunter with my hands on his chest, backing him out of my yard. "Get the fuck out."

Marcy's hanging on my arm and crying. "I'm sorry. He made me. He made me."

Hunter spits, "Get the fuck off me. You're just as useless as that fucking bitch."

I stop. "What did you just say?"

"The bitch likes it rough. Likes to be slapped, although I doubt you'd know about that. Frigid cunt."

When my gaze shifts to Marcy, she tries to grab Hunter's arm to pull him away from us. Before I can even move, he slaps her so hard across the face that she falls to the ground. "You'll get more of that later."

The fuck?

He grunts, "I didn't get to meet Outlaw."

Fuck him. Shoving him to the ground, I finally connect some dots. A musician. Hannah's reaction. *He hit her? Slapped her?* I'm about to pummel him when my brothers yank me backward. "I'm going to fucking destroy you," I yell, my voice booming. Anger courses through every muscle in my body, driving me forward to obliterate his punk ass.

I'm grabbed again and pulled backward. It's not my brothers that keep me back.

It's Hannah.

She runs in front of me and pushes her hands against my chest. "Jet, don't. Please. He's not worth it."

Everyone surrounds me, but I never take my eyes off him. Hannah whispers, "Please don't hit him. Think of Alfie—"

I close my eyes, trying to control my breathing and calm down.

Alfie.

Alfie.

Alfie.

When I look into her eyes, I see her secret. I can see how much she cares about me. I say, "He hurt you. He hit you."

Hunter spits, "Pussy!"

She touches my cheek. "He can't touch me now, but he can ruin everything for you."

Marcy's scream startles us. Her hands are over her mouth, and she crawls toward Hunter. He's staring up and touching his nose before I realize what has happened.

Standing over him, Johnny cracks his knuckles. "Motherfuckin' asshole. Get the fuck out of here before we call the cops."

As Hunter struggles to get up, he shouts, "I'm calling the cops on you for assault. I'll own that fucking Hollywood mansion of yours when I'm done suing you."

"I said get the fuck out of here." Johnny's anger is palpable.

"I'll get you for assault—"

"You'll get him for nothing, Hunter." Dave steps up out of the shadows. "We have more on you. Hannah barely survived what you did to her in Dallas." *What the fuck?* I look at her, and I think it's only her anger keeping her upright at the moment.

"You've got nothing on me, traitor."

Hannah says, "He has his word, and I've got photos."

"What the fuck does that matter?" Hunter stammers, wriggling his jaw back and forth from the punch.

"Let me fill you in, asshole," says Tommy. "Scum like you who hit women eventually go down. *You* stepped onto private property, attacked the owner, smacked around your girl. Come near anyone here again, and you'll be behind bars for a good decade or three. Get. The. Fuck. Out. Now."

"Fuck you guys. I'm out of here."

Tulsa shouts, "Stay a stranger."

Hunter replies with a middle finger in the air just as they round the corner of the house and disappear.

When Johnny turns back to me, he says, "Welcome to the family."

"And here I was going to welcome you to our brotherhood."

"An honorary Crow Bro? Cool. I can dig it. Do I get a band shirt?" He knows how to lighten a mood.

Rivers chuckles. "I'll make sure you get one."

Everyone starts gathering their stuff, the party clearly over. I look at Hannah, and she says, "We'll talk about it later, okay?"

I nod, watching her walk away. When Johnny pats me on the back, I say, "You didn't have to hit him for me."

"Sure, I did. He can't touch me, but you and your son, he can."

"Thank you." We shake hands and bring it in for a bump. "I mean it. Thank you."

"You're welcome." He shakes his hand out. "It's been a while since I've been in a fight, and I'm glad it was for a worthy cause because Holliday is going to kick my ass."

The thought of someone hurting Hannah—physically or emotionally—stirs my anger. "I don't know if I'll be able to restrain myself if I see him again."

"Until the hearing is over, think of your son first. Don't lose him because you lose control."

"Wise advice."

Patting me on the back, he laughs. "We're taking off, but we'll see you in LA." Once we're inside, we say goodbye to the guys, sending them on their way when an SUV arrives to pick them up.

My brothers hang back a bit on the porch. Leaning against the rail, Rivers asks, "Is she going to be okay?"

"Hannah's strong."

Tulsa asks, "How about you?"

"I'll be fine. Thanks for having my back, little brother."

"Always."

Rivers says, "The car's here."

I walk them out, and we do our usual handshake and push off before I go back inside. When I shut the door, Hannah's leaning against the kitchen bar. "Alfie's still sound asleep. Thank goodness."

"That is good." I'm not sure what to say. I don't want to push her away by demanding something she doesn't want to tell me. But it was going so well and I'm not ready to let that slip away. "How are you feeling?"

Her fingers tap on the bar with impatience, and she looks down as if time's up. When her eyes find mine across the room, she says, "I was once crazy. I was the girl everyone loved to hang out with. But you know what happens to crazy girls?"

I move across the room, wanting to be close to her, but giving her the space she needs to vent, confess, or whatever she feels the need to do. "What?"

"They end up alone. Marcy. Me. We're the same. She just hasn't realized it yet. She won't until she's bleeding in an alley beaten by someone she trusted, by someone she loved."

Tears she's been restraining slide down her cheeks, revealing her pain. All this time, her silence has held in the hurt, her words a release that's long been coming.

"Tell me what happened, Hannah."

"Will you hate me if I tell you I'm not in the right place? I don't want to be drinking. I don't want to be drunk. It makes the memories worse."

Covering her hands with mine, I stop the tapping beneath my embrace. "You don't have to tell me tonight, but I'll be here when you're ready."

"Why are you so good to me?"

"I'm just me. If I'm good for you, that's all I want to be." *And I'll be here for you forever if you'll let me.*

21

Hannah

I'm not naked but feel bare. Pulling the covers up to my neck, I can't cover up enough not to feel exposed. Like I see the real Jet Crow, he sees the real me. Alcohol reveals my fears and weakens my strength, but when I feel vulnerable, I don't mind feeling it with him.

The bedroom door opens, and he says, "I checked on Alfie. He's still sound asleep."

"I envy his ability to fall asleep so fast."

Coming to the side of the bed, Jet flops down next to me. "I'm so tired."

Looking over at me, he squints his eyes. "You know what I think, Hannah?"

Rolling to my side to face him, I say, "I'm sure you're going to tell me."

He laughs, and I love the sound, always finding comfort in his happiness. He says, "I think you're hiding under all these covers."

"From what?"

"Me. The conversation we started out there." He tugs the covers down just enough to expose my shoulder. "The future."

"That's a lot of hiding."

"Sure is, but I don't want you to hide." Reaching out, he opens his arms to me, offering himself. I move into the crook of his arm, a place that feels as if he were made for me.

Draping my arm over his middle, I snuggle close, safe in his arms. "Everything you tell me, you mean, don't you?"

"I do." The tips of his callused fingers scrape against my upper arm, causing goose bumps to form in their wake. "You don't trust easily. What happened?"

"I think we've had enough heavy tonight, don't you?" I close my eyes, hoping to hide some more.

"I think our heads are swimming with stories and pain, happiness and fears. I think if you really want to know that, you should talk about what happened because I don't think you have yet. I think whatever you went through, you've tucked deep inside, so tightly bound that when someone gets too close you explode."

He's too close. I want to pull away. I want to hide again. I don't want to talk to him about it . . . but I'll lose him if I don't. I'll scare him away because I'm scared to share. Screw it. "I'm not special, Jet. If I tell you all my secrets, you'll realize how not special I am, and you'll have no reason to stay."

"It's not your secrets that keep me here." He sits up and hovers over me. Looking right into my eyes, he says, "It's your secrets that are pushing me away."

The way his palm cups my cheeks—possessive but tender—matches his eyes and how they're set on mine. I'm tempted to open up, but I still struggle. "If I say it out loud, I have to relive it."

"If you tell your darkest secrets, you release them from your soul."

"My story is not extraordinary." I wiggle, trying to find the comfort I felt when I climbed into bed, but I can't. Suddenly, the sheets are too itchy, the pillow is too lumpy, and his dark eyes too intense. I was cold when I came into the bedroom, but now I'm sweating.

I push him away, needing air, needing a reprieve. My breath comes out harsh, and my throat is dry. The window. I need fresh air. It's too stifling in here. Too hot. Too damaging to my protective walls. Brick by brick, I built them up. Each day, I laid a new brick on top of a cracked foundation in hopes of making myself stronger.

Jet's right. I'm not making myself stronger. I'm hiding from the rest of the world, hoping to protect myself from the pain that was trapped inside all along.

It was only a matter of time before my walls came tumbling down. Leave it to this dark-haired knight to destroy them in an effort to save me from myself.

I climb out of bed and open the window. Jet is watching me, taking me in, but not in the way I like. He's analyzing me, watching me fall apart.

Because I have nothing left to hide, I stand in my panties ready to give him the rest of me. I take a deep breath, ready to give him this last part of me, not because I'm strong, but because I'm tired of being weak.

Holding up the pack of cigarettes on the windowsill, I whisper, "Will you smoke?"

The beauty of Jet Crow is more than skin-deep. He doesn't ask me why, though I know it's a strange request I've made of him. He just comes to the window, stands next to me, tugs his T-shirt over his head, and then pulls it over mine. I slip my arms through the sleeves and let the shirt swallow me, finding safety in the way it engulfs me.

How did he know? How does he know I need his comfort? Covering me, protecting me with the shirt off his back.

He takes off his jeans and toes off his socks until he's standing in his boxers. Sitting down in the chair by the window, he pulls the pane back down but leaves it cracked open. A cigarette is pulled from the pack and lit while his eyes stay on mine. Exhaling, he takes my hand and pulls me to his lap.

"Talk to me, Hannah."

"I fell in love with the boy across the street."

His chest rumbles with a growl. "He's a fucker."

He's right. He fucked me and then tossed me away when he found someone else to fuck. "We went to prom together, lost our virginity to each other, and when he landed his first tour, I left college to follow him. I thought we were in love. I thought we were forever."

Somehow, my breath doesn't feel as heavy in my chest. I angle around so I can see him, so I can watch him smoke one last time since he'll want no part of me tomorrow. "We lasted seven cities. Seven. After four years of dating, we lasted less than three weeks on the road."

"What happened?"

"He hi—" I stop cold in the tracks of where I was headed. Jet would never hit me like my ex, but what if . . . what if he blames me as my father did. Looking into Jet's soulful eyes, I don't believe he would. Maybe these things come out in time, releasing them bit by bit so they don't drag me down with them.

I know one thing for sure. I don't want this to be the last cigarette I see him smoke. Health wise, yes, but I don't want this to be the end of us. I don't want him to realize I'm too much trouble. I like Jet too much for us to end whatever this is between us.

"He what, Hannah?"

Next time, maybe I'll be ready to tell him the uglier parts. "At first, he cheated. Not shocking. I found him fucking a groupie in Oklahoma City."

"And that's when he hit you?"

"Can we not talk about that part tonight? Please."

He nods.

Shame for letting myself down coats my stomach. Now I have to confess how weak I was to Jet. *Will he see me as weak now too?* I hope not. I have to trust him. "I let him convince me I was the problem, that I drove him to cheat." I watch him smoke; a sad distraction I needed so he wouldn't focus on me.

He sighs. "So he threw stones in a bad attempt to break you. He's an asshole. You realize that, right?"

"I realized two tour stops later in Dallas that it wasn't just groupies I needed to watch out for. He was having sex with Dave's girlfriend the entire tour. She confessed to Dave who confronted Hunter. But Hunter didn't take it well, and he didn't take his anger out on Dave, he took it out on me."

"I want to fucking kill him," he mumbles. His body is tense, though his arms still hold me loosely. "He's a complete asshole, Hannah. How he disrespected you . . . used you . . . hurt you . . . Fuck, it makes me so angry."

I like that it makes him mad to hear how I was hurt. I like that he looks at me like he believes me. I like this . . . this sharing stuff. He doesn't need to hear the other side. He just needs to hear my side of the story. He has my back.

But there's so much more I like about him. I like how even when Jet shaves, he's got stubble by the time night rolls around. I like the hair on his chest—not thick but dark and masculine. I like how small I feel in his arms, but he makes me feel worthy and confident, not a shrinking violet. I can tell him how I truly feel without judgment. "He finally broke me."

"No, he didn't, Hannah. You're right here, all in one piece. He didn't win. You did. You got out. You're the hero of your own story, and you didn't even know it."

"I'm at the mercy of my own pen."

"You're not a character in your story, but the author that creates your life. You're not at the mercy of your pen, but the one who decides how it all plays out."

"How does this story end?"

"You write the ending to your fairy tale."

"You should write music," I tease, feeling better in his arms while taking in his emotional wisdom.

That makes him smile. As the cigarette burns out, the hate I've carried inside me for so long lightens, but the shame that burdens my soul remains. "He let me leave. After all those years together, he let me walk away, and he's never looked back."

Jet's arms hold me a little tighter as if he can tell I want to run away. "He didn't fight for me. To him, to everyone, I'm not worthy of keeping."

My body is maneuvered to face him when he sits straight up. His eyes are firm on mine when he says, "You were never meant to be kept. You were meant to be free until you found something more, something worth staying for."

Running my fingers over his chest, I ask, "Are you my more?"

"I'm whatever you need me to be, but you have to promise to always be honest with me." *Honesty. I haven't seen a lot of that from my family, but it is what I've craved the most.*

"Such a simple request in exchange for so much. Why are you so good to me?"

"Because what we have between these four walls is more than I've had in years. Selfishly, I hope it can go beyond this bedroom. I just need you to trust me. I'm not him. Although you might think I sleep with different women all the time, I don't. You were my wild night, a wild thing that I gave into. You were the wildflower demanding to be seen. And then you were gone."

"I'm here," I say, leaning my forehead to his. "I'm here. I'm here as long as you want me."

"I don't want you to stay for me. I want you to stay for you." Pushing my hair back from my face, he holds my head in his hands and looks at me. My lips. My nose. My forehead. My freckles. My chin. My eyes that can't lie to him ever again. Satisfied with what he finds, he smiles and it's just for me. "If you stay, I won't hurt you, wildflower."

Wildflower.

I hate it.

As he said, they're weeds, but it fits me better than a flower more pristine.

With a quirk of my lips, I ask, "So what you're saying is that you want me?"

"Finally. You see the light."

"It wasn't the light that drew me to you." I kiss the edge of his mouth.

"What drew you to me, baby?"

"Do you have all night?"

His smile broadens, and I kiss the gentle lines beside his eyes. "And all day."

I laugh. God, it feels good to feel good again. He's done that for me. He's taken my heat, my ire, and turned it into embers. I feel lighter. "The way you hold the microphone when you sing and there is no music. Just your voice haunting me. When you play your guitar, you don't think about the notes, only the melody. That's how you treat me. As if I'm a song, you hear me. Listening to make sure I'm on key."

"You should write music," he whispers, not teasing.

"Careful or I might fall in love."

He dips me into his arms, and I'm reliant on his strength. This predicament is not lost on me. With my head resting firmly in his hand and my body tilted to the side, he leans over me and says, "There's no being careful when it comes to love. You're either willing to fall in the moment or the opportunity passes you by. What will you do, wildflower?"

With my arms secured around his neck, I ask, "Will you fall with me?"

"I've already fallen. I'm just waiting to catch you."

I pull him to me, wanting all this man as much as he wants me. We kiss, exchanging our hearts and uniting our souls. I've been burned before, but something tells me he's a risk worth taking. Something tells me that he will catch me when I fall. Knowing he's already there . . . *He thinks I'm worth catching* . . . "I love you, Jet."

"I love you, too, baby."

22

Hannah

How'd I go from being in a new relationship to falling in love?

Three words. Or should I say one name.

Jet Mercury Crow.

I only recently discovered his middle name was Mercury when I ran across an online article about the band announcing they had signed with Outlaw Records.

The name fits his unpredictability and his profession. When I think he's going to react one way, he reacts the other. From discovering he has a son and his immediate acceptance to not judging me because someone else found me unworthy. But he lacks the temperament of an anger brewing deep inside. So mercurial moods do not apply.

I grab my charger from the wall and am winding it up when Eileen walks into my bedroom. Holding up the letter I left for her in the kitchen, she asks, "Do you think you're going to get away with this?"

"Yes, because both I and Jet have approved the trip, and

we're the only ones who legally have a say. I left that for you, so you wouldn't worry."

"You can't do this, Hannah. You can't take my grandson away from me."

"I'm not. We'll only be gone three weeks and then we'll be back."

"But when you come back, that only leaves two weeks until the hearing."

I set my shirt neatly on the other clothes in my suitcase. "This is the only way we could hold up the judgment. How can he see his son if he's there and we're here? How would I see Alfie if he's with him in Los Angeles?"

"What about me?"

"I'm doing the best I can in a bad situation," I reply, not letting her know that she's the reason the situation is bad. I turn my back to grab my underwear out of the drawer so I can pack them.

"What are you doing, Hannah?" I don't have to see her face to hear the distrust in her voice. "Are you trying to take him away from me?"

I stop sorting through the drawer and look down. Is that what I'm doing? It might be. Am I doing it for Alfie? Or for me? When I turn around, I reply, "No, I'm doing what the judge ordered, sharing custody."

"Are you sure?" Her eyes narrow on me. "The tension between us lately feels a lot like you're going to betray me."

Looking away, I say, "I'm doing what's best for Alfie."

"Where were you the past few nights? I called around looking for you, and no one knew."

What? "Who did you call?"

"Your father. Your friends—"

"You don't know any of my friends."

Her hand waves me off like a bothersome gnat. "Friend, boyfriend. Whatever he is."

My heart starts pounding in my chest, the irregular beat causing discomfort. "Hunter?"

"Yeah, that loser."

"He's not my friend. He's not my boyfriend. You know that. Why would you call him?"

Shrugging like she doesn't even care about me, she crushes the letter from the judge in her hands. "I had to make sure you weren't involving my grandson in anything that could lead to trouble."

Trouble.

The word reverberates around my head.

Trouble.

Hit.

Trouble.

Slap.

Trouble.

Slam.

Trouble.

Trouble.

Trouble.

My hands are shaking, and my breathing is shallow. She watches me in rapt fascination as I'm unable to hide my reaction to the abuse I once suffered. Coming closer, she brings me to her and hugs me. While rubbing my back, she says, "It's a pity that you're so weak."

I push away from her, my back hitting the dresser, my shoulder blades banging into the open drawer. "You're despicable."

"You know what I also am, little girl? Dangerous. You'll return in three weeks or I'll come after him. We were in this together. Remember? It was going to be the three of us."

"I now see that Cassie wanted otherwise, or else she wouldn't have named me in the will."

There's a plea to her tone when she says, "She was not in her right mind at the end. You know that."

"I know that her dying wish was for me to care for her son."

"You can't even care for yourself!"

The sting remains long after the words were spewed. I'm so tempted to say something just as harsh in return, but I hold my tongue. I can smell the red wine on her breath, and her teeth are a grayish purple shade of drunk. I'm hoping she'll leave me alone.

I knew I wouldn't be that lucky. And she's off . . . "No judge will deny me my flesh and blood. Neither will you or that man Alfie calls his father."

She turns around to leave. Makes it as far as the door when I ask, "Why are you so mean?"

I see the way her shoulders rise and fall with each breath, her anger visible through her body language. She turns back to me. "Your mother was never good enough for my brother." She gets reminiscent when she drinks and that never ends well for me. She says, "He could have had anyone. I still don't know why he chose her, and you're so much like her. You look like her, and you're weak like her."

Her hand twitches at her side, and I cringe, though I know she's too far to hit me. I level my eyes on hers. Jet's new nickname embodies me. I'm a wildflower, a weed sturdy enough to endure the harshest conditions. I'm a survivor. "You may think you won because you ran her off, but who is the real winner? My bets are on her."

"Your father is going to be very unhappy to hear about all of this."

"He can go to hell right along with you. And before

you tell me to get out. Don't worry. I'm on my way." I'm not done packing, but I've got enough to survive. I grab my backpack and swing it over my shoulders. The suitcase is zippered closed before I tug it onto the floor from the bed. I take my purse, putting the strap over my head, and walk to the door where she still stands with her arms crossed.

She steps to the side, and I wheel by, but stop just on the other side of her. "I used to love you. I used to love my father. But you're both too bitter to see that I was all you had left, and now you have nobody but each other."

"I have Alfie. I thought you would have a better chance of winning against that monster of a man, Jet Crow. I was mistaken, but it won't cost me my grandson. Your father will help me win custody."

"Just make sure you're fighting for Alfie's best interest and not out of revenge." I drag my suitcase down the hall and pick the small one I packed for Alfie up in the other hand. As I work the cases out the front door, I add, "Per the letter, I'll keep you updated on Alfie's well-being, and he'll be able to call you whenever he would like. The fate of your relationship now rests in his hands."

The door slams behind me, but that's okay. I'm good. I'm so good. Another mountain is behind me. One more battle won. I'm not just saving myself from this horrible way of life, but I'm also saving Alfie.

Walking away from the house, I felt strong, but driving away, I let the doubt creep in. My aunt is one thing. She needed me, not just physically to be there to help with Alfie, but financially to help her because of Cassie. Eileen lost her job for missing too many days of work. She's working again, but she's still in the hole because of medical and legal fees.

If she asks him, my father will bail her out and then help

her fight for Alfie. There's only one way to save him. I need to make sure that Jet wins full custody.

I parallel park on the street and walk to the front of the school. I'm so ridiculous, but that dark-haired man makes me smile uncontrollably. Jet stands out in a crowd, but really stands out at school pickup among all the moms in their yoga gear. I sidle up behind him, slipping my hand around his.

Eyeing me up and then down, he tightens his hand around mine. "Aren't we supposed to be a secret?" he asks with a mischievous twinkle in his eyes and a roguish smile on his face.

"I suck at keeping secrets." I shrug.

Two women without wedding rings move along. Good thing because I didn't want to stake my claim on him. Our hands. Oops. Guess I already have.

He says, "I didn't expect to see you here." Leaning down, he kisses me, and I let him linger loving every second of it. "But I'm happy to see you."

Glancing toward the door, I see the classes start to come out. Our hands part, and I say, "I need to talk to you about a few things, but in private later tonight."

"Does that mean you're coming over?"

"I packed a suitcase, so I hope it's okay if I stay overnight since we leave for LA tomorrow."

We try not to touch in front of Alfie, not quite ready to break the news of what we are to each other when we barely know what this is. When my foot is tapped twice, my heart flutters because he still touches any way he can.

"You can stay as long as you like. Are you okay?"

Always worried about me. He's the hero of my story. "I'm fine. Better than fine actually. I'm good."

"I'm going for great."

"It turns me on when you go—"

"Jet! Hannah!" Alfie comes running with wide-open arms for both of us.

His little arms don't reach around us, but ours do, and I close my eyes, enjoying the little family we've become. When our arms part, I spy Alfie's teacher staring at us. She quickly looks away when she's busted. "Is this what it's like with you?"

"What?"

"Women always staring at you."

Looking at us, Alfie asks, "Who stares? You told me it was rude to stare, Hannah."

I rest my hand on his shoulder. "It is. That's what I mean."

Jet chuckles. "C'mon, let's go."

We each take one of Alfie's hands, and he tries to swing between us. He's getting tall. When he's not successful swinging, Jet and I help out. Soon we're crossing the street while swinging him between us. I love seeing Alfie so happy and hearing his laughter. He may not have dealt with the death of his mother the way he needs to, but I'm happy he can still be innocent and find joy in such a simple thing.

We reach the corner, and Jet says, "I'm over here."

"I'm down there." I signal over my shoulder.

A low whistle is heard when I turn to leave, but I turn back to catch Jet call, "Hey?"

Floating on cloud nine, I ask, "What's up, Crow?"

"I'll see you at home?"

Home. *Home.* He's welcomed me into his home, but I'm starting to think it's not a location, but a person. Two people when I look back and see a man and his son bonding. Jet didn't just hang the moon and the stars for Alfie. He created the universe, every star another note played on his guitar.

Does cloud ten exist? I hope so because I'm walking on air, or maybe it's love. Love? Who would have thought when I least expected it, a musician would be the one to sweep me off my feet? For as handsome and tall as that man is, I truly never saw him coming. "See you guys at home."

23

Hannah

Jet is always calm. He's the voice of reason when I struggle to hear my own voice, much less express my emotions out loud. Unless he hides his worries in other ways. Does he keep them locked down tight in a place he visits when he's alone?

I'd understand.

I'd become adept at that myself until I met him. I'm not sure how long I can hold onto the darker memories when he's so insistent on me being free from them.

What about him?

The eldest brother.

The kid who stepped in as a dad to his younger siblings when his father left.

The man who had to bury his mother because his family looked at him to handle the arrangements.

Nineteen.

He was a kid himself.

We've not talked about that time too much. He's a

master at glossing over the details of the dark parts of life he doesn't like to think about. But there are stress lines carved into his forehead. He's too young so they won't stay for long.

Jet is punishing his poor knuckles—pulling and popping—one by one. Leaning against the kitchen counter, I ask, "What did your hands do to you to make you so mad?" I'm teasing, but curious what's going on with him.

His dark eyes do a onceover on me before he appears to catch himself from getting too deep. But I caught it. A look. A feeling. Anguish. It was only a flicker, but it was there for one split second. "Nothing." He reaches for the remote. Such a guy move. I thought he knew better than to try to tune women out when they wanted answers.

I sit down next to him, click off the TV, and take his hand between mine. Wanting to relieve his stress, his worries, and him, I start massaging it. "I feel like nothing means everything is on your mind right now."

"I don't really want to talk about it."

"You don't have to. We can just sit here in awkward silence with me staring at you if you prefer."

My joke is rewarded with a smile. "That feels good."

"Yeah?"

"Yeah. Sometimes my hands hurt. A bad side effect of playing so much."

"Are you still going to play tonight?"

Leaning back into the cushions, he starts to relax. "The show must go on."

"You have a kid relying on you. Don't do too much damage to yourself."

"Is the kid the only one . . .?" He leaves the question hanging out there, letting the words fade off as he closes his eyes.

I take his other hand, and he looks at me briefly before

closing them again. His breath evens, and the lines of his forehead soften. I run my thumb up the main vein on his hand and then turn it over and rub his wrist until he falls asleep. *No. The kid isn't the only one. But he should know that by now.*

Tonight is the last show before the band flies out tomorrow morning at dawn. Alfie and I fly out tomorrow after school. The packing is basically done except the few items we'll need before we leave, but I still wonder if we're doing the right thing. Our relationship went from zero to sixty as if the cops were going to catch us if we didn't speed ahead.

I set his hand down gently on his leg and cuddle against him. His arm comes around me and he plants a kiss on my head. But soon enough, he's asleep again. We've all been through a lot, all in different ways.

The broken pieces of me fit together so nicely with his that I sometimes wonder if this is the way it was always supposed to be. I'm learning that out of tragedy can come joy. Months ago, I felt trapped, in agony that I was going to lose my cousin, and fearful for the future. Yet somehow, here I am. With Alfie, who is the sugar to our tea, the sweetest boy. *And* with Jet, a man who's carried an anvil on his shoulders for years yet is still ready and willing to carry even more in Alfie and in me. *How did I get so lucky?*

A hand squeezes my shoulder, and Jet asks with a raspy voice, "What are you thinking about?"

I haven't told Jet about some of the things he missed because I don't want to upset him, but I've started to realize that if I share my memories, he can live them through me. "Jet, I know you're tired, but do you want to hear about the day Alfie was born? I was there. I saw him kicking and screaming into the world."

"Yes. I'm so pissed I didn't get to see him, Hannah. I still don't understand why Cassie didn't let me know."

I can see he really is hurt about that. Will I ever really know why? "I held him just an hour after he was born." And he was so adorable.

"Did he have a lot of hair or was he born bald like Tulsa?" He chuckles, but the question is sincere.

"He had a head of dark hair, just like yours, and the bluest eyes that turned green like Cassie's."

"Why did she name him Alfred?"

"Cassie hated the name Alfred, but she loved Alfie. Eileen told her that he needed a proper name, a lawyer or a doctor name. When the nurse asked what name, Eileen told her Alfred. But Cassie sat up and added Jet. She said, 'I want Jet to be his middle name,' so Alfred Jet it was, much to Eileen's chagrin."

"I'm surprised she let that slide."

"Cassie could be as stubborn as Eileen when she chose to be." Angling so I can see his face, I ask, "I once asked what happened to you, to Alfie's father. I remember it so clearly. Cassie glanced toward the door and then started to whisper, but Eileen came in with her lunch, and we never seemed to get back to a moment of freedom to talk candidly."

"Does it make sense to you that a woman who supposedly hated me named her son after me?"

"No. It never did, but if I'd bring it up, hellfire would be the price to pay." I lift just enough to kiss his cheek. When I pull back, I say, "Do you want to know what I always thought deep down?"

Rubbing my arm, he says, "Of course, I do. I always want to know what you think."

"I think Cassie was scared of her mom. Don't get me

wrong. They were super close, and I don't discount the fact that she had to care for her dying daughter. I can't imagine the pain she's endured."

"That's something no parent should ever have to experience."

"I still always had a weird feeling in my gut. Sometimes, I felt like Cassie was trying to reach out to me, but then Eileen would come in. It was odd. I could sit in her room and talk for hours about nothing, but if Alfie's father came up, whether I was asking his name or about their relationship, anything to do with you, Eileen was suddenly there. A busybody with food or medicine, drinks or wanting to sit with us. She wasn't so bad then. She got worse as Cassie got sicker. The thing is, Cassie would shut down and talk would turn to nothing important—the house hunting show or a recipe or somewhere Cassie wished she could be instead of in that bed."

"She liked live music."

"She liked corny jokes and P. Terry's burgers with jalapenos and onions."

"She liked prairie dogs and candy canes." We both turn to the sound of Alfie's voice.

I sit up and put space between Jet and me. "She did. She loved those peppermints you get at restaurants. All things peppermint."

Alfie says, "I gave her a candy cane I saved from my Christmas stocking for Valentines."

Patting the couch next to me, I call him over. When he does, he snuggles into my side.

We both look at Jet when he says, "She loved Trident original gum. When I'd run into the store, I'd buy spearmint for me and Trident for her."

I think I'm supposed to be jealous hearing about him

and someone who was important enough to remember the gum he bought for her, but I'm not. We all lost when she lost her life too young to really live it fully.

Alfie starts crying, and I pull him closer, wrapping myself over him as he leans down, looking smaller than his usual small form. We lift when Jet shifts, and he opens himself for us sit on his lap. With his arms wrapped around us, the weight of her loss bears down, my tears falling with Alfie's.

This sweet little guy cries for the mother he'll never see again except in pictures. "I want my mommy." His arms fly out as he pushes off us and runs to the bookcase. Grabbing a frame from the middle shelf, he stares down at the photo.

I look at Jet, looking for answers. He says, "It's a photo of him and Cassie."

How had I never noticed? Just when I thought he couldn't amaze me more, he does. The bookcase next to the TV is full, but I never saw the photo in the slim silver frame. Jet adds, "Alfie picked that frame out."

I cross in front of the TV and peer over Alfie's shoulder to look at the photo. Amazement morphs into shock. Why would he have this one in a frame? Why would he display a photo of her at her weakest, near death, at her worst?

Trying to calm down, I take a breath before I speak, knowing if I don't only anger will come out. "Why this photo?" I ask, looking back at Jet.

I'm about to tell him that this isn't how she should be remembered, but Alfie answers, "What's wrong with this pitcher?"

When I see the sincerity in his eyes, I had it all wrong. "Did you choose this photo, Alfie?"

He nods and then looks down at it again. "We were

giggling when Grandma took it. Mommy was the best tickler."

"She was. She used to tickle me when we were little."

He may be a kid, but he's *her* kid. He sees through the illness and only sees his mom. My heart just melted for both of these guys. I say, "She loved you so much. On her worst days, you would climb into bed with her, and she would read you a story. I remember hearing you both laugh at Curious George and her telling you how much she loved you. I would come to take you to bed, and you'd be holding the book and turning the pages. You would always have this big happy grin on your face." I exhale and rub his back gently, bringing him against me.

He says, "I remember. Will you read that book to me tonight, Hannah?"

"I don't have that book here."

"Can we get it?"

"Not tonight and we're leaving tomorrow."

Tears fill his eyes, and his arms wrap around me. "I want the monkey book."

"We can buy you a new one when we get to California."

"I want the one Mommy gave me. Can we go to Grandma's and get it?"

I doubt I'll ever be able to get that actual book for him. I'm not sure Eileen will let me back in the house. Not that I want to go back. Kneeling in front of him, I say, "I can go over there to get it when we return, but not before we leave. Do you want to get another copy in California or wait?"

"I'll wait. Can we read the bear book tonight?"

"Yep, the bear book it is." I steer him toward the hall. "Let's get you in the bath, buddy. It's getting late."

He's about to dash off, but I glance at Jet again. He sits up. "Hey Alfie, come here."

Alfie goes without asking twice. Jet says, "You can talk about Mommy anytime you need, anytime you want. Okay?"

"Okay." He climbs back into Jet's arms and says, "I don't like that Mommy went to heaven. I wanted her to stay here with me."

My heart is breaking, watching this precious boy try to work out life without his mom.

"I know, buddy. I didn't like it when my mommy went to heaven without me either. I still don't like it, but I feel a little better now."

"Why?"

"Because now my mommy has your mommy to keep her company while she watches over us."

Who is this incredible man? How does he do that?

"She's not sick anymore in heaven, is she?"

"No. She's not sick at all."

"I'm glad she doesn't have hurting anymore, Jet."

"Me too, buddy."

"And I'm glad you're my daddy."

At that, Jet looks up at me with what looks like awe in his eyes. He takes a deep breath and squeezes Alfie closer to him.

"I'm the luckiest daddy in the whole world, Alfie. Because I've got you." He kisses his hair and then sniffs loudly. "But you stink. You really need that bath."

When he then tickles Alfie, we both hear the best sound of the day. Alfie's giggles.

I come over and take his hand. "I'll start the water. You grab the toys you want to play with in the tub."

He runs off and I walk to the hall. Leaning against the corner of the wall, I take him in, admiring not just his good looks, but him, the man inside. "You're a good dad, Crow. You're good for him."

"You're . . ." He leans his head down with a smile on his face like he just lost a friendly bet. When he looks back up, he says, "You're good for all of us, Nichols."

"Charmer."

"You know it."

"Boy, do I know it," I flirt and give him a wink for good measure.

24

Hannah

The gates of the estate open, and I lean out the rolled down window of the Suburban to get a better look. "Wow." I've never seen a home like this before.

Alfie is peering out his window with his mouth hanging open, but he closes it, and repeats me, "Wow."

When the SUV comes to a stop, the driver hops out and opens my door. I see why it's called the Sunshine State. Not a cloud floats in the sky. Tall palms and a gentle wind welcome us.

I may be used to the warm weather in Texas, but it's like a spring day in LA. He starts pulling our luggage from the back, and I unbuckle Alfie from the car seat. When I help him down, I hear, "Hi. Hannah?"

I turn around to find . . . Oh. My. God! "You're Holli Hughes."

Holding her hand out, she says, "You know who I am?"

"Everyone knows who you are."

Even her laugh is amazing. I imagine that's the sound of

angel wings fluttering. I take her hand, and in total fangirl mode, I reflexively add a little curtsy before I turn ten shades of red when I realize what I just did. "I'm Hannah, and this is Alfie."

She smiles, all white teeth and California tan. The messy bun on top of her head was probably styled by some famous hairdresser, every strand looking perfectly tousled or tied back. She leans down in front of Alfie, getting right up to him, and taps his nose. "I've heard a lot about you, Mr. Alfie." She then shakes his hand.

"About me?" he asks under her spell I'm sure just like every other man on this planet and probably most females like me.

"Yes, I heard that you like ice cream."

"I do. I do. I like ice cream." He looks to me like she just performed a magic trick.

"Great. Your daddy told me you like banana splits. I was thinking we could talk Hannah into letting us make some before we head out to Ojai."

Alfie is jumping up and down and tugging on my shirt. "Can we, Hannah? Please?"

"Yes, that sounds yummy."

As we walk inside, I marvel at this mansion. "Holy—"

"Wow," Alfie finishes.

"This was Dalton's house before we were married. It's too big for three people."

"Dalton?"

"Johnny. I call him Dalton."

"I call Jet by his last name sometimes."

"It's good to keep them grounded. If I called him Johnny, I'd be feeding his ego, and we can't have that." Her carefree laugh is contagious.

Alfie reaches for my hand, and we walk together past our suitcases.

Holli has such a welcoming air about her. Being a mogul, model, and married to one of the most famous men in the world have not gone to her head. "I once read that you're originally from Houston. I'm from Austin but lived a few years in Dallas."

"I am. I love Austin. We spent a little time there a few years ago. Dalton played some local shows."

"I remember hearing about that."

She leads us into the kitchen. As soon as we enter, Alfie stops and steps behind me, feeling shy by the way he's peeking around me.

A woman with long brown hair and a tiny frame holds up a handful of spoons. "James dragged out all the spoons again."

Holli laughs. "C'mere, ya little troublemaker."

The boy runs into her arms. With him situated on her hip, she says, "James, this is Alfie and Hannah." Smiling at us, she adds, "This is my son, James, also known as a troublemaker."

I shake the little mister's hand. "Well, how do you do, Mr. James?"

Then I tickle his tummy.

Holli says, "I also want you to meet Rochelle. She's the rock to the band's roll. She's been with them since before they were The Resistance."

Rochelle comes forward. "It's so nice to meet you, Hannah. Dex said wonderful things about you." Her eyes go to Alfie. "It's nice to meet you, Alfie. Your dad talks about you all the time and showed me pictures of you. You're even more handsome in person."

He steps out from behind me and says, "Hannah says I look like my daddy with my mommy's eyes."

"You sure do look a lot like your daddy."

It's not Rochelle's kind and soft approach I note, though I do notice it. What Alfie said is worth a whole sky worth of notes. He called Jet his daddy. He didn't stumble over the word as if it was unnatural. Nope. He just said it like it felt right at home on his tongue. I wonder if he'll ever call Jet daddy one day. He'll be thrilled.

Rochelle asks, "I heard we get to make banana splits. Who wants one?"

James and Holli both say, "Me," along with Alfie and myself because yum.

Over ice cream, James and Alfie start goofing around. I love seeing this side of him. He needs to just be a kid for a while after dealing with the grown-up stuff he's had to face in the past few years and especially the past few months.

Once we all finish, Holli opens the back door, and the kids get to run and play. "There's a playscape at the ranch. Dalton built it." She grins to herself as if there's more to that story—a great memory—than she can share.

"Is it a real ranch?" I wonder since I didn't pack my boots. I didn't have time to when I left Eileen's.

"It's set up for one. We have a horse out there, but it's not a working ranch. We're out there quite a bit but not enough to keep farm animals and the upkeep that comes along with them. We pay a neighbor to take our horse when we're not there. He just opens the gate so he can go over. If you ask me, that horse prefers the neighbors anyway." She rolls her eyes. "He hates rock, and our neighbor plays strictly country music. The horse will go to their property for George Strait or Dolly Parton. Sometimes he'll mosey over for Johnny Cash. I once had a talk with him about his traitorous ways of supporting the wrong Johnny. He's a stubborn horse, though. A lot like my husband."

Rochelle says, "I need to get going. I pick my kids up from school in an hour, and traffic in LA is awful." She hugs Holli and tells me, "It's so nice to meet you. I handle the band's business affairs—"

"And pretty much their lives," Holli adds. "Rochelle is the glue."

"You don't have to sell her on me. The Crow Brothers already signed," she jokes and then hands me a card. "Anyway, if you need anything while you're here in LA or Ojai, just give me a call, and I'll help. My cell number is on the card."

"I'll talk to you tomorrow, Holli."

"Don't forget to schedule those days off for Dalton."

She laughs as she heads inside. We can't see her, but we can hear her. "I won't. Don't worry. Talk laters."

"You're close," I say.

She sits on a bench watching the boys run in the grass. "We're a family, not by blood or by marriage, but by choice."

"That must be nice." I sit down near her. "I've never had people I could trust like that." I laugh, realizing what I just said, out loud, to a virtual stranger, to the famous Holli Hughes. I bet she's never been alone before. She's too gorgeous to be alone or abused or rejected.

"What about your family?"

"My mom. I could trust her. My little brother I could trust. They're in another state, though. My aunt is an alcoholic who sees things how she wants to, and my father never had the patience to be a dad. I think I went from a verbally abusive home right into a physically abusive relationship."

"How'd you get out of it?"

"I threatened to leave, had every intention of it after

catching him having sex with his best friend's girlfriend. We had a huge blowout outside a club in Dallas. He said I was trouble, trying to ruin the tour and kill his dreams. The first hit I never saw coming." I find comfort in the sympathy residing in her eyes. "The second and third time, I fought back, but he won. Two band members pulled him off me when they found us outside fighting. My ex had his fist raised a fourth time."

Reaching over, she covers my hand with hers. "That's awful. I'm so sorry."

"I walked away beaten to a pulp with no money and no friends."

"What did you do?"

She makes me feel comfortable in sharing my story, the parts I never want to burden Jet with. "I called my dad, and he proceeded to tell me that I had chosen my ex over my family the year prior, so I had to deal with the mess I made on my own."

"Terrible. Even after he knew what happened to you?" I see the worry forming on her face. "God, I can't imagine turning on my child like that."

"He was right at the time. I shouldn't have trusted my boyfriend. My ex's arrogance was getting bigger with every gig he played. I was blinded by fake promises and what I thought was love. I had left college to chase my boyfriend's dreams against my dad's demands to stay. What he didn't realize and doesn't to this day is that I left because of him. Just like my mother, another little fact he's always thrown in my face."

"Did you ever reply to him?"

"I replied goodbye and sent him a photo of my face so he'd have something to remember me by." Her gasp is audible, the shock on her face evident. I start talking faster. "The irony of the whole thing is he thought I was asking for money. I just wanted to come home."

"I'm so sorry, Hannah. It's heartbreaking."

I shouldn't have told her this . . . *why did I?* My defenses were down, and now I feel awkward. The heat of embarrassment covers my chest, and my hand follows trying to stave it off. "I shouldn't have said any—"

She moves to sit closer and rubs my back. Keeping her eyes on the boys ahead, she says, "I'm honored you trusted me with this information." With her hands back in her lap, she looks down. "We all go through battles in life. Scars may show on the outside, but they define our insides. You're here. You're strong. You walked away when so many would have stayed. It's very admirable."

Holli's easy to like. Sounds like she's had some dark times too, but she still manages to be so genuine in her intentions and authentically herself. I'm just a girl she just met, a nobody in the glamorous world she lives in, but she treats me as if I'm important, as if my story matters, as if she cares. I see why she's portrayed so positively in the media.

"Thank you for listening."

"I appreciate you sharing with me." Standing up, she walks to the rail and leans on it, looking up at the sky. "We Texas girls have to stick together. The music industry can be tough, the gossip, the press, the fame—it's not a yellow brick road leading to Oz as much as it's paved with broken dreams and broken hearts. You've already experienced it with your ex. Here you are, though, supporting another musician in his pursuit. You know why you can do that?"

"Love?" The word comes before I gave it permission, my heart quicker than my practical side.

Turning around, she replies, "Yes, most definitely love. Also, a little of that home state strength is needed with the men we fall for. Not everyone is cut out to be with a musician. They don't need a groupie. They need someone who will tell them the truth when everyone else is paid to lie. Lies that can damage them, you, and your family. Lies that will destroy their careers and passion. When everyone wants to make money off a piece of Jet by selling paparazzi photos or filling their blog with gossip, magazines that sell lies to sell copies, or to convince him to go down the wrong path, you will be there for him. He will always see the truth in you."

She laughs. "That got heavy. Sorry. I'm apparently full of unsolicited advice today."

"No, don't be sorry. I appreciate it." She speaks to me as if she knows we're together and meant to be. I'm starting to believe.

"By the way, you're exactly how Jet described."

My eyes go wide. I understand him talking about Alfie because that's his son, but me? "How did he describe me?"

Waving to the boys, she shouts, "C'mon guys. We need to get on the road." Turning back to me with a smile on her face, she adds, "Beautiful and brave." Holli goes inside with the boys running after her, leaving me with his words to savor in this stunning setting.

Beautiful and brave.

Love indeed.

25

Jet

Dex scowls.

I can't hear what he's saying on the other side of the glass that separates my brothers and me from Johnny, Dex, and Tommy, but Dex is clearly pissed. His sticks are tucked under his arms while he points his hand at us and gripes at the other guys.

The sound tech working the board is looking on but is clearly staying out of it.

Looking back at my brothers, Tulsa mouths, "What?"

Our mics are on, so Rivers shrugs.

I ask loudly, "What's up, guys?"

Dex leans over the soundboard, punches a button, and says, "You can't have a rock band without a drummer."

He's taken personal offense to our situation. We were upfront with them before we signed, so I'm not sure why this is an issue. We can just hire a drummer.

Letting my guitar hang, I speak into the mic this time. "I know enough to get by, but I'm rusty. Also, I can't sing, play guitar, and add drums into the mix, so Tulsa gets relegated to the kit some nights when we're short a steady drummer."

Dex pushes the button again. "Get on the kit, Tulsa. Start from the top of 'Evermore' and let Tulsa kick off the song instead of Rivers."

Tulsa is a pain in my ass most days, but his heart is always in the right place. He eyes me, and I nod once. When he takes off his guitar, I hear him sigh. "You can do it, bro."

"I'm not as strong on the drums as I am on guitar, and now I'm playing for one of the best drummers out there."

Dex's voice comes over the speaker. "*Rock Magazine* named me Drummer of the Decade."

We laugh. Tulsa spins on the stool and then adjusts it to the right height. With sticks in his other hand, he points at Dex and says, "That doesn't help."

"Sorry, man," Dex says, chuckling. "Just do your best. I can work with you if we decide to keep you on the kit."

Tulsa shakes his head. I know what he's doing. He's building his courage. He has to let the beat flow free. He's just the vessel, the messenger of music. Let it flow. He says, "Here goes nothing." Tapping his sticks together, he counts down and kicks off the song.

WE'VE BEEN in the recording studio in Ojai more than four hours. We're all starting to get worn down, but Johnny says, "Play 'Wildflower' once more, but this time, I want more bass from Rivers and hit harder on that first chorus, Tulsa. I want the impact felt in the bleacher seats. You're not just playing for front row VIPs. You're playing for everyone. They've all bought a ticket to hear you play live. Jet, try going up an octave on the word stay, then lower on the second verse again."

Tulsa mutters under his breath, "Damn, dudes, we must suck."

Johnny adds, "You don't suck. If you sucked, you wouldn't be here. Now from the top."

We must have played this song twenty times making tweaks, but this time it's different. This time, I'm moved by the song, the words, and I recapture the feeling I had when I first wrote it so many months ago.

Call it kismet, but my wildflower walks in when I'm singing about her. *Beautiful and brave.*

Hannah's the most gorgeous woman, her smile just for me. My heart beats faster, and I try to control the tempo, but I struggle when she's near.

Next to her, our kid waves. *Our kid.* Hers and mine.

Alfie's so happy to see me. I keep playing but watch as she leans down to whisper in his ear and point at me. They both smile, holding hands—my biggest fans.

Leaning into the mic again, I play my guitar and start to sing:

My wildflower grows free.

Free.

Free from worry. Free from me.

Leaving me craving the things she took away.

Stay.

Why can't she stay instead of wrecking me?

Her happy fades, but she smiles—softer, sweeter—just for me. I've never played this song in front of her. We've never performed it live. This is for the album. This is for her. My wildflower. My sweet Hannah.

When we finish the song, I turn around. "Fuck, that was perfection."

Rivers says, "You nailed it, Jet. It's evocative and—"

Laughing, Tulsa hits him with a drumstick. "Evocative?"

"Not sorry," Rivers snaps, "for using words you don't understand."

"Fuck you, Riv."

Tommy announces, "Take a break."

The door swings open, and Alfie runs into the studio. Slamming into my side, he hugs me. "Miss me, Jet?"

I swing my guitar around to my back and pick him up, hugging him. "Missed you tons. How was the airplane?"

"Boring."

Hannah comes into the room, looking shy, unsure what to do or maybe what her place is in this situation. I'm failing her. Going toward her, I say, "Couldn't be that boring. You had Hannah with you."

"Hannah's not boring," he replies.

"No, she's not." I set him down, and he runs to Tulsa. To Hannah, I tilt my head and smile. "Were you bored, too?"

"Nervous."

"I know a way to help with those nerves."

"I bet you do."

"Are we still keeping us a secret?"

Johnny comes over the speaker. "You two suck at keeping secrets, and by the way, your mic is still hot."

Fuck.

Hannah laughs and grabs me by the guitar strap. "Since the secret is out already, c'mere. I missed you."

I am all for this kiss, but we both freeze when Alfie asks, "What secret?"

Shit.

Her hands fall to her sides, and we both sigh while taking a step back. We were almost caught. I'm ready to tell

Alfie, stepping out of secrecy's dark shadow, but there are other things to consider than how I feel.

She whispers, "We'll talk later?"

I nod. Since we're taking a break, I take my guitar off over my head and set it on the stand. Alfie comes back. "What secret, Jet?"

"Nothing you need to worry about, buddy." Checking the time, I ask, "Are you getting hungry?"

Rivers walks by. "We all are. How long are we breaking?"

Alfie's hand slips into mine, and we walk out of the studio and up another level to the main house. Johnny's wife is loading a tray of sausage onto the table. "We have enough barbecue to feed an army. Help yourselves to brisket, ribs, sausage, and all the sides you want. There's potato salad, coleslaw, and fruit. We have other stuff if you're not digging this." She casually strokes the top of her son's blond head. "If you need something special or have allergies, just let me know."

Johnny picks up his kid and grabs a plate, letting him point at what he wants for his dinner. Tightness in my chest causes me to look down at Alfie, wishing I had those early years with him.

I've been muddling through this since the day I found out I have a son. Watching the bond Johnny has with James makes me wonder if one day it will come more natural for Alfie and me. I feel like I'm still stuck in shock that I have a son, much less being all that he needs in a dad.

I grab a plate, totally copying Johnny, and we start moving around the table with everyone else filling their plates. "What would you like to eat, Alfie?"

He shakes his head no.

"Brisket?" I'm answered with a scrunched face. "Ribs?" A gagging sound is heard, and we get the kind of attention I don't like. Squatting down, I take in the table from his eye level. Wow, I'm surprised how much you can't see from down here. I'm about to ask Hannah what he will like but then give it one last shot. "How about a sausage?"

He nods enthusiastically. "And fruit."

"Grab a fork and napkin." We load some fruit and a brownie on his plate, and then he joins Rivers outside on the patio. Though by the size of the patio, I'm thinking technically it might be called a terrace. Either way, this place is decked out.

The sun has set, but it's not too cold outside just yet. With full plates on laps or at the table, everyone is spread out. By the silence of the first few minutes, we're all starving. We've all stayed close enough to be a part of the same conversation. After cracking open a can of soda, Tommy says, "We're keeping the last track."

"Wildflower?" I ask.

"Yeah, and the recording of it."

"What? I thought we were warming up, not recording for the album."

Pushing away an empty plate, Johnny settles back with his arm over Holli's shoulder. Next to her are James and then Alfie. He says, "It's going to blow your mind, man. I had complete faith when we signed you, but that song in there is pure gold. It's going to hit big. Wait until you hear it."

"Is it supposed to be that simple? Just go in and record."

Dex puts his hands behind his head as he lies on a lounge chair. "When it's right, it works like magic."

Johnny adds, "We're not going to fu—" Holli's hand flies to her right, landing smack dab against his middle. Glancing down at the kids, he corrects himself, "*Mess*. We're not going to mess with perfection. If you guys don't like it, we're open to hear your ideas, but I'm telling you, you guys nailed it."

Rivers asks, "A song a day. May not even take three weeks to wrap the album."

Laughing, Tommy says, "Slow down. Trust me, you're going to be sore, tired, and hoarse once we're done here, but don't worry. We have some days off built into the schedule."

When Holli starts to stand, Johnny stands with her and pulls out her chair. He watches her walk inside with their plates, and then scoops James into his lap. I look at Hannah who's sitting a few feet away. "Hi," she says silently.

Dex says, "I think we had a good day. Maybe we should call it a night for the studio work. I want a beer." He pushes up and goes inside.

Johnny adds, "I'm good for the night. I feel like we're off to a good start. Make yourselves at home." He swings his kid onto his back. "Ready, kiddo?"

"Weddy," he replies.

Before they reach the door, Johnny looks back. "This is your home for the next three weeks. If you need anything, just let Holli or me know. We'll get some rental cars brought out tomorrow so you can come and go as you want."

Alfie says, "All done."

"Take two more bites, buddy. This is dinner. You're heading to bed soon, and I want to make sure you're good and full."

He shoves two pieces of sausage into his mouth and then darts inside. I know he wants to find James before they both have to go to bed. An awkward silence settles. My brothers and Tommy are up and out of their seats. Tommy says, "Rivers. Tulsa. Let's go, umm . . . yeah, not stay here."

Hannah starts to giggle. "How are you doing, Crow?" She gets up, comes to me, and runs her hand over my shoulder. Her touch feels good. My body stirs, a twisting in my gut, wanting some alone time with her, wanting to be deep inside her. I cover her hand, and taking her by surprise, I pull her into my lap.

Her hands, those same soft but strong hands, latch behind my back and her feet go up in the air. When her head tilts back, her hair almost touches the ground. It was only one glass of wine from what I saw, so she's either tipsy or happy. I'm going with the latter.

Her laughter is carefree, her smile relaxed. When she lifts up, she tightens her hold on me. I tuck some hair behind an ear and pull her close enough to sneak a kiss on her cheek. "I'm happy to see you. How are you, Nichols?"

"Amazing. I haven't felt this good in a while. Is it bad if I say I think it's because . . ." She pauses, but then says, "I'm not on my family's watch?"

"Is this how you're going to be the entire three weeks?"

"Like what?" She sits up concerned.

I squeeze her ass and smirk. "Gorgeous in your happiness? 'Cuz if you are, I might keep you here forever."

The tension lifts from her body, and she laughs. "I don't think I'd mind staying here. Will you give me this life of luxury, Jet?" Although I know she's teasing, I love how she also sounds dreamy and peaceful.

"I'll give you whatever your heart desires, baby." Her lip gets pulled between her teeth. I can see the need in her eyes. The more time I spend with her, the more I learn about this beauty. I know so much about her sexually, but now, I want to know everything about the woman. "What's your favorite candy?"

"You're asking me about candy?"

"Yeah, what do you like?" Her hand cups my jaw, her thumb running up and down my scruff. "I need to shave."

"I like it like this."

I hold her a little closer. Glancing toward the door, I

check to see if the coast is still clear. "I like you like this." I lean in and steal a kiss. Wine and barbecue. Sinful.

When voices carry from the inside out here for us to hear, she moves slowly off my lap. Before she goes, her hand touches my shoulder, and she says, "Red Hots and Hot Tamales."

"Cinnamon." Sweet and spicy, matching her personality. After tasting her sweet, I'm willing to get burned to taste her fire.

26

Jet

"Puberty hit early. I was tall and fairly developed by sixteen. Born with a face like mine, my mama warned me to be leery of girls and their intentions because I was bound to attract the good and bad. As much as I could appreciate a good girl, the bad girls were a lot more fun."

That was then.

This is now.

I rub Hannah's thigh. She's a good girl in a bad girl's body. Pure sin and sweetness. *Cinnamon*. Fuck, I'm horny.

A bottle cap nails me in the neck. Tulsa. Little fucker. He finishes his beer and makes a joke. "He only asked how tall you were, bro. And while we're on the subject of you. You were an asshole growing up and let's talk about that 'fairly developed' part." He chuckles when he does the air quotes.

Dex is still laughing when he says, "Damn, you guys are rough."

Rivers can sling a comeback, but he's more Switzerland

lately. He's spread out on a chair, kicked back. "You have any siblings, Dex?"

He seems to mull it over before answering. "I have a half-brother. He's an asshole but not the good kind like yours." Standing up, the sticks are stilled. "I'm off. Just a word of warning. Johnny likes to start before lunch. I wouldn't get too wasted or stay up all night."

"What time do you think we should head to the house?" I ask.

"I'll be up around ten. I need to eat before spending hours in the studio." His gaze shifts to Tulsa. "What do you prefer—guitar or drums?"

"I'm more comfortable on the guitar."

"That's not what I asked."

Tulsa sits up. "I'm okay with either."

"If you're okay with either, then why haven't you been hitting the skins?"

I've never made him stick to the drums. Doesn't mean he wasn't talented, but this was always a democracy. "He was free to do what he wanted as long as we were covered for the shows."

Dex shoots me a look before returning his attention to Tulsa. "You have talent, Tulsa. The arrangement of your band is on the agenda to discuss tomorrow. It's up to you which instrument you want to play, but we need to know in the morning."

Tulsa can be hot-headed, spontaneous, and more stubborn than a mule, but I see how much he values Dex's opinion when he asks, "What do you think I should choose?"

Dex doesn't hesitate to respond. "I'd like to see you continue drumming. You have good rhythm and you're strong, but you're wearing out. There's fading at the end of each song you played. You're getting tired and slowing the tempo. You may not notice, but Rivers and Jet are slowing to meet the beat. Drumming doesn't work like that. I can teach you some patterns, and we can increase your striking speed with practice, get you in the gym and make you stronger with more endurance." He opens the door to the guesthouse and adds, "Good skills to have all around. Good night."

When the door closes, we all crack up except for Tulsa who says, "Trust me, nobody's complaining about my rhythm, speed, or endurance. I'm going to bed. I have a feeling when Dex says teach he means torture." He's the first to stand followed by Rivers and Hannah.

Hannah offers a hand. I say, "Like you can pull me up, little thing."

"Let me try."

I take her hand and pull her onto my lap. "That worked out nicely." Rolling her eyes, she pushes off me with a laugh. I'm quick to add, "Guess size does matter."

"I won't argue with you there. C'mon, big boy. Take me to bed and have your wild way with me."

That's an invitation if I ever heard one. I grab the walkie-talkie and scoop her into my arms before we start for the stairs. "Night, guys."

Their good night is heard faintly in the distance as I run up the stairs. She says, "You're the one doing all the work, but I'm the one out of breath."

"I've stunned you. It happens. It's not the first time."

I'm whacked on my arm. "God, you're so arrogant."

"Remember what I said about calling me God. Jet will do." Her head leans against my chest as she laughs. As much as I want to carry her to bed, I have to set her down. Whispering, I say, "I'm going to check on Alfie first."

Taking my hand, she says, "I want to come too."

When I open the door, I walk in after Hannah, my eyes slow to adjust to the low light. The nightlight helps guide us to his bed where we stand together watching him sleep. Hannah leans against me, her head resting on my arm. I tuck the blanket under his chin like at home and make sure no feet are hanging out. I also check to make sure the walkie-talkie is working.

He's not a baby, but we're in a strange place, and I was worried he might get scared. Holli brought us walkie-talkies to use. Alfie said he felt better knowing he could contact me if he got too scared to come two doors down. The upstairs master bedroom was the only room with a king-size bed and only a large walk-in closet separates our rooms.

Watching him now, I see he looks peacefully asleep, so we quietly leave. I shut the door behind me as Hannah takes the walkie-talkie from me, sets it on the nightstand, and walks back to the end of the bed. Sitting down on the edge, she glides her hands over the blanket on either side of her. "So this is where you're going to have your way with me?"

"We have a shower if you prefer, or a marble bathroom counter I can bend you over." I nod toward the couch. "There's another option, Ms. Nichols. Choose anywhere you like."

"Is the door locked?"

I reach behind me and turn the lock. "Yes."

"Come here."

"No."

Her eyebrows rise. "No?"

Shaking my head, the left side of my mouth lifts. "Take off your clothes."

Her lips barely part, but I see the smallest of space between them as her chest pushes out and slowly retreats again. I can hear her breath deepen and then her tongue dips out—wet, ready, and teasing. Crossing her arms in front of her, she reaches for the hem of her shirt and pulls it off. I'm not a guy who needs sexy lingerie to get off. The basic beige bra is just as erotic. The way her tits are pushed together and how they spill just over the top draws me to them, and to her.

I resist, wanting to enjoy the show first.

Taking off her shoes and pulling down her jeans, she steps out of them and stands before me and then spins once around for me. "Is this what you want to see?"

That ass. It sits high and tight, making me want to fucking bite it. "Not quite."

Both hands fly to her hips, those hips that curve out like the bottom of an hourglass. "What do you want?"

"You."

"You have me, Jet. I'm right here."

Quirking an eyebrow, I take this opportunity she's handing me on a silver platter. "I can have you?"

"You have me."

"Any way I want?"

Reaching behind her back, she loosens her bra and starts sliding the straps down her arms until it joins the rest of her clothes on the floor. The little strips of lace wrapped around those luscious hips glide down next. She eyes me up and down, raising her own eyebrow. "Are you going to stand there and gawk or come and get what's yours for the taking?"

I don't need to be asked twice. "Turn around and put the palms of your hands on the bed." She doesn't hesitate, and even takes it a step further by sliding forward just until her tits touch but are pressed against the blanket.

My jeans are becoming painfully tight. I take my belt off, pulling it through the loops. I toss it behind me. I've never been into spanking. I'll do it if a chick wants it, but I don't get off on it.

I'm thinking about fucking her right now. I can just drop my jeans. But she's putting a lot of trust in me positioned like that, so I should make her feel good in return. I strip off what I'm wearing because if she's naked, I want to be naked with her. Touching her waist, I run my hand along the curve. "If you're mine for the taking, can I take you like this?"

Resting on her elbows, she keeps her eyes forward. "I'm getting cold. Touch me. Cover me. Take me. Fuck me, Jet. Just fill me. Please."

"Such a dirty fucking mouth. Do you know how much that mouth of yours turns me on?"

Her voice lower, her eyes on the pillow just out of reach. "How much?"

"Almost enough to make me want to fuck it first."

"Do it."

"No, you're not running this show, baby. I am." Dragging my hand slowly down her spine and lower, I stop when I reach between her legs and find her wet and ready for me. "So damn sexy." I coat my cock with her slickness and position my erection just as I remember I'm not covered. "Fuck, I forgot a condom. Stay right there, baby."

She giggles. "You don't need one."

I'm about to go rummage through my suitcase to find my Ziploc full of bathroom stuff, but I pause instead. "Really?"

Looking back, she says, "Really."

"You have birth control?"

"I take the pill." She wiggles to get more comfortable. "I'd really like to move this along if possible."

It'd be rude to keep the lady waiting. Still positioned where I want to be, I lean over her from behind and slide my hands from her shoulders to her hands, resting my weight on my wrists and legs. I kiss one shoulder and then the other while holding her in place. "You don't want me to go easy, do you, sweetheart?"

"You know I hate being called swee—

Thrusting, I push myself deep into her supple warmth. Her hands anchor her to the bed, taking every thrust I give while her body begs for more. My eyelids dip closed as I lean back and drive forward.

"Tell me everything you hate while I fuck you, baby."

"I hate when you call me sweetheart."

"Why?"

"Because my ex called me that."

For a guy who earns his living from his great rhythm, mine is thrown off, but only for a millisecond. Can't let her see me sweat. "What else do you hate?"

Her breaths come out in pants, and she moans. "Um."

I love that she struggles to focus. Me too. This feels so damn good that I know I'm not going to last much longer. I want her to come with me. "Tell me, Hannah," I demand.

"I, uh . . ." She drops her head. "Feels so good." *So good.* She says, "I hate saying goodbye to you."

Stopping, I draw back. "Turn over for me." She scoots up the bed and lies on her back. Her chest is flushed and goose bumps scatter across her skin. I move over her and sink back inside, the heat melding us together. Slowing my pace, I start making love to her.

I kiss her cheek and everywhere else on her face. I stop kissing her neck just long enough to whisper in her ear, "Tell me what you love, wildflower."

"I love the way I feel whole when we're like this."

Kissing her chest, I say, "I feel it. Whole." *Complete.*

"I love . . ." She reaches up and holds my cheek in the palm of her hand. "I love you."

She's been strong since I met her, even tough sometimes when she had to be, but when she lets you in, you're all the way in. She exposes her vulnerabilities and opens her heart, not just a little, but wide open to be hurt.

Trust.

This is trust in shades of giving. *One of the best gifts she can give me.* She's giving me her heart but doesn't realize she's had mine all along. The words don't seem enough, but they need to be said. They need to be heard. "I love you."

Her light shines in her eyes from her heart.

Just for me.

I bow my head to my love's shoulder. Twisting. Tightening. So close. Her breath blows across my ear—mews of pleasure, the pleasure she gets from me. "I love you. I love you. I love . . ." The curve at the base of her neck takes my final breath as I grind out my orgasm, releasing all of me with a harsh exhale. "You."

The tips of her fingers dig into my shoulders. Her hold tightens, her head pushing into the pillow behind her. Still caught up in her, I lick the base of her jaw as her body speaks for her—back arching, moans that come from deep within, her fingers weaving into my hair demanding my eyes on her.

When she gives me all of her, I kiss her. I kiss her until her outsides twist with her insides and then back again. Tension escapes her, and we fall, fall, fall back together.

I stay.

I lie on top of her, too weak to move. I lie on top of her, feeling her breath coat my skin like a breeze on the beach. I lie there until her fingers loosen and soothe my body. I lie there while she holds me so tight I can't leave.

A kiss lands on my neck, and I shift, taking the bulk of my weight off her but leaving enough to still cover her.

I always smoke after sex, and the craving is there in the pit of my stomach, but it doesn't feel right to leave her. I like this. I *love* this.

"Jet?" she whispers so quietly, so unsure.

I hate it. "Yeah?" Keeping my eyes off hers to give her enough room to find surety in the space between us again.

"This is real for me."

Space isn't needed. Lifting up, I lean over her and then dip my head down, closing my eyes and feeling our cheeks pressed together, feeling us together. I whisper, "It's always been real for me." Fuck. I squeeze my eyes, refusing to give into the surfacing emotions I didn't even know existed until she came along.

Pushing up, I get out of bed because I need to clear my head. I need air. I need a smoke.

27

Jet

Pacing the length of the pool, I light up.

Hannah watched me pull on my jeans and shirt, not saying a word. I grabbed the walkie-talkie and a jacket and left the room.

I meant it when I told her I loved her the first time and this time and every time in between. What was that in her eyes—fear? Her words—*this is real for me*—making me wonder if real for her stirs her fears. Will she hold back or give in all the way, be all in like I am?

Me?

That I'm a musician?

That she's been burned by a musician before?

The situation with Alfie?

Her aunt?

Her father?

Fuck. I can name a dozen reasons that might be holding her back. I shouldn't have left her. I turn to go back, but she's standing there, an angel standing in the dark wearing a white dress that illuminates her in the moonlight. The lightest of breezes cause the fabric to float into the air.

"Are you leaving me?"

All the other reasons go away. That's the fear I see in her eyes, the sadness that still resides. "You think I could leave you, wildflower?" I tear my gaze away and blow smoke into the inky black sky. "I'm right here," I repeat her words from earlier.

"Your mind isn't. Where did your thoughts run off to?"

"What is this, Hannah? This between us?"

"We just said we loved each other inside. Was that not real?"

"It's all been real. Don't you see? It's always been real to me." I take a drag hoping to calm down. When I sit, she remains too far away. "I didn't damage you, but I'm paying the price for someone who did." My heart beats too fast to remain. I start to pace again. "This shouldn't be complicated. We fucking love each other. They aren't just words. I feel it when you say it. Do you feel it when I tell you?"

"Why are you upset?"

Why am I upset? Why am I fucking upset? "Are we still pretending we're a secret?"

The question seems to surprise her. "How can we be a secret when everyone knows?"

"Alfie doesn't."

"Alfie's not blind. He can see we're close. Do you want to tell Alfie?"

"Yes." I take a breath, calming my heart with every step I take. She's a goddess in a white dress soothing my restless soul.

I stand before her with my arms at my sides, waiting for her to say something, anything that will make this turmoil inside me go away. Reaching up, she takes the cigarette from my mouth and tosses it to the concrete. "I don't want you smoking anymore." Moving my jacket to the side, she presses the palm of her hand over my heart. "When I love, I love hard, fully, with all of me. You don't understand the damage you can do to me. The power you have. With that power in your hands, you also hold your health and your life. You can't risk your life because you're damaging my heart and my life when you do. Alfie needs you, but I do too. I love you, Jet."

My arms wrap around her as my jacket covers her shoulders. She wraps her arms around me, resting her head on me, and says, "I feel it."

And there she is, the girl I always saw beneath her struggles and the burdens life had dumped on her. My brave and beautiful woman.

"I don't want to be a secret. We were already the worst kept one around anyway." Resting her chin on me, she looks up. "We can talk to Alfie, but we need to be careful and manage his expectations of dating versus . . ." Her eyes leave mine.

"Versus something more permanent? Something like marriage?"

Just a nod. So small, but I see it.

Running the back of my hand over her cheek, I ask, "It's fast, all of this is so fast, but where do you stand with marriage? Is that something you want in life?"

"I do."

"I like the sound of that." I put a little pressure on her ribs until she giggles, the sound echoing into the night.

By her hand, I spin her out and bring her back to me. Then I slow dance with her under the California stars. "We're more serious than we intended."

Smiling down at her, I hold her hand in mine and her

waist in my other. "Good or bad, intentions are commands of the heart."

"What are we? Good or bad?"

Dipping her, I kiss her and whisper against her lips, "The best."

When I bring her up, we're pressed together again. No music, only the wind is heard, but we still sway together. She asks, "Why did you ask me to tell you everything I hate?"

"I wanted to fuck the hate out of you so you're free from it."

I like her smile too much. Seeing it now reassures me. Yeah, we're going to be fine. "You were making love to me."

"I want to replace that hate with the love you deserve, Hannah. I want you to feel it long after we leave that bed."

"I feel it with you." Holding my hand, she trails away until only the tips of our fingers touch. "I hated the life I was leading."

"When?"

"Before Alfie." I love when she suddenly turns shy. "Before you," she whispers.

The words float through the air between us. She twirls, her skirt ballooning free like she wants to be from the worries that plague her.

I'll give her what she needs. I'll do my best to take her worries and bury them. I'm sure of all these things. I'm sure of her and me. One day, we'll get married. She's not just my heart, but she holds my soul captive inside her.

Going to her, I sling my arm around her shoulders. "C'mon. It's too cold out here for you." Her arm slips around my back, and we walk to the house. "So you want me to quit smoking?"

"Yes, I do. My cousin died of cancer, and it doesn't matter how good you look doing it, your health is more important."

"So is yours. No asking to smoke my cigs anymore."

"You never let me anyway."

"So how about I try to quit after the album wraps?"

Jumping in front of me, she places one hand against my abs, halting me. The other is between us. "Shake on it, Crow."

"You're a tenacious little thing."

"A weed." Her eyes reveal the happiness bubbling up inside her, and she laughs. "Weeds are persistent."

"Wildflower," I correct with a chuckle. "And yes, they are persistent." Taking her hand in mine, I shake, a big and official shake. "You and Alfie got yourselves a deal."

"He'll be thrilled."

Wrapping my arm around her waist, we go inside the house. "How about you? Will you be thrilled?"

"I already am." Her hand rubs over my stomach, and I hear one of those little dreamy mews of hers that makes me hard. "I really like your body. Is that terrible to say?"

I scoop her up and put her over my shoulder. With a firm hold of her ass, I carry her upstairs. Just outside Alfie's door, I stop, but she pulls the walkie-talkie from my jacket pocket and wiggles it in her hand. "He's okay."

"Okay." She's right. He is. I just worry. Wow. Maybe I'm not so lost on this dad thing after all.

Inside the room, I ask, "Shower?"

"Yes," she replies with a little lift onto her toes and kissing me.

I start the water so it can warm up and take off my clothes. She comes into the bathroom naked already. I catcall her because damn, she's fine. "You have a really fucking amazing body. You remember how you told me you stay in shape?"

She bursts out laughing and shakes her head. From that reaction, she clearly remembers. "I can't believe I told you from fucking. I also can't believe you didn't throw me out of your bed right then." Her hand goes under the water. The temperature must be right because she moves under the spray. "Ahhhh. This feels so good. Come in here with me, baby."

Baby? *Fuck.* Who knew I'd like being someone's baby so much. I move behind her and run my hands all over her stomach while kissing her neck. "It's been a while since we did it in the shower. Hint. Hint."

"Good God, Crow." She laughs and cups between her legs. "My vagina needs a break."

"I'd make apologies but yeah, I'm not sorry. You knew what you were getting back into when you seduced me with your charms and tight little pussy."

"Who's got the dirty mouth now?"

"Dirty." I lower my voice. "You're so dirty. Let me help you and make everything feel so much better." I lower to my knees and turn her around, making her call my name while she praises the heavens above.

Twice.

Once we're thoroughly exhausted and clean, we lie under the covers. She's curled against me. She has her arm and leg draped over my body as I hold her.

"You're a good guy, Jet." Her eyelashes are feathers brushing against my skin. "You'll always tell me the truth, right?"

"You have no reason to doubt me. I'm loyal to those I love."

"I know you are. It's my personal insecurities, not anything you've done."

"Time." I kiss her head. "It will take time, but I'll give you no reason to ever doubt me."

Snuggling closer, she closes her eyes, and then her breathing deepens and steadies. "Love you."

"Love you."

I LEFT Hannah sleeping when I rolled out of bed to the sound of Alfie stirring around seven in the morning. My head is groggy as I pull on some boxer shorts and a T-shirt and head down the hall.

His door opens, and he smiles.

It's hard to be annoyed at this early hour when you're greeted with pure, unadulterated joy to see you. "Morning, buddy."

"Morning. I'm hungry."

"Go get dressed and brush your teeth. I'm gonna do the same and meet you back here in a few minutes. We have food in the kitchen, but I heard there's going to be breakfast in the main house this morning."

"I want waffles."

Walking back to the room, I say, "We get what we get—"

"I know. I know. And we don't throw a fit."

A few minutes later, we're walking across the property to the big house and I'm taking in the scenery. It's a place I can only dream of having one day. Dreaming doesn't cost a thing, so I'll keep doing it. "You think you'd like living at a place like this?"

"Yes. Ms. Holli said we get to visit the horse today. I've never seen a real horse. I heard they're big."

"They are." I hold out my hand, and he takes it so naturally as if we've been father and son forever. Guess we have. We just didn't know it before. "Are you happy, Alfie?"

"I like it here. Are you happy, Daddy?"

My feet come to a stop, and my chest feels thick with hopes that can be destroyed with something as simple as questioning myself. *Did I hear him correctly?*

He asks, "What? Why'd we stop? I'm hungry."

"What did you say?"

Looking up at me, he rubs his stomach. "I'm hungry."

"Before that."

The seconds tick by as he ponders my question. "Are you happy?"

I smile. "I am happy. When you asked me that, you called me daddy."

Nodding quickly, he asks, "Is that okay? Am I in trouble?"

"No," I say, bending down. Looking into my son's eyes, I say, "You're not in trouble. You called me daddy. Thank you, son." I bring him in for a hug, and he hugs me. When I pull back, I add, "I like that. I love being your daddy."

"I love it just like Mommy told me I would."

We start walking toward the house again. "Hey, buddy?" When he looks up at me, I ask, "When did your mommy tell you about me?"

"When Grandma would go to bed, I would sneak into Mommy's room and she'd let me sleep with her."

"That's nice of your mom. So you'd talk when your grandma was asleep?"

"Yeah, Mommy told me we had to keep our talks a secret because it would upset Grandma if she knew."

On the terrace, we stop. I sit in a chair, which puts me

eye level with him. "Why do you think Grandma would be upset about you talking?"

"Grandma says she loves me, and if you ever found out Mommy died, you'd take me away forever."

The fire in my gut rolls into anger. *How could she be so cruel to her grandson? Can she not see how damaging her words can be?* "Do you remember what else your mommy told you?"

"I didn't have to. She wrote it down so I wouldn't forget."

"She did?"

Looking away from me, he looks guilty, so I ask, "What is it?"

"I forgetted. Do you think she'll be mad at me in heaven?"

I don't need to correct his English right now. I need to hug him. Pulling him to me, I do just that. Sitting him on one of my legs, I say, "No, your mommy won't be mad at all. Also, if you remember anything else, let me know. Okay?"

"Okay."

Setting him on his feet, I stand. The back door opens, and Holli says, "You guys are up bright and early."

"I've got an early riser," I say.

She smiles and points at James as he speeds by on his push car. "I can relate." Holding her hand out, she asks, "You hungry, Alfie?"

"Yes."

"Come on in. I've got the waffle maker out. I could really use some help in the kitchen. Are you up for the job?"

He looks at me, looking for permission.

"Go on, kid."

Running to Holli, he says, "My daddy gets the first waffle."

"Absolutely, he does." She takes him into the kitchen,

but I stay a few minutes, watching the fog rise above the trees in the distance.

Man. That kid knows how to hit me right in the feels.

Daddy.

Best name ever.

28

Hannah

Heaven.

I'm in heaven.

Was last night real or just a dream?

Rolling to my side, I ache in all the good ways. I miss my personal heater as the chill from the room starts to seep in through the covers. I miss Jet's weight on top of me, the steady hum of his heart beating next to mine, and the way his arm holds me tight like he's afraid he'll lose me in the night. I feel safe in his arms and in his bed.

I never did with Hunter. Even when I believed I was happy with my ex, I was living a lie, one he would eventually prove right.

Hunter Hix was the boy who lived across the cul-de-sac from me. He moved in when my parents were still together and kept me company back when I felt alone. The friend who was always there for me even when I was brace-faced and moody from changes in my body. He's the one who comforted me when my mother left, the one who went to court as my mom fought for me, the one who sat behind me when the judge ruled in my father's favor because he was the one who could support me.

At thirteen, I started looking at Hunter through new eyes, through teenage girl eyes. He was cute with his lanky body and a smile too big for his face. I thought I loved him then, but I was convinced two years later when playing doctor with him was totally different than when we were little.

He grew into his body and that smile. Other girls noticed, but he only noticed me . . . until he got a taste of fame.

Touring.

It's a necessary evil of any musician who wants to get discovered or support an album. I thought Hunter loved me until the crowds increased with each tour stop. More fans. More girls. More groupies. Tickets were selling out before the band arrived in each city. It was fun.

At first.

Until it wasn't.

Sex became about getting him off, feeding his ego. Too rough. He couldn't do anything without a hit of something, without a high or a pill to stave off a low.

Weed wasn't enough. Alcohol made things worse. A good mood could change before my eyes. Suddenly, I wasn't enough. Everything I did was wrong.

I shouldn't have quit school. *What kind of fool was I?* Young and so carelessly dumb.

That I have this second chance with a man who is so good to everyone he loves is incredible. I won't blow it. I'll be the woman he needs. Strength. As Holli said, I'm not a groupie. I'm his partner. When it's painful for me, the scars reveal themselves, reminding me of a bad past, so I can't hide or go quiet. I have to speak up, speak freely, and voice my fears. Fears that Jet helped put to rest last night.

My thoughts are changing, my self-worth growing, my body opening back up, and my soul healing. He did that. He doesn't jump every hurdle I throw his way. He tramples it. Each act of love, his caring, and his forgiveness proves he's the real deal, the one who will work for what he wants and then cherish his reward.

I want to be that for him too.

Opening my eyes, I see a note where Jet should be, and then I gasp. *Alfie.*

Checking the time, I realize he is surely up already. How did I sleep past nine?

Smiling because I know why.

Jet Crow.

I even swoon a little just thinking about him. The crazy thing is normally I'd be running into Alfie's room, but I know I don't have to. If Jet's not in bed right now, that means Alfie's already up, and they're together. He's truly embraced what it means to be a father—he's showing up.

Reaching over, I take the little white note to read.

GOOD MORNING, *Wildflower,*

Don't worry. Alfie's with me. Take however long you need and enjoy your morning.

Love,

Your former dirty little secret.

EVEN WHEN HE'S not here, he has me rolling my eyes.

I'd love to lounge around all day, but I know he'll be

working in the studio, and knowing Alfie's six-year-old attention span, Jet will need me.

It feels good to be needed. But taking advantage of his offer, I don't rush through my routine. I spend a few extra minutes getting ready—makeup, hair, and a pretty dress that feels like Southern California, matching the clear blue skies.

This estate is amazing, so much of Johnny with Holli mixed in—it feels so them, built with love for their family. I'd usually stop myself from dreaming of having the same, but I don't today. I let my mind wander as I mosey across the vast lawn.

I walk in the back door but don't see anyone around. There's food on the table, which makes my stomach growl.

Taking a plate, I load it up, deciding it's best to eat first before fully starting the crazy of my day, and Jet did say take my time. I pour a cup of coffee and sit on the terrace to enjoy the morning.

Holli and James soon find me. "Good morning. How'd you sleep, Hannah?"

When she's seated on a chaise, her sunglasses come down from the top of her head to cover her eyes. Her hair is down, but she twists it up with a few flicks of her wrist and a rubber band she was wearing around it. Boom. Perfection. Disproving my theory of it being styled professional altogether. She's the professional.

If I didn't feel so good this morning, her beauty would intimidate me. But I've never felt more beautiful because of Jet and how he makes me feel inside.

"I love your dress," she says.

And suddenly, I'm blushing. "Oh, God. This old thing. I just threw it on." I take a sip of coffee just to make myself shut up.

Laughing, she says, "I had to learn to take a compliment. I used to be so uncomfortable with them. I felt like people were just being nice, not necessarily genuine. I never received the words they were gifting me. I never felt good enough, pretty enough, tall enough, short enough, thin enough, blond enough, brunette enough, tan enough, pale enough. Never enough. One day I looked in the mirror and liked what I saw. I saw me. I finally realized that what everyone thought of me was their business, not mine. To me, I was enough. That's what mattered."

I want that. I want to erase the words that I'm trouble. That I wasn't beautiful enough to hold his attention. I need this for me. "Did things change?"

"It changed my whole life. I finally started living, living for me. I don't tell this story much, but I thought Dalton was a one-night stand." She laughs again while watching James play with big blocks on the ground. "I left his room thinking I'd never hear from him again. We had our night, and that's all the expectations I put into it. I wanted that one night as much as he did, and that was before I knew he was famous."

"Would you have slept with him if you'd known?"

"Yes, but I liked that he worked for it. We talked, got to know each other a little before. It's funny because even though I didn't know he was famous, that night I got to know the real man. Not the showman or the musician. Just Dalton. That's your superpower when it comes to Jet— knowing the man behind the image."

"You're saying this as if you already know he'll be famous."

She bends over to help James just as he starts getting frustrated with the wooden blocks. Looking back at me, she says, "He's going to be famous, Hannah. He's got everything going for him—the voice, the band, the songs, the looks, the charisma. Johnny sees it too, or he wouldn't have signed them. The Crow men may be brothers, but they're all unique. They're the full package and are going to drive the fans wild."

"That's my fear."

When she realizes I'm not joking, she comes to sit with me at the table. "Don't fear fame. That's a by-product of the career. It doesn't have power over you or him, though it may feel like it does some days. If you feed it, it will grow. If you feed your souls, all the other stuff will be left outside the front door."

"What about secrets? Things we don't want people to know about. How do I hide those things?"

"You can't. It's just best to face them head on and then stroll right on by, leaving them in your past."

Rolling a strawberry around my plate, I watch as the berry starts to lose its seeds. I don't want to be a distraction to Jet's career or for my past to haunt his future. "Can I ask you a favor?"

"Sure, anything."

"What I told you yesterday, the story about my ex."

"Of how he abused you?"

"Yes. Jet doesn't know all the details."

"Oh, honey. That's a terrible burden to have to carry yourself. You should think about telling him."

"It won't do him any good. He's here and needs to focus on his music. Not me and a past I could have prevented."

She angles away, checking on James, and then back again. "We just met, but I heard so many good things about you from Jet that I felt like I already knew you. Then when we met, my instincts were right. When you trusted me with your story, I was touched and will respect your wishes. But it doesn't matter how busy he is; he needs to know your life story too. You will have to trust him with your secrets. If you don't, he might find out another way and where does that leave you?"

"I have a feeling the answer is alone." *I'm not alone.* My little man loves me, and my big man does too. I survived. And I will continue to do so.

With a bottle of water in hand, Jet walks outside to join us. "Trust me with what secrets?"

My first thought is to flee the scene, but I fight through it, my fingers holding the chair and keeping me there.

Holli stands and walks over to James to pick him up. "Daddy's taking a break. Can you find him first?"

James takes off running inside with Holli hot on his heels. Jet takes the seat she vacated across from me. That look of concern I didn't want to see is firmly in place. He asks, "What secrets, Hannah?"

"Nothing really. I heard they have a horse," I say, changing the subject.

"Nice try, sugarfly."

"Sugarfly? Really?" I try to laugh, playing it off like my gut isn't twisting with anxiety.

"Sorry, I thought of it . . . *on the fly*."

Scoffing so hard that my head even goes back, I say, "That is a terrible pun."

"It was awful." He laughs, but it's short-lived. His eyes stay on mine, so I look away. "I didn't get enough sleep. Some chick was keeping me up all night begging for a banging."

"She's a hooker. You should really spend your time on something more worthwhile," I joke.

"Hey. Hey. Hey. That's the woman I love you're talking about. Speaking of my woman, what secrets are you keeping from me?"

Communication is key. I know this. Holli just gave me another reason to be up front with him now, so our relationship doesn't pay the price later. Secrets don't stay buried forever, as much as I wish this one could.

Here goes everything . . .

29

Hannah

The great debate begins.

If I tell him, he'll flip out. But will his anger only be directed toward my ex, or will he look at me differently?

My aunt is wrong about my mother. She was never weak. She was smart. But she was right about me being just like my mom. I was strong enough to walk away.

Jet will see that. *Beautiful and brave.* He already does.

"You know my history with Hunter. You know it was more than cheatin—"

"He hit you. Say it, Hannah."

"He hit me." Saying it is easier these days. "If I tell you the details, please don't get upset."

"I can't make that promise."

"Nothing can harm us now."

When I try to wrangle my thoughts, to make my words concise with enough details to be honest, he reaches over and taps the table twice. "Hey, it's okay. You can tell me anything. I'm here for you."

"I know you are, Jet, and thank you for being my rock when others just thought . . . I don't know what they thought. I just know that no matter how disappointed I was with someone I loved, I could never turn my back on them when they needed me most." I look at his hand, palm up and open for me, and set mine on top. "I struggle to trust people because it's not only my heart that was hurt." I hate remembering.

I hate that I didn't blackout and take each hit without my knowledge. I would rather deal with the consequences of the abuse then relive it over and over in my head. My jaw starts aching, so I move it back and forth.

"Hannah?"

Looking up, I realize he's still here while I was trapped in my head. "He beat me until I started to black out."

"Unconscious?" He mutters swear words under his breath.

"He was out of his mind, high as a kite. I didn't know him at all that night. I'd never met the devil until I caught him fucking someone else."

"When you say beat, you mean he tried to kill you?" The words are hard for him to swallow, a look of disbelief on his face as he chokes them down. "I knew it was bad because of the night he came by, but fuck, Hannah, it's worse than I imagined."

I can't sugarcoat what Hunter did to me any longer, not if I want to heal and move on. Move on. *Move forward.* That's what I want with Jet, for me and for Alfie.

I've protected my ex for too long. I've hidden secrets behind a façade of better memories and excuses, pretending it could never happen to me while trying to remember who he used to be when he was just the cute boy across the street who adored me. I believed my own deceptions, candy coating the truth to make the lies more palatable.

Jet's eyes never leave mine, and I shift under the intense stare. The deeper hues of his widened pupils engulf the sweet caramel of his eyes, taking me in and inhaling every word and breath I take, and move I make.

The hand that holds mine, slips out, and begins to curl into a fist. Before it disappears under the table altogether, I lift and grab it. His gaze softens, and he gives in to me, resting his hand on mine again.

"I love you." I don't know why I say it other than I just feel how much he cares, and I want him to know what that means to me.

"I love you, too," he replies, some of the fight leaving his body. His shoulders don't relax entirely, but he's calmer. "Was hitting you a regular occurrence for him?"

"One time was all it took. I was lucky I could walk away. He didn't cause permanent damage—"

"He didn't leave any visible scars."

"Yes, visible."

"Promise me you'll never defend him or his actions again. Not ever, Hannah."

"I won't." I didn't realize I had until I said the words, making excuses for him. I hate feeling like a victim, but I hate being a victim even more. I will never own that title. I will never be labeled less than beautiful and brave again.

With Jet by my side, I know I'll never have to.

"Sometimes, I remember how distant his eyes were when he was hitting me and how the blows came faster. I wonder what would have happened if his band wouldn't have found us when they did. If Dave hadn't been there, would I be dead?" My gaze shoots back up to his. "I fought."

A little squeeze of my hand reassures me. "Even though you never should have had to, I have no doubt you did."

"The band went on to play that night, and he never even washed my blood off his hands."

"*What the fuck? They pulled him off you.* What—"

"Dave helped me. He never took the stage. Instead, he took me into the bathroom of the bar by shielding me under his jacket. He washed my face and let me cry on his shoulder."

"Fuck. Glad he was there. Did you go to the hospital?"

"No. I had no money. My credit cards were maxed. No insurance. Nowhere to go."

"Where'd you go?"

"We left and found a cheap hotel about a mile away. Dave went and got food, and we watched TV. Well, I listened because I had bags of ice on my face, and my eyes were too swollen to see anything anyway. He was worried I had a concussion, so he kept me up all night talking. I don't even remember what we talked about, maybe a little of everything. Anything other than our exes and what happened." Unburdening my soul lightens the worries that weigh me down. "The next morning when the sun rose, we slept. He held me all night." Making sure he understands it was purely platonic, I add, "As friends. Nothing more. We didn't do anything then and never since."

Jet nods his head. *Loyalty.* He gets it. "He is a good friend to you. I have no doubt you are to him as well. What about your family? Where were they?"

"In Austin. I had been on the receiving end of my father's cold shoulder most of my life. He was all work and no play. Still is. I realize he only had one kid for a reason, but deep down, if he had none, he might have been happier. Not everyone who can reproduce should."

"So he knew and did nothing?"

"My father and aunt were bred from cold parents and inherited their traits."

He nods, looking away, and then turns back to say, "If I could punch your father right now, I would."

"He's not deserving of my time or energy. He most certainly is not worthy of yours."

"What happened with you and Dave after that night?"

It sounds like he's a little jealous by how he phrases it like that, but he's met Dave. He knows we're just friends. I see genuine curiosity as he waits to hear more.

"The next day we went our separate ways. Dave left the band the night before, but they still had all his stuff in their van. He asked me if I wanted to go with him and then head back to Austin, but something just felt in my gut wrong about going back. I think it was my dad. Dave gave me enough money to cover another few nights at the hotel, and I had enough to buy food. I had to pay daily, so when I went downstairs the front desk clerk, Sherri, took pity on me. She even let me stay two extra nights for free. After that, I waitressed at the diner next door and rented a room in Sherri's house. After a few months, I found a job as a receptionist and moved into my own place. It wasn't that nice, but no one knew where I lived. I liked the anonymity. I liked feeling safe because monsters don't just live in your nightmares. In Dallas, I was safe from them; the monsters I knew in real life."

"When I was fifteen, my mom dated a guy who walked into her house, seizing an opportunity to take over." He scoffs and rubs his face. "He sold used computer parts he found in dumpsters and on bulk trash pick-up days. He labeled them as new without packaging. He forced us to help him once. The next time, he was smart enough not to take the three of us."

"He sounds awful."

"He hit my mom across the face, backhanded her for not having dinner on the table when he was ready to eat. He told us that you have to get a firm hold on your household or it falls apart, that women would look at us for direction and it was our job to dole out rewards and punishments so they fall in line."

That's not the Jet I know. It's not Rivers, and even though Tulsa's sowing some wild oats, his heart is good. All of them are good. They've shown me nothing but respect. That awful man's lessons were never learned. Thank God.

Jet continues, "Then he looked at the three of us with our empty dinner plates on the table and pointed his fingers like a gun, shooting us one by one."

He reaches for a cigarette, gets as far as pulling one from the pack, but then stops. Glancing at me, he puts it away. "To this day, I remember the sound he made as he shot each one of us." His voice is so low as he replays the memory for me to hear.

My body knows to still, my mind focused on the man across from me. My heartbeats slow to a stop, and my breathing has ceased altogether.

The shift in his mood as he comes back to me this time is with a devious glint in his eyes. "The doctor told him his fingers would only take two months to be good as new. He could have pressed charges against us, especially me being fifteen, but I had a little talk with him as we walked back to the car. I told him if he ever came near my mom, my brothers, or my house again, he wouldn't have fingers to heal. He dropped us off, and we never saw him again."

This man astounds me at every turn. No wonder he took to

Alfie so quickly. No wonder he didn't shirk his responsibilities. When he loves, he loves fiercely, and in that, we are so very much the same. *How did we get so lucky?* "Your mom was fortunate to have you."

"We were fortunate to have her." He gets up and comes around, taking the chair next to mine. "Our break's almost over, but why didn't you go back to Austin? Why did you stay in Dallas so long?"

"I had enough for the bus fare to get back home in hotel money, but there was no point. I didn't want to go back. There was nothing and no one worth wasting my life on. Except for my cousin. I came back for her because she asked me to. As you know, Eileen needed help with Alfie while she cared for Cassie."

"So you left the life you created, gave it up to be there for the family who wasn't there for you?"

"I came back for Cassie and Alfie, not my aunt, despite what she believes."

"Where does that leave you now?"

"Right here with you." I reach over and rest my hand on his leg. "I'm sorry you have to deal with the aftermath of the emotional damage from my ex. It wasn't fair to you."

"I'm not sorry. It just means words won't be enough. I'll show you how a real man treats a woman. Every day. And one day my love for you, shown through my actions, will drown his out."

"They're already starting to."

"That's not enough. I want you to forget the other life and live in this one with me."

"You talk as if we're already set in stone. As if we're eternally meant to be."

A sliver of a smile appears, that arrogance I tease him about, but secretly, love shines through. "I've never felt like this about anyone. We're what legends are made of, written in the stars for all time. There's no shaking me. I've had a taste of forever, and I'm not willing to lose you now."

"What does forever taste like?"

"It tastes like you, Hannah. Wildflower and cinnamon."

Oh God. How I love this man.

30

Jet

Two weeks.

We've worked long days and sometimes into the night. With ten songs recorded, we have one week left to record the last three tracks and wrap up this album on our end. Then our music is in the hands of the great musical gods themselves.

Being here in Ojai has been a nice break from the grind of playing five or six nights a week to get by. I don't have to worry about money for the time being. The advance was enough to sustain for a while, though not enough to retire.

But who's looking to retire? This has been amazing. Being around the members of The Resistance has fueled my ambition. My brothers are stoked. We want this. We want the career, the fans, the money, the life that they can afford. We want it all. I want it for me, Alfie, and Hannah.

So I'll play this fucking guitar into the ground ten, twelve, fourteen hours a day to get the songs right. Other than breaks and the two days off we've had, I haven't been able to do a lot of things like go to the beach or visit some of the touristy sights. But I did take Alfie and Hannah on a surprise trip to Disneyland.

Standing in the studio today makes me glad we got to do something fun together as a family.

Family.

My family. That's why I'll work this hard. I'll do anything to give them the life they deserve.

Johnny stands next to me with his guitar in hand, learning the song by watching me play. "Hit the twelfth fret on that last note," I say, checking out his finger positioning. Alfie's taken over the captain's chair in the sound room, and from the looks of it, he has been talking the tech's ear off.

I check my watch. Hannah was supposed to be here twenty minutes ago. "Can you give me five?"

"Yeah, sure. I think I've got it. It's a good melody. Did you write it alone or with your brothers?"

"That riff is mine. Rivers has a lot of cool ones he wants to incorporate into some songs."

"That's a lot of talent for one family." The drums are hit, the bass booming. We both look back at Tulsa rockin' out. Dex looks pleased, proud even. "Tulsa sounds good. I think it was smart to move him to the kit."

"Watch out, *Rock Magazine*. You might have your next Drummer of the Decade back there."

Johnny laughs. "Just don't say that to Dex. Drummers are a sensitive bunch. It will fuck up his day, and he'll get an attitude."

I set my guitar on the stand and tell him I'll be back in five. With two fingers, I point at the door so Alfie understands to meet me in the hall. When I leave the studio, he's already there and running up the stairs. "Come on, buddy. Let's go see if Hannah's in the guesthouse."

Once we're outside, he runs free across the lawn and down the slight hill. He beats me long before I make it. When I open the door, I find Alfie hugging Hannah, who's on the couch. Her face is streaked with tears and her eyes puffy from crying. "What's wrong?"

"It's my family."

Family.

I want to yell that I'm her family, but I don't.

She says, "My father . . ."

"What happened, Hannah?"

"He's siding with my aunt." She looks at Alfie, and says, "Let's go outside and play, okay?"

Alfie's worries disappear, and he asks, "Can we play tag?"

Getting up, she takes my hand and replies, "Jet and I need to talk, bud. Let's just go outside and you can run around."

Holding hands reminds me again that we are truly the worst kept secret, and Alfie either supports us together or doesn't think twice about seeing two people in love. We still have to talk to him about what's going on between Hannah and me, but for now, I need to know what's going on with her father.

Alfie is already climbing the playscape when we walk up the hill. Sitting down on a bench, she says, "My father is giving Eileen the money to fight me and you for custody."

How can he side against his own daughter? *Fucker.* "How do you know?"

"He called me." She looks at her phone with expectation. Only a black screen is seen. "I thought he was calling me to talk to me, maybe he was checking on me or was worried since we hadn't talked or saw each other in a while."

I wrap my arm around her. "He doesn't matter. I understand you're hurting, but he's an asshole, baby. You don't need him. Anyway, I have the advance for the album. I'll use every penny to fight for Alfie. There's no way in hell they're going to take him away from me."

Standing abruptly, she walks a few feet and then turns back. "Where does that leave me, Jet? You're his father. I'm not his mother."

"It leaves you exactly where you're meant to be, with me and Alfie. It doesn't matter that you didn't give birth to him. You are a mother figure to him. You're the only mother in his life."

"But I have no rights."

"You have Cassie's wishes. Those matter."

"I have no money. I have no job. I don't even have a place to live." Her hands go to the top of her head. "What am I doing?" She starts to cry, but when she sees Alfie nearby, she walks back to me. Standing next to me with her back to the playscape, she wipes away her tears.

I reach up and take her hand. When she looks down, I say, "Unlike the custody hearing, my love doesn't come with any conditions. I'll take the bad with the good. I'll take you broke or making money. Happy. Sad. Calling me out on my dumb puns. I'll take the way you love with your whole being, the way you love me and the way you love *our* son. I'll take it all as long as I get you."

Sitting down on my lap, she hugs my neck and kisses the shell of my ear, and then whispers, "The words *I love you* don't feel like enough for how I feel about you."

When I catch Alfie's eyes on us, I say, "Hey, Alfie? C'mere."

He runs over and sits on the bench next to me. Patting his back, I stop wasting time and start claiming the life I want. "Hey buddy, I love Hannah."

"I love Hannah too," he says with a smile as if we've found something in common.

We have. I add, "I want Hannah to live with us. Since it's our home, I thought maybe we could ask her together."

His eyes go wide, the sunshine highlighting the happiness inside. "Yes. Yes. Yes, please. Please, Hannah. Live with us. Then I wouldn't have to live at Grandma's."

Hannah's expression falls, and she touches his cheek. "You don't like living there?"

He shakes his head, and I'm about to speak, but he says, "Mommy's gone, and I want my books, but I don't like feeling sad, and when I'm there, I do."

If I were listening to an adult, it would have been a lot of beating around the emotional bush, but this kid nails his feelings and speaks his truth.

Hannah says, "I'll get your books. I'll make sure I do."

I wish I could give him some guarantees, but nothing is final until the judge rules in my favor. With Hannah's father stepping in to fund this feud, I need to talk to someone who knows more about the legality of this situation. "You can go play, kiddo."

He runs off as if we were holding up his fun all along. I look at my woman, holding her on my lap. "We were never on opposing sides. You and I want the same thing—what's best for that little boy. Your aunt just wants to win. This is not about slow and steady. This is about a full-on war. I'm not going to lose my son, and I need you by my side when we walk into that courtroom."

"I'll be there. I'll be whatever you need me to be, babe." Glancing once at Alfie, she says, "You called him *our* son."

"He is. He's *our* son, Hannah. Will you raise him with me?"

She's going to cry again. At least I can tell these are

happy tears. Her head falls to my shoulder, and her arms tighten around me. "Where have you been all my life?"

"Right where you left me."

A gentle smile graces her face. "Will you ever forgive me for not staying that next morning?"

"There's nothing to forgive. You had your reasons for leaving, but I had mine for wanting you to stay."

Cupping my face, she leans down and touches her nose to mine. "You had reasons for me to stay?"

"I did, baby. I had many."

"Tell me just one, Jet Crow, and I'll be yours forever."

"I like the way you look in my bed."

She tilts back, laughing. Swinging her hair to the side, she looks beautiful in the sunshine. "Does everything always end in sex with you?"

"No, sex was just the beginning, baby. The end remains to be seen."

"I can't wait."

I kiss her and lean back. "Hey," I say, giving her a little squeeze. "I'm sorry about your father."

"I should have expected it."

"That doesn't make it right."

"No," she says. "It just makes it what it is."

"What are you going to do?"

"I'm going to fight him with you."

I stand and set her on her feet again. "I should probably get back." I kiss her cheek and with my lips pressed to hers, I say, "I love you, Hannah Nichols."

"I love you, Jet Crow."

"Hey Alfie," I call out. "You coming with me back to the studio or hanging here with Hannah?"

"Hannah." He giggles, sliding down the slide.

"Okay, I tried to tempt him away. You win, Ms. Nichols. See you later, gators."

A kiss is blown my way, and I reach up to catch it because the prettiest girl I've ever seen loves me.

THE THREAT from her father and her aunt was taken seriously, but not enough. A letter arrived summoning Hannah to return to Austin with Alfie immediately. I thought it was unwarranted. We only have a week left, but Ivan Nichols doesn't play nice. He lawyered up against his own daughter.

Hannah talked to the lawyer she and her aunt were using, but Eileen fired him. He gave Hannah some free advice—return to Austin to show our cooperation and willingness to put Alfie first.

"The game has changed," I say, trying to reassure her two days after we received the letter.

"How are we going to fight them, Jet? My father's a very wealthy man."

"Yet he never helped."

"He helped me but only on his terms."

"That's not how parenting works. If we don't have that love . . . My father left when I was little. I never felt a hole in my life because my mother's love filled it. You don't need the man who helped create you. You just need to find the love that fills your soul. Alfie and I love you. I'm not sure if that's enough. Only you can know that. But you have us, and we'll help you however you need."

"I don't deserve—"

"You deserve everything good. You just believed their lies for too long."

"I saw the truth in you, and I fell in love." She snuggles up to me on the couch but looks over at Alfie who has teamed up with Tulsa to play pool against Rivers. "We'll leave tomorrow because I don't want to waste legal fees fighting this. My lawyer said he would discount his fee for us for the final hearing. He knows the case. I think we should stick with him."

I'm selfish. "I don't want you to go." I look behind us when Rivers laughs loud enough to get our attention. Alfie's a Crow. He fits right in. Teasing Tulsa, the three of them remind me of when I hang with my brothers. "I think you're right. I like having him near. I like this routine we've fallen into, but the advance isn't enough to fight a long drawn out legal battle."

"We won't have to," she says, resting her hand on my chest and looking at me. "My attorney said he wants to recommend custody remain with you with my support. If we want, we can ask the court to appoint an attorney for Alfie. Someone to represent *his* best interest as well, but I don't think we need to. The judge will see that we're a family. That matters."

"I'm counting on it."

"You showed up when no one thought you'd even care." The pressure of her hand over my heart brings me comfort. She kisses the edge of my jaw and whispers, "I know what you're thinking. I see it in your eyes. You want to fight and so do I, but you need to stay and finish the album. We'll go, and everything will be okay, but know that I'll miss you."

Closing my eyes, I savor the feel of her lips on my face. Tilting my head up, I want to see her gorgeous eyes. "I'll fly back as soon as we're done."

"We'll be waiting for you."

I kiss her quick and shift to get up. "I want to spend some time with Alfie before you guys go."

She settles down onto the couch as I walk around. "Alfie, how about you and me versus your uncles?"

"Yes!" he exclaims, running into my arms. "I want Daddy on my team."

Tulsa and Rivers do a double take and then look at each other with grins on their faces. *Daddy.* I freaking love when he calls me that. "So which stick do you want to use?"

I set Alfie down, and he takes off to grab a stick from the rack, giving me a chance to check on Hannah. Resting on her elbow, she watches us over the back of the couch with a smile on her face. Keeping her voice low to keep things between us, she says, "Go get 'em, Daddy."

I've already won. She and Alfie are my prize.

31

Jet

My world left on a plane two days ago. Alfie and Hannah. Hannah and Alfie. We've been a family for too short a time to have it ripped away.

I'm booted in the ass, and Rivers says, "Play the fucking intro, Jet."

Snapping back to reality, I look up to find all the guys in the studio standing with their arms crossed and staring at me. Not one friendly face found in the bunch. "Sorry. From the top."

No breaks come for another hour, and when I go to smoke out back, I'm followed by Derrick Masters—guitarist for The Resistance. He's not been around much since he's not producing our album like Johnny, Dex, and Tommy. He's sat in a few times, though, and drank and jammed with us afterward. He's a badass musician with the fastest fingers I've ever seen move across a fretboard.

My cigarette isn't even lit when he sits in a chair, keeping some distance. I nod, acknowledging him. "What's up, man?"

"Getting fresh air, like you, even though you're the one polluting it."

He doesn't laugh and neither do I. Since Hannah and Alfie left, I've been smoking more than I ever did before. At this rate, I can't imagine quitting. It's the only thing I have right now to help keep me calm. It used to be my music. But with Alfie and Hannah gone, the pressure of trying to get custody, the album along with this interview we're doing tomorrow, nothing else is working.

Derrick says, "Want to talk about it?"

"Not really." I walk a little farther, down the steps, and stand on the grass. Johnny Cash's "I Walk the Line" is heard in the distance, and I watch the horse working its way over to the neighbor's pasture at the back of the property. I don't know what that's about, but I don't think I'll ever see a weirder sight than that.

I take a drag and look over my shoulder. Derrick sits, soaking up the sun. "Fine. Let's talk about it."

"I know what it's like to be where you are now."

"Where am I?"

"You're caught between this dream that seems too good to be true, questioning your abilities on this instrument that's gotten you this far, and where your heart used to be."

I tap my chest. "It's right here."

"No, it's not. It's in Texas, but we need it to be here, to be heard in the music. You told us she's fine. Your kid's fine. Don't get distracted from the right you've earned to be here."

"How do I focus?" *How do I not think about them?*

"They're with you." He taps his temple and then his heart. "They're just not physically here. I know you have a lot on your mind right now, and these concerns for her have weighed on you for the past few days. But she'd want you to be present at the moment, not worrying about her, which doesn't do anybody any good anyway."

He moves a little closer but still keeps some space between us. "We're the same age, you and me. I was picked out of obscurity and suddenly living a life most dream about. You know why they chose me to join the band?"

"Why?"

"Because I had nothing to lose, and I played that way."

"I have everything to lose."

"That's what makes your music different from mine. You have the soul I was missing in my earlier days. It's something I had to learn."

"So you want me to learn to play like nothing else matters?"

"No, I want you to channel the wasted energy you're expending and pour it back into your music where it belongs. Call your girl. Call your son. Then give us three good days, and you can be on the first plane back on the fourth."

He starts to walk inside, but the guy's a mystery, so I ask, "What's your story?"

"My story's too long to tell on a ten-minute break, but if you'd asked me five years ago, it would have been full of highs and lows and a lot of rebellion. Asking me today, I think it's a lot like yours in some ways. I've had a few surprises along the way, but I eventually found my way. You will too."

I know he's right. Hannah's had no news since her return. Eileen and Hannah's father, Ivan, haven't even bothered to see them or call after they found out she returned.

They don't care about her or my son. They just want to control them.

I have to trust that she would tell me if something's wrong. It's her family I don't trust.

Texting her, I type: *I miss you.*

Her response comes fast: *Good.*

I laugh, and type: *That's all I get?*

Her: *If I start now, I'll never finish. There are just too many things I miss about you to text them all.*

Me: *Good.*

Her: *LOL*

Her: *I miss you.*

Me: *What happened to all the other things?*

Her: *Figured YOU encompassed everything and went with it.*

Me: *I'll give that to you. How are you?*

Her: *I'm helping Alfie with his workbook. I think we should re-enroll him in school since we're back sooner. He's missed three days more than allowed, but we've stayed on track with the homeschooling, so I can petition the absences.*

Me: *I agree. I wish I were there to help.*

Her: *Don't worry about us. We're fine. Just be your amazing self, finish the album, and come back to us.*

Me: *I love you. YOU encompasses all of you.*

Her: *I love you. That's the all-encompassing YOU too. Call you later.*

Derrick was right. They're here in my heart. Now I can focus. Now I will make them proud.

I go inside, tucking my phone into my back pocket, and grab a bottle of water on the way back down to the studio. The guys are settling back in here and in the booth. Tulsa asks, "You with us, bro?"

"I'm with you." I am too. All in and focused. I sling my strap over my shoulder and settle my guitar in my hands.

Dex comes over the speaker. "Ready to work?"

I look back at Rivers. "Let's do this."

Then I give a nod to Tulsa, who counts us in. "Four. Three. Two. One."

32

Hannah

Staring at the TV, I've lost track of what cartoon we're watching. My mind has been wandering for the past hour.

My gaze shifts to the framed photo of Cassie on the bookcase. The air becomes stale with her lost life and how isolated we are from our family and from Jet. The loss of Alfie's mom being there for him, watching him grow up and love, and just being his amazing self hangs over my head, clawing at my heart and making me feel guilty. But what's troubling me is how we got here—why did Eileen turn against us?

I love Alfie so much that it's inconceivable for me to imagine Eileen loves him less—her flesh and blood, the legacy of her daughter that lives on.

She says she wants custody but then doesn't bother to come see him or even ask us over. This is so confusing and twists my heart. Something's wrong—more than Cassie's death. This mission to destroy Jet ultimately makes no sense if she really doesn't want to see her grandson. Does it bother

her that Jet cares? That he stepped up? That if he'd been told, he would have been there all along? Why would she ever want a child to have less love in his life?

I hate her. I hate her for keeping Alfie from his father. I hate her for keeping Jet in the dark about his son. I hate her for treating me like I mean nothing to her. I hate her. I just hate her, but I hate that I feel this much anger, this much discord toward my aunt.

Alfie's been asking for his books again and seeing an available spot on the bookcase, I realize I need to get them for him. A confrontation with her is worth it when it's something good for him. He misses his mom. He needs those books to hold since he can't hold his mother.

I get up and open the front door, not wanting to darken the air that Alfie needs to breathe. The cartoons still play inside, but I sit on the swing outside.

My fingers run over the places I remember Jet's touching that night I came over, the night I foolishly thought I wasn't in love with the man. *I was.* I was the minute I saw him on that stage.

There was no saving me, my heart already his the moment he opened his mouth and sang that first song. That first night feels like forever ago as his fingers skated over me, each of my heartbeats becoming notes he played in his melody. Sultry. Sexy. Rolling the words he was singing around on his tongue as if they were me.

The lights shined in his eyes, but somehow, he found me. A girl lost in a shadowed sea of people. He found me like I found him as if we were always meant to be.

There was no reason I should have been out that night. A fight with my aunt made me walk out, trying to forget my life, and walk into the bar just as the opening act ended. *The*

Crow Brothers came on just as two shots of Fireball began warming me through.

I never intended to stay. But once they took the stage, I couldn't leave. As soon as Jet held the microphone, I knew he was singing to me, for me, because of me. And I did what I swore I would never do. I fell quickly for a musician, but not because of his voice or the way he held me captive throughout their set. It was because when the lights shined on him just right, I could see he was just like me.

Jet Crow sang about drunken nights under a moon tower and having his brothers' backs. But he also sang about finding something that was missing, not knowing what it was until it walked right in.

When the set ended, I ordered another shot for the singer—

"Hello?"

I look up, my shoes dragging along the wood porch until the swing comes to a stop. A woman stands on the top step. Her bleached hair is smooth instead of teased. Her lips are nude instead of being deep red. There's no cleavage pushed up under some too tight shirt, and her skirt is church appropriate. She looks different than I remember, but I know who she is from the other times I've seen her. *Marcy.* Before I have time to brace myself with concern to why she's standing in front me, she asks, "Is Jet here?"

Standing up, I move toward the door I left open. I reach in and close it enough to hide Alfie from her view. "No, he's not."

"Oh, darn." She looks at her watch like she's late for something more important.

"Why are you here?" I can't control my rude tone. This woman is dangerous because of her connection to Hunter, but also because the first time I saw her, she was clawing at

Jet for his attention. So I save the courtesies for someone who deserves them.

A quick onceover covers me from head to toe and once more for good measure it seems. I'm not dressed particularly nice, not realizing I had to prove my worthiness to be here to a woman who was a two-time thing for him. I'm too exhausted to make an effort and play these games.

Then the clouds seem to clear, and she says, "I'm sorry."

"You're sorry?"

"I'm sorry for bringing Hunter to the house that night. I had no idea about you and him until I saw it—the fear in your eyes, the painful memories, the . . . I'm just sorry. He used me to get to Jet and Johnny Outlaw."

"If you weren't in on his plan, you don't have to apologize. I just hope that night showed you what you were dealing with when it comes to him. He's not a good person."

"He hit me in the car when we left. I hit him twice as hard back, then he stopped the car and pushed me out the door, leaving me there." She looks ashamed. *Shame.* I remember feeling the same. Sometimes I still do. I shouldn't, but I'm a work in progress.

"You didn't deserve that."

"It was the wake-up call I needed, though. My life had been spiraling out of control for a while. Hitting that street was my rock bottom. The next day, I went home for a few weeks. I'm going back to San Antonio tonight, but I owed Jet an apology. I owe you one too. I'm glad you were here."

"Thank you. I appreciate that. I'm sorry Jet's not here, but I can tell him or . . ." As much as I don't want women texting or calling Jet, I trust her. "Or you can call him."

"Not sure if that's wise." She gets it. "Do you mind passing along the message for me?"

"Not at all." We stand there in awkward silence, so I

break it because she deserves credit for making the effort to make amends. "Your hair is pretty like that."

She touches it and looks down, feeling shy from the compliment. I can see how we may not be alike on the outside, but on the inside, we have a few things in common. Holli's words ring back through my head about learning to take compliments. I get what she meant. I am enough. I am enough because I like who I am. I am enough because Jet loves me. Despite the prickly parts, he always finds my soft side. "You deserve to be treated well, Marcy. Find someone who loves you for who you are and not who you know."

When she turns to go down the stairs, she stops. "Thank you, and Hannah?"

Standing there, I almost expect the showdown that never happened. "Jet's an amazing man, but you're an amazing woman too. I'm glad he found you."

"Thank you."

We don't hang out and chitchat or become besties, but I go back inside and feel happier that we've both found our way. But more importantly, when I sit on the couch and Alfie climbs onto my lap, I've found him. I didn't know if I'd ever be a mother, but I've been given this child to raise, and he's become my heart.

And soon, Jet will return to us, to his home, to our hearts right where he belongs. Together, this is family.

My family.

The only family I need.

33

Hannah

I knocked twice just to be polite, but my aunt doesn't answer her door, so I let myself in. I'm here after promising Alfie I would finally come get his books while he's at school. The time had come because Jet flies home tonight.

If he were here, he'd insist on coming with me, and I don't want him and my aunt together. That war would end in bloodshed. Since the custody hearing is coming up, it's best to keep them apart.

I have to be quick. In and out. If I can avoid her, that's probably best as well. I'm in no mood to fight, and there's no way she's not going to start one with me.

I don't see the books in his room. I dig around and then find one on his nightstand. I grab it and toss it in the backpack, but anxiety fills my stomach because I realize if the books aren't in his room, that means they're in Cassie's. Her room is off-limits . . .

Alfie. It's for Alfie. Cassie would want him to have his

favorite books because he shared them with his mother. Eileen will understand, but maybe if I'm super quick, she'll never know I was here.

It's been a few months since my cousin's death, and the room still smells of her perfume and the faint scent of cleaner that was used to keep things sterile. I tiptoe in as if I'll wake her and try to avoid looking at the bed. I remember the last time I saw her and some of the things we talked about before she died.

Eileen was at the grocery store, so I asked the questions I'd always wondered and had never gotten an answer before. "How did you come up with Alfie's name?" I asked.

Cassie had a few rough nights and was struggling to keep her eyes open, though she held my hand tightly in hers as if begging me to keep her there, to keep her awake. We all feared she'd drift off to sleep and never wake up, but over the past few days, I had prayed she'd go peacefully. A smile, though weak, shined on her face. "I had the worst crush on Jude Law."

I had no idea how the two were related, and before I had time to ask, she added, "Jet is Alfie's father's name."

Her lids dipped closed, and I was relieved. If I'd been standing, I would have stumbled. Jet. Not a common name. I was always curious if it was possible that she knew the same Jet I'd met and fallen for him as I had. Walked away with more than the regret that I didn't stay. She walked away with a baby.

My thoughts spun around my head. I'd heard such bad things about Alfie's dad—lowlife, love 'em and leave 'em, heartless— which was why I struggled to connect that Jet to my Jet. The name may be uncommon, but how they described him could never be the man I'd met. He was nothing less than caring and responsive, romantic, and kind.

She said, "Promise me you'll find him and tell him about Alfie."

"Cassie—"

Her grip on my hand tightens, and the words rush from her mouth through heavy breaths. "Promise me, Hannah. Promise me."

"I promise."

She relaxes and says, "I have a will that my mom doesn't know about. Make sure the lawyers get it."

"Where is it?"

"Under a box in my dresser."

My gaze flicks across the room. She's been bedridden for at least a month now. She says, "Alfie put it there for me. He knows all my secrets."

"What secrets are those?"

I know I'm not mistaken. I see the light in her eyes, the happiness shining through. "About his father."

"What about his father, Cassie? You can tell me. I won't tell your mother anything."

"She hates him. I get it. I made her hate him by sharing too much with her. But Jet and I were young, so young. I didn't know better. I just wanted my mother to help me through the breakup. I lied to her—"

Oh, my God! I remember now. Eileen came home so we stopped talking, but I remember Cassie trying to tell me everything. She lied to Eileen. She lied to her about Jet and the breakup.

I have to find her journal. No wonder Eileen was looking for it. I just hope she never found it. I go to the dresser and open the drawers until I find her box of mementos. Needing to be quick, I open it and dig through—prom flower, Alfie's christening pamphlet, a bar flyer. I stop and look at the lineup. The Crow Brothers were the opening act. With nothing that can lead me to the journal, I put the lid back on and move it aside to search the drawer.

When she passed away, I got the will as promised and her wishes inside is what sent me seeking out Jet. At the time, I didn't remember that short conversation with Cassie. I was too buried in my grief and all I could hear were Eileen's words being whispered in my ear. I owe him an apology. So many.

After searching the drawers, her closet, the nightstand, and around her bed, I know I don't have enough time to continue. I want out of here and need to remember my mission—Alfie's books. I grab the stack I find beside her bed and fill my backpack. Looking around the room once more, I don't think there's anything worth keeping other than a photo album I found with the books.

I take it and leave as fast as I can.

"Hannah?"

Jet's behind me, so I turn around. "Huh?"

"I've called your name three times."

"You have?"

"Yes." He stirs the vegetables in the pan. "What's wrong?"

"Nothing." I grip the counter behind me. "Just a lot on my mind."

"Want to share?"

I glance once more at Alfie who's been sitting on the couch for the last hour quietly reading his books. "I think I'd like a glass of wine." I don't drink much, but something's unsettled inside me that I can't pinpoint and the need to calm this twisting is strong. I check on the chicken in the oven and then grab a bottle of wine from the fridge.

Jet sets a glass in front of me and twists the cap. I start to pour when Alfie says, "Here it is. My favorite part."

Seeing him so content, so happy makes me happy. "You're such a good reader. Will you read it to us?"

He says, "I can't read what Mommy writes sometimes. Her letters are curly."

Jet asks, "Your mom wrote it?"

Alfie nods. I'm fast, sitting next to him as soon as I reach him. "Show me what your mommy wrote."

Opening the book wider, there are pages of handwritten notes tucked between the pages of the nursery rhyme book. My hand covers my mouth as I try to hold in my surprise.

Jet's leg presses to mine as he leans over us and reads. "Jet Mercury Crow. This is about me."

Alfie nods again with even more excitement. "Mommy told me all about you and said I would know you when I met you." He holds up a picture of Jet laughing. Looks like something from a magazine or article that was printed from a computer. That is why he ran to him straight away when they first met. "That you'd want to be my daddy."

"I do, buddy."

I look up at him, his hand running through his hair and the other rubbing the inside corners of his eyes. He's standing, but I still wrap my arm around his legs. I want him to know I'm here for him however he needs.

Alfie hands him the notes, and Jet begins to read, "I fell in love with your daddy the first time we met. And he loved me . . ."

My heart begins to ache, and I bring my arm back to my side. I'm not sure what to do or how to feel. I feel like an invader into this private moment. But worse, I feel like an impostor, a replacement in this family. *My family.*

Standing up, I walk to the front window and stare out as he reads silently while sharing some lines here and there. They had their ups and downs, but she was in love with him.

He was recording an album. He explains they never did finish due to money and time, so it became their EP. I hear him, but the words become muffled as I shrink inside myself, wanting to hide, knowing I was never supposed to have this life, a life I've come to love. This is a life of dreams come true and now . . . I'm unworthy of it just like so many have said. She was supposed to be in my shoes. Cassie deserved this happiness, not me.

"Hannah?" My eyes meet Jet's, worry creasing his forehead. "Did you hear that?"

"No. I'm sorry. What?"

Getting up from the couch, he comes over and wraps his arm around my waist. With the paper held in front of me, he says, "Second paragraph."

I read it to myself.

I'm sorry for pushing him away. I only wanted what was best for him. I wanted to see his dreams come true and not be the reason they're taken away. He's an upstanding man who would drop everything if he knew, but what he has to offer the world and his child later is worth more.

Turning into him, I rest my head on his chest. Cassie lied to everyone to help Jet make his dreams come true. "She knew you'd quit performing to be there for her, so she made it so you would never look back."

"She started that fight with me to seal our fate, and I fell for it."

"These are notes from her journal. Eileen's been searching for it, and here, they were hidden in Alfie's books." I see that kid with the big smile sitting on the couch not even realizing how epically big this is. "You knew, pipsqueak, didn't you?"

"I pinky promised Mommy I wouldn't tell anyone."

Jet says, "You did good, Alfie." Giving my waist a little squeeze, he kisses my head. "Read the next paragraph."

I wrap my arm around him and continue to read. "Hannah Lynn Nichols, my cousin. I think she's in love with Jet. She spent a week reliving every moment with me. She never said his name, but I knew from how she described him. That's destiny, Alfie. You're going to be the one who brings them back together. If he can make her that happy after being together once, imagine how happy she'd be if they had a lifetime together."

Jet whispers into my hair, "You should have told me. I knew I loved you then."

"I wanted you together too. Did I make Mommy happy?"

We turn to Alfie at the same time, and Jet says, "You did."

"You brought us together, Alfie," I say, "just like she wanted." Tilting toward Jet, I look up. "She saw through it all."

"I don't like that I didn't know about Alfie. I missed a lot and have a lot to make up for, but we're getting there. As for Cassie, she was good for me when my mom died. She may have loved me, and I loved her in that I cared about her, but it's not the same as what we have. I'm *in love* with you, Hannah."

"I'm in love with you, too." The lump returns to my throat when I read the last part, and I tear up all over again. "My sweet Alfie, you will be with your daddy, but you will have Hannah. She loves you like I do, like I always will, but she'll be the mommy you need when I'm not there."

Like he knew already, he nods. "She told me that." Maybe he did know all along.

"About me being your mom?"

Nodding again, he says, "She said I can call you mommy if I want, and it won't hurt her feelings."

I sit next to him. "You can call me that if you like."

"Okay." He pops up and off the couch like I didn't just have the most emotional conversation of my life. Kids keep the levity in check.

Once Alfie goes to bed, Jet and I sit quietly in his room going through every book and pulling the journal papers from between the pages. It's a big stack, and something we'll always cherish. I'll protect them and keep them safe for Alfie. He knows when he reads them, he gets to be with his mommy again in a way. It's quite a gift she has given him.

"Cassie was hiding these from Eileen. It was the only way she could tell Alfie about you. She was preparing him to be with you, to accept you, and love you."

"She was preparing him for her to be gone and for us to be together."

"This could have been her sitting here with you."

"No," he says, rubbing my leg. "We were kids. Neither of us knew what it meant to be in love. Whereas, I knew I loved you from the very beginning. You didn't step into her position in my heart, Hannah. She never claimed a spot. Only you. Just as it should have been. Only you."

I rest my head on his stomach, staring up at the pages I hold above my head. "This is proof, beyond the written will, that she wanted you to have custody of him."

"Yes. I'm showing the lawyer in the morning. But the one thing I don't understand is why Eileen is so adamant about winning custody. She must have known her daughter's wishes. She read it in the will. Who I was at nineteen, hormonal and high-strung isn't who I am now. So we had a fight. Would her mother really still hold the grudge from lies she was told?"

"Seems extreme." My eyes scan the pages, and then I see it. Sitting straight up, I say, "Oh, my God."

"What?"

I point at the page. "It's here. All right here."

34

Hannah

The judge looks back and forth between our side of the table and theirs. My aunt with her expensive lawyer by her side stares at us. Her eyes on me are dull and emotionless, not even anger seen in the dark centers. It's as if she doesn't know me at all.

I guess she doesn't anymore. *Maybe she never did.*

I don't feel the loss either. I feel sorry for her. I feel sorry for how she'll have no one but my father to care about her. I feel sorry that she'll miss out on the love I have to give. But I feel most sorry that she won't get to see that amazing grandson of hers grow up. Her hate will keep her at a safe distance from ever being in our lives.

She thinks she's going to win because her lawyer charges more per hour than ours. The judge doesn't take that into consideration, though.

So as we sit at this table, and the judge is about to begin, I just feel sad for the woman who was once my aunt and now is nobody to me.

Our clasped hands are starting to sweat, our nerves getting the better of us. I pull my hand away but leave it on his thigh. *I'm here for you* whispers between our touches. *I love you* felt in each beat of our hearts.

The judge stacks a file of papers loudly on the table in front of her and says, "I've reviewed everything from the will to each of your individual wishes. I've talked to Alfred Jet Barnett about his wishes because it matters what he thinks. We are here to find what is the best environment and situation for the child. We've already taken financial stability into account, and upon Mrs. Barnett's request, we did a secondary formal evaluation of Mr. Crow's assets and monies."

I don't know how much Jet's advance was for the album. I don't know what his royalty cut will be after it releases. So I'm surprised when the judge says, "Congratulations on your record deal. That's very exciting and the money in the account at the time of evaluation was recorded in the file."

"Thank you," he says, his voice deep but soothing, calm even though I know he's worried.

The judge continues, "The situation has had a dramatic change that was not predicted, but is in the child's best interest so I'm ruling full custody be given to Mr. Crow. As Ms. Nichols has given him her full support, no formal visitation schedule will be granted at this time. As a family, it is up to you to make sure this child receives the love where it's given." She looks at my aunt. "And if it's given, which I hope it is, please put your differences aside for this child."

Jet's head drops down, and he rubs his brow. His worries are expelled from his chest as he breathes out and relief is inhaled. "Thank God," he mumbles under his breath. Taking my hand, he brings it to his mouth, kissing me openly.

My aunt's hands slam down on the glass table between us. "No!"

Her lawyer is quick to warn her, "It's not over."

Jet and I both turn back to the judge not sure what else there is. She says to us, "We understand that sometimes money can create issues among family members. Thank you for providing a copy of the insurance policy for the records—"

Eileen asks, "What? Where did you get that, Hannah?"

"I didn't. I haven't actually seen the policy, but you have, haven't you?"

"That's none of your business."

"Alfie's my business. Cassie told us who the sole heir of her policy is, and it's not you."

Jet's relief turns to rage. "That's the only reason you wanted my son? Not because he's your own blood from your only daughter, but because he inherits a policy she was wise enough to take out right after having him and before she had cancer. Think about that, Eileen." He stands, his fingers whitening as he presses on the table. "A twenty-year-old girl knew to protect her child, to take care of him in case anything happened to her. The question that remains is why she wouldn't include you. But I think you've made your motive and intentions more than clear. She knew you best and didn't trust you with her son or his inheritance. That's what you're left to live with."

"Mr. Crow, sit down," the judge cautions.

He does, but never takes his eyes off my aunt. She slides a file to our lawyer and then one to Eileen's. "Alfred loves you very much. My opinion in custody cases is based on the children's thoughts and preferences. Alfie has a lot of wonderful things to say about you and Ms. Nichols, who has helped him work his way through a very difficult time in his life. His love for you is obvious in the way he speaks about both of you. Take care of him and live happy lives. This case is resolved and will be recorded as I've already stated, giving full legal rights to Mr. Crow."

She wraps up with the formalities so they're on the record, but then our lawyer taps our arms, telling us to go.

The last time I walked out of the courthouse, it was with Eileen by my side. This time, it's different. Not because I chose Jet over her, but because she chose money over blood. I'm tempted to stop and talk to her, extend an olive branch to make peace. I hate feeling unsettled in my emotions and the pain that frequently circulates inside me.

I don't stop.

Holding Jet's strong and protective hand, I walk by his side, knowing I've found the love I never thought I deserved. He saw me through the sadness and the pain of my past. He loved me when I didn't love myself. He taught me we are worthy, whether together or apart.

I am enough.

Three Months Later . . .

I'm restless in this sterile hospital waiting room. After three days of being here, I need good news. "I thought a stroke affected his motor skills and his speech. Why isn't he coming back from this?"

The doctor replies, "Your father has had a series of minor heart attacks. We were waiting for the tests to come back to confirm our suspicions."

"What does that mean?"

"It means we keep him here a little longer and supervise. He's awake if you want to visit with him. The nurse will be in with his dinner shortly."

"Thank you." When the doctor walks away, I hold out my hand to Alfie. "Come on. We can go back in now."

"I want to go home."

"I know, but let's stop by for a few minutes to say hi." Going home to an empty house isn't something I'm particularly looking forward to either. It's a lose-lose situation.

He huffs expressing his unhappiness and drags his feet. "Your dad will be home tomorrow."

"I want him home now."

Jet's been gone for two weeks doing promotions for the single they released. The day after hearing it played on the radio, he had to hop a flight to LA for interviews and to meet DJs around the country. "So do I, buddy."

He wanted to come home, but I told him to stay. This is what he was working so hard to do, and he had to be there to support his dream and his brothers.

Once we're in the hospital room, my father is awake. "Hi." I almost called him Dad but stopped myself. I don't want to be that person. I don't want to live with grudges or regrets. It's been a daily battle for me for years. After walking out of the courthouse with full custody, I hadn't heard from my dad. Not until I got the call from his secretary that he had collapsed during a meeting. The anger suddenly subsided, and my heart softened. "How are you feeling, Dad?"

Even though I know he can't speak, his blinks at least let me know he hears me. When he looks at the table next to him, I track his gaze to a pen and pad. "You want to write?"

Fast blinks and a grunt. Yes.

I move the rolling table in front of him, and he moves his right arm, picking up the pen. Alfie is restless and bored, making noise over on the chair behind me as I wait to see what my dad writes.

The paper is pushed toward me, and I pick it up. He's never had particularly neat handwriting, but his struggle from the stroke is evident. The two words, though, are very clear. Two words I never thought I'd hear, much less read. But now that I'm seeing them and looking up at his tear-filled eyes, I realize they are all I need.

I'm sorry.

My tears fall, landing on the note and seeping into the paper. He holds his hand out, and just as I slip mine into his, his eyes close and his body shakes. Alarms sound, the ringing making me jump.

Alfie pops up, pressing against me. "What's happening, Hannah?"

The terror in his voice causes me to turn and grab him, holding him to me. "I don't know."

Nurses run in, the door propped open. One turns to me. "Please wait outside the room."

"No."

When she glances at Alfie, I realize it's best for him. We wade through the nurses and get out just in time for the doctor to run in. Alfie asks, "What happened?"

"I don't know." I almost lie, telling him everything will be okay, but I can't bring myself to do it. My heart is racing, and all I want is to find someone who will lie to me.

We make it to the waiting area, and I stand, not sure what to do. Alfie goes to the basket of books. I hear him talking to me, but the words are muffled, the light too bright, my hope stolen from me.

Looking down at my hand, I'm still holding the note. The two words precious to my well-being two minutes prior feel even more sacred now. I read them over and over, tracing the lines of the black ink until each letter's complete.

I'm sorry.

I'm sorry.

I'm sorry.

I'm sorry.

I'm sorry.

A little hand covers the words. "Hannah?" Shifting my gaze, Alfie's wide eyes are on me, and he says, "I'm scared."

I bring him to me, holding him against my body and bend to hug him. "Me too."

As soon as Alfie's asleep, I start the shower and strip off my clothes. The water's not hot, but I don't care. I step under the shower spray and let the tears fall and wash down the drain.

I'm sorry.

I got those, but I will never get the three I realize I've been desperate to hear.

When I dry off, I crack the window open and sit in the chair next to it with my legs curled under me. I've tracked the moonlight crossing the yard for hours.

With a cigarette butt tucked in the corner of my mouth, I can taste Jet. *My heart. My home.* Spearmint to my cinnamon.

"I hope you're not smoking."

My eyes flicker across the dark room to the man standing in the doorway. "I wouldn't. It causes cancer."

When he comes out of the shadows, I swear Jet's ten feet tall. My big man with the bigger heart. He lifts me as if I weigh nothing and sits in the chair beneath me. "Why are you sitting in the dark with old cigarettes in your mouth?"

"Because I missed you."

Removing the butt, he puts it in the ashtray. "Is this all you have to remember me by?"

I don't know why that makes me smile and feel equally bad. "Your scent has faded from the pillow."

"I came home to remedy that."

Wrapping my arms around his neck, I lean my head on his shoulder. "He died, Jet. He died before he ever told me he loved me."

"He probably wouldn't have ever said those words to you. My guess is that he loved you in a way that he thought was enough. But in my opinion, you deserve the world, so I'll never forgive him for abandoning you." His hand warms up my leg, the other rubbing my back

My sobs are quieter, less forceful, but my hurt, this pain, still holds me hostage.

He says, "Your mom did the right thing to run. I hate that she couldn't keep you with her, but she was right to leave such a toxic environment. Somehow, you became strong within that environment."

"I wish I was weaker and had a dad who told me he loved me."

"No. Don't. You're a survivor. You survived everything you went through because you lived in spite of needing his permission. His love."

Lifting my head, I look at him, surprised by his line of logic. "You're saying how he treated me was a gift?"

"No, he treated you like shit. But you took that shit and turned it into gold. Don't let the lack of words from him ruin you. You love because you feel, not because you speak." My forehead is kissed and then my nose, my lips, my lips, my lips . . .

Sweet kisses feel good, but him holding me begins to take away some of the pain. "You're home early."

"I caught the last flight of the night out of Sacramento. I'm sorry I wasn't here sooner."

"How did it go?"

"Let's not do that. Not tonight. I'm here for you."

"I'm better now that you're home."

"I am home. Right here holding you in my arms. You're my home, wildflower."

Home.

My heart.

My home.

We don't move to do more. We don't need to. This is enough, just holding each other until the moonlight shines in someone else's yard.

35

Jet

Four months later . . .

"WE WERE THINKING you might consider going on the road with us?"

Dave's head about spins off in shock. "Me?"

"Yeah," I say.

"Why me?"

Rivers says, "Because none of us could play that Van Halen solo, and you nailed it while you were drunk."

He laughs. "I can only play it drunk."

Tulsa adds, "Then stay drunk, but we need a guitarist, and we like you."

"And you're damn fucking good," Rivers adds.

I ask, "What do you think?"

"You're paying me?" he asks, still blown away.

I drink my beer while Rivers covers the business side of

things. "We're paying a lot more than the recording studio is paying you. Plus, you'll be part of the band. The album comes out next month, and we'll be touring all winter and early spring to support it."

"Fuck." He stands. The table wobbles when he bumps it. "I'm not going to say no to that."

Tulsa shakes his hand. "You'll be an honorary Crow Bro because the band's name remains."

"Sold," he says. He shakes Rivers hand, and then I stand to shake his hand.

"I also wanted to tell you that I appreciate everything you did for Hannah. When she had no one, you stepped in. You saved her, man. I'll always be grateful for that."

"I did what any real man would do. I just wish I had been there a few minutes sooner."

He's a solid guy. Good character. Values. Badass guitar player. He's a respectable addition to the band. "You were there. That matters. Thank you."

"When you sent me the album to listen to, I was already jamming with it. It's gonna be huge, but if I'm coming on board, we'll make it epic when we play live."

"Fuck yeah, we will." Tulsa flies from the chair and orders another round of shots. When they arrive, we hold them up, and he gives the toast. "To fame, fortune, and women with big tits. To rock and roll music and mosh pits. To my brothers by birth and my brother by band, here's to us. Fuck yeah, life is grand."

The shot is downed, and the laughter begins. "You're a fucking poet, little brother," Rivers says, rubbing Tulsa's head.

"Don't mess the hair. The ladies are liking the new coif."

"I can't with this kid," Rivers says, laughing to me.

Two Months Later . . .

Hannah

I'M ABOUT to boob punch a woman if she grabs between Jet's legs again. How dare she. Not only is he mine, but he's also not a piece of man-meat for her to eat. Screw her.

I slide into the SUV, but Jet stops to sign autographs. The door is opened, and I'm called a bitch and whore. I think this is what Rochelle warned me about. Women are vicious to each other. Doesn't matter that Jet has publicly declared his love for me at two shows, in three TV interviews, and on five blogs. I'm apparently the bad guy.

I'll play the villain for him. It could make for interesting role-play in the bedroom anyway. Catwoman could be fun to his Batman.

The door opens, and Jet flies inside, his head hitting my shoulder before he rights himself. "Fuck, it's crazy out there."

"Life of a superstar."

He laughs. "Yeah, not quite."

"But getting there."

"We'll see," he banters back. "I hoped the album would do well, but I never expected this."

Slipping into a more comfortable position—straddling him—when the SUV takes off from the concert venue, I wrap my arms around his neck. "I did. All those people are discovering what I knew all along. You were born for this."

"The Resistance being tied to us and having us open for them helps."

"It's your music, babe. Your debut album hit top five on

the charts. That's why everyone is here. Not your connections. You still wrote the songs and played them."

His large hands cover my ass and squeeze. "I need you around all the time."

"Am I not going to be?" I know what he means. I just like to fish sometimes.

"We're going to be touring. I want you and Alfie with me."

"We're there then." I'm kissed, the back of my head held as he devours me kiss by kiss until I'm a writhing mess on top of him. "I want to feel you inside me, Jet." Leaning to whisper in his ear, I say, "Fuck me hard and fast in the back of this car."

I watch as his gaze goes past me to the front. A button is pushed, and the security glass slides up. "Take those jeans off before I rip them off your body."

Scrambling to get up and find room to peel these tight jeans from my body, I fall onto my knees in front of him, my ass to his legs. I'm about to get up, but he touches between my legs. "You're wet. So fucking wet for me. My horny woman. God, that's so fucking hot."

"You turn me on," I reply, lowering my head and not looking back.

"Does this turn you on?" Slowly, he slides his fingers between my cheeks and circles my anus, which tightens, though I can feel my body getting wetter from it. "Do you like me touching you here?"

My breath comes harsher, uneven, the car getting warmer as I let him take me in, and I remain wide open for him. "Yes."

"You're so dirty. So fucking sexy. You're mine, all mine, beautiful." I hear the pause at the moment, his breath deepening, all my senses hyperaware. A button is pushed, and he asks, "How long until we're back to Ojai?"

"At least an hour, sir."

"Perfect. Thank you." When Jet's hands return to my body, he says, "We have an hour to kill. What should we do?"

The tease.

What is it about musicians? Why are they so damn sexy?

I'm lifted by the hips and slide down his steel erection until I'm seated on his lap. I could stay like this for days. So full. So complete. So everything I'll ever need.

His hands are under my shirt, squeezing my breasts, and his breath covers my bare shoulder. I lift and come back down. With my eyes closed, his name comes in exhales of sin and inhales of ecstasy as I feel him in every part of me.

As I pay homage to the blissful perfection of this connection, I know it's not just the sex. That was just the spark that kindled the flame. Together, we're a full-blown blaze.

I used to worry about getting burned. Now I realize that I'm the one who handed him the match because Jet Crow ignites my soul on fire.

———

I WANT to run to him, to wrap my legs around him and kiss his face silly. It's only been a week since I've seen him, but I still want to jump him . . . I mean, jump *on* him.

I don't.

Alfie gets first dibs as I stand back and watch a son jump into his father's arms. I see the way Jet embraces him, the way he closes his eyes just to take him in. I see the smile that's big and too handsome for every woman in the world to not want him. That's what the journalists write about him.

The Crow Brothers aren't just taking the music world by storm, but they're also winning women's hearts at every stop of the tour. It's a smaller tour to launch their album, but Outlaw Records is ready to plan a large stadium tour for next summer. That means another album, but I plan to leave this summer wide open for him. I can't wait to tell him the news.

With Alfie on his back and his suitcase in hand, he comes up the steps and kisses me on the porch. "Hey," he says against my lips with that smile still on his kissable lips.

"Hey."

He cups my face and leans his forehead against mine. "I missed you."

"I missed you," I reply with a matching goofy grin. "Welcome home."

We're not inside the house, but just standing there holding each other with Alfie's arms wrapped around both of our heads. Jet says, "It's good to be home."

After lugging the case inside and showering, Jet sits at the bar across from me while I wait for the lasagna to cool on the stovetop behind me. Alfie's out back with his uncles, jumping on the trampoline, so I take advantage of the time alone and ask, "What do you think?"

"About?"

"The fame."

"The women?"

I reach across and smack his arm while he laughs. "The fame. All the attention and the women, yes."

Catching my hand before I pull back, he kisses the top of it. "I don't think of them at all because I have you at home."

Swoony. Resting on my elbows, I say, "I have news."

"Yeah?" I love that he always is genuinely interested in everything I have to say.

"I got accepted back into college for the fall semester."

"That's fantastic, baby." He gets up and comes around to hug me. "Congratulations."

I love getting lost in him and his scent. He's more spearmint than nicotine these days just like he promised. Maybe I'm becoming more spearmint instead of cinnamon as well.

"Want a beer to celebrate?"

"I'm good. Go ahead."

Grabbing a bottle from the fridge, he sits back down and rigs the cap off using the underside of the counter. "To you, Hannah." After taking a large swallow, he asks, "What are you going to study?"

"I did my basics before quitting last time, so I'm going right into my major. I've decided on social work."

The grin that appears gives me all the approval I need. "I think that's great."

"After everything, I feel like I have something to offer, something to give back. But I won't make much money."

"The first time I saw you, I could see your heart right there on your sleeve. It's what drew me to you."

Swoony all right. Although I love what he just said, I have to give him a hard time. "That's what drew you to me? My heart?"

"Okay, your killer little body, beautiful face, hair that I couldn't wait to mess up, and makeup I wanted to kiss right off your face." He gets up and comes around, pulling me by the waist right into his arms and spinning us around once and then again. "And your heart that I swore right then and there to protect. You, the all-encompassing version of *you*, drew me like a bee right to your honey."

"You sure know how to sweet talk a girl, Jet Crow."

"I'll do you one better." He pulls his shirt off in that magical way, and while I admire every damn sit-up this man finds the time to do, he says, "Eyes up here, beauty."

When I look up, there are two more crow tattoos that match the ones for him and his brothers. The two new ones are on his chest, flying high toward the sky. I'm gentle when I touch the freshly inked skin, but I can't help but want to run my fingers over the raised design. "I love them. They're different. Beautifully done. The other three represent you and your brothers. And these?"

He covers my hand with his and kisses my fingertips. "One is for Alfie."

Tears fill my eyes. "Jet . . ." My throat thickens thinking of how much this gesture will mean to his son. "He'll love it. He'll love it so much."

"I'm going to ask him if he wants to take my name. He can keep Barnett. That's a link to his mother, but I'd like him to be a Crow if he wants to be. I want him to know that he's a part of this family as much as any of us."

I squeeze this man. Holding him as tight as I can, I kiss his chest. "You are amazing."

"No. I'm just a dad who feels damn lucky to have a son."

"I love you."

"Why do you love me, baby?"

"Because you didn't just show up for him, but also for me when I needed you most."

His strong arms come around me, keeping me close. "And here I always thought you were the one who saved me."

A kiss is placed on top of my head just before I lean back. "We never needed saving. We just needed each other." I lift and kiss him.

Touching the other bird, I ask, "Is this for Dave, the honorary Crow Bro?"

"No." His arms slide from around me, and he kneels on one knee. Pulling something from his pocket, he then holds a sparkling diamond ring before me. "I was thinking about asking you to change your name as well."

The waterworks begin, but I play along anyway. "Just thinking about it?"

"No. I want you to change your name. Hannah Crow sounds really nice. What do you think?"

My gaze volleys back and forth between his eyes and the stunning ring. I love the ring, but I prefer the soulful eyes that I fell in love with, so I admire them instead. "I think it's a beautiful name."

"Hannah Lynn Nichols, I fell in love with you the moment I saw you, but it was your beautiful heart and kind soul, caring side, and feistiness that made me realize I wanted to be yours forevermore. Will you be mine and stay?"

"There's nothing I'd rather do than spend a lifetime and more with you. Yes, Jet." The tears dry as excitement takes over.

This time I jump into his arms and wrap my legs around him. I kiss him silly and find myself being kissed right back just as much.

Love.

He taught me what love really is. It's not about the words. It's about the action, about showing up and being there when someone needs you most.

Love.

I used to think it was only for those more worthy. But Jet taught me, through Holli's words, that I don't have to be anything but me. With him, I'm happy. With him, I am enough.

With him, I am home.

EPILOGUE

Jet

Hannah insisted on paying for the wedding, wanting to burn through the money she felt was tainted somehow. Eileen and Hannah were both left equal shares of her father's estate, which included mostly money he kept in banks and rarely spent.

Hannah never knew how much Ivan Nichols had amassed until the will was read.

Eight hundred thousand dollars.

Her share.

She told me she would have rather had his love.

There's not a lot anyone can say to that, so I held her a lot tighter and promised her she would never be without love again. I intend to keep that promise every day and night for the rest of my life.

The day she received the money, she paid for the wedding in full.

It's not lost on me that on a day full of love she's spending money that holds none. What's mine is hers and hers mine, but I would have liked to pay for something more than the rings. My ego doesn't need stroking . . . *often*, so I'm okay marrying a rich woman.

Anyway, with album sales skyrocketing over the past six months and our fame growing—we were nobodies last year, and this year, we're everywhere—the band's made a lot of money, more than we ever thought possible. I'm not Johnny Outlaw rich yet, but we never really have to worry again about watching our spending.

A little snag Hannah's come upon is that when you plan a wedding on a friend's estate, you find that the owners tend to be too generous. Holli loves to plan a party, and apparently, she and Johnny got married here, so her and Hannah have been gushing over the memories.

That's usually my cue to head to the studio with the guys and jam.

But today is different. The planning is over, and although I got a few hours in with the guys to record, I'm now standing in front of a large floor-to-ceiling mirror next to my son, teaching him how to tie a four-in-hand knot with the sage tie around his neck. "You almost got it that time. Want to try once more?"

"Yes," he mumbles, frustrated.

This time, I kneel beside him, and I go slower, tying my black tie while his hands mimic mine. "Dude, you did it!"

"Yes!" He fist pumps, which has Tulsa written all over it. "You were right. I just needed to be seven."

His birthday was a month ago, and we've been celebrating ever since. It's my first with him, and we went all out —Nerf battles, laser tag, cake, ice cream, and presents. Hannah pulled some from our pile to store for Christmas. She said there's a difference between spoiling him and caring for him.

The only surprise was that all the moms stayed. I thought they would just drop their kids off and go, but their kids are seven, so I get wanting to stick around. My beautiful fiancée wasn't so sure that was the reason they hung around, but she has nothing to be worried about.

Except for the money, apparently. I call her because I miss her. She sounds stressed. "You're going to look just as gorgeous as you always do," I say.

"Stop being charming. I already said yes."

"You've got a lifetime of this charm coming your way. Best prepare, my love."

"Ohh, I love preparing, especially with you." She's laughing one moment and not the next. She huffs instead. "What am I going to do with this money?"

"There are worse problems to have."

"I'm paying for Alfie's college and mine. And I'm buying a house."

"For us or investment?"

"We'll see."

"There you go," I say, trying to calm her down. "That should cover the rest of it."

The sigh I hear on the other end of the line is happy. "I'll see you in a little while?"

"I wouldn't miss it for the world."

Unlike Eileen, who was sent an invite on Alfie's request. He doesn't know she wanted his inheritance or the evil she's capable of. We haven't heard from her once since we won custody, not even on his birthday.

I'm not sure what's wrong with that woman, but her heart died the day Cassie did because a black soul is all that remains. Alfie will find out eventually, but for now, we keep our opinions to ourselves in hopes that one day she'll find a way to make amends with him.

I turn my phone off and tuck it into my pocket. Looking at Alfie sitting on the couch trying to show Tulsa how to knot his tie is quite the sight. Rivers stands by the windows looking out at the lawn where the wedding has been set up. I shove my hands in my pockets and stand alongside my middle brother. He says, "You ready for the big day?"

"I'm ready."

"No nerves?"

"No nerves." What is there to be nervous about? I've lived with Hannah for a while now. I can't imagine there will be any surprises or changes when it comes to that. "I love her so damn much." She's a Crow even without the legalities in place.

"What do you love about her?" This time, he turns and looks me in the eyes, genuinely interested in my answer.

Before now, I hadn't noticed he'd grown taller than me. Not by much, but an inch or so. My little brother isn't so little anymore. He's become a man; someone I'm not only proud to call my brother, but also my friend.

His question is easy to answer. "Everything—the good, the bad, the in between. All of her."

"Yeah?" Half a smile slides up.

"Yeah. I remember driving her back to her car. I dreaded that goodbye. Every second I felt like I was driving in the wrong direction. I should be taking her home, not letting her leave. I felt like I was losing a part of me. It was wrong. Everything about that morning was wrong except one thing."

"What?"

"When she woke up in my arms." I should feel embarrassed for admitting that. I sound like a sap, but I can be truthful with him. He's been there. He knows what I mean.

Rivers only asked for one invitation to be sent out. We

never heard back despite how much I know he held out hope. Just in case he's heard otherwise, I ask, "Is she coming?" carefully broaching the subject.

"No. I don't think so."

"Did you call her?"

"The call went to voicemail."

I give his shoulder a squeeze. "Sorry, man."

Shrugging, he replies, "It's all right. What's done is done." Turning to me, we do our handshake and then bring it in for a hug. When he pats my back, he says, "Mom would be proud of you. Hannah's a good woman."

I know she is, but it's good to have the family support behind me. He adds, "And you're a good dad. You always were."

"I'm twenty-seven, but I sound old."

"Not old. Wise. I hope I'm as wise as you at your age."

"Thanks, Riv." It's time, so I announce, "Come on, guys. It's time to get hitched."

Alfie runs up to me and hugs me. "Uncle Tulsa says I can get bird tattoos like all of you when I turn eighteen."

I shoot a glare in his uncle's direction. I'm obviously not against tattoos. "Can we let him be a kid for a few more years?"

Tulsa rolls his eyes. "Yes, Dad."

"Good, son," I say, patting his head, which spurs Alfie into a fit of giggles.

Reaching over, I wrap my arm around my youngest brother's neck and pull him into a semi-headlock and part hug. "Hey, Tuls?" He usually fights it, but this time, he stops wriggling. "You guys are the best brothers anyone could ever ask for." Releasing him, I pick Alfie up. "And you, sir, the best son a guy could ever wish for."

Alfie's arms fly around my neck, and he rests his head on my shoulder. "I love you, Daddy."

"I love you, too."

Tulsa pats my shoulder. "Thanks for being a great big brother."

We stand there, letting the quiet sneak in. We've come a long way. I'm just glad I got to experience life with these guys by my side. "We should go. I don't want to worry my bride by being late to the altar."

Hannah and I decided on a small ceremony with just a few close friends, family, and our band families. We didn't need a big party. We just need each other.

As I stand there with my best man by my side, I glance at my brothers once more who represent my family in the front row.

Johnny, Holli, and their son sit on the front row on Hannah's side. Family is who we choose regardless of relation, blood, or bone. The people who matter are here.

Her mother.

Her half-brother.

Her stepfather.

I met them yesterday when they arrived, and I see so much of her mother in Hannah. She's clever and confident, a survivor.

It's good to see some other familiar faces staring back at me who made the trek from Austin to Ojai, but it's the woman who stands at the end of the aisle that steals my attention and my heart all over again.

On Dave's arm, Hannah Lynn Nichols is an angel on earth. Her dress billows to the side as the winds blow. The sun shines off her chestnut hair bringing out the gold as it catches in the breeze under a halo of a mixture of pale and deep pink and white flowers. She walks toward me with grace, a classic eloquence and beautiful bohemian.

I'm eternally grateful to the man on her right who saved her life—not just for Hannah, but also for me—so we could share the destiny we were always meant to have.

I take her hands, looking into the blue windows of my forever. "I love you."

Hannah smiles and whispers, "I love you."

We're not supposed to be talking yet, but how can I let the moment pass me by without telling her how much she means to me? I can't.

The traditional wedding vows are read as we stare into each other's eyes. When it's time for the rings, my best man leans his head against my hip and says, "Am I allowed to talk now?"

"Yes, Alfie," I reply with a smile. "You can talk. What did you want to say?"

He moves to Hannah and tugs on the dress that hangs loosely at her hips. "Can I call you mommy now?"

"Oh Alfie," she says, kneeling and hugging him tight. "You can call me mommy whenever you want. I love you, sweetie."

"I love you, Mommy."

There's not a dry eye in the vicinity, including mine. The kid has great timing. Maybe I'll let him play drums after all.

When he returns to his spot beside me, I slip the ring on her finger. "I didn't know I was lost until I found you. In a sea of stormy weather, you are the anchor that saved me. In gratitude, I will spend my life being an anchor for you."

Her eyes were watering from what Alfie said, but the tears finally tip over her bottom lids and slide down her porcelain skin. She takes my ring, slips it on, and then looks up at me. "I could spend my days regretting walking away that day, but instead, I celebrate every day I've been given since returning. You've given me your patience and kindness, your support, and your love. But what you've given me the most is your heart and a family. Both of which I will forever honor and cherish, taking care of them with all that I am. I love you, Jet. The big encompassing you."

The I do's are done and rings are on fingers. My gaze slides from her eyes to her lips, delicate pink petals calling me home. I cup her pretty face and lean in to taste the cinnamon once again. Just before our lips meet, I spy dandelions in her hair and smile, not just because of the flowers, but because our lives our finally entwined forever.

My beautiful wildflower.
My love.
My wife.
My home.

IF YOU ENJOYED MEETING Johnny Outlaw, Holli, Dex, Tommy, Kaz, Rochelle, and the Derrick, make sure to read all about them in The Resistance and the Hard to Resist Series.

The Prologue and Chapter 1 of The Resistance is included in this book after the BONUS Epilogue.

TURN the page for BONUS SPARK.

BONUS EPILOGUE

Jet

We haven't been in Hawaii but for two hours and the first round of newlywed lovin' was good. Can't wait to see how the second round goes. Hannah promised to let me try something new in the private pool on our balcony overlooking the beach.

Naked and breathtakingly gorgeous, she reaches over me and grabs a box from the nightstand. I grab hold of her hips, ready for that second round now. But she starts laughing and swatting my hands away. Setting the box on my stomach, she says, "Open it."

"Is this a wedding gift?" I ask watching a mischievous glint spark in her eyes. *Seductress. Tease.* Flipping her down onto her back, I maneuver between her legs, already hardening again. "I thought we agreed no gifts?"

"Being married to you is gift enough, but this is something that can't wait until your birthday or our anniversary."

"What about Christmas?"

"Definitely not Christmas." After setting it on her chest, she nudges it. "Just open it."

After kissing each one of her perfect tits, I take the unusually shaped box and turn it over. "Is it a watch? You trying to keep me on time?"

"It's not a watch." She smiles. "Jet, you're impossible you know that?"

"My mom called me a knight in shining armor with a ladykiller smile."

"Your mom filled your head with nonsense," she says, laughing. "Now open it."

I lift the lid but then set it back down. "So you're saying I don't have a ladykiller smile? Are you telling me my mama just told me I was handsome because she was my mom?" I try to hold back my laughter, but fail miserably when she rolls her eyes.

"Oh my God, Jet. Just open it all right already."

"Fine. Fine." I lift the lid and look inside the long skinny white box.

I sit up still staring down at the box. Hannah rests her chin on my slumped forward shoulder, her hand rubbing lightly over my bare back. No jokes come to mind. The teasing has stopped, but then she whispers, "That ladykiller smile gets me every time."

Taking the present out of the packaging, I ask, "This is real, right?"

"Yes, it's real."

"Two pink lines?"

"Two solid pink lines."

Swallowing becomes harder as realization sets in. "You're pregnant?"

With a wide and smug grin, she replies, "I sure am, Mr. Crow."

"I'm going to be a dad again?"

With a laugh, she kisses my arm. "Yes, and this time I'm going to let you do everything you never got to do the first time like change those middle of the night diapers."

"Happily, but might I remind you that this is all new to you too."

"How about we do this together?"

Her hair's a fucking sexy mess, her lips swollen from kissing. The makeup she wore for the wedding is all but lost in the sheets. But when I look at her, I see the most beautiful woman I've ever seen. There's a glow that shines from the inside. Sincerity when she looks at me that gives me peace. A welcoming smile that accompanies her warm embrace. How did I get so lucky? "I wouldn't do this any other way." Leaning back, I bring her with me. The smell of her cinnamon mixes with the ocean breeze as she snuggles with me.

"Are you happy?" she asks, her breath blowing across my chest.

I struggle to answer such a simple question. Not because I'm not happy, but because I've never felt such a strong reaction. My breath doesn't come easy and her head pops up to look at me. "Jet," she says, stroking my cheek. "Aww."

There's no hiding the water in my eyes, so I close them hoping it returns to where it came from. When I reopen them, I say, "Happy isn't a big enough word for what feel. I just . . . I can't believe we're going to have a baby. I can't believe you're having my baby."

The tips of her nails scrape lightly along my scalp as she lies back, comfortable in who she is, not just exposing skin, but exposing her heart to me. Sliding down the mattress, I lean over her and kiss her stomach. "That's my baby in there. My baby carrying my baby."

That makes her laugh. "So I've been thinking about names."

My gaze shoots up to catch her eyes on me and that glint is back. "And?"

"I thought that maybe we should continue the Crow tradition."

"Which tradition is that?"

Sitting up abruptly, she straddles me. With her hands on my chest, she's clearly excited by how she starts talking faster. "Naming the baby after the place where she's conceived."

Thinking about all the places we've had sex . . . and fucked, I start to tick off every major appliance, room in our house, in the Ojai guesthouse, and praying it's not in some of the other places we were too impatient to wait. "Do you know where the baby was conceived?"

"I do."

Please don't let it be that time we did it in the bathroom, or on the pool table, or in the bed of my truck. "Where?"

The Crow Brothers Books Coming Soon:

Stay tuned for the other Crow Brother's books coming in April and June.

Add these hot rockers' books to your Goodreads TBR so you're in the know when more details come.

Tulsa Crow

Rivers Crow

PART I

THE RESISTANCE

ISBN: 978-1-940071-15-2

PROLOGUE

Johnny Outlaw

I'm a fucking fool.

I'm not even sure how I got into this mess, but I know I need to get myself out of it. I look down at the hand on my thigh inching up higher and my stomach rolls. Squeezing out from between the tight confines of the third row in this van, a girl on each side wanting a piece of me, I fall over the seat into the cargo area and move away from their astonished stares. They're speaking German and I don't know what the fuck they're saying, but I've been in this type of situation enough to know how it will end, if I let it.

Everything has changed... or sometime around my last birthday I changed.

I didn't invite these chicks. Dex did. He'll fuck'em all before the night's through and the bad part is, they'll let him. Thinking they're special, that they'll be the one to tame him. They'll let him do what he wants just to be close to him.

Beyond this set up being predictable at this point, it's

really fucking old or I am, probably both. I ignore their taps on my shoulder and them calling my name. I ignore everything to do with them and focus on my phone.

On the inside, I'm freaking the fuck out that I'm sitting in the cargo hold of a huge van in Germany with attractive girls willing to do anything I want them to, but I prefer to look at a photo of a little blonde with hazel eyes. Freaking the fuck out might be an understatement.

I'm a player or was, supposed to be, maybe still am. I don't keep score or anything like that, but I've slept with plenty of women, sometimes more than one at a time. I used to blame my lifestyle, but more recently, I realized I'm the common denominator in the bad relationships I've had.

The car comes to a stop and the driver rushes around to the back to let me out. I stumble while climbing out, and hurry inside away from the sound of my name being called. The girls will be upset when they realize I'm not staying to play, but Dex will be thrilled—more pussy for him.

Cory hops out from the front, and follows me. "Wait up," he says, jogging to catch up.

When we reach the elevators, we look back. Dex is helping the girls out of the vehicle one-by-one. With a cigarette hanging from the corner of his mouth, he's sloppy, already drunk. He never lacks for female companionship. By the way he acts, I don't see the appeal, but I don't think that's why they're hooking up with him anyway.

Cory looks at me and nods once. "What's up? What happened back there?"

The elevator doors open and we step in, pushing the button for our floor. "Over it. Over it all."

"The girl from Vegas?"

"She's not from Vegas, but yeah, I've kind of been thinking about her."

When the brass doors reopen, we walk down the hall to our rooms. Cory and I don't do small talk. We've been friends for years, best friends if I think about it.

"Maybe you should call her," he suggests as we open our doors.

"Maybe I will."

"Night."

"Night," I mumble and shut the door behind me.

CHAPTER 1

Holliday Hughes

*"Comfort zones are like women. You have to try a few
before you find the one that feels right." ~ Johnny Outlaw*

That damn lime and coconut song has been playing on a
loop in my head, driving me nuts for hours. I make a mental
note: Fire Tracy in the morning for subjecting me to that
song twenty-thousand times yesterday. She called it inspira-
tional. I call it torture after the first two times.

Rolling over, I look at the time. 4:36 a.m. I have four
hours before I need to be on the road. This may be a business trip, but it will still be good to get away for a few days. I
need a break. I've been in a bad mood lately. The spa and I
have a date I'm really looking forward to. The thought alone
relaxes me. I close my eyes and try to get a few more hours
of sleep before I need to leave for Las Vegas.

I get two tops.

I tighten my robe at the neck. Just as I open my front door to get the paper, I hear a male voice say, "Hello?"

Peeking through the crack, I hold the door protectively in front of me just in case I need to close and lock it quickly. "Hi."

"I'm your new neighbor. I just moved in last week. I'm Danny."

Curious, I slowly stick my head out to get a better look at this Danny. Strands of my sandy blonde hair fall in front of my eyes, so I tuck it behind my ear and get an eyeful. To my surprise, he's quite handsome and has a big smile. "Oh, um," I say, dragging my hand down the back of my hair, hoping to tame the wild strands. "Hi. I'm Holli. Welcome to the neighborhood."

He nods toward the paper on the bottom of the shared Spanish tiled steps that lead to our townhomes. "I'll get your paper since you're not dressed."

"Thanks." I watch him. He looks like he just got back from a run or workout—a little sweaty, but not gross, in that sexy kind of way. Or maybe Danny's just sexy. He's well built with short, brown hair and when he bends over, I notice his strong legs and arms. Well-defined muscles lead to—*Oh my God!* Not just my face, but my entire body heats from embarrassment. Hoping he doesn't say anything about me checking him out, I turn away and start picking at a piece of peeling stucco near my house number. "Um, so are you settled in, liking your place?"

His chuckling confirms I was busted. But he's a gentleman, so he acts as if it didn't happen. "I like the neighborhood. The place is great," he says. "I like all the space, especially the patio. I'm thinking of having a party to break it in, maybe in a few weeks after I finish unpacking." He hands me the paper and takes two steps back. "You should stop by."

Nodding, I look into his eyes. I think they're brown, lighter than mine, more honey-colored. His offer is friendly, not a come on, which is good since we're neighbors now. "Thanks for the invitation."

Walking back to his door, he steals one more glimpse over his shoulder. "Have a great day. See you around, Holli."

"Yeah, see you around."

I shut the door, paper in hand, and fall against the wood with a smile on my face. One of my golden rules is not to date where I sleep, but I still appreciate that my new hottie neighbor is easy on the eyes. He might know it, but he doesn't seem arrogant.

I lock the door and get ready to leave.

Los Angeles is hot, smoggy, and grey at this hour and I have a feeling it won't be much different a few hours from now. I close the patio door and lock it, double checking for safety. After pulling the drapes closed, I take one last look around to make sure I'm not forgetting anything. I text Tracy and let her know I'm leaving. She doesn't reply, but I'm not surprised. Her boyfriend proposed last night after six years of dating. Being the kind boss and friend I am, I let her out of this trip, so she could spend the weekend with their families to celebrate the engagement.

There are selfish reasons as well for letting her off the hook. I really don't think I can handle hours of sitting in the car with her as she reads bridal magazines and plans every detail of her big day. After too many dud dates in the last couple of months, I'm not in the right frame of mind to plan her happily ever after.

With my garment bag in one hand and my suitcase in the other, I click the button, disarming my car's alarm as I walk to my parking space. I've lived here a couple of years. I wanted a place near the beach that also had space for my office, and I was fortunate enough to find both in this townhome.

A meme I created went viral three years ago this month. Who knew a snarky-mouthed fruit would be the way I make my fortune. I took it though and ran with the brand, building it into a small empire I named Limelight. The company is lean and I keep my costs under control. My fortune has grown by a few million in the last year alone.

I back out onto the street and take the scenic route, one block up to the beach. Driving slowly along with my windows down, I let the sound of the waves and the smell of the ocean center me. At the first stoplight, I take one deep salty air breath, roll the window back up, and leave for Vegas.

An hour into the trip, Tracy calls. I answer, but before I have a chance to speak, she asks, "Can I please tell you all about it again?" Happy laughter punctuates her question.

"Of course. Tell me everything." I'll indulge her wedding fantasies because that's what friends do... and because I have four hours to kill in the car. Listening to her takes my mind off the time and the miles stretching ahead of me as she relives every last detail of the proposal. Fortunately for me, she skims over the engagement sex.

Her excitement is contagious and because I've known her and her fiancé, Adam, for so many years, my happiness exudes. "Congratulations again."

"Thank you for letting me stay home this weekend. You'll be great and don't be nervous. It's just a rah-rah go get'em presentation and cocktail party. The rest of the time is all yours."

"You know how much I hate these kinds of events."

"You don't have to prove anything to anyone. Your company's success speaks for itself."

"Thanks. I'll try to remember that."

"Drive safely and squeeze in some fun."

I laugh. "You know I'll try. Bye." When we hang up, I turn on some music and let the miles drift behind me.

After a stop for gas half-way and a coffee later, I enter the glistening city in the desert. Pulling up to my hotel, I valet my car and take my own luggage to my room after checking in. I like this hotel because of the amenities, but the men aren't bad to look at either—a little edgy, a lot sexy—lucky for this single girl.

I spend a couple of hours checking emails and work on a proposal before I realize the time and need to get ready for the night. It's Vegas, so I mix business with some sexy. I pull on a black fitted skirt that hits mid-thigh, an emerald green silk camisole with spaghetti straps, and a short black jacket. I slip on my favorite new pair of stilettos and after one last check of my makeup and hair, I head out.

The meet and greet isn't long, but I slip out at one point to use the restroom. As I'm walking back toward the ball-room, I'm drawn to a man standing with a group of people nearby. His magnetism captures me. He might just be the best looking man I've ever seen—tall, dark hair, strong jaw leading me up to seductive eyes aimed at me. His head tilts and for a split second in time, everyone else disappears. I break the connection by looking away, everything feeling too intense in the moment. When he laughs, I add that to his ongoing list of great attributes.

When I pass, the feel of his gaze landing heavy on my backside warms my body. With my hand on the door, I pause, wanting to look back so badly. I resist the urge, open the door, and return to the party. The presentation portion of the evening is interesting. Despite that, my thoughts repeatedly drift back to the hot guy in the corridor—fitted jeans, black shirt, leather wristband. *Damn I'm weak to a leather wristband.*

I'm mentally brought back to the presentation when my company is recognized as one to watch. The acknowledgement is nice, and it feels good to be among my peers.

The dinner becomes more of a party as everyone wanders around instead of taking their seats. I'm not hungry and need to psych myself up to mingle. Tracy is awesome in these types of situations. Me, not so much.

The ballroom is dimly lit, I'm guessing to set the ambiance, but since this is business, I can do without the romance. I head straight for the bar just like everyone else— one big cattle call to the liquor to make the rest of the night a little more bearable.

"I usually hate these things," I hear from the guy behind me. When I look over my shoulder, he gives me a half-smile —half-friendly, half-creepy. "But they don't usually have attractive women either."

I roll my eyes while turning my back on him and his cheesy pick-up line.

"I'm sorry. That was bad. I know," he says with a weird nasally laugh.

His breath hits my neck and I jerk back. "Do you mind? Ever hear of personal space?"

"Sorry. You're just really pretty." He shrugs as if that makes everything better. "Your beauty is making me stupid."

"You think?" *Big mistake.*

He actually takes my sarcastic comment as a conversation opener. "Yes, I do. But I can't be the first to be dumbfounded by your beauty."

Standing on my tiptoes to see how many more people

are in front of me, I exhale, disappointed by the long line. One person in line would have been too many at this point. "Excuse me," I say and slip out of line. I find the table with my name tag on it, set my purse down, and take off my jacket. This hotel ballroom is crowded and too warm.

Saved by a friendly face, I see Cara, a marketing strategist I know from L.A. Weaving between the tables, I sit down in a chair next to her. With her eyes focused on the paperwork in front of her, I ask, "Working during the party?"

She looks up, smiling when she sees me. Opening her arms, she leans in and hugs me. "Holli, it's so good to see you."

I went with a different company than hers for a campaign a while back and glad she's not holding it against me. "Good to see you again."

"Congratulations on your success. Well deserved."

"I'm not sure if a smartass lime deserves the success it's gotten, but I'll take it."

She taps my leg. "You deserve it. It's funny and quite catchy. Just take the accolades."

"Thanks."

Looking over my shoulder, she leans in and whispers, "I'm skipping out of here early, but I'm meeting a few people for dinner tomorrow. If you're still in Vegas, you should join us."

"I'd love that. Thanks."

She stands up and grabs the papers in front of her. "Fantastic. I'll text you the details tomorrow. I'm so glad we ran into each other."

"Me too. See you tomorrow."

I'm left sitting alone. When I look around the room, like Cara, I'm thinking that skipping out early might be the way to go. If I do, I know Tracy will kick my ass, so I decide to suffer and give this party one last chance. But I definitely need a drink and the line for the bar in here is still way too long.

I head for the doors to buy a drink in one of the many hotel bars—any bar without a line. Guy from the bar line jumps in front of me as I try to exit, startling me. "Hey, hey, hey. You're not leaving already, are you?"

Since my glare and earlier hints didn't work, I reply, "I'll be back, no need to worry yourself."

His head starts bobbing up and down, confidently, and a big Cheshire cat grin covers his face. I start walking again as he keeps talking... again. "Cool. I'll see you later then."

I feel no need to respond to the come on, and will try to avoid him when I return. Following the wide-tiled path through the casino, which reminds me of the Yellow Brick Road, guiding me to what feels like Oz, a bar in all its gloriousness with no lines in site. Inside the darkened room, the sounds of the casino fade away as current hits play overhead. Still on a mission for a cocktail, I step up to the bar and wait.

If you would like to continuing reading The Resistance and meet Holliday and Johnny, download The Resistance today from Amazon.

ALSO BY S.L. SCOTT

Talk to Me Duet

Sweet Talk

Dirty Talk

Welcome to Paradise Series

Good Vibrations

Good Intentions

Good Sensations

Happy Endings

Welcome to Paradise Series

From the Inside Out Series

Scorned

Jealousy

Dylan

Austin

From the Inside Out Compilation

Stand Alone Books

Everest

Missing Grace

Until I Met You

Drunk on Love

Naturally, Charlie

A Prior Engagement

Lost in Translation

Sleeping with Mr. Sexy

Morning Glory

A PERSONAL NOTE

There are so many people, amazing humans, that make my life amazing and that allow me to live in this fictional world where my dreams run wild and the stories come to life.

My family is just everything to me. It's not about the big adventures but the day to day that they make life so wonderful.

My friends, loyal, supportive, and inspiring. I'm beyond fortunate to have such amazing women in my life. Amy B., Andrea J., Heather M., Irene, Jennifer S., Kerri, Lynsey, Melissa K.

The team that surrounds me, that I can call on, and who are always there for me to help where they are needed, you are the reason I can release books, an amazing team of women that amaze me all the time with their brilliance. Andrea J., Jenny S., Kim S., Kristen J., Letitia, Lynsey, Marion, Marla.

Dear Bloggers, I couldn't do this without you. Thank you for your time, your dedication, and your love of books. XOX

Dear Readers, you make this such a fun journey. Thank

you for reading my books and all the support you continu-
ally show me.

Love,

S.

www.ingramcontent.com/pod-product-compliance
Lightning Source LLC
Chambersburg PA
CBHW020509260626
47156CB00006B/1942